Kathleen Rowntree grew up in Lincolnshire and was educated at Cleethorpes Girls' Grammar School and Hull University where she studied music. For the last seventeen years she has lived on the Oxfordshire/Northamptonshire borders. Her husband is also a writer, and they have two sons. She has written four previous novels, *The Quiet War of Rebecca Sheldon*, *Brief Shining*, *The Directrix* and *Between Friends*, and she has contributed to a recent series of monologues for BBC2 TV called *Obsessions*.

Also by Kathleen Rowntree

BETWEEN FRIENDS
THE QUIET WAR OF REBECCA SHELDON
BRIEF SHINING

and published by Black Swan

TELL MRS POOLE
I'M SORRY

Kathleen Rowntree

BLACK SWAN

TELL MRS POOLE I'M SORRY

A BLACK SWAN BOOK : 0 552 99561 4

Originally published in Great Britain by Doubleday,
a division of Transworld Publishers Ltd

PRINTING HISTORY
Doubleday edition published 1993
Black Swan edition published 1994

This book is set in 11/12pt Linotype Melior by
Phoenix Typesetting, Ilkley, West Yorkshire.

Black Swan Books are published by Transworld Publishers Ltd,
61–63 Uxbridge Road, Ealing, London W5 5SA,
in Australia by Transworld Publishers (Australia) Pty Ltd,
15–25 Helles Avenue, Moorebank, NSW 2170
and in New Zealand by Transworld Publishers (NZ) Ltd,
3 William Pickering Drive, Albany, Auckland.

Reproduced, printed and bound in Great Britain by
Cox & Wyman Ltd, Reading, Berks.

To Mark

CONTENTS

1
FORMING UP

i

'The difficulty is,' said Liz, of her daughter Rosie, to
her friends Chrissy and Nell, 'she's no longer a child.
She's eighteen. There's not a helluva lot we can do
about it. What makes me mad is the effect this might
be having on Nathan. After everything he's had to
contend with lately – the new management, those
nasty little pricks coming over from Harvard; and
his . . . his angina.' The word hurt her, she could
never get it out easily, casually. She pushed it away
– 'But you know all about that.' Of course they did.
Hadn't Chrissy dashed off a letter to her with a helpful
booklet, *Eat your way to a Healthy Heart?* Hadn't Nell
telephoned – 'Bring Nathan to London *at once*. Consult someone who knows what they're talking about'
(because no consultant who did could dream of practising Up North), 'and if you're stuck for the readies,
don't worry, I'll help'? She sighed – of course they
understood; which was why she needed to talk over
this new worry with them. 'It's the suddenness that's
the worst of it,' she went on, concentrating on the
subject of Rosie. 'From Go-for-it to Get Lost in a matter
of days – surly, secretive, monosyllabic – total transformation. I'm sure she's got involved in something
she's not happy about. And now she's refusing to go
to university . . .'

She paused. Nell and Chrissy had exchanged glances;
were now frowning at her. 'What is it?' Really, though,
it was obvious. 'All right,' she conceded, thrusting her
hands deep into her jeans pockets, 'I admit it. This

9

thing with Rosie – it's brought back – you know, the Poole business. Not that it'll be anything like that . . . But it has started me thinking back to that time. Which is why I was so desperate to talk to you – you're the only ones who *know*; we were in it together. So if the Poole business *is* coming back to haunt me, you can damn well help me cope . . .'

'Liz? Am I supposed to be cooking this for two of us, or three?'

Her mind blanked. It was like someone leaning over and tripping a switch. She saw with shock, and considerable disappointment, that she was alone in her own Northumbrian garden, and not on The Old Rectory lawn in Fenby-cum-Laithby, just south of the Humber, with Chrissy and Nell. Furthermore, they were not taking their ease in the shade of the horse chestnut with a bottle of Vouvray. And it had been such a relief telling them. Such a *relief*. The disappointment made her mouth tremble.

'Liz?'

'Oh – for three. If Rosie isn't back we can keep hers warm. Or chuck it away.'

She'd better go in. It was a sunless early evening, chilly for August. Yes, better go in.

Nevertheless, she was reluctant. Indoors, nowadays, it was necessary to tread carefully – thin glass everywhere, prickly draughts lurking, the ominous thump of Rosie's sounds machine, or the quiet threat of time being bided. Which was all very unfair, for she loved her home; had invested a lot of time and care making it a place where she could expand and relax, shrug off the downside of her professional life. As a clinical psychologist she was jammed up against people and their emotions every working day, mostly in cupboard-sized rooms (just herself, the patient and a dusty cheese plant), sometimes in ugly sitting rooms where damaged people sat in a therapy circle, or in tiny offices conferring with staff – everyone perching on chair-arms or on patches of cleared-off desk top. By the time she got home she craved space to stretch her eyes in and plenty of unused air. So the house was fairly spartan; flooring an expanse of stone flags or oak boards softened here and there by thin frayed rugs, walls plain, ceilings low and beamed. The furniture was largely of old polished wood, cracked leather or faded chintz. There were a few paintings, many books, some pieces of china. The stone fireplaces, alive with burning logs in winter, lay at rest all summer with dried flowers in their hearths like graves awaiting the trump.

She went in through the yard door.

Nathan, in the kitchen, was making lovely smells – onion, tomato, basil.

'She took your car again,' he observed. 'Didn't ask, I suppose?'

'No.' She moistened a finger, ran it over the bread-board on which he'd been cutting up crusty bread, gathered crumbs to her mouth.

'What if you'd been called out?'

'I could've taken yours.'

'Not if I weren't here.'

'Oh, Nathan, never mind the car. She hasn't eaten a thing today, as far as we know. I hope she'll come home and have some of this.'

'Food's not exactly the most pressing problem, either.'

'I expect,' she said, pausing to breathe in heavily, 'this is something to do with a man.'

'Man?'

'Boy, then. Bloke, fella.'

'Don't know why we went in for kids. I remember saying I'd rather have dogs.'

She laughed, went to the stove, put her arm round him, rested her head on his shoulder. 'We can't complain about Jon, never had any trouble with him. And only these past few weeks with Rosie.'

'Mm. I've always thought it odd, how most people we

11

know, Bob and Denny, Annie and Tim, the Rawlins . . . My God, their eldest was done for drug pushing, wasn't he?'

'Supplying.'

'How they're always tearing their hair out over their kids, while ours were so easy. Perhaps it's our turn.'

This was terrible. She ought to be in control, sorting out Rosie in a sensible manner, bringing her skills and training to bear, taking it off Nathan's shoulders. Nathan shouldn't be worried. 'Darling, it's just a thing she's going through. It's not the end of the world if she takes a year off before university. Jolly good idea, probably. Stop brooding about it. Leave it to me, I'll sort it.'

'You're rattled, too.'

'No, I'm not. Not really. It's just the suddenness. Shall I open a bottle?'

'Why not? Make it Chianti.'

Rosie came in much later, when Nathan was watching TV and Liz was washing-up. The car's headlights glanced across the window. Liz rushed to feel whether the left-over food was still hot, then returned to the sink affecting nonchalance. 'Hiya,' she called, as Rosie came in and shut the door behind her. 'There's something in the oven if you're peckish.'

Rosie went to the kettle and switched it on without bothering to check if it had water in it. Then she sauntered to the oven, opened the door, lifted a corner of the foil covering. 'Might as well,' she mumbled, reaching for an oven glove; and Liz put a brake on her hands and feet which were itching to go charging about getting things, like a clean fork, a mug of coffee ('or a glass of wine, dear, there's still some in the bottle.') Not a word, she warned herself. Not yet.

When her leisurely washing-up was done, she said, 'I think I'd like some coffee too,' as if surprised to discover this wish. She made it, brought her mug to the table.

12

Rosie had removed her jacket and cast it over the back of her chair. Liz noted her long-sleeved black T-shirt – *our* T-shirt, she thought, the expensive one Rosie had persuaded her to buy on the grounds that two of them sharing it would in some way reduce its price. Liz had acceded to this cheerfully. Rosie was always borrowing her clothes, indeed, confessed that for some mysterious reason she often preferred her mother's things to her own; and Liz, hiding her pleasure with mock long-sufferance, would tell herself she knew the reason. It was because they were such good mates. Now she could only marvel at her previous confidence. How long since they'd bought the shirt? Two months, three? It felt like yesterday – Rosie's arm through hers pulling her into the shop, Rosie urging, 'Try it on, Mum; if it doesn't look good on us both, we'll forget it.' Unbelievable that such a short passage of time could take them from *that* to *this* – Rosie scarcely able to bear her company. Liz felt her brain had not entirely grasped the new situation, was lumbering behind events as if still half-persuaded that what was occurring was an aberration and at any moment life would revert to normal. Disbelief – the classic reaction to shock, she told herself mechanically.

Rosie was now scraping at burnt-on cheese round the sides of the empty dish. 'Something else?' Liz suggested. 'Piece of cake?'

'N'hanks.'

'Well . . .' She looked into her mug of coffee. 'Aren't you going to tell us about him?'

Rosie's scraping fork fell still. 'Who?'

'Your boyfriend.'

'*Boy*friend,' she scoffed.

'I meant "friend". What's his name?'

'Simon,' said Rosie after a pause.

'How long have you been seeing him? Going out?' she amended nervously.

'Going *out*?' Another sneer.

OK, going to bed, almost snapped Liz, and was immediately taken with fright. Striving for calm, she persisted. 'Is he a student, then, or what?'

'Teacher.'

'Oh,' said Liz. 'Which school?'

'What the hell is this?' cried Rosie, scraping back her chair. 'I don't see why I should tell you anything after you called me a liar.'

'I didn't.'

'You did. Last night. You said I was lying about not wanting to go to university.'

'I said that wasn't the whole story − and so it's proved.'

'You get on my nerves, you think you're so clever. Stop trying to trip me up. I'm not one of your nutcase patients.'

'Hang on a minute, Rosie.'

'Oh − piss off.'

The reason for this defensive outburst seemed clear: Simon was a teacher at Rosie's school. As her daughter fled, Liz sank back in her chair − her hands folded in front of her on the table − to think about it. Was their affair going on while Rosie was still a pupil? Technically, yes, she decided; it probably got going during the last weeks of term when sixth-formers' lessons had finished, coinciding with Rosie's character transformation. A memory came gliding − and with it a queasy sensation: I bet he's married, she thought.

Suddenly, she was in a driving panic to get hold of Chrissy and Nell. Imaginary chats weren't good enough, she'd really got to tell them − why she hadn't done so already was a mystery . . . Oh, please, she remonstrated with herself; do come on. The reason she hadn't told them was simple: fear of losing face. She feared they might say (or at least, *Nell* might say), 'Aren't you paid to sort out things like that?' − not comprehending that her expertise would actually be a hindrance. Rosie could see it coming a mile off, found it infuriating,

14

and no wonder. The only aspect of all this she'd stake money on was that she was doomed to make a hash of it. 'For the one thing we can't stand,' she heard her professional voice coolly explaining, 'is our children making the same mistakes that we once made.'

Now she'd put her finger on it. There was more to her feeling of panic than fear for Rosie. It was definitely the Poole business lurking at the back of her mind. Which made it imperative to see Chrissy and Nell. Chrissy, she was sure, would make herself instantly available. Of Nell, always so busy and in demand, she was less certain. But damn it, they owed her; at times in the past she'd dropped everything on their behalf.

She rose to go to the upstairs phone. No need to get heated, she soothed herself, because at times like this, getting together was what they did. It was a habit. Natural. Like going home.

ii

The first day of the new school year. In classroom Lower Three B at the Girls' Grammar School, girls wait their turn to meet the form mistress and have their names and particulars checked against the list on the register. A similar process is taking place next door in class Lower Three A, for these two classes comprise the successful candidates in the recent eleven-plus examination. Some of the queuing girls are from the same primary school; you can tell this from the way they chat and joke together. Liz is silent. She knows no-one here, only Jane Benton, who, as the possessor of a surname beginning with a letter in the first half of the alphabet, is standing next door in the Lower Three A line-up. Of the new intake, Liz and Jane are the only girls to have come from The Lawns Preparatory School. Their former classmates have gone off to boarding school or, if they failed the eleven-plus, to the local fee-paying convent school (secondary moderns being beyond the pale). After careful enquiry, having been persuaded of the examination's effectiveness in eliminating undesirable elements along with pupils of lesser intelligence, Alderman Stockdale has sent his daughter here with an easy mind. Liz is not so sure. Listening to the unpolished voices around her, she suspects her new classmates are what her mother and former friends at The Lawns would term 'rough girls'.

Some who have already presented themselves to the teacher are sitting at desks in the main body of the classroom. Chrissy Thomas is one of these. She has dreamt of this day, longed for the chance it will bring to meet girls from schools other than her own neighbourhood primary, girls who do not know about Dad and Auntie Julie, girls who have never set foot in 142 Lister Avenue and smelt Auntie Julie's vests airing in front of the back living-room fire or seen senna pods soaking in a basin in the kitchen or disembodied teeth in a glass of Steradent. Chrissy has never had trouble making friends, but she resents the way her friends, once they gain admittance to 142 Lister Avenue, are thereafter subtly changed towards her, becoming faintly pitying, always calling for her subsequently in the safety of a group. Not that hers is a shaming address; on the contrary, Lister Avenue is a respectable tree-lined road, the house a substantial semi-detached villa of the sort built before the war for the captains of fishing vessels – approved of locally as 'skippers' houses'. It is the two dour and eccentric adults occupying the house who are the cause of her humiliations. Today, she has set her sights on acquiring a new friend from further afield, one who, by dint of means so far not worked out, will be prevented from ever crossing number 142's threshold.

'Good morning. You are . . .?'

'Elizabeth Stockdale.'

'Ah, yes. From The Lawns.' Miss Wormold's pencil comes to rest beside Liz's name. 'And your address is The Mount, Wold Enderby. A charming village, Wold

Enderby. Do you know Doctor and Mrs Furze by any chance?'

'Yes, Miss Wormold.' Liz is the first pupil this morning to use the form-mistress's name.

Miss Wormold beams. 'They are dear friends of mine. Now, have you brought gym kit and hockey stick?'

'Yes, Miss Wormold.'

'Everything name-taped?'

'I think so.'

'Jolly good. Go and sit down – wherever you like.'

The room, it occurs to Liz, has fallen quiet. She wonders what has caused this, fears it may be her voice which has had its Lincolnshire accent trained out of it by Miss Millicent of The Lawns. Or perhaps it was the mention of her surname; *Stockdale, builders of repute* and *Hennage & Stockdale, funeral directors* are slogans constantly displayed on the sides of corporation buses, and the phrase *Alderman Stockdale, the former mayor* is a familiar one in local press reports. Her posh address, too, has no doubt been noticed. Help me, God, she prays, nervously surveying the room, anxiously seeking a place to sit.

Some of the seated girls are 'saving' a neighbouring desk for a friend still in the queue. Chrissy has placed a possessive hand on the desk next to hers in the hope of spotting her dream friend. If no such friend materializes, well then, she will absently withdraw her hand and effect not to notice when the seat is finally taken. She, like all the girls present, has noted Liz's classy voice and personal details, and particularly the country address. Now, as Liz turns and Chrissy takes full measure of her glossy black hair and black-fringed blue eyes, her neat elegant little body, she experiences a leap of recognition. 'Here,' she hisses, patting the desk beside her. Girls who know Chrissy exchange glances, snigger. Chrissy and Liz are oblivious of this: Chrissy's heart is beating too distractingly, Liz is too grateful.

'I like your satchel,' Chrissy whispers, as Liz

hauls this splendid receptacle on to the desk.

'Thank you.' Liz turns to examine her neighbour. 'I like your hair.'

'Oh that,' says Chrissy, tugging a long curl and grimacing as if her hair were the bane of her life. 'Yours is much nicer. My name's Chrissy Thomas.'

'Mine's Elizabeth Stockdale.'

'I know. I heard.'

'At my last school the girls called me Liz. It's just relations and teachers who say Elizabeth.'

'Liz is my favourite name.'

'Gosh, what a coincidence.' They widen mouths and eyes at this encouraging omen. 'I've got an apple. We can share it at break.'

Chrissy smiles, her brown eyes gleam, she's certain, now, she's met her new dream friend. Furthermore, she's starving; Auntie Julie hardly gives her enough to eat at meal times, never mind for break.

Returning the smile, taking this skinny girl in, Chrissy's eleven-year-old morning look – all freckles and teeth and untidy brown curls – pings on to Liz's brain like an arrow with a suction-pad tip; bonds so tenaciously that twenty, thirty years on it will still be the image conjured by her voice on the phone and will always seem her truest representation.

The apple is red on one side, green on the other. At break, Liz and Chrissy stand correctly buttoned into their new school gaberdine macs on the asphalt playground beyond the quadrangles amid sixty or so other shivering first-formers, considering it.

'You eat the red side,' Liz says, holding it out.

Chrissy draws back. 'No, you have the red.'

Liz decides the matter by sinking her teeth into the middle of the green part. Chrissy, transfixed, watches the glossy rosiness come abruptly towards her. It's like biting into the sun. The apple goes to and fro, diminishing. As they chew, they swap pieces of information about themselves and stare around at other girls.

A drear day. Now and then, a spitting wind off the North Sea drives over the playground flapping the unbuttoned macs of the more sophisticated second and third years. These older girls charge about and shout, or stand in gangs arguing and joking. Some stroll arm-in-arm in pairs along the paths of the quadrangle. Liz and Chrissy walk to the far end of the asphalt bounding a second quadrangle. This is the territory of the senior girls, the fourth, fifth and sixth-formers. Many of these have not deigned to put on a mac at all; do not even bother to leave the open-sided corridor between classrooms and quadrangle, but lounge against walls and pillars, gossiping. They are arresting creatures; amazingly tall some of them, and spectacularly developed. The watching first years are filled with awe. They feel undersized, childish, and soon drift back to the area of the junior quadrangle.

'Hello, Liz,' says Jane Benton, catching her arm.

'Oh, hello.'

They eye one another warily. Never the closest of friends at The Lawns and now placed in different classes, there is nothing to be gained today by clinging to one another. Jane gives Chrissy an appraising look, then turns to walk back to girls in Lower Three A – at the precise moment Liz chooses to turn away.

'She was at my school.'

'I can tell. She talks like you.'

'Which girls did you come up with?'

'Um, Angie Hutchings, Valerie Dove, Beryl Ogden, Gilly Banks, Pamela Pettifer . . .'

'Shall we go and talk to them?'

'All right,' Chrissy concedes without enthusiasm. 'Pam Pettifer's not very nice, but the others are OK.'

Lunchtime arrives – or dinner, as it is called here. It is the moment Liz has been dreading, her fear of being made to eat food she cannot fancy intensified by the cabbagey stench which has been wafting towards the classroom during the latter half of the morning. The dining hall is a single-purpose building of painted brick walls, linoleum floor and raftered ceiling. An eating area is separated from the steamy cooking area by a counter. The place swims with condensation; benches, tables, utensils feel slimy. Liz's stomach knots. She looks hopelessly at the plate put in front of her, eventually takes up her knife and fork, rearranges the food. 'I'll have yours,' offers Chrissy, noting her friend's discomfiture. Liz cradles the plate from prying eyes while Chrissy scoops. But the third-year monitor spots what is going on. 'You should've asked for a small,' she reproves Liz. 'And you,' she addresses the other miscreant, 'can stop behaving like a pig.' Exertion knits Chrissy's forehead as she bolts Liz's dinner in thirty seconds flat.

Liz talks to other classmates and survives their taunting curiosity. She quite likes some of them, finds herself mildly popular. But none of the girls charm her like Chrissy. By the end of the first week, it is accepted that they are best friends, a pair like Valerie Dove and Angie Hutchings, like Beryl Ogden and Gilly Banks. Henceforth, their peers will speak of them in the same breath. 'Chrissy and Liz,' they will say; 'Liz and Chrissy.'

'Will you come to tea on Saturday?'
Chrissy's heart leaps. A month has gone by. She has begun to anticipate this invitation. She nods.
'Will your father bring you?' Liz asks diffidently, unsure as to whether the familiar Lawns routine of daughters chauffeured by parents (usually the male parent) is the norm in her new circle.
'Dad?' Chrissy looks bewildered. 'I'll get the bus.'
'But there's only the country bus and it doesn't go very often. Don't worry, I'm sure my father will fetch you. Where do you live, exactly?'
'142 Lister Avenue. I'll wait at the traffic lights

on the corner with Barton Road.'

'All right,' says Liz, unperturbed. Evidently, this is the way things are done. 'We'll come at half past two.'

'At the traffic lights?' Alderman Stockdale has never heard of such a thing. 'Nonsense. Tell the lass we'll pick her up at her house.'

'But she said at the traffic lights.'

Over delicate china teacups, Alderman and Mrs Stockdale exchange glances.

'Never mind,' says Mrs Stockdale comfortably. She is a comfortable looking woman (well-upholstered, as her husband unkindly puts it); also unruffled looking, bejewelled and powdered, swathed in one of her shiny floral frocks, her hair's crisp waves and tight curls preserved by a night-time hairnet. 'I'll give her mother a ring. What's their name, love?'

'Thomas.'

'In Lister Avenue, you said? Another cup of tea, Daddy? Pass Daddy's cup, Elizabeth. Lister Avenue's a decent enough road.'

Receiving back his cup, Alderman Stockdale notices his daughter's frown. 'Nothing wrong with Lister Avenue,' he confirms. 'Nothing wrong at all. Good day at school? What've they been teaching you?'

He has turned his special look on her, the look that sends Carol in the office and Miss Millicent at the Lawns and the mothers of her friends into a girlish dither. He is a strikingly handsome man, tall, broad, craggy featured, faintly weather-beaten, with hair as black and eyes as blue as her own. Understanding the requirements of the situation, Liz clears her forehead and smiles prettily. 'We had science. Pamela Pettifer singed her hair in the bunsen burner.'

'Did she, by heck? Mind you don't singe yours, princess.'

'Course I won't, Daddy. Pamela Pettifer messes about.'

21

* * *

'Hello. This is Mrs Stockdale speaking. Is that Mrs Thomas?'

A pause. '*Miss* Thomas.'

'Ah. Well, I'd like to speak to Chrissy's mother, please. My little girl has asked Chrissy to tea on Saturday.'

'You'll have to shout pretty loud, then, duck. Chrissy's mam ran off nine year ago. No-one here's had a peep from her since. There's just me and her Dad – that's me brother. Oh, and Chrissy, of course.'

'How very sad. Well, I trust the arrangement for Saturday meets with your approval, Miss Thomas?'

'Oh, aye. She can go if she likes.'

'Mm, Chrissy told my daughter,' says Mrs Stockdale with a confiding little laugh, 'that she'd wait to be picked up at the traffic lights.'

Silence – as Auntie Julie peels a smouldering butt from her upper lip. 'There you are, then.'

'Oh. Well, my husband will bring her back afterwards, to the door, of course.'

'Right y'are.'

'Well, it's, er, nice to have spoken to you.'

'Cheerio,' says Auntie Julie, dropping the receiver, stabbing the cigarette end into a conveniently positioned lid off a Bird's custard tin. 'Chrissy?' she yells. 'A woman just rang, says she was Mrs Stockdale . . . What's that in your mouth? You been in the larder? If you don't stop all this picking and pinching, you'll get a good tanning, my girl.'

'What did she want?' asks Chrissy, crossing arms over chest, stuffing hands under armpits.

'Well,' says Auntie Julie, stalking purposely into the back sitting room to hunt for her packet of Players, 'she wanted your mam. I told her she'd have to shout pretty loud.' She laughs at the memory, a harsh cackle which disintegrates into the inevitable cough. Still hacking, she fumbles for a cigarette and jams it in her mouth. When a lighted match is put to it, her face is illumined

22

– the yellowy upper lip, the dangling white yellow-streaked hair, the fierce lines centring on, drawing energy from, the live red tip.

The visit is a success. After all, Chrissy does not suffer the cross-examination she has been dreading regarding her personal history. No-one mentions the phone call to Auntie Julie. In fact, the Stockdales seem wonderfully incurious, their only concern is for her to enjoy herself, particularly at the tea table. And in truth she cannot remember more delicious or abundant fare. In such a hurry is she to consume as much of it as possible, and in such an agony of pleasure, that little moans escape her. The Stockdales are entranced. 'Try a slice of this, dear.' 'Come on, you can manage another.' 'My, that found a good home.' Vastly amused, Alderman Stockdale is reminded of a starving pup. And Mrs Stockdale silently rehearses what she will tell her friend and bridge partner, Mrs Garth: 'Poor little waif. I said to Elizabeth, I said: you ask her here whenever you like. Let her come and stay in the Christmas holiday. Honestly, Elsie, if you'd seen her, you'd feel same as me, you'd be itching to feed her up.'

It becomes the practice for Chrissy to visit Wold Enderby most weekends, chauffeured by Alderman Stockdale or one of his trusted employees. She no longer waits at the traffic lights, but watches for the car from the front window in Lister Avenue, and when it draws up, rushes from the house, slamming the door. More than the luxurious Stockdale house and its extensive garden, more even than its laden tea table, her imagination has been captured by the lady of the house, though she conceals this preference from Liz who is always rather off-hand with her mother. If, when they are reading their books, they are interrupted by Alderman Stockdale coming into the room, Liz will look up and answer him brightly. But should her mother come in, she will ignore her, even say

'What?' crossly when Mrs Stockdale speaks. Alderman Stockdale is kind and handsome, but he makes Chrissy uncomfortable; he seems always to be laughing at some secret joke, it's hard to tell when he is serious and when teasing. Mrs Stockdale, on the other hand, is the most comforting person imaginable. If Chrissy's own mother were to miraculously return, though she may not look wonderfully plump and squashy like Mrs Stockdale (Thomases, in Chrissy's experience, being without exception bony), Chrissy imagines her with the same fine attribute – motherliness oozing from every pore.

The moment arrives when she feels some explanation is owed her friend for not being invited back to Lister Avenue. They are in the orchard at Wold Enderby at the time, searching for fallen Orange Pippins. Liz has just passed on her mother's suggestion that Chrissy should come and stay next Friday and join the Stockdale party for Bonfire Night. It's a wonderful idea, she's about to accept, when the awkward thought drops of her inability to reciprocate. 'Oh, it would be lovely . . . But, but, I'm afraid I can't ask you back to tea or anything. Auntie Julie, you see, doesn't hold with visitors.'

Liz is very pleased to hear it. She can't tell how she knows about Auntie Julie's fearsomeness, she just does know. Perhaps it's the way, when her mother talks in an undertone about 'the poor little girl's aunt' to Mrs Garth, Mrs Garth shudders. Perhaps it's the way Chrissy lets drop an amazing snippet and then clams up. ('Gosh, you're allowed a top sheet as well as a bottom one,' she exclaimed one afternoon when Liz raised her bedcovers to retrieve a book. 'But everyone has a top sheet, otherwise the blankets would scratch,' Liz retorted; and Chrissy went pink and changed the subject.) Perhaps it's also the sly hints of girls at school. 'Have you been to Chrissy's yet?' asked Gilly Banks one day. And when Liz said 'No' and asked 'Why?', Gilly said 'Oh, nothing,' and turned and clutched Beryl

Ogden. They staggered off, splitting their sides. Obviously, some insult to her friend had been intended and it frustrated Liz, having nothing concrete to go on, to be powerless to stick up for her. She relieved her feelings by writing *G. Banks smells – true, signed B. Ogden* on the cloakroom wall.

Liz pictures Auntie Julie as the archetypal wicked stepmother, dark, crone-like, malevolent. It is perfectly fine with her if she never goes to tea at Chrissy's.

The trouble is, it does not seem altogether fine with Chrissy, who at this moment is standing hunched with her arms crossed over her chest and her hands stuffed under her armpits. Liz has come to recognize this posture as a distress signal. Hunting for something consoling to say, she works the toe of her shoe into the orange pulp of a rotten apple. For a time neither speaks. They are two small shapes under the apple trees; motionless, save for Liz's foot which they both study intently and their breath coming in faint puffs from their mouths and noses.

'It doesn't matter *whose* house, really, so long as we're allowed to be together.'

They look up and smile with relief. Liz had phrased it exactly, put parents and guardians in their place in the background, and they two – their friendship and the excitement of discovering the world together – centre stage.

One Monday morning in the middle of the Easter term, a new girl is found in the classroom. It is an event no-one has foreseen. In twos and threes they come running in from the cloakroom, then halt. There she sits, at a desk squeezed on to the end of the front row, staring out of the window. Stunned, they go to their seats. 'Who's *that*?' 'What's *she* doing here?' She looks most unpromising. And her name ('This is Monica Nelson, girls') – ugh, *Monica*. 'Natalie, will you show Monica the ropes?' asks Miss Wormold of the girl placed nearest the newcomer. Shielding her face with her hand, Natalie pulls a feel-sick look at the rest of the class who grimace back sympathetically.

In class 5B, Monica's beautiful elder sister is being given an easier time. Though her arrival is disturbing – unheard of in the fifth-formers' experience for someone to arrive slap-bang in the middle of term – this eccentricity is soon overlooked. She smiles shyly and apologetically, says, 'I hope I haven't taken anyone's place. I'm Marion Nelson, by the way,' and is at once overwhelmed by greetings and offers of help.

(Down the road at the Boys' Grammar School, Michael Nelson is nervously confronting a third-year class. And in the playground of the scruffiest primary school in town, the two younger Nelson boys are squaring up to rougher elements. Their trauma is the fault of Mr Nelson, a fiery-tempered man, who, after an accident at work in the Clyde shipyard, has obtained less strenuous employment in the local fish docks. With the compensation money paid by employers overjoyed to be rid of him, he has acquired a tiny house in a back street near the docks, and into it crammed his large family.)

Monica Nelson manages to look disagreeable without in any way ruffling the smooth surface of her face. It's the way she doesn't look right at you, but somehow beyond you, Liz decides. Her pale green eyes are lazy-lidded, never wide open, and are often directed upwards. She speaks in a hurried throw-away fashion, so fast you can hardly catch it, and with a peculiar accent hard to define. Though she has come here from Scotland, she doesn't speak Scottish like Miss MacBride who rolls her rrs and swings her voice up and down but whose every word is clearly enunciated. Monica, it appears, has lived in many places, places quite foreign to the girls in Lower Three B, such as Wearside, Merseyside and most recently Clydeside. Perhaps all this travelling has affected her speech; in fact, the way she gabbles it's as if she's trying to keep up with something.

During the succeeding weeks, Liz and Chrissy study her closely. Monica is taller than they are, and heavier but not fat. Her hair is mousy brown; lank wisps of it are forever escaping from its hair ribbon. Her face is very like her beautiful sister's in 5B, but on her it has gone wrong somehow and resulted in pudginess; and while Marion has an engagingly lively air, Monica always looks sleepy.

Gradually it dawns on them that Monica Nelson is unusually clever. Not clever like Janice Maw who is a swot and a teacher's pet; Monica's cleverness has an edge to it. Sometimes it wins her praise; sometimes, inexplicably, wrath or laughter. For instance, Miss Braithwaite, the student teacher whom all the girls adore, who wears blood-red lipstick and a tight sweater over her uplift bra, whom the girls draw in the margins of their notebooks and would die to please, Miss Braithwaite seems to find things that Monica says and writes hilarious. Handing back class essays one day, she comes to Monica's. 'Loved yours, Monica,' she says with an admiring grin. 'Specially the bit about Morning Assembly. Know *just* what you mean.' And Monica smiles secretively, turns her head to stare out of the window. Miss Cummings, head of English, has been driven wild, though. 'I thought yours was in very poor taste, Monica Nelson. Kindly do not descend to vulgarisms. Good construction. Nine out of ten.' And once (Miss Cummings on the verge of apoplexy): 'I can't think where you have been grubbing for information, Monica Nelson, but it is sufficient for gels in this class to know that a eunuch is a male servant.' And to the class's utter mystification, for they understand nothing of the matter and only Miss Cummings's displeasure, Monica is again awarded a generous nine marks out of ten. But then, everything to do with Monica Nelson seems strange and unsettling.

Most girls, most of the time, ignore her. She continues to feature as she began, as an intrusion. Sometimes, girls gather in front of her desk and shoot questions at her; generally, they leave her alone. Though they are forced to notice her when a teacher singles her out – moments they endure with disapproval – it's as though she doesn't properly belong, as though her late entrance into the class can never be forgiven. Only Liz cannot ignore Monica, or the *idea* of Monica. Of course, being 'different' herself in the way she speaks and in her private-school background, she feels lucky to have been accepted and is careful not to jeopardize her good fortune; so she indulges her curiosity discreetly, breaks off if other girls notice when she is exchanging a few words with the newcomer. But she watches her when she ought to be watching the blackboard, speculates about her as she rides home on the school bus.

'Have you noticed how she's always drawing and scribbling, and when you try to look she covers it up?' Liz asks Chrissy. 'Do you think she's poor? Her gym slip's all saggy and faded. She told me it used to be her sister's.'

Liz's interest puzzles Chrissy. 'So what?' she replies. 'Who cares?'

Every day after school, Chrissy watches Liz go off on the bus that ferries country children home to their villages, then searches for other girls with whom to while away some time. She is never in a hurry to return home to Auntie Julie. Sometimes, girls she walks home with invite her in; sometimes, she persuades them to join her for a game in the Robinson Rec, to play on the swings there or watch boys kicking a football. Often, long after other girls have vanished indoors, Chrissy is still hanging about outside, staring into shop windows, trailing her fingers to make them judder along garden fences, crouching to fondle dogs through the bars of a gate. Now and then as five o'clock approaches, she catches a glimpse of Monica Nelson, similarly employed. One afternoon they find themselves side by side in front of the surgical appliances shop.

Everything in the window – the rude shapes, the preponderance of naked pink and pervasive hint of mysterious unpleasantness – combines to sicken Chrissy; she has an unwelcome intuition that Dad and Auntie Julie are the sort of people the display is aimed at, people who are always moaning about their dentures and waterworks, their bowels, bunions and bronchial tubes.

Monica, who is staring in with gleeful appreciation, lets out a chuckle.

'What're you laughing at? It's all horrible.'

'No it's not.' She puts her head on one side, waves a hand. 'It gives you ideas.'

'What ideas?'

'I'll show you if you like. Want to come to our house?'

Chrissy hesitates, then, summoning a picture of the home awaiting her, agrees.

They set off, cross the busy main road dodging buses, cars, bicycles, leave the better area of town and head for the dockside. Until now, Chrissy has never thought of the main road as a divide between respectable and down-at-heel areas, but now she sees this is what it is. She grows apprehensive. 'Where *is* your house?'

'Maud Street. Where's yours?'

'Over there,' says Chrissy, trailing a hand behind her. 'Lister Avenue.'

'Posh, is it?'

'Not really,' she says defensively.

At last Monica swerves right, and they enter a street of terraced houses which ends abruptly in a house-high wall. Beyond the wall, tall cranes loom. Gulls swoop and scream. Monica goes through a gateless entry beside a tiny square of untidy grass. She pushes at the front door which is unlocked and opens with a slack lurching. Inside, a narrow passage heads straight for stairs. Two doors are set in the right-hand wall. The

29

first of these is open, and Chrissy glances in. The room is full of packing cases dwarfing a narrow table where a bespectacled youth sits with a pile of school books. Monica has gone straight upstairs. Before Chrissy can follow her, the farther door opens and Marion Nelson comes out carrying a cup of tea with sandwiches balanced in the saucer. She seems to float out. 'Hello,' she says brightly. But Chrissy, gawping, has lost her tongue. Marion does not pause but continues seamlessly – like a queen or a ballerina, thinks Chrissy – into the front room and closes the door.

'You coming?' hisses Monica from the landing, and Chrissy hurries up the steep flight.

In the small room at the top of the stairs are two beds, a chest of drawers and a tiny alcove with a clothes rail. Monica flops on to her stomach on the floor and reaches under one of the beds. A large rectangular sketchbook is retrieved, also a tin full of pencils and crayons. She flicks open the sketch book and presses flat an unused two-page spread, selects a pencil, lies on one hip with a knee brought up in front of her, and, propped on a forearm, begins to draw.

Chrissy squats beside her on the freezing lino, her back against the other bed. 'Is this Marion's?' she whispers; Monica nods. An overhead light bulb and a dingy window combine to give poor light. Monica squints at the page with her face close to it, and when her nose drips because of the cold, impatiently brushes the moisture over the paper. Chrissy gropes for her handkerchief.

'Monica?' someone calls, and Monica sits up and blinks. 'Come on,' – she gathers everything up, scrambles to her feet, then leads the way downstairs.

Chrissy is full of dread, not knowing whether her visit has official sanction. But Monica goes confidently through to the back room, and Chrissy, following, finds a bright fire, an easy chair containing a sleeping man whom she supposes is Mr Nelson, a dining table and

30

several hard chairs. A boy is seated at the table copying a textbook drawing of a galleon. A smaller boy is crouched on the hearth-rug reading a comic. Monica sits down at the table, motions Chrissy to join her, spreads out her work.

A door at the rear of the room opens and a lady, presumably Mrs Nelson, looks in from the kitchen. Her face is pleasant but crumpled. 'Monica – oh, hello, love,' she adds, seeing Chrissy who flashes the wide smile she has perfected over the years on the mothers of her schoolfriends, 'Want a drink? Something to eat?'

'Mm, please,' says Monica without looking up, and Mrs Nelson goes back into the kitchen.

Soon she reappears, a forefinger of one hand crooked through the handles of two brimming mugs, her other hand bringing a heaped plate of jam sandwiches. 'I have sugared 'em, petal,' she says reassuringly to Chrissy, who, pleased and surprised to be included, overlooks her dislike of sugared tea. 'Are you a friend of Monica's?'

'Yes,' says Chrissy, darting an embarrassed look at Monica, who is taking no notice of the conversation whatever.

'That's nice. And you live close by here, do you?'

'Fairly.'

The boy drawing at the table looks up and stares at Chrissy. Also, Mr Nelson's noisy breathing quietens.

'Well, you come and play with Monica whenever you like.'

'Oh, thanks, Mrs Nelson.'

As soon as their mother has gone, the two boys rise and swoop on the plate of sandwiches. Monica is too quick for them. 'Gerroff,' she growls, swiping at them with her free arm. She drops her pencil and takes a handful – four or five of the quartered slices – and puts these in a heap at the side of her work. 'Go on,' she urges Chrissy, who catches her sense of urgency and snatches three for herself. In a trice, the boys have cleared the remainder. 'Pigs, you've had yours,' Monica grumbles to the boy opposite. But then her face clears as her eyes fall on his drawing. 'That's really good, Keith.' She watches him working for a moment with a pleased expression, then returns to her own effort.

Chrissy leans back and puts her head on one side to view Monica's drawing from Monica's viewpoint. Then she gasps, and looks uneasily across at Mr Nelson in fear that he might wake and demand to view his daughter's handiwork. For it is extremely rude.

'It's Miss Cummings,' she whispers, shocked, but also awestruck at her friend's cleverness. 'It looks just like her.'

'Of course.'

'I mean, it *is* her, yet it isn't. She doesn't look as horrible as that, so why's it look like her?'

'It's a caricature, like in a cartoon.'

'Oh.'

The longer Chrissy looks, the more items she recognizes from the surgical appliances shop, and the greater becomes her sense of unease. Miss Cumming's attire, for instance, consists of knee-length rubber knickers and horrible cup things attached to her chest with tubes dangling; supported by a crutch, she stands on one surgically booted foot and waves the other leg, artificial and bandaged, jauntily in the air; balanced on her head is a huge bedpan. 'What's that?' asks Chrissy fearfully, pointing to the figure's chest.

'It said *breast pump* on the box. Didn't you notice?'

As if to deny the possibility, which in any case she cannot begin to understand, Chrissy violently shakes her head.

At that moment, with a great shout and flinging about of limbs, Mr Nelson comes to.

Monica and her brothers look up. Calmly, they observe him; unmoved, receive the torrent of spat-out words, the whiff of sour breath. Some of the words are swear words, Chrissy suspects, for the kitchen door opens and Mrs Nelson rushes in calling, 'Jock, Jock, we've a visitor, mind.'

Chrissy is suddenly afraid that an alert Mr Nelson might rise up and march on the table to see how his daughter has occupied herself; his half-asleep wrath is fearsome enough, a fully roused and provoked Mr Nelson doesn't bear thinking of. To her great relief, Mr Nelson closes his blood-shot eyes and subsides; Mrs Nelson, darting a sad little smile at Chrissy, returns to the kitchen.

'It's his work,' Monica explains. 'It wears him out. He has to clock on at five in the morning. Sometimes it's so cold his gloves freeze to the fish boxes. He's a victim of exploitation.' This last is stated matter-of-factly, and Chrissy assumes it is a job description which may have something to do with lorries, 'exploitation' putting her vaguely in mind of 'transportation'.

'I'd better go,' she says.

'All right.'

Evidently, there will be no ceremonial leave-taking, so Chrissy stands up and buttons her school mac. No-one comes with her into the hall passage. The front door is sticky to open and slams abruptly when she tries to close it. Hysteria mounts as she flies to the end of Maud Street. She pictures Mr Nelson giving chase, or the breast pump reaching its tentacles after her. Along the busy main road she calms down, walks sedately, watches for a chance to cross to the other side.

Liz burns to get herself invited to Monica's house. She has made Chrissy recount her visit again and again, pouncing on any new details.

'Jam sandwiches – just jam? You never said that before. Are you sure just jam?'

'Yes, strawberry.'

'And three brothers? I thought you said two. Gosh, that's five of them, seven with her parents. And the room's only how big?'

Chrissy indicates a portion of the Stockdale's sitting room. 'But not as wide. Only up to the front of the settee.'

'You wouldn't think you could get a table in and still walk round. Tell me again about the drawing.'

Hearing once more the shocking details of Miss Cumming's likeness, Liz is provoked to devise a plan. She will tell her parents she is going to tea at Chrissy's place one day next week – Thursday, say – but instead she and Chrissy will walk home with Monica and wangle an invitation. Mr Stockdale will be persuaded to fetch Liz later at a given time from Chrissy's.

'But Auntie Julie won't like it,' protests Chrissy when the plan is outlined. She blushes as she says this, for it is Chrissy who won't like it; Auntie Julie couldn't care less how many amorphous little girls are about the house so long as nothing is expected of her and she can go on exactly as usual – cutting her corns over the hearth, hawking up spit, shouting enquiries to Dad (who is deaf) as to whether he's had his bowels open yet. Chrissy feels it is still too soon to risk an encounter between her aunt and her brilliant new friend.

'I needn't come in. I'll wait outside in the porch, and tell Daddy it's because I didn't want to keep him waiting.'

'All right,' says Chrissy dubiously.

Since Chrissy's visit to Maud Street, Liz has thrown caution to the winds. She talks openly to Monica in the classroom, invites her to join Chrissy and herself in the playground. She purposely brings three of everything to school for break – three apples, three oranges, three of Mrs Stockdale's melting moments. All because she thirsts to get a peek at Monica's drawings.

On Tuesday her persistence is rewarded. When Chrissy and Liz come charging into the classroom after dinner – which is an illegal thing to do because the bell hasn't gone and officially they should be outside in the playground – they find Monica scribbling at her desk. (She sits at a different dinner table composed of faster eaters, so is always let out before them.)

Liz goes quickly to her side. Monica, after a moment's hesitation, withdraws her shielding hand.

Liz is not disappointed. The page is crammed with familiar faces: Valerie Dove and Angie Hutchings clinging together like dopey twins, Gilly Banks with an ape's body swinging from a climbing rope, and Pamela Pettifer splitting her pants vaulting the horse. Liz dwells for some time on her own likeness – she has a basket over an arm and is dispensing goodies – but decides the depiction is favourable: after all, she hasn't been given outstanding spots like Natalie Smith or had her ears hideously enlarged like Beryl Ogden. Chrissy has been depicted quite kindly, too – cramming food into her mouth, which is fair comment.

'Gosh, you are clever, Monica.'

Monica, putting her head on one side, seems pleased.

'I'm playing with Chrissy after school on Thursday. You can come with us, if you like. We're not going to her house exactly, just sort of messing around. I might get some money for crisps.'

'Mm. All right,' agrees Monica.

When Liz has told her parents about going to Chrissy's after school on Thursday, Mrs Stockdale slips from the room. Liz opens her geography textbook and starts to learn by heart the names of American states. Alderman Stockdale reaches for the evening paper to check whether the new *Hennage & Stockdale, funeral directors who care* advertisement is correct in every particular.

In the hall, Mrs Stockdale consults her telephone book. Then she lifts the receiver and dials.

'Oh, hello, Miss Thomas. Mrs Stockdale here, Elizabeth's mummy.'

Auntie Julie, caught with a new purgative concoction nearing the boil on the gas ring, says impatiently, 'Aye?'

35

'Um, Elizabeth tells us Chrissy's invited her to play after school on Thursday.' And when this provokes no comment, she continues, 'It's very kind of you to have her.'

'Oh, that Chrissy does as she likes.'

'Then it is all right with you, Miss Thomas?'

'No skin off my nose. That it then?' – for the bubbling sound has grown agitated.

'Just to add that, of course, her daddy will collect her at half past five.'

'Right y'are, duck. Cheerio.' Just in time – Auntie Julie's dash into the kitchen allows her to grab a cloth and sweep saucepan from stove barely a second before the seething brew flows over.

'How did you get it?' asks Monica.

They are standing in the Robinson Rec, each holding an open bag in one hand and with the other conveying crisps to their mouths. Monica is curious to know how Liz got so much money, for Liz has bought three bags of best quality crisps at fivepence each, not twopenny bags of broken crisps. Liz, who can always get money via the simple expedient of asking for it, munches in silence, fearing that a truthful reply may sound boastful. Chrissy dispels her embarrassment by changing the subject. 'Gilly and Beryl are on the swings. Shall we go and play with them?'

'No,' say Monica and Liz, and Monica suggests going to look at the shops. Her companions, who recall how a visit to the surgical appliances shop window led to Chrissy visiting Maud Street, readily agree. Today, Monica leads them to M and B Modes.

'Who'd want to wear them?' marvels Liz, surveying the gowns displayed in the window.

'My sister, probably,' Monica regrets.

Chrissy complains that a yellow dress puts her in mind of sick. A strapless ballgown in red particularly disgusts Liz for the way it presents the dummy's bosoms. 'Like putting them on a shelf,' she shudders. They agree, squirming at the shame of it.

'Be funny on the wrong person, though,' suggests Monica. 'On Miss Thirkettle, say.'

They collapse with mirth imagining the wiry, mannish little games mistress thus tricked out, and make such a row as they howl and shove one another that Madame M and B Modes comes angrily to the window making clear-off gestures.

'I bet you could draw Miss Thirkettle in it,' Liz says artlessly as they move away.

'I could try. Want to come to our house?'

'Yeah,' they shout, and set off in the manner of those inclined to waste time no further.

Mrs Nelson sits by the fire, knitting needles tucked under her arms, fingers flying. 'Wait while I get to the end of the row,' she tells the girls, who have come downstairs, not in the expectation of sustenance, but because the patch of floor between Monica's and Marion's beds is too small to contain the three of them.

They sit at the table and Monica spreads out her sketchbook.

'I haven't seen you before, have I, love?'

'No, Mrs Nelson. I'm Elizabeth Stockdale – Liz.'

What a nicely brought up little girl, thinks Mrs Nelson, and hopes there is some cake left.

When she's gone, Liz and Chrissy give Monica's busy pencil absolute attention. Mugs of tea and a mountain of sandwiches ('Sorry, no cake today, lasses; the boys've had it') are temporally diverting, but gradually, with some debate as to who should wear what, several teachers striking unlikely poses materialize – one astride a sit-up-and-beg bicycle, another wielding a hockey stick, another conducting morning assembly – wearing gowns like the ones in M and B Modes' window.

Liz, who was mildly disappointed to find only

Mrs Nelson at home, is pleased when Marion appears briefly; and pleased but at the same time apprehensive when she hears Mr Nelson's voice in the hall (sounding roughly Scottish, unlike Mrs Nelson who has a Lancashire accent – no wonder Monica speaks so peculiarly).

'Dad's back,' calls Monica to her mother in the kitchen. Liz picks up the warning tone in her voice, but is reassured when Monica goes on placidly drawing.

'Cup of tea, dear?' asks Mrs Nelson, putting her head into the room. She sounds anxious.

Mr Nelson grunts, and Mrs Nelson closes the door.

'What have we here?' growls Mr Nelson, looking not at his daughter's work but at her two visitors.

'Liz Stockdale and Chrissy Thomas. They're in my class at school.'

'Is that so?'

They nod eagerly.

'Let's hear you then. Which one's which?'

'I'm Chrissy,' says Chrissy, showing her best smile.

'I'm Liz.'

'And where d'ye come from, Chrissy and Liz?'

'Lister Avenue.'

'Wold Enderby, actually,' says Liz, suddenly nervous.

'Wold Enderby *actually*. D'ye hear that, Monica? We've a proper young lady here unless I'm very much mistaken.'

Liz's ears go hot. She considers the merits first of denying, then of conceding the description. Mr Nelson has put her in a panic; she doesn't know how to be with him. She recognizes him as the sort of man who labours on her father's building sites, whom her father would address as 'Nelson' or 'You, man'. Hitherto, this sort of person has always spoken to her deferentially. No sign of deference here. Mr Nelson looks challenging and speaks sarcastically. She is alarmed and at a loss, she wishes he would go away or pick up the newspaper.

38

'Didn't know you were mixing with the high and mighty at this new school of yours. What's that yer doing, lass? Show us here.'

Monica obediently turns her book to afford her father a clear view; then, to her friends' utter consternation, proceeds to explain who the models are and why she has clothed them as she has. Mr Nelson is interested. He doesn't laugh but after one or two sharp questions begins to praise her. 'You ought to sign it,' he adds. 'That's quite a talent you've got there. You could work for the papers doing drawings like that, but you don't want some naughty wee fella passing yours off as his. Mark my words – all my life I've watched other buggers make brass outta my sweat – always claim what's yours.' He thumps his finger down on the page. 'Sign it.'

'Right, Dad. What shall I put? Not Monica . . .'

'Something short and snappy. Like the fella I always like in the *Worker*.' He seizes a newspaper from the side of the easy chair, begins to hunt in it.

'Dad reads the *Daily Worker*,' Monica tells them proudly. 'He's a Communist.'

'Here we are – *Bic*. Because his real name's Bicknell or somesuch.'

Monica stares dreamily into space, then picks up her pencil and in the corner of the page writes *Nel*.

'Nel,' they murmur, looking up for Mr Nelson's approval. But he's no longer interested in schoolgirls' doings, a headline in the *Daily Worker* has drawn his eye.

Monica is still contemplating her new name.

'*Nell*,' cries Liz suddenly, clapping her hands.

And Chrissy gets the idea. 'Yeah. Nell's a much better name than Monica.'

The centre of attention looks up with a glassy expression; they laugh and clutch her arms. It's like a christening. From now on, whatever she calls herself in future, Nell she will always be to them.

'Hello,' drawled a smoke-ruined voice, familiar to thousands. 'This is Monica Nelson.' Its owner leaned back languorously, assumed her tele talk-show pose – little finger pressed to quizzical eyebrow, lids drooping under the weight of frankly false lashes, teeth bared ready to snap up anything the world cared to throw.

'Hello, Nell?' said Chrissy, nervousness turning the greeting into a question.

The famous columnist swivelled in her chair. 'Bog off, would you darling?' she hissed to her young male assistant, who dropped what he was doing and left the office. The door safely closed, she slumped, shedding the Monica Nelson look entirely. 'Chrissy,' she said in Nell's voice, sounding genuinely pleased. 'It's been weeks. How are you?'

'Sorry to ring you at work, but all I ever get from the flat is your answerphone.'

'Ah. And I've been too darn bushed to play the thing back. But listen – how are you?'

'Oh, all right. How about you?'

'Tired, permanently past it. But business is good so mustn't grumble.'

'We watched you on *Question Time*. You looked terrific.'

'Hours in make-up, lovie. How're Tony and the kids?'

'We're all fine. I told you about Davey getting a research fellowship?'

'Yeah – great stuff.'

'Thanks ever so for all those cuttings you sent him; he was so pleased, saved him no end of bother.'

'Glad to be of use.'

'Amanda sends her love . . .'

'Returned,' murmured Nell – she'd put Chrissy's daughter up for a few weeks last year while the girl was searching for a bedsit, found it a daunting experience.

'She's landed a super job at the new leisure centre

here. You should see her, Nell – full of it.'

'I can imagine. Where is this new leisure centre?'

'Where the bathing pool used to be.'

'You mean they've got rid of the open air swimming pool – where we displayed our young charms to an unappreciative populace? Bloody sacrilege.'

'Oh, it's all change here. You must come and see.'

'I will – soon as I can fit it in.'

'Um, I was rather hoping . . . The thing is, something's up with Liz.'

'Oh no, not Nathan. She wrote and told me about his heart trouble.'

'It's not that. She *says* it's to do with Rosie and some man, but she's in such a state about it . . .'

'State? Surely, a thing like that's right up her street? Good grief – a clinical psychologist? She's paid *not* to get into states. Anyway, Liz doesn't.'

'She doesn't *usually*, but she has now. That's why I suspect . . . Mind you though, if it were Amanda . . .'

Nell reached for a cigarette – there was always a packet within reach kept open at a handy angle – stuck it in her mouth and lit up, thinking, as Chrissy fretted in her ear about the end of the world as the great earth mother saw it, that at least she had managed to avoid one of life's pitfalls. 'Uhuh,' she put in soothingly through her ciggy; 'frightful, must be.'

'But I agree, it's not like Liz to go over the top. Nell, you remember the Poole business?'

Nell removed her cigarette. 'You don't mean the *Mr* Poole business?'

'She brought it up.'

'But I thought she told us we were never to talk about it.'

'Well, now she has. Seems to be on her mind. Nell, I really think she needs us.'

'Right,' breathed Nell. She reached for her diary – 'Hang on a sec,' – and leafed through the coming days with increasing gloom. 'Doesn't look good. I suppose,

Chrissy, it's best if we meet at your place – as it's home and all that.' (She meant that, of the three of them, only Chrissy still resided in the territory where they grew up.)

'Of course. Liz is tied up for the rest of the week, but she's hoping to come after that.'

'I'll just have to cancel something. Towards the end of the next week *might* be possible.'

'Oh great. That's super. Shall I tell Liz or will you?'

'You. She and I are always edgy over the phone – don't know why – we're terrific correspondents. Even when we meet it's dodgy for the first half hour or so, till the veneer rubs off. Unlike you and me.'

'Mm,' said Chrissy, who often heard a similar complaint from Liz. 'But I know it's important for her to see you too.'

'Naturally,' Nell said, for anything of deep significance in their lives required the scrutiny of all three. It always had.

'I'll phone her, then let you know. 'Bye, Nell. Take care.'

'You too, Chrissy, flower.'

Fenby-cum-Laithby is a pretty village not two miles distant from Wold Enderby where the Stockdales used to live; travelling in another direction, it lies eight miles south of the part of town where Chrissy and Nell grew up. That afternoon, in The Old Rectory, Fenby-cum-Laithby, Chrissy Duckenfield (née Thomas) rose from the study chair where she had been sitting talking to Nell on the telephone. It was her husband's study, lined with law books and books on local history, reflecting both his profession as a solicitor and his spare-time enthusiasm. (The tools and regalia of another enthusiasm were locked away in a drawer of the old oak desk, safe from the profane eyes of women and others not on the square.) Chrissy's own 'study', more of a junk room on the second floor, didn't contain a telephone. Hence, seeking time and privacy – for it required courage to ring up a national newspaper and demand to speak to a national institution – she had come in here, her husband being safely out of the way at work. With the school holidays in full swing, neither the hall nor her bedroom could be relied on: one never knew when a daughter might burst in to borrow a hair-drier or a son arrive in the house with half a dozen noisy friends.

Children were always in evidence in this house, their own five children and other people's. So far, none of the Duckenfield brood had shown any inclination to decamp permanently. Of the two who had made a stab at leaving home, Davey returned every vacation often accompanied by chums bearing sleeping bags, and Amanda, on completing her training in London, powered straight home to reclaim her room and shape up the locals. Now, in the brand new leisure centre in town, most mornings and evenings found Amanda pacing, stretching, beating her naked feet before classes of fifty persons trying to emulate her – an indiarubber vision of perpetual motion, leotard and tights like an ultimate dream skin, glossy, crease-free, endlessly elastic. 'To the left, to the right – strrretch – go for it,' squeaked her amplified voice over blaring music.

The younger three were still at school: Neil attended the local sixth-form college, Joy and Clare the comprehensive. There were also two cats, and a pony in a rented paddock. For herself, Chrissy would enlarge the family further, but she'd decided not to push her luck; Tony had been very fair and was only occasionally complaining. And when Davey and Amanda left school it was a shock to discover how, if anything, they grew more expensive. Three further young adults queuing up for tranches of Tony's income (sizeable though this was with his services indispensable to some of the wealthiest businessmen in the region) seemed quite enough to expect of him.

She had always thought of their marriage as a system

43

of negotiation. In her mind was a pair of scales: on one side of the balance was the premise (adhered to by both) that she had done him a terrific favour by marrying him in the first place; on the other was his work rate and subsequent material success. She had trained as a teacher and practised the profession for a few months here and there, but her ambition was always to surround herself with a family as far removed in character as could conceivably be from the one she herself was raised in. Her children's lives consumed her, their every enthusiasm – football, horse riding, films, rock, t'ai chi, astronomy – became her enthusiasms. God forbid that her children's friends should discover an eccentrically self-absorbed adult in the Auntie Julie mode: rather, she prided herself on dispensing warm hang-loose welcomes. 'Your mum's nice; I wish mine was such a sport' – the exact words, according to Amanda, of a friend she'd once brought home from London. Chrissy wasn't sure who had charmed her most – the girl for the remark, her daughter for reporting it.

While arranging things so well to her taste, Chrissy was scrupulous about being fair to Tony. His tolerance and generosity – every bicycle, every pony, every school trip abroad and expensive extra – she weighed in his favour; in her own she reckoned good looks and reasonableness and, very heavily indeed, such sacrifices as joining the Ladies' Circle and taking part in hideous tomfoolery like Rotarian Quiz Nights. When, as sometimes happened, her photograph appeared in the local press above such captions as *Rotarian and Mrs Tony Duckenfield arrive at the Winter Gardens* or *Circlers look on as their new president receives her jewel of office*, the scales went against Tony with a great thud, for Chrissy could picture only too clearly the scene in the Fairfields Nursing Home – Mrs Stockdale snipping out the photograph and posting it on to Liz. In a day or two, she would receive confirmation:

'Dear Chrissy,' (would write Mrs Stockdale)

'What a thrill to see your picture in last night's *Telegraph*. Mrs Garth and I showed it round to everyone and they all said what a beautiful dress and what a gracious smile. I've cut it out and sent it to Elizabeth, I know she'll be interested. Your hubby must be very proud of you, dear, as would Alderman Stockdale be, if only he were still with us. I was telling them here about how you used to come and stay with us at Wold Enderby. What a dear little poppet you were . . .' (Here would Mrs Stockdale pause, as thoughts, impossible to write, ran on in her head along these lines: 'and what a poor little waif with no background to speak of. Yet there's our Elizabeth with all those piano and elocution lessons behind her, never once had her photo in the paper, wasting her life on loonies and ne'er-do-wells. Her Daddy tried to warn her: there are some folk in this life it doesn't pay to waste time on. But you never could tell our Elizabeth anything. And when she married that man . . . I don't mind telling you, dear, it was a great disappointment – not that we're prejudiced or anything.') Omitting these confidences, confining herself to a sorrowful sigh, Mrs Stockdale would conclude prosaically. 'Do come and visit again soon. Mrs Garth and I often talk about you. You're a real burst of sunshine, Chrissy. Though I know you must be busy, Tony being such an active man about town.'

Mrs Stockdale's letters, though they propelled Chrissy to the Fairfields Nursing Home with a winning smile and a box of All Gold, gave her horrible misgivings. She imagined on Liz's doormat the reproachful letter accompanying her photograph. At times like these it took more than a teenage rave-up or a new pair of jodhpurs to restore equilibrium to the marital scales.

She looked at her watch – no good, now, phoning Liz who would be still at work in the clinic. If they weren't back too late this evening she'd try and catch her then. She went out of the study, through the hall, into the roomy kitchen. Here she stood leaning against the pinewood table; no need, she remembered, to cook for herself or the kids. Tonight, she and the younger two children planned to visit the leisure centre, Clare to swim, she and Joy to join Amanda's aerobic class; afterwards they would go to a pizza house where Neil had a holiday job waiting at table. Amanda would come home and fix her own meal of nuts, fruit, tofu and vegetables. Davey and his friends were away on a walking trip for a few days. Which only left Tony to accommodate. Tonight was his Masonic night; she'd fix him something tasty on a tray, for she was feeling mellow towards him, the satisfactory evening ahead tipped the scales marginally in his favour. She began to set out the wherewithal to make his favourite leek and sausage pie.

Rolling out the pastry, Chrissy's mind returned to her marriage. It was a good one. A useful and productive vehicle. Not exciting or romantic (and how could it be, considering the relationship's antecedents? – her snootiness to him, years of Nell and Liz pouring scorn) but it had enabled both to get what they wanted from life. Which was as much as she and Tony had hoped for all those years ago. More than once, Chrissy had tried to explain this to Liz and Nell. She remembered accidentally letting drop about Tony being a Freemason and how Liz and Nell had hysterics, told her she ought to put her foot down. 'But it's *his thing*,' she protested, having no need to indicate her own things which were everywhere they cared to look – all the trappings of a rich home life, of adolescents and babies. Guiltily, she recalled lapsing into disloyal giggles as Nell speculated on the scene in the Lodge – little Tony with his skinny chest and legs all bare ('I wonder if they keep their socks on?') swearing blood-chilling oaths. That was really bad of her, she thought; disloyal. Still, she must have impressed them with her equanimity over the

Masons because they never mentioned it again.

('Tony's another child to her,' Liz said afterwards to Nell. 'She likes indulging him. She'll go to his ladies' nights as fondly as she goes to Davey's football matches.'

'Of *course*,' breathed Nell, much easier now they had managed to explain and pigeon-hole a bizarre and worrying aspect of one of their lives.)

A laden Liz pushed down the door-latch with her elbow. In one hand she carried a briefcase, in the other two bulging carrier bags. A key ring dangled from between her teeth. 'Managed to get to Sainsbury's at lunch time,' she said, dropping the keys on to the table. Carefully, she lowered the bags. 'Cor – something smells good.'

'Matzo meal fish cakes with spicy tomato sauce.'

'Nathan Learman, the working woman's dream-man,' she cried, going to him, sliding her arms round his waist, laying her head on his broad chest. He hugged her. She heard his heart going and thought of its lesion. 'Love you,' she growled.

'And me, you, babe.' He smacked her backside. 'Go on, go and change. You know how I get when you're not down for the dishing up.'

'Right. I'll just put the shopping away.' Not until she had completed this task and started towards the hall did she suddenly recall her uppermost thought on the journey home. 'Rosie in?'

'Nope. Soon as I got back she asked to borrow the car. I said OK. We agreed we don't want her cycling in the dark or waiting around for buses.'

'Absolutely,' she confirmed, her face smooth and untroubled. 'Be down in a tick.'

Fifteen minutes later she was back, showered and changed into track suit and trainers. Her hair was hooked back behind her ears, her face naked and pearly; she looked, he thought, about twelve years old.

When he put the food before her she made keen

noises, but forked it up wearily, her head propped on the splayed fingers of her left hand.

'Hard day?'

'You could say that.' She paused, added shortly, 'Drug dependency unit.'

'Uhuh.' He didn't press her. She was always cagey about her work. Sometimes this annoyed him, made her seem primly secretive; but it was a very minor irritation, on a level, he guessed, with her dislike of his habit after all these years of never replacing the lavatory seat. In any case, usually he was too eager to discuss his own doings to care about Liz holding back. 'Guess who came to see me this afternoon?'

She was glad he'd changed the subject. The reason for her reluctance to talk about work was simple – she wanted to forget it. Early on in her career, she'd had a hard time putting it out of her mind; flashing images haunted her, arguments re-ran in her head; by bedtime these were taking over and ripe for a night's rampage through her dreams. Only by willing a huge mental effort in the peak of her exhaustion, did she train herself to blot out work as she entered the house. 'Who?'

'Brendan Foyle.'

'Brendan? How's he making out?'

'Very well. It's ironic, but the firm's using him. And it's costing us. He's got more work than he can handle. In fact, he's asked me to join him.'

'And are you going to?'

He reached for extra vegetables. 'I might.'

'Good,' she said encouragingly, watching him. Could this be a way out, an escape route? Or would it be a case of out of the frying pan? Three years ago, the firm had been bought by an American outfit, the British management team was dismissed, sharp suited young men moved in. Brendan and Nathan, the two top design engineers, applied to other firms without success – their work was good, but they were getting on. A year ago, unable to stick the new situation, Brendan set up on his own as a design consultant.

'What wouldn't I give to tell the Boston boys where to stick it? Anyway, I said I'd go and see him on Saturday – if that's all right with you.'

'Of course. Make a weekend of it, if you like. As a matter of fact, I'm thinking of taking a couple of weeks' leave. I've got quite a lot due. Next week I'll go to Chrissy's for a few days, then maybe you and I could do something. I really feel I could do with a break . . .'

But he wasn't listening. 'It'd be a risk . . .'

'So what?' she asked, putting aside her fork. 'The children are very nearly off our hands. The mortgage is piddling – we could pay it off now if we wanted to. My job's OK. It's not big bucks, but we can bank on it – I can't see my customer source drying up, can you? So, if it's what you really want, take the plunge. Do it.'

'Yes? Of course, if the symptoms come back I may have to have this angioplasty. Anyway, I'll take a look at Brendan's books; phone a few people. But thanks, Liz.'

'Darling – for heaven's sake.'

He started to gather the plates.

'Leave it,' she commanded. 'You cooked, so I clear.'

'Let's do it together. You're tired.'

In her bedroom, perched on the side of the bed, Liz dialled Chrissy's number. She was already with Chrissy in her mind, and when the ringing stopped, anticipated her sing-song 'Hel-lo'. So a stream of numbers rattled off in breathless triumph took her aback. 'Um – Amanda?'

'Yes, hello,' confirmed a brisk baby voice.

'It's Liz Learman here. Is Chrissy about by any chance?'

'Oh, hello. Sorry, Mum's out. She went for a pizza with Joy and Clare. Can I give her a message?'

'Just that I rang. Congratulations, by the way, on the new job. How's it going?'

'Oh, brill. Super-tremendous. We've had to put on three extra classes. People here are terribly keen. Amazing.'

'That's good,' said Liz, feeling all the enthusiastic words had been used up.

'Yes, isn't it? Do you want Mum to phone you back?'

The fire-cracker delivery was making her head spin. 'Er, yes, please – if she's not too tired. Otherwise tomorrow will do.'

'Tell you what – I'll leave her a note. Two notes acksherly – one by the phone, the other on her pillow. I always do that, then she's bound to see one of them. I won't be able to tell her myself 'cos I'm going to bed. Did you know that one hour's sleep before midnight's worth three after? It was in my *Health and Fitness* magazine. Amazing.'

'I'll have to remember that. I'm a bit of a night hawk and I do get tired.'

'Oo dear, then you ought to make up with some early nights. I'm nearly always asleep by ten and I'm never tired – really. Everso nice talking to you, er, Liz. I'll write those notes for Mum straight away. *Ciao.*'

Liz's grin lasted all the way downstairs and into the sitting room.

Rosie was there, staring over her father's head at the television. She started when her mother came in, said, 'Thanks, Dad,' and dropped the car keys into his lap.

'Had a good evening?' asked Nathan, looking up from the newspaper he was half reading while inattentively watching the screen.

Rosie grunted.

'I say, I've just been talking to Amanda Duckenfield,' Liz began. But without a word, indeed, without a look, Rosie pushed past her into the hall and ran upstairs. Liz's amusement withered.

An hour or so later, Liz said she was expecting a call and would wait for it upstairs.

'If you don't want this on . . .' Nathan offered.

'No, go ahead and watch. I'll be down later.' She kissed the back of his neck and went off, glad of the television's noise trailing her which would drown the sound of any altercation. For she had decided to tackle Rosie.

First, she went and sat on her bed. She'd already thought this out once and reached the conclusion that there was no need to feel guilty or go and eat humble pie. Rosie was behaving badly, treating her parents' concern as if it was of no account, having for years taken full advantage of it. Think, she urged herself, of all those far-flung universities Rosie had asked to be chauffeured to last year while she was making her choice. Liz had used up precious holiday taking her. And think of all the times she begged Nathan to help her with her Maths. And then, after all that, just blurting that she wasn't going and they'd better get used to it. Damn it, the Learmans' was a democratic household. She and Nathan always consulted the children when they'd a mind to do something or other. No need to kid herself, the fault lay with Rosie.

Liz sighed. Trouble was, Rosie was ignoring her, creating an atmosphere. Sooner or later this would get to Nathan.

She stood up, walked to the wardrobe, frowned into the long mirror at her pale face, dark eyes, her neat small body and swingy straight hair – not quite as black as it used to be; turned and walked back to the bed. Just remember, she said sternly to the unbleached woven counterpane, the poor kid's having a tough time at the moment. Her first love affair. Probably, with complications. A *harrowing* time, she insisted, gearing herself up to feel really bad for Rosie.

Her mind arranged along corrected lines, she went

quickly to Rosie's door and gave it a tap. No answer. She tapped louder.

'What?' came the inauspicious reply.

'Can I come in?'

There was a pause, then the door jerked open, Rosie's face showed. 'Wha-for?'

'I'd like to talk . . . First of all, though, I'd like to apologize if I, well, gave the impression I thought you were lying.'

'So?'

'Well . . . can I come in, Rosie?'

'I'm tired. I want to go to bed.'

'For goodness sake, you seem so hostile – I've said I'm sorry.'

'Want a prize for it? I told you, I'm going to bed.' She closed the door.

Liz stood looking at it, remarking hitherto unnoticed features – pock marks in the paint, a faintly discernible wood knot. Noise from the downstairs television bore gently in on her. Leave it, she decided. Try again tomorrow.

Back in the bedroom, she lay on the counterpane, waiting for Chrissy's call.

iv

'Daddy, what's a Communist?' asks Liz, pouring milk over her cornflakes.

A small convulsion ripples the *Daily Telegraph*.

'Don't slouch, Elizabeth,' says Mrs Stockdale, employing the tone understood by nice little girls to mean *'I'm sorry you asked that; abandon the subject at once.'*

But Liz doesn't even glance at her less-sensible parent. 'Did you hear, Daddy? I asked, what's a Communist?' And for the moment she placidly tucks into her breakfast.

This is too much – page six cleaves to page seven, the whole thing collapses. 'And why, might I ask, do you require to know?' demands Alderman Stockdale over his defeated newspaper.

Liz's spoon is stilled. A feeling is born that she has miscalculated. 'Just wondered.' She decides to finish her meal rapidly.

Her problem has been how to introduce Nell to the Stockdale household. She and Chrissy are eager to include their new chum in their weekend get-togethers. The difficulty is, will Maud Street meet with the chauffeur's approval? The very thought of the big black aldermanic Humber drawing up before the dockyard wall makes Liz nervous. Nell says her father works on these docks. This is bad news. The word 'docker' is a term of abuse as uttered by Alderman Stockdale. Desperately, Liz has been casting in her mind for other ways of describing Mr Nelson, who seems to her an interesting, albeit faintly alarming, man. On her way down to breakfast this morning, she suddenly recalled Nell confiding proudly, 'He's a Communist.' Liz isn't sure what this means but thinks it may refer to a club or organization like 'Rotarian' or 'Mason', and anyway it sounds better than 'docker' and might persuade Alderman Stockdale to keep an open mind. Having uttered the word with hopeful calculation, she now knows it was a mistake.

'Very well,' says her father with menace. 'Just tell me where you heard it.'

Oh no. She's been through this sort of bother before, soon after starting at the grammar school, in fact. Emerging from the school toilets one day, she asked the girl nearest to her, 'What does fuck mean?' Gilly Banks gasped and turned and whispered in Pam Pettifer's ear. 'It's the worst word you can say,' Pam said sternly. Chastened by her classmates' reaction, Liz dropped the matter, but kept thinking about it. The idea that words can be good, bad or even 'the worst' – never mind their meaning – was new to her; not a whisper of it ever reached her at The Lawns. And no wonder, she decided, for it seemed a daft idea. Surely Pam and Gilly were mistaken. 'What does fuck mean?' she asked her parents later that day at the tea table.

Though she was not to be enlightened, the consequences of her innocent enquiry were instantaneous and frightening. Her father tore into the hall to ring the headmistress at home. Next morning during Prayers, Miss Devlin ranted for fifteen mystifying minutes about girls who write on lavatory walls, and declared that from henceforth prefects would patrol the toilets and all satchels (presumably because of their contents – pens, knives, sharp instruments, etc.,) must be left outside. Liz, the instigator of this bitterness, hung her head and felt the blood mount in her ears – all because of an odd little word of which no-one could tell her the meaning. Perhaps it didn't have a meaning. Perhaps you could just open your mouth and say something terrible without meaning to – 'Blat', for instance, or 'Goop'. Clamminess broke out on her forehead. She might have fainted had not Miss Devlin announced the hymn and the two girls next to her, thinking her laggardly, hauled her to her feet. A very dismal rendering of 'He who would valiant be' followed, and ever since the hymn has provoked in Liz a quagmire of queasy feelings associated with early morning rows and involuntary wickedness.

'I'm waiting, young lady,' declares her father; and her mother urges, 'Answer Daddy, dear.'

'Got to go,' says Liz, pushing back her chair. 'The bus went early yesterday; I nearly missed it.'

'Sit down. I'm not sure whether you'll be going to school this morning. I may be going instead. Now then. Who's been talking to you about Communists? That History teacher, was it? Hurton, Horton, or whatever she calls herself? (Saw her last council election', he says in audible aside to his wife. 'She was with the Labourites, bold as brass, red rosette, the lot.) It was her, wasn't it?'

'No,' cries Liz, as inspiration arrives like clouds parting; 'I heard it on the wireless. The man on the news said someone was a Communist and I wondered what it meant.'

'There – see? Really, Daddy, you do work yourself up about nothing sometimes.'

Alderman Stockdale breathes easily again. 'Well, it's nothing you should worry your pretty little head over, princess. Run along. And if the bus has gone, I'll drive you to school myself – then I'll call at the bus station and give the manager a piece of my mind. Chap's got no business going early.'

Gladly, Liz goes. But her legs feel wobbly.

A miserable journey. Liz stares out of the window, ignoring the boys who are throwing someone's cap about, imagining her friends' crest-fallen faces and her own embarrassment. It's her parents' fault. After all, they sent her to this school. Not that she wants to be anywhere else. Not now. During the first couple of weeks when things were strange and peculiar she sometimes wished she'd gone with Betty Harris to the convent school; but now she couldn't bear to leave, not after meeting her two best friends in the whole world. With a start, she realizes what she's just thought. Her *two* best friends. And it's true – though it's happened without Chrissy or herself really noticing: the friendship has become three-sided; any permutation of just two of them would now seem very flat.

Luckily, the bus is late arriving at school so there's no time for a chat before registration and Prayers.

'Did you ask?' mouths Chrissy during the register.

'Tell you later,' she mouths back.

During French she is reprimanded for inattention.

At last the bell rings for break and they run to squat on the concrete steps leading up to the netball courts, which is their usual place for a conference. Then, miraculously, the problem melts away.

'I've been thinking,' says Nell before either of the other two gets a word in. 'It'd be better if you picked me up from Chrissy's on Saturday. You can tell your dad I'm playing at her house.' (She, too, has recoiled from a vision of a posh car arriving for her in Maud Street, also from the ever present danger of her father lurching along it the worse for beer.)

'But what about afterwards?' objects Liz, her spirits rising nevertheless. 'He'd want to take you home, too. He wouldn't just drop you.' (It's amazing how Nell has somehow sensed the problem and is showing not the slightest hint of resentment. What a marvellous, sensible friend.)

'Say I'm staying at Chrissy's for the weekend while my mother's away visiting my nan in hospital.' (This is not as creative as it sounds, for while the Nelsons were living at their last address, such an event actually happened and the children were dispersed among the neighbours.)

'Gosh, that's clever. Because if you're supposed to be staying at Chrissy's she'll have to bring you on Saturday – it'd be only polite.'

'Well, I hope your mother doesn't ring Auntie Julie again,' says Chrissy.

'I don't see why she should; it's not *me* coming to stay.'

'It's not Nell either – only pretend,' Chrissy reminds them.

'But don't you see,' Nell muses, 'it's so much better when they don't really know where we are and what we're doing? It stops all their stupid questions; stops them messing things up.'

This is a shrewd remark. Liz endorses it with examples of her mother's interfering attitude, and Nell, listening avidly, detects a kindred spirit. 'I can't stand my mother, either. She's pathetic, never stands up to Dad.'

'So's mine pathetic,' cries Liz, pink with the pleasure

56

of at last shedding a burden. 'Daddy despises her, you can tell. All she thinks of is food or new curtains or getting a hostess trolley like Mrs Garth's or something better than Mrs Turnbull's. She really gets on my nerves.'

Chrissy will not be outdone. 'Your mums aren't as bad as Auntie Julie. Nobody could be.'

'You know,' Nell says slowly, 'Three is so much better than two. It'll be easier to confuse them, to cover up where we are and what we're doing. It gives us more scope for excuses.'

The notion excites. They explore the scope for excuses thoroughly, and a gratifying sense develops of their gaining the upper hand.

When the bell goes and they clamber to their feet, Liz suddenly recalls Scottish Miss MacBride declaring ringingly in Maths: 'A triangle is a *strr-ong* shape.'

Nell is thrilled with Liz's home. She walks round it with a pleased smile, fingers plush velvet chairs with tassels, knobbly brocade curtains with ties, watches her feet sink into carpets, leans over her reflection in the mahogany dining table, sounds the keys of Liz's piano; is finally brought to a halt by the view from a tall window overlooking the garden. 'I never realized you were actually *rich*,' she says, staring at the striped mown lawn. Terrified this may be held against her, Liz tries to belittle the splendour, but the more she describes even greater ostentation to be found in the homes of her former preparatory school chums, the more Nell is dazzled.

'She doesn't *mind*,' says Chrissy, acutely. 'You like it here, don't you Nell?'

'It's terrific.'

Liz is amazed. Her idea of a really terrific home is Molly Greene's at Wold Enderby Rectory, a rambling, echoing, shadowy house furnished with battered chairs, sagging tables; and strangely haunting pieces such as an oak dresser with carved ivy, acorns, birds, and columns and secret cupboards. However, if her friends are truly pleased with her home this is no bad thing; after all, she wants them to like coming.

Mrs Stockdale is visible from one of the windows, or rather Mrs Stockdale's rump is visible as she stoops over the rockery planting alpines.

'Is that your mother?' Nell asks.

Liz nods. Mrs Stockdale straightens, looks round for a watering can, strides across the lawn in her galoshes to collect it. 'Crikey,' says Nell as a picture of Mrs Stockdale in full sail is obtained, her voluminous skirt several inches longer than her gardening coat which, ten years and several sizes smaller ago, was her best coat. 'She's a giant.'

Turning back into the room, Nell is suddenly struck by an omission. 'Where do they keep the books?'

Books? 'There's my mum's gardening books,' says Liz doubtfully, indicating a rack full of magazines by the side of the fireplace.

'They don't count,' says Nell scornfully. 'You must have some proper books somewhere.'

'Dad's got some in his study, but they're not very interesting, all about building and stuff.'

'Is that all? Gosh, we've got hundreds, there isn't room to put 'em all out. They're in those cardboard boxes in the front room.'

Chrissy, whose home also suffers from book deficiency, jumps to her friend's support. 'You've got some books in your bedroom, haven't you Liz? Shall we show her?'

'All right,' says Liz doubtfully, wondering whether the *Girls' Own* annual counts, or *Young Ballerina*.

Upstairs, they watch tensely as Nell flops down in front of Liz's bookcase. In fact, several books pass muster, the Alice books, *Oliver Twist*. 'Dickens is good,' Nell says; 'my dad reads him quite a lot.' She thinks *Wind in the Willows* looks interesting, but hasn't come across it before. This was a book heavily relied upon for elocution purposes by Miss Millicent at The Lawns ('*Ducks are a-dabbling* – drop jaws on *dab*, and please not dabberling, girls'), a fact Liz keeps to herself.

At teatime, Alderman Stockdale pays Nell flattering attention. He has heard about this girl's cleverness from Liz (who, after her near-disaster with Mr Nelson's Communism, plumped for erudition as a characteristic likely to tell in Nell's favour) and wishes to test it.

'So, Miss Nelson,' says he, after a period of general banter, 'where do you hail from?'

Nell blinks. 'Do you mean immediately, today; or originally?'

'Wherever you like to start, m'dear.'

'Born in Liverpool. Lived in Cardiff, Sunderland, Greenock . . .'

'Docks,' cries he, pouncing on it.

Nell looks at him from under her eyelids – 'Of course,' – and suddenly Alderman Stockdale feels less confident about enquiring as to Mr Nelson's precise relationship to these docks. 'Liz tells me you're clever. Is that so?'

Nell turns to her friend with a modest expression. 'Very kind of you. Yes,' she answers him, 'I suppose I am.'

'She is,' confirms Chrissy. 'She's always top in tests – except in maths. Janice Maw comes top in maths.'

'So what do you plan to do with your cleverness?'

Nell looks vacantly across the tea table. 'I'm not sure.' Then adds as a hunch strikes her, 'Though I'll probably be famous.'

Liz, breathing more easily as her father laughs, discovers a lump of egg sandwich gone dry on the roof of her mouth during the moments of inquisition. Glancing round to be sure no-one notices her finger dislodging it, she sees that her mother, too, thinks the danger past, for she has returned to a favourite preoccupation – urging someone to eat. 'Come on, Chrissy, love. You can manage another; they're only small. Then we'll cut the cake.'

This passion of her mother's to stuff food into people is one of the things Liz can't stand. She watches her mother watching Chrissy eat. It's not because her mother specially likes Chrissy that she goes on like this, Liz knows; it's because she's driven. And all the tut-tutting she does about Chrissy's aunt not feeding her properly is a sham; she enjoys exclaiming over it, is secretly glad of the excuse it provides to indulge herself. She's specially nice to Chrissy because famished Chrissy doesn't mind being pressed to overeat. Liz often steals food to take to school for her, over and above what her mother doles out. No doubt her mother would augment the supply with pleasure; but Liz begrudges her the satisfaction. Another thing – Chrissy doesn't have to listen to Mrs Stockdale going on and on about food every mealtime of her life – how she bought the sprouts from Tate's because the ones on the market looked grubby, how she had morning coffee at Mrs Turnbull's and her sponge was light as a feather though her shortbread left a lot to be desired, and don't forget the Shaws and the Hubbards are coming on Sunday, should she order beef or lamb? – though that sirloin was nice and juicy last weekend; cut like butter, didn't it, Daddy? and you do get a good feed from beef, feel as if you've really had something; never mind if Mrs Garth always swears by pork – which reminds her: Mrs Garth's started taking a new cookery magazine; perhaps she should order it, too, it's such a fag copying out the recipes . . . Elizabeth, eat your pastry, duckie; it's lovely and short, made with that new whipped-up fat: well, put some more custard on it, then . . .

Liz looks from one end of the table to the other, from Chrissy sparkling her eyes at Mrs Stockdale and cramming food into her mouth like a demented cuckoo, to Nell flushing with pleasure from Alderman Stockdale's teasing attention, and reflects on the strangeness of it

60

all. These friends obviously don't see her parents as she sees them (though neither can Liz understand Nell's scorn for Mrs Nelson who seems such a mild and pleasant person), yet their faults are all the more outstanding to Liz as a result of her new friendships. For instance, after years of unease, she can now put a name to the thing about her parents she most despises. Snobbishness. Their knowing they're better than most other people, more important, more in the right, more deserving, and always, after meeting people, running them down, sneering. The two events which have enabled her to pin down this nasty outlook were overhearing her mother gossiping to Mrs Garth about Chrissy's background, and the panic she underwent preparing her father for Nell.

After tea they go exploring round the village. When Nell is full of how wonderful she finds Alderman Stockdale, Liz is not at all surprised. She takes a swipe at a stone with the toe of her shoe and listens to its hollow clatter up the lane, then the quick stuttering echo. 'But you don't know him,' she objects mildly. 'Not really.'

Nell thinks about this, puts her head on one side. 'Mm, I know what you mean. I suppose it's like my dad probably seems interesting to you because he's sharp and reads loads of books and says interesting things – and I'll give him that, he *is* clever. But living with him day by day you get to see what's wrong with him. He can't put his brains to good use, gets drunk, starts throwing his weight around. Yeah, I suppose when you live with them, you see their bad side.'

'You could see Auntie Julie's bad side without living with her,' says Chrissy bitterly and incautiously. 'You'd know straight off.'

Nell comes to a halt. The other two, having moved ahead, turn and look back. 'I think,' she says, coming up to them slowly, 'it's about time we took a look at this aunt. Don't you agree, Liz?'

Liz isn't keen and stays silent. Chrissy wishes she'd kept her mouth shut.

'I could come in tonight when Liz's dad drops me off.'

'You can't, you're not expected. You're only pretending to stay, remember.'

'Just for a few minutes.'

'Not tonight.'

'When then? You've been to our houses. Why can't we come to yours?'

'Leave her alone, Nell. It's not her fault.'

'All right then,' says Chrissy, afraid to find herself the lesser friend, the one who can't have anyone round.

'Great. I'm dying to see her. When can we come?'

They walk on seeing little of the village, too busy with the pictures and schemes inside their heads.

'Coo-ee – ' Mrs Stockdale comes running down the lane, pink with the novelty of placing one foot rapidly in front of the other all the way round her garden and orchard and then halfway round the village. 'Come along, girls. Elizabeth's daddy is waiting to take you home. We mustn't make him late; he's got a function.'

'Oh,' says Liz, disappointed. 'Does that mean I can't go with them?'

'Afraid so, dear. But you've had a lovely long time with your friends. Buck up now, there's good girls.'

They jump down from their perch on a five-bar gate and hurry back to The Mount where the big black car is standing on the gravel. Alderman Stockdale is waiting on the topmost step before the front door, smoking a cigar and showing his dinner jacket to great advantage. The visitors are visibly impressed.

'Does anybody want to spend a penny?' hisses Mrs Stockdale, arriving rather breathlessly behind them.

Chrissy and Nell shake their heads, mesmerized by Alderman Stockdale running down the steps in his shiny shoes and pulling open the rear door of the car. 'At your service, young ladies.'

They scramble inside. Liz, feeling flat and already lonely, goes up the steps and waits at the top to watch them leave. They peep at her through the car's rear window and wave shyly. At once Liz's dullness fades. Affection pierces her; she wants to express this, make them a present, give them a memorable send-off. She comes tottering down the steps with an outstretched hand and a half-blind screwed up face in the manner of their art mistress approaching somebody's easel. (Liz can be as accurate with her body as Nell with her pencil.) In the slowly moving car they clamber on to their knees on the back seat to watch the performance, shriek their appreciation, fall about, clutch each other – which inspires Alderman Stockdale to toot the horn and accelerate round the bend shooting up gravel. Through her squinting grimace Liz glimpses their hilarity. The next moment she's alone.

'Elizabeth,' comes a premonitory cry from inside the house.

But it's much too soon to relinquish the scene. As noiselessly as possible, she speeds round the side of the house and down the garden path towards the orchard. Here there's a hut – big enough to live in, as Nell pointed out. She goes inside and closes the door and flops down on a pile of old newspapers. When she closes her eyes, Nell's face and Chrissy's laugh at her again from the rear of the car. Their heads have encircling auras, she perceives, and when she opens her eyes suddenly, two large holes where their faces have been superimpose on the slatted wall of the hut, blanking out fork and spade handles. Her friends seem to exist more potently than ordinary mortals. There's magic in them. Merely conjuring them creates so forceful a sense of presence that her heart races. For the first time in her life she is moved, awed, delighted, struck with wonder by another's (in this case two others') sheer existence.

Some time later, on stiff and shaky legs, she returns to the house and spies in the drive a likely reason for her mother's call. Mrs Garth's Morris Minor is parked there alongside two larger cars. A bridge party: and her mother will have been anxious to dispatch her to bed beforehand. Fortunately, Liz knows very well how to retrieve the situation.

She opens the drawing room door, looks in apologetically, then goes forward with a pleasant expression. 'Excuse me,' she murmurs as the card players look up. 'I've come to say goodnight. And to thank you very much for giving my friends such a lovely tea,' she adds, kissing her mother's cheek prettily.

Mrs Stockdale is disarmed. Already she can hear Mrs Pockerington murmuring 'ah' to Mrs Garth. She reaches for her box of All Gold. 'Take a goodnight sweetie, dear.'

'Thank you, Mummy,' says Liz, selecting a foil-covered chocolate.

'Goodnight, darling,' the ladies coo. And the gentlemen are moved to stand.

Upstairs, she opens her satchel and takes out a box done up with rubber bands. She puts the chocolate into the box, returns it to her satchel. Tomorrow evening the chocolate will be joined by further items filched from the larder ready for Monday morning break. It is very satisfying picturing handing the box over to Chrissy. But she remains restless. If only she could think of something which would give equal pleasure to Nell. Then an idea comes to her, and she slips out of her room and creeps downstairs and lets herself into her father's study. Some nice paper or sharp pencils she thinks, looking round; and finds just what she seeks in a desk drawer. Making off with her father's belongings, sliding them under the box in her satchel, her violent desire to give, to demonstrate her depth of love, is at last quieted.

* * *

At ten past four on a warm May afternoon, entering Chrissy's house is like stepping into gloomy evening. This is because the curtain is drawn over the window on the stairs. They stand in the hall and peer at Chrissy while she wonders what to do with them. On the left is the closed door to the little-used front parlour, on the right are the stairs and behind these the kitchen; straight ahead, the back-living-room door is ajar. 'She's in there,' Nell whispers helpfully.

Chrissy starts towards it like a condemned person, but at the last minute veers away and leads on into the kitchen.

There is a bad smell in here, emitted, Liz thinks, by a steaming saucepan on a gas ring. Most of the surfaces are covered with stuff not immediately recognizable as kitchen clutter, so they stare about them curiously. Liz looks into a basin of water. 'What are they?' she asks, clutching her throat, for under the water lurks a heap of fat black pellets like sheep turds.

Chrissy shrugs. 'Senna pods, I expect.'

'I say, your aunt doesn't half smoke,' remarks Nell, totting up the tin lids and stained saucers cradling fag ends. 'And what the heck . . .' She looks into the steaming and heavily encrusted saucepan. 'Whatever is it?'

'Hankies?' Chrissy hazards. 'Might be her stockings.'

'Stockings?' they gasp.

A rasping shout makes them jump – 'Chrissy?', and a pain darts in Liz's stomach; even Nell's keen expression vanishes. When Chrissy goes into the living room, the others hang back in the hall, and for a moment Liz imagines getting away with it, remaining here while Chrissy deals with her aunt and then all three escaping to the Robinson Rec until it's time to come back and hang round the gate for her father's car. But Nell, suddenly recalling why they are here, shoves Liz into the room ahead of her.

Auntie Julie is sitting on one side of the hearth with her stockings off and her skirt rolled back, one foot soaking in a bowl of water, the other propped on a knee while she prods at it with a metal instrument. Near to her at shoulder height, a smouldering cigarette juts from the mantelpiece. On the opposite side of the hearth, a man is lying in an armchair with a tartan rug drawn up to his chin. Chrissy is being harangued by Auntie Julie. 'I didn't,' she protests. 'Honestly. We were just . . .'

Auntie Julie cuts her off. 'I see you've brought your pals,' she observes with a particularly fierce jab at the sole of her foot. A piece of foot flies off and lands with a plop on the newspaper spread around the bowl where several horny bits are already lying.

Chrissy, stuffing hands under armpits, says nothing.

'Who are they?'

'Just . . . girls from school.'

'I can see that. I may be daft,' – she gives an abrupt cackle – 'but I'm not blind.'

This is dreadful, thinks Liz, mortified by all those nice manners and correct forms of address instilled into her at The Lawns. The impoliteness of just standing here and not making herself known – Chrissy, apparently, having lost her tongue – brings her out in prickles. Propelled by shame, she steps forward. 'How do you do, Miss Thomas? I'm Chrissy's friend, Liz, Elizabeth Stockdale. I believe you've spoken to my mother on the telephone.'

'Oh yes, duck; so you're her little lass. I thought Chrissy was bringing you some weeks back. Never mind, you've got here at last. Pleased to meet you. That's Chrissy's dad, but he's deaf; it's no good talking to him.' (Liz turns and nods to the man in the chair who stares back blankly.) 'He's been like that – neither use nor ornament – ever since Chrissy's mam ran away. Did she tell you about that? Ran off when she were three – she hardly remembers her, do you Chrissy? – leaving me stuck with these two. Aye, it all fell on me. Who's t'other one, then?'

'Nell,' says Chrissy.

'Never heard of her. Aye, as I was saying . . .'

They stand and listen to Auntie Julie outlining the sacrifice her life has been and watch her hacking at her foot. Her thin shanks are ribbed with veins, her inner thighs scorched beetroot from lengthy sittings over fires. 'Well, it's nice meeting you, duck,' she says to Liz at last, 'but you'll have to excuse us now while I see to Chrissy's dad.'

They all but stampede through the doorway. Chrissy leads the charge upstairs.

'What's she going to do to him?' Nell half-fearfully thirsts to know as they gain the landing.

But Chrissy can't answer, she's too moved by Liz's plucky behaviour. She grabs Liz's arm, hugs it, lays her cheek on Liz's shoulder. Hitherto, Chrissy's friends, confronted by Auntie Julie carrying on regardless, have always behaved as Nell just did. Without exception, they've hung back, fallen dumb unless overtaken by nervous giggling. Until now. Until smooth-speaking, gentle-mannered Liz. *Brave* Liz, thinks Chrissy, recalling how white her friend turned in the kitchen over the senna pods and how Auntie Julie must have come as a shock to her (for sometimes Auntie Julie comes as a shock even to Chrissy); yet Liz swallowed her nerves and saved the day. 'She liked you,' she marvels, happy and very relieved.

Liz, too, is relieved, and warm with the self-congratulatory rush which follows the doing of a thing long dreaded and discovering it not half as bad as imagination conjured. Auntie Julie's appearance is certainly unappetizing – gaunt and bleached-looking with fierce eyes and chin, and hair the colour of dirty candle wax. And her behaviour is extraordinary. (Usually, in Liz's experience, friends' relatives make some show of welcome, are never undressed and never do things downstairs which ought properly to be done upstairs behind a closed door.) But once she'd got over her shock, Liz perceived a sadness in Auntie Julie which quite touched her. She's glad to have made a favourable impression. Returning Chrissy's squeeze, she almost skips beside her into a bedroom.

'I say,' says Nell, looking round. 'Isn't this the *best* bedroom?' It's a large bow-windowed room on the front of the house.

'It used to be my parents'. Then it was mine.'

'But why've you got the big one?'

'I don't know,' says Chrissy, who has never questioned the arrangement. 'Auntie Julie sleeps in the little room over the landing. Dad's is the one at the back.'

'And it's a double bed, too. Gosh, all this to yourself,' marvels Nell.

'Do you want to see some photos of my mum?'

'Yes,' they cry emphatically.

She takes an album from a drawer and spreads it open on the bed. They clamber up, heads towards the photographs.

A merry looking young woman with tumbling curls and bright eyes hangs on to the arm of an expressionless man as they pose on the sea front or under a tree in the back garden.

'Is that your dad? He looks ancient beside her.'

'She's very pretty, and sort of fun looking.'

Time flies. When Chrissy closes the album, the house strikes them as particularly still and silent.

'You know, we could easily be here without her knowing,' Nell remarks. 'She hasn't come near us.'

'She hardly ever comes up during the day.'

'See? We could've just slipped upstairs and she'd be none the wiser.'

Liz latches on to the idea at once. It's another of those exciting fantasies in which they carry on a secret existence beyond the reach of adult authority. 'You mean we could hide. You and I could nip upstairs while Chrissy maybe had a word with her, and they wouldn't know. No-one would. We could smuggle food in . . .'

'Yeah,' breathes Chrissy. 'Have a feast.'

'One day we will,' Nell declares, and they grin at one another, picturing it.

Soon after this, a car toots outside. Liz flies to the window and sees her father waiting below in the street. 'Got to go. See you tomorrow.' She runs downstairs, grabs her satchel from a corner of the hall, lets herself out.

Nell decides she, too, must go. Chrissy accompanies her to the gate where they stand gossiping for a while, then Nell heads off towards the main road and Chrissy goes indoors.

In the shadowy hall Auntie Julie is waiting. At first, Chrissy doesn't notice her, then, as she drops the front-door latch, live cigarette smoke floats across. Her heart leaps. But Auntie Julie is not, after all, about to confront her niece with a misdemeanour. She simply demands, 'What d'you want for yer tea, then?'

A shrug shows that Chrissy isn't prepared to commit herself.

'There's some meat paste left in the jar.'

'All right.'

'Go and make yerself a sandwich, then.'

In the kitchen, Chrissy removes several slices of bread from a packet and smears each slice with margarine. 'Can I finish it?' she asks, holding up a small, half full jar.

'Aye. Go on.' Auntie Julie watches from the doorway.

The greyish pink paste is stretched over four slices. Chrissy tops each of these with an unpasted slice, and without further ado bends her face towards the table and fills her mouth while her right foot hunts for the leg of a stool. When the stool is located, it is drawn deftly into position under her. With every swallow she refills her mouth; there is no pause in her seamless mastication. Now and then small groans give a hint of the effort involved.

'That's a nice lass you brought back. I like a lass

with summat to say for herself.' So saying, Auntie Julie comes briefly into the kitchen to make use of a tin lid. When her fag end has been thoroughly stubbed, she returns to the living room leaving Chrissy to finish her meal in peace.

When her more savage pangs have abated, Chrissy gets up and puts the kettle on. While the water boils, she eats at a more leisurely pace, reviewing the events of the late afternoon. Liz and Nell, in her mind's eye, sprawl once again on her high wide bed. 'We could be here without anyone knowing,' says Nell. 'Smuggle food in,' says Liz. 'Whenever we like,' embellishes Chrissy. Suddenly, number 142 Lister Avenue undergoes radical, irrevocable change. Until half an hour ago it was the place she is shut in at day's end, away from the normal world of mums and dads and brothers and sisters and bright comfy rooms and clean well-stocked kitchens, into this pinched, cluttered, smelly old place where no-one ever smiles or gives you a hug and where you feel sort of ashamed. No more. Not since she came here with Nell and Liz, and the three of them weighed the place up together, made themselves at home in her bedroom and pronounced its future as one of their secret places.

The kettle whistles. She jumps up and makes the tea, then returns to the table and starts to cram down the remaining sandwiches in a tearing hurry to get back upstairs to their part of the house. For she's no longer a part of that sad old threesome, Auntie Julie and Dad and Chrissy; really and truly she belongs with Liz and Nell. It gives her a soaring feeling, as if her chest's going to burst with the joy inside.

Nell, having crossed the main road, stops thinking about how Chrissy's room can be useful to them in future, and turns instead to the start of the visit, recalling the clammy feeling she got in the kitchen and the shivering shock of entering the living room. Phew, it was suffocating in there, and thick with horror – like being shut in the stuffy cupboard under the stairs. She seemed to die on her feet, felt it was never going to end until Liz spoke up. What a relief that was. And tremendously impressive. Liz is good at that sort of thing, it comes to her naturally. Nell has often noticed how a teacher's attitude softens when Liz speaks up, and how, in class, a word from Liz can change the atmosphere. It's because she's posh, thinks Nell. Nicely brought up, as her mother puts it. The phrase puts her in mind of something she saw once at the pictures in a supporting feature about the Potteries. She imagines a slip bath full of rough clay pots, a hand reaching in and finding not one of the pots but a china figurine; then the figurine tenderly drawn out, the milky liquid wiped away and finally a painstaking polish – nicely brought up. Like Liz: clean, fine, burnished. Sometimes, Nell feels dingy in comparison, a touch sweaty and stale. She doesn't resent this: certainly not; it's what makes Liz interesting. Nevertheless, as she turns into Maud Street, a dreamy smile lights her face. She's thinking it'd be quite good fun seeing Liz smudged up, getting just a tiny bit dirtied.

Then she pushes at her shuddering front door, and the wide shining space where her fantasies fly (all the wider and shinier for knowing Chrissy and Liz) shrinks and dulls as the tiny overcrowded house envelops her. The door closes her in with a dispiriting thud.

V

It was dark, now, in the bedroom, but Liz hadn't bothered to get off the bed and put the light on and draw the curtains; nor even to stretch out her hand and flick on the bedside lamp. She would put the lamp on when the phone rang.

Must be getting late, though. The hall clock struck ten some time ago. What was the betting that Chrissy, having come in tired from an energetic evening out with the kids, had decided to postpone phoning Liz till tomorrow?

Her eyes pricked. She felt let down, full of unreasonable anger, like a child railing at absent parents who escape their duty of sympathetic suffering. I want them to bloody well care, she raged; and if this was pathetic – too bad. Weeks she'd spent helping out Nell – the ghastly pregnancy business, putting up with her agonizing over whether to leave Fred, boosting her morale when Fred finally beat her to it. And she'd damn near broken her neck getting to Chrissy before her breast operation. Yes, one way or another she'd done her bit – so where were they, the bastards? They could at least ring. A picture of Chrissy and Nell wilfully neglecting her, going on with their lives, saying 'Oh, Liz'll be OK. She's a coper,' made her so mad and sorry for herself she had to sit up and force her mind on to a sensible tack. Like, for instance, trying to work out why she was feeling this.

It eased her to recall that they were just the same – always desperate to see the other two when something bad happened. Generally, letters and phone calls sufficed. At some periods of their lives, whole years had gone by with only Christmas cards passing between them. She could remember a time when she felt quite distant from Nell and Chrissy, rather despising how Nell made a living from the tabloid press ('Prurient drivel,' she'd scoff to Nathan, 'reactionary platitudes shrieked like they were freshly minted truths.'), regularly infuriated by an endless account of Chrissy's civic activities in letters from a disappointed Mrs Stockdale. They were travelling in different directions, she'd thought, foreseeing the death of their friendship with containable sorrow. But even then, at a very deep level of her consciousness, she'd carried a mental picture of herself as part of a three. It was like imprinting. Nothing had ever changed it – not becoming part of a couple, not becoming a parent. She suspected Nell and Chrissy were similarly marked. It was as if at the age of eleven, caring little for the families they'd been landed with at birth, they took on one another instead. Not always with happy consequences. But that was the way with families; it was pot luck whether or not you thrived in them.

Why now? Why was this business with Rosie *her* crisis? Because she suspected she was going to fail despite her supposed talent for dealing with people? Because it came on top of months of worry over Nathan's health? If she were honest there was a good deal more to it than that. Suspicions as to what Rosie was up to had reactivated her tiresome guilt (she'd never erased it entirely, it was still liable to very briefly slip over her, like flesh creeping for no apparent reason) and spawned a superstitious dread that this, belatedly, was her punishment. Ridiculous, of course . . .

The phone rang. She scrambled off the bed, snatched at it – 'Yes?' – and fumbled for the lamp switch.

'Hel-lo-Liz,' came the reply – a falling tune.

'Chrissy.' Now the longed for call had come, she felt dazed, pressed a hand to her temples; hair fell round her face.

'Sorry to be ringing so late, but the town's full of trippers. We went to a place on the sea front – you know how it gets.'

'Yes, well, the weather's been nice. Always brings them out. Good evening, was it?'

'Lovely.' And while Chrissy gave a brief description, Liz pushed the pillows against the bedhead, climbed on to the bed, hauled up the phone.

'I spoke to Amanda earlier. She's obviously enjoying life.'

'Oh, she is. Now, how are things with you? Did you try again with Rosie?'

'Yeah,' she said thickly. 'Another brilliant failure. I don't know what's happening – or how it all started. If only I'd done something straight away as soon as she began withdrawing. But I thought, this can't last, it's not Rosie. We've always been such mates, never had hostilities. I still can't believe it. Driving home I tell myself, it'll be over when you get back, we'll talk properly to one another, it'll be life as normal. I tried to have it out with her this evening but met with the proverbial brick wall. I just don't know. Did you ring Nell?'

'Yes,' said Chrissy carefully. 'And I think she's coming.'

'But she must. I need to see you both.'

'Of course. It's a matter of *when*, not if. She's going to try and cancel things towards the end of next week.'

'Oh, good,' said Liz, mollified; and continued, 'I know you and Nell can't do anything exactly, it's just I really do need to talk.'

'We know. And anyway it's time we three got together. I'll let you know precisely when in the next few days. Meanwhile, go cautiously, Liz. If I were you . . .'

'Yes?'

'Oh listen to me – telling *you*, for heaven's sake.'

'Please go ahead. What would you do if it were Amanda?'

Chrissy caught her breath and her quick advice fled. 'Help,' she floundered, 'it's so difficult. Um, I suppose, well, really I think I'd try to be much as usual – friendly, warm, interested but not inquisitive; and I'd try not to act hard done by. Oh – and it'd probably kill me.'

Liz sighed. 'One thing though, Chrissy: wouldn't you try and find out why this involvement's had such a devastating effect? I mean, it can't be a straightforward attachment. There must be something else, something about the fellow, something not right. Surely you'd try and find out?'

'I'm not sure.'

'Chrissy, I've got to. Don't you see? Discreetly, without Rosie knowing, I must at least discover who he is.'

'Mm. I suppose so. But do be careful.'

'Oh, I will,' promised Liz breathing out heavily as though she had been given permission. 'I'll be very careful. I'm just so .... in the dark. I haven't felt like this – like I'm drowning – since, well, you know when.'

'I'm so sorry, Liz. Have you and Nathan talked about it?'

'Up to a point. I don't want him worried.'

'Of course not. Look, I'll phone again very soon.'

'Thanks ever so, Chrissy. Goodnight, chum.'

'Night, night, Liz. Take care.'

Before she went to bed, Chrissy sat down to write.

Dear Nell,
Whatever happens, be here next week. Sounds like Liz is tearing her hair. Obviously, there's more to this than she's letting on. I'm certain it's something to do with the Poole thing. She referred to it again – not in so many words, but I caught the gist. I'm sending this to your office to spur you on about making those cancellations. I'll phone at the weekend to hear when you're definitely coming. I mean it, Nell – *be* here.
Love, Chrissy.

Nell read the letter a second time and a third, then laid it on her desk and slumped back in her chair. Her eyes grew unfocused.

Tearing her hair, she thought – mm. She could envisage the hair all right – silky-smooth and reliable; never known to frizz, curl, matt, tangle, stand on end, grease up, or hold any shape other than the swingy Liz Stockdale bob. But *tearing it*? That was harder. Come to think of it though, Liz had certainly got it in her to go suddenly wild. Very, very occasionally. When greatly provoked. Nell fingered a small round scar between two knuckles of her left hand; an old

75

scar; her fingers could no longer detect an indentation, but she knew where it was, didn't need to look. Breath shot explosively down her nose, half-sigh, half-laugh. She hoiked herself up over the desk to turn on the word processor.

Dear Chrissy, (she tapped)
Of course I'll be there. Wild horses, etc. How about Thursday? Tell you what – find out exactly when Liz plans to arrive and I swear to get there first. We'll wait on the doorstep together with outstretched arms.

Writing this last bit, intended facetiously, in fact made her come over chokey. She signed off, reached for a tissue. As she was blowing her nose, her assistant came in. 'Print that would you darling, and pop it in the post?' she asked, muffled-voiced, then composed herself and raised a finger to check her eyelashes. 'And keep the coffee coming. Got to get ahead of myself, workwise. It's going to be a bitch of a day.'

2
SCRUMPING, STALKING, PULLING A STUNT

i

'You're going in late.' – Nathan stating the obvious, for Liz at the kitchen table was still in her dressing gown.

'I'll be going in late and coming back late for the rest of the week. It's my Redmond House stint.'

'Oh God, here we go,' he groaned, irritably feeding bread into the toaster. 'Well, please remember your promise. Not that I'm crazy about you being on that estate at night, even with other people.'

'Di or Les will be coming with me,' she soothed, reminding herself to fix this up with one of them. 'If you're pouring coffee, I'll have another.' She watched him filling the cups. 'Thanks. Anything we need from town? There's a gap in my afternoon.'

'Can't think of anything.'

'In that case, I might get my hair cut – if Josie can fit me in.'

'Looks just right to me.'

She sighed. He never could understand about hair – how the result of hanging on when it was 'just right' for a moment too long was an overblown appearance. 'Any sign of life upstairs?'

'Not a peep.'

When Nathan had gone, she washed and dressed then went round the house, tidying. Coming face to face with the hall clock, she saw that only half an hour remained before she, too, must leave for work. It was now or never. Still no sign of Rosie; even so, when she went into the study and closed the door, she turned the key in the lock.

After consulting the directory, she didn't pick up the telephone straight away, but sat hunched on the edge of a chair with her hands pressed together between her knees. At last, forcing herself, she snatched up the receiver, keyed the number.

'King Edward's School. The secretary speaking.'

'Hazel, I thought you might be in school. How are you? Liz Learman here. Can you spare a minute?'

'Hello, Liz,' Hazel answered warily. 'You, er, you're not ringing a day early, by any chance?'

'I don't think so . . .'

'Oh, good. I've already had two anxious mums and a bluffing dad ringing in, jumping the gun. The kids are glad enough to put off the evil day; it's the parents who lose their nerve.'

'Oh my God, A-level results. Are they really out tomorrow? Honestly, I'd clean forgotten.'

Hazel laughed. 'Well, I suppose you can be pretty confident about Rosie's. Anyway, you've other things to think about. If it's about the Friends of Redmond House, I'm sorry, Liz, but I can't spare the time for committee work just now. Maybe, when we've finished this blessed reorganization . . .'

'No, no, just a query.' She swallowed. 'Have you by any chance got a Simon somebody on the staff?'

'A Simon?'

'It's daft to worry about these things, but I think I snubbed someone unintentionally the other day.'

'Oh, I see. Well, yes – Simon Goodridge. Tall, fair, youngish?'

Her ears caught no hint of embarrassment in Hazel's voice, which would surely be the case if intimacy between Rosie and this Simon Goodridge had attracted attention while Rosie was still a pupil. 'Probably,' she said, feeling more confident, 'As a matter of fact, though, it wasn't the man but his wife I may have offended.

She seemed to know me; referred to her husband as Simon, and I sort of gathered that he taught at King Edward's. This Simon Goodridge is married, I take it? You haven't any other Simons?'

'Yes, he is, and I'm sure . . . No, I'm sure there isn't another Simon. But look, don't worry about Ellie Goodridge; she's a perfect dear, the last person to take offence. Mind you, I've heard her pregnancy's not suiting her. Perhaps it's a bit soon after their sad little tragedy. You know about that, of course?'

'Uh, no,' said Liz, reluctantly. That the man was married was all she wished to know.

'Their second child was born with a heart defect. Only lived for a few weeks. I suppose being pregnant again might, you know, stir up bad feelings.'

'Gosh, yes,' she muttered, feeling cheap and caught out. 'Anyway, I'll know her name if I meet her again. Probably won't, that's usually the way it goes.'

'Well, best of luck for tomorrow.'

'Oh, sure. Goodbye, Hazel.'

Goodridge, she repeated to herself, turning the pages of the telephone directory; Goodridge, S. Her finger came to rest on Goodridge S.J., 35 Claremont Drive. She wrote the address on a scrap of paper, then hurried out of the room to stow it in her briefcase.

Damn, fumed Liz when she stalled on the ring road. Beat it, Ellie Goodridge. Scram.

This wife of Rosie's fellow, whom, the moment her existence was confirmed, she immediately envisioned as an attractively independent young woman grown tired of her teacher husband, was now stubbornly presenting as a heavily pregnant mother with lank hair, large bottom, hopeless clothes, tragic eyes. She dropped down a gear and pressed the accelerator, hoping to chase off the image with a spot of dynamic driving. Because her daughter was at stake; Rosie was being messed with by a married man with kids. So stay single-minded, she implored, turning into the clinic car park. For once in your life, stick to the one point of view. Honestly, she was so predictable she made herself sick.

By ten to three in the afternoon, Ellie Goodridge had insinuated herself into the persona of a depressed patient called Brenda. For one scatty moment, it was a teenage hussy called Rosie who was driving Brenda to despair, and not the scheming bitch at her husband's garage, after all.

When Brenda, who was her last patient, had gone, she all but ran down the corridor and out to her car, still fooling herself that she was going for a haircut. She started the engine, even moved off a couple of feet, then braked and reached into the glove compartment for the street map. Claremont Drive. A mere ten minutes away.

She drove from the town centre, through streets of Victorian and Edwardian stone terraces blackened decades ago by spewings from chimneys, into once-decorous post-war avenues where single trees alternated with lamp-posts and the best homes were signalled by leaded lights and garages, on into 'sixties territory. Along Bewick Way, past Tennyson Close, Wordsworth Close and Shelley Gardens, into Claremont Drive. Number 35 leapt at her all of a piece: its strip of white-board facing, its wide featureless windows, its white-painted glazed front door, its bright yellow Mini under the car-port. She drove past, braked, turned round in somebody's drive, then crawled back and stopped three houses distant on the opposite side.

Some papers brought out of her briefcase and slapped against the steering wheel gave her confidence. She pretended to study them, thinking how ridiculous it was to suppose either Goodridge would oblige her with a sighting. Yet when the front door opened, Liz felt it had been inevitable. Not that Ellie turned out at all like either of Liz's previsions – except for the obvious pregnancy, of course: she had shiny brown hair, a nice frock and looked pretty pleased with life as she came briskly down her driveway hitching the strap of her bag higher on to her shoulder while putting on a pair of sun-glasses. She turned away from Liz's car. Liz watched her head bob out of sight down the incline of the road, then got out of the car, grabbed a shopping bag from the back seat, locked up. At the crest of the hill she spotted Ellie crossing to the far side of Bewick Way. When she reached the corner, Ellie was turning into a cutting between two houses.

Alternately hurrying and dawdling, Liz followed. Further on, the cutting widened, was lined on the left by a wooden fence bordering gardens, on the right by the high wire fence of a school playground. The garden fencing was overhung with branches and had greenery poking through; the wire diamonds on the other side criss-crossed an expanse of asphalt. People were gathered near the top of the cutting, mostly young women busily exchanging news. Standing singly were a lone man and a couple of older women. The crowd had formed in front of a long hut on stilts just inside the playground. Liz was puzzled: this was obviously a school queue, yet the schools were on holiday. Then her ears caught the babyish cries, the soft thunder of small feet on wooden flooring, an encouraging adult voice ('Hurry up Jamie, your mummy'll be waiting. Oo no, dear, that's Emma's.') – nursery sounds, everyday to her once, now almost forgotten.

She stood on the edge of the group. No-one took any notice of her. I could be just another waiting mum, she thought, and then, making a subtle adjustment to her mode of standing, changed 'mum' to 'older aunt or youngish granny'.

The door to the hut opened. A woman brought out two youngsters and stood on the top step looking down into the crowd. When the children's mothers stepped forward she handed down their offspring then went

81

back inside for more. Ellie Goodridge claimed one of the next pair – a sturdy boy with a red face, brandishing a painting; as ecstatic to see her as she him.

'Look, Mummy. It's me and Blackie.'

'It's lovely, Tommy. Won't Daddy be pleased?'

The voice was artless – Liz shot her a look – so, too, the face; the reference to Daddy came without trace of strain or emotional blackmail. She's totally oblivious, muttered Liz indignantly to the absent Simon. An unclaimed child had started howling. 'It's all right, she can wait with me,' called Ellie. 'Come along, Sarah, Mummy won't be long.' The child's tears vanished as she clambered down the steps to join Ellie and Tommy.

Just then a hot-looking woman propelling a pushchair arrived, gasped her thanks to Ellie, gathered up Sarah and admired Tommy's painting. After a few moments, they all moved off together, dawdling back down the cutting. Liz watched them go. Suddenly, a commotion broke out; the women grabbed the children and pressed close to the wire fence as three lads – one on a bicycle – charged past. Drawing level with the remaining parents, one of the lads leapt up and snatched an apple from an overhanging branch.

'Hey, you. That's someone's property,' yelled the lone waiting man.

The apple thief looked back, took aim, bowled at the complainant. The man ducked, there were ironic adolescent cheers; the apple, having struck Liz's shoulder, dropped with a thud at her feet.

She stared at this apple for what seemed a long time.

ii

Apple scrumping. They can't remember how or why the craze started, or who was the instigator or how they came by the term; all they know is scrumping's the thing they're mad to do this summer. And not because they're particularly desirous of apples or any of the

82

other fruits they steal – there's plenty to be had legitimately in the Stockdale orchard and garden; it's taking them that counts, trespassing on other people's property, sneaking about, making off. Such a lovely name, too, scrumping. Like scrumptious. Juicy, dark, bad. No, they certainly don't do it for the sake of the apples.

Chrissy and Nell are staying at Liz's for a week, which means virtually all their time is devoted to it. It's possible to go scrumping when they're at Chrissy's, too, through the leafy gardens backing on to the Robinson Rec, but it's not as rewarding as scrumping in the country where the opportunities are boundless. Today, Liz has suggested walking over to Fenby-cum-Laithby to select a target, saving challenges closer to home – the Hall, maybe, or Mrs Garth's – for later on. Evening raids are the best.

'Lunch at one,' Mrs Stockdale reminds them through the kitchen window when she spies them setting off.

'Blast,' says Liz to her friends. They pause, frowning.

'We don't want any,' she yells back.

'What? Just a minute.' Mrs Stockdale's head disappears from view and reappears a second later with her body on the doorstep.

'We're going for a long walk. Um, a nature ramble,' embroiders Liz. 'We probably won't be back by one.'

'Then take a picnic, dear. You mustn't starve your friends just because you can't be bothered. Wait there and I'll cut some sandwiches.'

Parcels of sandwiches don't gel with their picture of the day's activities, creeping through shrubberies, diving from walls, swinging from branches. 'We don't want a picnic, Mummy.' In any case, they've already removed eight shillings from the sideboard drawer where Mrs Stockdale stashes her card money, for buying refreshments with at Fenby-cum-Laithby Post Office.

Mrs Stockdale is in a torment, desperate to go back into the kitchen and make piles of nourishing sandwiches, afraid to stir from the doorstep in case the girls vanish while her back is turned.

Liz sets off defiantly. Less confidently, her companions follow.

'Elizabeth . . .'

'We'll eat extra at tea,' Chrissy promises over her shoulder. With which Mrs Stockdale must be consoled.

They set off down a lane where beech trees dig their toes into the banks on either side and loom to a giant height despite their precarious footing. Overhead, the leafy branches intermingle; light through them dazzles and dapples.

Liz is disgruntled with Chrissy. 'Did you have to say that?'

'Uh?'

'About tea. Say we'd eat extra.'

'So?'

'I just don't know why you had to say it.'

They trudge up the hill staring at the weathered road, at earth crumbling over it from the spilling banks, at their dusty forward-thrusting sandals.

Nell puts her head on one side. 'I think it was good Chrissy said it. It probably satisfied your mother. If we'd walked away without saying anything, we'd only catch it later on. It was rather bright of her.'

Liz and Chrissy continue walking with their heads down, but Chrissy is feeling better.

'Mind you, I can see how Liz feels. I'd be flippin' mad if it was my mother and one of you two encouraging her.'

Chrissy chewed her lip. 'Sorry, Liz.'

'It's all right. It wasn't your fault – it was her's, going on about food.'

Disputes are invariably settled like this. The one who is least involved listens to the other two arguing or complaining, then pronounces judgement and extends, by way of a codicil, understanding to the loser. The formula has never let them down, though so far it has not been severely tested.

They arrive at a T-junction and take the right turn along a flattish road lined with rough greensward and low hedges, open to the breeze and sky. Once again light-hearted.

In the village, they go straight to the Post Office stores. No discussion, Liz knows where it is and the others know where she is taking them; they're not even hungry: simply, there is money in their pockets nagging like an itch. As they cross over the road, eyes and nose tell them it's the right sort of shop. A sweet soapy staleness wafts out, heady as beer fumes to a six-pints-a-night man. The windows are smothered in faded handwritten notices and advertisements for Hovis, Winalot and Typhoo. Sunlight through the open doorway shines the nail heads in a patch of grubby floor-boarding, but fails to penetrate the farther gloom. They take a long time making up their minds; finally select crisps, doughnuts, liquorice sherbets and chocolate toffee éclairs. Also home-made ices – wet buttercup domes balanced on cornets fished out of a box by the postmistress (whose mail-sorting fingers are still encased in blackened pink rubber thimbles).

Licking assiduously, they go slowly over the green with their bags of goodies to a long wooden seat beside the war memorial. Here they sit with spread bare knees. A horse comes into view. Its rider smiles and nods across the green; they stare back sternly. When a woman comes out of the shop, the rider hails her and reins in her horse. 'Good morning, Mrs Megget. Splendid weather. How're the children?' By now, horse and rider are presenting their not dissimilar rear ends to the girls. While the pedestrian mumbles and the rider exclaims – 'Splendid; that's the ticket,' – the horse lifts its tail and copiously excretes.

This is explosively amusing. Hilarity makes their limbs go haywire; legs thrust, arms fling, heads, spines go floppy, and Chrissy's face lands in Nell's ice cream. A shaving foam ring round her eye is so apoplectically funny to Liz and annoyingly funny to Nell that they shove Chrissy off the seat; she falls, grabbing hold of Liz's legs, Liz hangs on to Nell, and they sprawl shrieking over the grass.

They have no idea of the stir they are creating. The postmistress comes running to the store doorway, an elderly farm hand jumps from his bike to obtain a prolonged view, and they join Mrs Megget in threeway disparagement – which persuades the horse rider, who cannot allow herself to be accounted with the lower orders, that it is time to trot on.

At last, spent, they clamber back on to the seat and open the crisp bags.

'What's black and steaming and comes out of Cowes backwards?' asks Nell. (She thinks of it as Cowes because that's how it was spelt in her joke book, though she knows nothing about the Isle of Wight or its steamer.)

'Pooh' say Chrissy and Liz in unison.

After a moment's hesitation – for the answer given at the back of the joke book was so inscrutable she promptly forgot it, Nell says 'Yes,' rather lamely; and they sit in faintly perplexed silence, contemplating the departing figures across the green.

Things have gone flat. They hunt in their minds for a means of restoring the hilarity. 'Good morning, Mrs Megget,' Liz cries shrilly, mimicking the upper-class tone of the departed horsewoman, 'excuse me half a mo' while I deposit this wacking great pooh.' And when the howling subsides, first Chrissy, then Nell, stoke up the merriment.

'Ta very much, madam. Just the thing for putting on me vegetable garden.'

'And come next spring when we're eating our spuds, we'll be eating a little bit of you, madam.'

They roar and roll about, stuff their mouths with crisps and doughnuts.

'I feel sick,' Nell says suddenly.

They study her. She is pale and greasy looking. Chrissy knows of a remedy. 'If we buy some fizzy it'll make her burp. Burping always makes you feel better.'

Liz counts the remaining money, then they go over to the shop to see whether it will run to a bottle of pop. The postmistress's manner has changed; her friendliness gone, she's disapproving and watchful as if she suspects they will try and steal something. At first they pretend not to notice, though they understand the situation perfectly: when they first came in they were taken for nicely behaved grammar school girls; since then they've displayed their true natures, rude, raucous, brazen. A spasm of shame overtakes Liz who fears the woman has recognized her, but this is far outweighed by a delicious feeling of shared wickedness. The purchase accomplished, they acknowledge their fall from grace with weak giggles and a bumping exit through the doorway like home-bound drunks.

They wander aimlessly through the village taking turns at the lemonade, after each swig courteously wiping a hand over the bottle before passing it, as though sweaty hand dirt must be less impure than mouth smearings.

The church further down the main street is so boringly churchy they scarcely take it in: they vaguely note its existence, but it's too predictable – a tower, a porch, some pointed windows – to merit attention and too obviously inviting – the 'welcome' notice, the open gate – to present a challenge. The house next door, on the other hand, positively leaps at them.

'That's it,' cries Chrissy, gazing at the looming Victorian hulk half hidden by laurels and a massive chestnut tree.

'Ee-normous,' breathes Nell (who has burped prodigiously and is now comfortable). 'Bet they're rich.'

'I shouldn't think so. It's the rectory,' Liz says,

thinking of the delightful shabbiness to be found in the Wold Enderby rectory.

Even so, the garden is huge and there are certainly scrumping possibilities. Her knowledge of the Wold Enderby layout leads Liz to suggest there may be a way in through the churchyard, whereupon they troop through the church gateway to test the theory.

Sure enough, there's a tall wrought-iron gate in the wall at the back of the graveyard, and beyond it lies a path through the rectory trees. The gate squeaks when Chrissy opens it. They flinch, look round, but the place is deserted. Quickly they slip through and close the gate behind, dash through the trees and shrubs, creep towards an expanse of green lying ahead. This is an enormous lawn, with a rising bank halfway across and steps with ornamental balustrades cut into the centre. At the top of the lawn a path runs across the front of the house. Facing them to the left is a huge square bay window, to the right a series of tall single windows. The glass is like dark water, fathomless. Perhaps eyes lie behind it. They crouch for a long time in the shrubbery. Nothing stirs.

To the side of the house, Liz spots some nets flung over bushes. Soft fruit, she guesses, redcurrants and blackcurrants, perhaps some late raspberries. They go quickly through the trees until they have a better view of the fruit situation, discover there is a window in the side of the house, directly opposite the fruit bushes. This turns the bushes into a particularly daring prospect. They steel themselves. Apples and plums are dead as a consideration; it's currants or nothing.

'The place looks deserted,' says Chrissy. 'Perhaps they're out.'

Liz isn't sure. 'They could be on the other side of the house, in a study or somewhere.'

'The thing is to check out this side. One of us must sneak up and look in the windows,' Nell decides. 'And it had better be Chrissy, because she runs the fastest.'

'Ay?'

Liz agrees. 'Yes, you do it, Chrissy, then if someone spots you and you come haring back, Nell and I can start running. You're bound to catch us up. We'll hold the gate open.'

'All right,' concedes Chrissy, pleased to be the best at something.

Bending low, she sets off over the lawn, scrambles up the bank, dashes across the remaining lawn and the path to flatten herself against the wall of the house between the windows. Her heart thuds so madly, she can't think what to do next. Then, recalling the critical eyes on her from the shrubbery, she acts like someone in a film, sidles along the wall with head and hands pressed back against it, and when she reaches the bay window, waits, listens, then stealthily peers in. It's hard to see anything beyond her reflection. She cups her eyes with her hands and a spacious sitting room springs to life, fortunately empty. The dining room, which lies behind the series of long windows, also proves empty. More confidently now, she steals round to the side of the house and the vicinity of the fruit bushes.

The window here is tricky. It's set too high in the wall to permit more than a sighting of kitchen taps. In the border nearby there's an upturned flower pot. She collects this, puts it beneath the window and stands with one foot on it. Now she can see rather more of the kitchen and it, too, appears deserted. She scampers to the corner of the house, beckons the others to come.

Halfway across the lawn it occurs to Liz that even now the Rector could be watching, gazing out from a bedroom window. Her eyes fly up, but the windows remain unruffled. They gather, panting, under the kitchen window, decide to take turns keeping a look-out, proceed to a ravaging of the fruit bushes.

Sun, currants and the possibility of imminent discovery are an intoxicating combination. Their heads swim, their hearts rush. The leaves are so vividly green and the fruit so darkly glossy that at widely spaced moments throughout their lives these images will flash at them on a bright day and the smell of blackcurrants rise and the earth become briefly unsteady. After a time, Liz craves a less-reckless exposure. 'Let's explore,' she suggests. 'Perhaps they're out.'

The front door is found on the other side of the house. As well as the kitchen door, there's another back door in a walled paved area near the dustbins and fuel shed. To the left of this door there's a window sill with a saucer on it. And the window, their popping eyes note, is imperfectly fastened. Half an inch gapes at the bottom.

With all their fingers inserted, and a joint heave, the window shoots up resoundingly. They dive for cover. No-one comes.

An upturned bucket from one of the sheds is placed under the window to provide a leg-up. Within seconds they are inside, clutching one another in a gloomy passage at the bottom of stairs.

'You go first,' whispers Liz to Nell.

But Nell pushes Chrissy forward.

They keep very close together as Chrissy leads the way upstairs. The stairs continue for a second flight, but they take a look at the first floor first, and discover a warren of little bare rooms – a broken bedstead here, a collapsed trunk there, piles of old magazines, boxes of jumble. Everywhere smells of warm dust and mustiness. Floors creak, doors groan. A dead bird by a fireplace in one of the rooms sends them racing and smothering screams down the corridor. The end of the corridor is barred by a door. It's locked. They try it repeatedly.

'Oh well, that's their part of the house,' says Liz, trying for magnanimity.

The others agree. 'This side's ours.' And they fall naturally into their seductive habit of fantasizing how they will stow away here, smuggle in everything they need, remain hidden for weeks. The idea of a secret existence is as entrancing as ever.

Shadows lengthen, sudden shivering besets them; they remember it's a long walk home. Vowing an early return, they hasten away, covering their tracks.

Back in the village street, they puff noisily, gasp 'Phew,' and 'We made it,' and 'Crikey, what if we'd been caught?' So quakey are their legs, they wonder whether they'll carry them home.

'Now, Elizabeth,' says Mrs Stockdale when the girls show signs of wanting to leave the tea table, 'Don't forget your piano practice. You promised to keep it up if your friends came to stay – not that we aren't glad they *have* come, eh, Daddy?' (A gleaming smile, here, for Chrissy who has just excelled herself as a trencherman.) 'And they won't mind watching telly while you do it, I'm sure.'

The girls politely shake their heads to show they won't mind. Television is a novelty to both. Chrissy's father could probably afford one, but Auntie Julie says television burns your eyes out and if they get one Chrissy will be blind by thirty. The Nelson budget simply won't stretch to one.

'Oh, Mother,' moans Liz.

'She didn't do her practice yesterday,' Mrs Stockdale tells her husband, who lays aside the evening newspaper.

'Now, come on, princess. Four distinctions in a row – you don't want to let yourself down in Grade Five.'

'But that's not for ages.'

'It's a tough exam, or so I'm given to understand.' He addresses his wife: 'If she gets a distinction in Grade Five, Mr Poole might take her on. I was talking to Charlie Bennet the other night. Apparently, that's how his lad got to be one of Poole's pupils. And look how well he's done, three first prizes at the

Festival, two columns and a photo in the *Evening Telegraph*.' He smirked – 'Handy publicity for Charlie's business, eh? – blummin' music shops. No, you keep it up, my girl. Mr Poole's choosey. He can afford to be. Best teacher in the area. She'd have to travel to Leeds to find a better one.'

'But I don't want to,' says Liz. 'I don't want to leave Mrs Andrews.'

Alderman Stockdale winks at his wife. 'We'll see about that when the time comes. Meanwhile, do as your mother says. Go on, jump to it.'

Liz flounces off. Chrissy and Nell help Mrs Stockdale clear the table, then sink without complaint on to the settee in front of the television.

Later, they set off on a scrumping expedition in the grounds of the Hall. Perhaps because they are tired, perhaps because the light is fading, they make a hash of jumping over the wall into the wooded area at the ground's extremity. Chrissy knocks out a couple of stones and sets off a rattling echo. Liz hurts her ankle, Nell's skirt gets torn. Doom-laden, they creep through the cracking undergrowth towards the orchard.

Their worst fear – that someone has heard them – is confirmed when a low white streak comes hurtling. Then they hear a shout, see the dog's teeth.

Liz stands rooted. Nell and Chrissy flee. When swift Chrissy reaches the wall, she looks back; Nell is loping towards her, Liz is farther back, hampered by the terrier's teeth in her skirt. At a further distance, a man is stepping through the tangle of fern and bramble and fallen branches. Chrissy starts back. Nell grabs her by the arm to stop her. 'We can't leave Liz,' cries Chrissy, freeing herself. After a second or two, Nell also turns back, terrified, half-resentful.

'You help Liz, I'll get the dog off,' pants Chrissy to Nell. With both hands she grabs the dog's collar; the dog hangs by it in a frenzied twisting. Its master whistles; the dog hesitates. Chrissy lets go and runs.

Afterwards, they can hardly recall hurling themselves over the wall, limping down the lane. They clearly remember the dog's breath on their legs, its yelping, the man's shouts.

'In here,' gasps Liz when they reach the rectory stable block. 'I know the people. They won't mind.'

They flop on to a plank, examine their wounds, wait for heart and lungs to recover.

Nell is the first to speak. 'You two look horrible.'

'So do you.'

Chrissy thrusts her arm out. 'It bit me.'

Liz squints at the wound. 'It isn't deep. We'll put iodine on it as soon as we get in. I think I've sprained my ankle.'

'Mum'll kill me when she sees this skirt,' Nell grumbles.

'My mother'll mend it for you. We'll say we were climbing trees.'

'At least we escaped,' says Chrissy.

Nell sighs, stares dreamily at the whitewashed brick wall. 'Yeah,' she breathes dramatically; 'we survived,' – which cheers them up, elevates their adventure to a higher plain.

'And tomorrow,' Liz declares, 'we'll do something even better.'

Twenty years on. In the bloom of their early thirties, they are tipsy once again in the Fenby-cum-Laithby rectory garden. Only this time it's glasses of Vouvray intoxicating them, not danger and blackcurrants. And it's The *Old* Rectory, now, the newly acquired home of Mr and Mrs Tony Duckenfield.

They lie in deck chairs on the lawn, idly watching Chrissy's two eldest children and Liz's only two build a tree house in one of the oaks beyond the shrubbery. It's a marvel, they keep saying as the bottle goes round, truly wondrous, a miracle. 'Here's to Tony, good old Tony, brilliant Tony.' And they giggle at the thought of scraggy little Tony in bicycle clips and horn-rimmed glasses (as all three women still secretly picture him) steaming ahead, seizing all the best local law business, selling the five-bedroom house in town, buying this gorgeous old rectory. *This* rectory, theirs.

'Funny how life turns out,' Nell muses. 'Chrissy's got all this, I've got my posh London pad, and poor old Liz is stuck in that bare little cottage on those God-awful moors. I mean, Chrissy and I've shot up from where we began, whereas Liz from a well-off home' (her voice starts sinking to *basso profundo*) 'has – gone – right – down.' Then she adds with an angelic smile, 'Though of course, she'll get her reward in heaven.'

Chrissy looks nervously at Liz. But it's all right, Liz is laughing so much she can't pour straight trying to recharge her wine glass. It's just Nell being Nell, airing her thoughts frankly as usual with no account for anyone's feelings. Good job they love her.

'You must plant some more currant bushes,' Liz tells Chrissy when she's recovered. 'In the exact same place.'

'Under the kitchen window,' Nell remembers.

'Oh, I shall.' Chrissy lies back, her head lolling to one side. 'I wonder why we did all that stuff,' she muses. 'All that trespassing and stealing and pulling stunts. We were obsessed with camping in peculiar places. Remember how we called the back room here "ours"? Do you think it was like saying: this is us; we belong together, not to people at home or school?'

Liz tilts her chin up and leans an arm across her forehead to shield her eyes. Overhead, the leaves with the sun on them have no colour, just gleam. 'I think we were trying to create our own space,' she says in a far-away voice; 'our own existence where no-one could reach us and interfere. Become secretly autonomous, secretly powerful . . .'

'Rubbish,' interrupts Nell, leaning over to stub her

94

cigarette out in the grass. Then she too lies back and closes her eyes, looking pleased with herself like a cat. 'We did it to get high. For the buzz.'

iii

While she was staring at the apple, Liz's mind was racing: of course this Simon wasn't *the* Simon – what an idiot, leaping to conclusions because Rosie baulked at naming the school where he taught.

'You all right?' asked the man who'd shouted at the apple thief.

The question threw her, until she remembered the apple striking her – it seemed to have happened so long ago.

The man – evidently a father – was now hand in hand with a child.

'Here,' said Liz, impulsively picking up the apple and holding it out. 'Your little girl might as well have it. Shame to let it waste.'

'Keep it for yours.'

'Mine?'

'Yeah. You're the one who got clobbered.'

'Oh, right.' Recalling that she was supposedly collecting a child, she smiled 'goodbye' and stepped nearer the hut. The man and his daughter went off, turned out of the top of the cutting. As soon as he was out of sight, she hurried off herself in the opposite direction, in the wake – trodden some minutes ago – of Ellie Goodridge.

After a few paces, she opened her hand and released the apple into some long grass.

The evening session at Redmond House finally dispelled Ellie Goodridge. Driving home afterwards, memories of her afternoon floated briefly back, but seemed tenuous, faintly pathetic, almost laughable after the problems which had occupied her since. She staggered into the house, went straight through kitchen and hall into the sitting room, fell against Nathan on the settee.

'I can smell that place in your hair,' he said. 'Institution.'

'I know. I could smell myself in the car. Just now I'm too tired to do anything about it.'

'Who went with you in the end?'

'Di. Honestly, love, it's daft of you to worry. There was even a policewoman there – Sergeant Wendy Marriot. Not to mention assorted social workers. Liaising's the name of the game these days.'

'I'm very pleased to hear it.'

'Make some cocoa,' she wheedled, 'there's a sport.'

'OK, Stinker. Put your feet up. Want the telly on?'

'Mm, OK.'

When he returned she was asleep.

Next morning she woke late in an empty bed, sprang from bedclothes into dressing gown in a single movement, hurried downstairs. 'Hey, did you forget to set the alarm? What time is it?'

Nathan was making toast.

'What's going on around here?' she protested, flopping, dazed, on to a kitchen chair.

'You needed to sleep in. You were shattered last night. In any case,' he added, trying to sound casual, 'it's results day. Thought I'd go in late myself.'

'Oh, Nathan. Fancy you remembering. *She* probably hasn't. Bet she doesn't show till noon, and you'll have waited around for nothing.'

'No I shan't. If Rosie can't be bothered, I'll ring up myself. Hell, I spent hours on her maths. I want to know how we did.'

She sighed, took the coffee mug he pushed towards her, sipped. 'Look,' she said when she'd thought about it. 'If there's no sign of her by ten, I'll give her a shout. I think it'd be better if she did the phoning.'

'OK. I'll be in the study going through those plans of Brendan's.' Plate of toast in one hand, mug in the other, he went into the hall calling, 'By the way, there's a piece in the local rag about Redmond House. You won't like it: *Girls climb out at night to go on the game.*'

'Not that old chestnut,' she said crossly, picking up the *Guardian* instead.

At ten to ten, Liz at the sink, Rosie, bleary-eyed, slunk in. 'Mu-um?'

'Yes?' said Liz, quite surprised to be spoken to.

'I think A level results come out today.'

'They do,' Liz confirmed. 'Breakfast?'

Rosie shuddered. 'N-hanks. Better phone.'

'Your father's in the study. You can use the phone in our bedroom if you like.'

'S OK,' said Rosie, shuffling towards the phone on the dresser. She put her hand on the receiver. 'O-oh, Mum?'

'Yes?'

'Wha's number?'

'How the heck should I know? The directory's in the study.'

Rosie didn't move. When Liz turned, she sent her mother a look of appeal. (Good heavens, thought Liz, she's really in a state. Can't face her dad, but doesn't mind me.) 'Shall I go and find it for you?'

'Oh, thanks, Mum.'

She stripped off her rubber gloves and went quickly through the hall to the study. 'Rosie's down,' she murmured in Nathan's ear as she searched for the school's number; 'but I should keep schtum for a bit if I were you.' She wrote down the digits, returned to the kitchen, handed them over in silence.

In silence, Rosie dialled – then crashed down the receiver. 'Bloody engaged.'

'Well, I expect everyone's trying. Sit down for a bit. Have some coffee.'

But Rosie dialled again – and again and again. 'Oh,

hello, Mrs Austin,' she said suddenly in a child's breathy voice. 'It's Rosie Learman. Oh, did you? Right. OK.'

Liz stopped breathing.

There was a joyous shout – 'Three As? Are you sure? Oh, thanks, thank you. Yeah, I will. Goodbye.' And her daughter turned back to her, restored. '*Mum* . . .' The shriek ended in a bear hug, which turned into a waltz for two. 'Three As, three As.' It was the old Rosie.

'Oh, Rosie . . .' Just in time she bit back the rest of the sentence – 'that means Durham will take you' – because, of course, Rosie had said she wouldn't go to university even if she did succeed in satisfying the entry requirements. She pushed her daughter away. 'Hurry and tell Nathan. He's terribly anxious.'

Rosie's voice came back to her – 'Dad, Dad,' – Rosie's clear, confident, happy voice. Awash with happiness, she flopped on to a chair and blew her nose.

Nothing lasts. Two minutes later Rosie was back, thunderous.

Nathan followed. 'I only said . . .'

'He said "That means they'll take you". That's all he cares about, sodding university. It's not enough what I've done already. "Where's the next bit?" Christ, you're never satisfied. I told you, I'm not going.'

'Right,' said Liz, getting to her feet in a determined way. 'We hear you, we understand.' She lowered her voice. 'It was a perfectly natural thing for your father to say, I almost said it myself. But we don't give a toss whether you go to university now or in the future or not at all. We're just glad you've won the right to go, if and when you feel like it. That's right, isn't it, love?'

'Er, I think I'll go up and shave.'

Liz waited for him to go. 'Now hear this,' she told her daughter softly. 'I want you to bear in mind two things about your father. One, he gave you a great deal of help with your maths. Two, he's by no means enjoying the peak of health. As for me, you can do as you please

98

so long as there's a pleasant atmosphere in this house. Not too much to ask, is it?'

She frowned, then shook her head. 'I'll, er, I'll make it up to Dad. I know he helped, I wouldn't have got A in maths if he hadn't.'

'Then tell him.'

'All right. And Mum, can I have a lift? Will you drop me at school? I want to see everyone.'

'Of course. So long as you're ready by half eleven.'

'I will be,' she promised, dashing away. Her feet thundered up the stairs. 'Dad?' she called.

Rosie was quiet during the journey, quiet but pleasant; spoke when it was polite to do so and not exclusively in monosyllables. It's an advance, Liz told herself, definitely an advance.

She turned in at the school gate and drove slowly along the drive, drew up in the wide space before the main door.

'You've got some money on you, I suppose?'

'Um, don't need any. Jenny's passed her test, she'll drive me home.'

'But have you arranged to meet her?'

'No, but there's always Fiona.'

'Pass me my bag.' She seized it, opened it, brought out her purse. 'If you're stuck for a lift get a taxi. It'll be no good ringing the clinic because I'm working elsewhere this evening. I'm not sure what your father's doing. Here.'

But Rosie wasn't attending. She was transfixed by a bright yellow Mini which had drawn up alongside. Liz peered across. Ellie Goodridge was tilting her head for her husband's kiss; she laughed at something he said as he climbed out of the car, backed, waved, drove away.

Rosie jumped out.

'Hey Rosie, the money . . .'

She slammed the door, called out an ominous 'Hello.'

99

Liz unbuckled her seat belt, struggled out. 'Rosie?'

The man – tall, fair, youngish, as Hazel had described – looked from Rosie to Liz, then hurried into the building.

'Take this, love.'

Rosie snatched the money.

'It's him, isn't it, your . . . friend, Simon Goodridge?' Her face bulged as though it could barely contain her hatred. 'You make me sick,' she said, and stalked away.

It was too late to ring Chrissy; much too late, she told herself repeatedly on the journey home that evening. But she knew she would. Mercifully, Nathan seemed to assume she was keener than she had been the previous night to soak away the smell of Redmond House. In fact, she showered in three minutes flat and, still towelling herself, ran into the bedroom and closed the door. Naked, she crawled under the duvet pulling the telephone on to the bed beside her. Two seconds later, the telephone in The Old Rectory, Fenby-cum-Laithby rang.

'Hel-lo.'

'I'm really sorry, Chrissy. I know it's late.' She broke off.

'Liz, whatever . . .? Look, why don't you come sooner? Tomorrow. Soon as you can. No need to wait for Nell . . .'

'Can't. Haven't made arrangements. Might manage Wednesday.'

'Great,' (she tried to keep the relief out of her voice, for she had just remembered the Rotarian dinner on Saturday) 'and Nell's coming Thursday . . . Liz, are you OK?'

'It's just . . . Rosie started being nice again. Her results came, three Grade As . . .'

'That's fantastic.'

'Yes, it was lovely. Such a relief – that she was more

100

herself again, I mean. Then I drove her to school and *he* was there, her chap, kissing his pregnant wife goodbye, a kid in the kiddie seat in the back. You should've seen Rosie's face. Chrissy, I just came out with it. You see, I knew it was him because I'd done some checking up. It's a long story. Anyway, I let her know I knew. Her expression when she looked at me – it was poison.'

'Liz,' said Chrissy after a pause. 'I really and truly believe you ought to leave it alone. Keep right out of it. I mean, she's eighteen. I know it's hard, but there's not a lot you can do.'

'You're absolutely right. Perhaps . . . I've been thinking. Maybe there's more to it – for me, I mean. Oh, I don't know. But you're right about Rosie; and I will try and keep out of it. Thanks, Chrissy.'

Chrissy's breath rushed out in a shy little laugh – such a familiar sound to Liz that it instantly sprang a picture of the schoolgirl Chrissy, even made her smile.

When she rang off she felt better. Just hang on, she thought.

iv

They are second-years. In the gym, the whole class is assembled in an embarrassed huddle in front of Miss Thirkettle – wiry, frizzy haired, dried-up Miss Thirkettle, whose lisle-encased legs are temporarily still under the mid-thigh length games-tunic in which she bustles along the corridors making out she's a mere slip of a girl. They shift their feet uneasily, hang their heads, sidle brief glances at one another. They know what's coming; they've been warned. Older girls have told them all about Miss Thirkettle's obsession with monthly periods. She's famous for it. As soon as they become second-years, the older girls warned, they too will suffer the Thirkettle lecture, followed by nasty moments when she gets you on your own, pins you into a corner and *asks questions*. Never, never give anything

101

away, even if you're dying of belly ache; throw her a crumb and she'll pester for more.

'Hands up,' says Miss Thirkettle, 'any girls who don't know what MPs are.'

Hands remain firmly attached to sides.

Nell wonders whether to venture 'Members of Parliament?', but doesn't bother; instead, she observes Miss Thirkettle. While other girls find relief letting their eyes roam the fine flecked lines in the oak-strip flooring, Nell commits every detail of the teacher to memory, her pale eager eyes, lip-moistening tongue, chicken-skin neck, tense craned-forward little body. She's never seen a more horrible sight: it's a treat, wonderful, she can't wait to draw it.

'Hands up,' says Miss Thirkettle, 'any girls who've already started.'

You could hear a pin drop. But yes, two, four, five hands creep into the air; then a sixth belonging to Pamela Pettifer. This creates a stir among those who know Pamela well, an intake of breath like affronted disapproval. They know she's lying, trying to draw attention to herself. They peer at her sideways. She has the grace to blush.

Miss Thirkettle launches into detail, more detail than any girl wishes to hear, especially from Miss Thirkettle. Chrissy gropes for the wall bars and hangs on tight. 'When your mother,' says Miss Thirkettle, and 'Tell your mother . . .' In her wildest dreams Chrissy cannot imagine Auntie Julie doing or suffering to be told any such things. In fact, Chrissy would die if it were otherwise, and finds comfort in the conviction that none of what Miss Thirkettle is talking about could possibly apply to her aunt.

An outsize negative is filling Liz's head. 'No,' she wants to scream; 'won't, can't, never.' As to most of the girls present, this subject is not exactly news, but up until now it seemed remote, a bit yucky, something the sillier girls joke about, no direct threat to herself. She is filled with loathing for the gym mistress. If this horrible thing really is going to strike, tact and taste surely demand silence, not someone publicly identifying you with it, gloating. She feels ambushed, branded. From this moment on she will always feel sickly when it's PE or games.

The bell goes for break. Miss Thirkettle reluctantly releases them.

'Argh, yurr, ker-ipes,' the class explodes, hanging tongues out, grasping throats. 'Wasn't she re-volting?'

'Pam Pettifer's lying, you can tell.'

'How?'

'Cos she's still flat. Jessica Bennet's started and she wears a bra.'

They fall silent, digesting this.

Liz, Nell and Chrissy drift away to their usual place on the steps by the netball courts. For once they forget about the possibility of titbits from the Stockdale larder, just crouch there privately brooding. Nell plans a drawing. Chrissy wishes Miss Thirkettle didn't teach games, which is her favourite subject. Liz draws on the sense of power she always derives from their three-way friendship. They three are different from the rest, stronger. I mightn't happen to us, she thinks.

But it does. A year later, give or take a month or two, all three have succumbed to what Nell's sister Marion calls the curse. Liz and Chrissy wince, pull resigned faces. Nell makes a fuss – groans, weeps, clutches her stomach, says what the hell are the medical profession playing at, why haven't they invented some way of stopping the beastly business which is barbaric and shouldn't have to be tolerated in this day and age.

Looking on the bright side, it can get you out of PE and games. No proof is required in the form of a letter from home: enough to shuffle forward, hang-dog or tortured looking, to earn an interested look from Thirkettle and be sent to do private study in the hall. Herein,

103

however, lie the seeds of the first difference to develop between them – that is, between Chrissy and the other two, for Chrissy loves PE and games; her dream is to be picked for the netball team. Nell and Liz, on the other hand, heartily despise every activity undertaken in navy-blue knickers and mucky-white aertex shirts.

There's a strange thing about games. Showing keen – better still, being good at them – confers a sort of badge on a girl; shows she's a good type, respectable. Thus it is that during their third and fourth years Liz and Nell become established as poor types, rebels, girls apart. By the time they enter the fifth they are no longer bothering to play the monthly period card, even though they've become past masters at fooling Thirkettle. They just bunk off. During PE lessons they sit hugging a radiator behind a partition in the library; on games afternoons they sneak out of the tradesmen's gate behind the canteen and stroll about in the nearby cemetery, perch on gravestones to philosophize, lounge on a bench with Colette (author of their favourite reading matter at the moment), smoke Craven A. Once or twice they've been sent for and asked to explain themselves. Unluckily for the games mistress's case against them, she cannot resist fishing for intimate information which she hopes may be offered in mitigation. Which is how they get the better of her. They lead her on a bit, then sort of crowd her in, stare eyeball to eyeball, imply without directly saying as much that they know what she's up to. They're not even sure what she *is* up to, nor how their intimidation works. But it does work. As Nell points out, Thirkettle can't very well report them to the Head without giving away her own negligence, because she's been letting them go AWOL for months. The success goes to their heads; they swagger and snigger and discuss matters in an undertone looking wise and cynical beyond their years. Other girls know they're getting away with murder and are thoroughly perplexed. Liz and Nell have mystique.

All this is trying for Chrissy. She runs off to games lessons looking back over her shoulder with a hopeless expression as though her heart isn't in it. This is for the benefit of Liz and Nell who may be watching. It's tricky with the rest of the class, too. Her useful participation is acknowledged with cries of 'Good shot,' and 'Well played, Chrissy.' And she's never one of those girls who don't get picked for five-a-side teams. Yet there's wariness in other girls' eyes; curiosity when she joins in the after-match banter. They're puzzled because, though she's such a good sport, she's a member of the dissident trio. Afterwards she has to nearly kill herself trying to make up for it to Liz and Nell. She'll pinch some of Auntie Julie's ciggies, suggest going for a smoke in the cemetery after school, even though she secretly hates the taste and never inhales.

Liz sometimes inhales, mostly she doesn't; it's the feel of the cigarette between her two fingers she specially enjoys, taking it to her lips in languorous self-embrace, tilting up her head and popping smoke rings. Nell inhales greedily, takes the smoke deep into her lungs, expels it gradually as she talks. This gives an added cachet to the things she says – added, because there has long been tacit agreement between them that what Nell says is particularly profound.

It's Nell who presents bunking off games as a matter of principle. Compelling people to risk injury – breaking a neck falling from the beam in PE, say, or getting legs bashed blue by steaming brute hockey players – is an abuse of authority, an outrage. They listen to her throbbing voice and remember the day, recently, when Nell got stung by a bee in a Geography lesson; her screams of disbelief ('I've been stung, it's left its sting in, I'm being *poisoned*,'), her furious indignation as she was led from the classroom ('Why'd it get me?' – as if the singling out were an added twist on her rack of pain); Nell is not a stoic, they recall. Even so, her argument is persuasive. Nell's right, says Liz fiercely

105

to Chrissy, and Chrissy hangs her head and mumbles.

Chrissy knows Nell is right; and that Liz is, too, in siding with Nell and doing as Nell does; knows this in her heart because she is one of them. She suffers their sneers meekly, accepts their implication that by meekly skipping off to games she's slipped from their standard, become the weak side of the triangle.

Nell demonstrates that she's right and teachers wrong on many occasions. For example, when the word 'eunuch' crops up again. This time Nell proves her understanding of the word correct by producing a large dictionary (not the cropped version issued to fourth and fifth formers) and thrusting it under Cummings's nose. Gratitude might have been expected from the head of English, but not a bit of it: Cummings shudders with rage as if knowledge were a box of tricks and mere girls not permitted to take the lid off. In spite of their faith in Nell, it is still quite a shock to Liz and Chrissy seeing her so thoroughly vindicated, to catch jealous authority in the very act of stifling and suppressing burgeoning young intellects. From now on they're wary in class, take nothing on trust, prefer Nell's guidance in literary matters.

Nell has been guiding their choice of reading matter for some time. Only sixth-formers are permitted free and unsupervised access to the school library. ('Pathetic,' says Nell.) After school, they often go to the town library, make for the teenagers' section to forestall objections, then sidle round to where the proper books are kept in tall wide bookcases, between which they can remain undisturbed for hours. Nell insists they give a decent chance even to books that at first glance appear dull; reading, says Nell, is not all about discovering what happens on the last page. They slip books into their satchels, morally justified, as Nell points out, by the absurd age limit on the right to tickets, bring them back a few days later and exchange them for others. It's their own unofficial borrowing system. Before they leave, while Chrissy and Liz persevere with *Sons and Lovers* or *Goodbye to Berlin* or *Anna Karenina* (as selected by Nell), Nell likes to wander over to the Art section, spread one of the big volumes open on the floor, sit with her eyes boring into the pages. She gets so carried away she doesn't always hear them when they speak to her. They peer over her shoulder to see what is so engrossing. Sighing because they are spoiling her light, she heaves herself up and carts the volume over to a table (always the same table, one round a corner out of the sight of librarians who may feel duty-bound to interfere). They sit on either side of her as Nell lingers over the pages. Prints of famous paintings which hang in school classrooms and public buildings and appear endlessly on calendars, so predictably that eyes notice them only as conventional wall decoration – these dead things are brought alive; it's as if Nell's gaze, her glancing finger, sigh, odd remark, can draw veils aside, switch on brightness. Nell shows them that you don't have to make paintings only in the manner taught by Miss Redmond (art mistress), which is to draw outlines and fill them in: there are endless methods, some without outlines at all. This freedom, which exists out there somewhere, which they are never allowed a peep of at school, takes their breath away. Thank heaven for Nell, Liz and Chrissy think tremulously. With her assistance they are getting to grips with the world, in spite of systems designed to prevent them.

They continue their day-dream of occupying places illicitly. Possible venues regularly crop up; they discuss their rival merits, decide first on the town library, then on the rear quarters of the rectory in Fenby-cum-Laithby. The plan they actually put into action is rather tame; they regard it as a starter, a trial. It's staying overnight at Chrissy's unbeknown to Auntie Julie. Liz and Nell's parents are told of the visit beforehand, but given to understand that Chrissy's aunt has sanctioned it. (Fortunately, Mrs Stockdale has long ago ceased making courtesy calls to Auntie Julie, and Nell's mother never began.) Everything goes as planned: Liz and Nell creep upstairs while Chrissy presents herself in the living room, they sate themselves on smuggled-in food, tiptoe to the bathroom and back with a delicious sense of subterfuge. Chrissy even manages to bring three mugs of tea upstairs. But around midnight, Nell's proposition that Jane Austen's Emma Woodhouse is an unworthy heroine, only the heroine, in fact, because she's the rich girl, a boring snob who plays with people, provokes a vehemence which carries to Auntie Julie. 'You're so prejudiced,' Liz hisses, feeling somehow under personal attack, 'that you can't see her good points, like, well, like she's good fun.' 'Fun?' all but shrieks Nell, fired up for revolution. Fortunately, Auntie Julie's cry of 'Chrissy' gets to them before she does, allowing Nell, who is lying on the far side of the bed, time to roll out and under. Thus, only Liz is discovered beside Chrissy, blinking in the sudden illumination.

Auntie Julie recognizes her at once. 'Oh, it's you, duck; I didn't know you were staying, you should have said, Chrissy. Don't mind any noise on the landing, it'll only be me traipsing up and down after Chrissy's dad – five times I was out to him last night with his waterworks. Ah well: night, night, sleep tight, mind the bugs don't bite.' Chortling to herself, she snaps off the light, leaves them.

They count it a partial success because Nell's presence wasn't discovered. Also, it's useful knowing they have a ready bolt-hole should one ever be required, no prior permission necessary. As a thrill, though, stowing away at Chrissy's is dead in the water.

108

They decide to pull a really big stunt to celebrate the end of O levels. Until these exams are safely over, it's hard to think of anything other than work.

None of the rest of the class and few of the teachers expect the trio to do specially well in the coming exams. (Some teachers say Monica Nelson will, because she's outstanding; though she won't deserve a good result, not with her attitude.) They've earned a reputation for negativity; never answer brightly in class, just sniff, mutter, argue points. But *they* expect to do well. This is because, unlike many of their classmates, they actually enjoy school work (though not all of it: they loath science and maths). Much of their free time is spent reading together, exchanging and looking up information, arguing and testing one another's theories. All three are devoted to English literature, competent in languages, interested in history and geography. And each has a specialization: Nell's is art, Liz's is music, Chrissy's is home economics. (Nell has always been a clever artist; Liz, who was indeed accepted as a pupil by the choosy Mr Poole after passing Grade Five piano, has become an accomplished musician; and cooking lessons have served as a beacon of hope to Chrissy: while other girls, thoroughly bored, slapped dough till it was tough and couldn't be bothered to cream fat and sugar properly, the prospect of something decent to eat has fired her execution, produced a passionate cook.) All in all, they confidently expect a decent crop of O levels, however others may estimate their chances.

When the last O-level paper is handed in, they turn at once to planning the celebratory stunt. The overnight venue they hit on is the school library. It'll be a way of cocking a snook, of establishing ascendency over an institution which has sought to cramp their style – only for a night it is true; but, they argue, once done it will never be undone and in that sense will live on. They'll have taken over.

They're in place in the library when the bell goes at ten to four. There's an immediate snapping to attention, books shut, satchels close, feet tramp through the doorways at each end of the library which straddles the top of the two-storey building situated between the quadrangles. On the ground floor of this central building are the staff and visitors' entrance, the office, the staffroom and the Head's study. The first floor provides the sixth-form classroom and cloakroom, also a small pantry and a sickroom. There are two stairwells: you can run up one side of the building, go through the library on the top floor and down the other flight. When the bell rings, Liz, Nell and Chrissy remain at a table between two bookcase partitions.

It's surprising how promptly the place empties, goes from noisy to silent in seconds. The room turns into a different character, from a provider of seating for dozens of reading, scribbling, day-dreaming, fidgeting girls into a brooding hall of books. They sit listening to the dwindling sounds below. When these become faint, they creep to the stairs and perch there. A sixth-former startles them by returning suddenly. They prepare to flee into the library, but she goes into the cloakroom on the first floor, collects something, runs down and out again. They squat on the stairs and listen to the cleaner on the ground floor. (Yesterday they had a practice run, so they know the pattern.) When the cleaner mounts the stairs with bucket, mop and broom, they wait in the library while she cleans the sixth-form area. As soon as she starts climbing to the second floor, they nip down the far stairs and hide in the small sick room until she's finished in the library. When she returns to ground level they creep back to the top floor. Sounds rise clearly up the stairwell: the cleaner calls to the caretaker, a key turns in the door on the staff room side of the building, heavy feet cross the ground floor. Words are exchanged. It's the Head speaking.

Nell has gone pink, Chrissy has turned pale. Liz's eyes smart with the heat of blood rushing double time round her body.

'I'll lock up, Mr Box,' comes the Head's cry ringingly. Crikey, if they make the slightest sound . . .

They seem to crouch on the stairs for hours straining after sounds that don't come. A conviction grows in Liz that they'll always be here, that an insidious heaviness has rolled over the world spreading inertia and they lack the massive energy required to throw it off. When noises sound at last they almost topple with shock and terror. But it's over in seconds – tap, tap, go the Head's feet over the ground floor, whoof goes the outer door, and a key clunks in the lock.

A hush eases over the building now: a sigh, a gentle rustle and creak; the place settles down.

After a time they become accustomed to the new atmosphere, talk more freely (though very quietly), move more fluently, set out their supplies – food, bottle of pop, torch, cigarettes, matches. From the sick room they collect blankets and pillows, carry them up to the library, spread them out.

Time passes. For a smoke they go downstairs and sit in the staffroom. (It's something everyone's noticed, how, when the staffroom door opens, a stink of fags wafts out.) They make black instant coffee in the pantry, eat the food they've brought from home. There's only one torch, so they take turns to read *Chéri* aloud to one another. A moon comes up; they stand transfixed at a window, grow giddy watching thin cloud speed by. When they try to settle down it's surprisingly difficult to get comfortable. Nell and Liz have a hissing quarrel; Nell accuses Liz of taking the best blankets and tries to pull them away, Liz struggles to hang on to them. Eventually, Chrissy sorts them out.

At last they lie still, stare at the bookcases looming like sentinels, marvel at their daring and how easy it has been pulling this audacious stunt. The conclusion is clear (they repeat it to one another and enlarge on it endlessly): given their outstanding pluck and imagination they could bring off just about anything.

V

Two other people waiting, not necessarily for the same doctor. In fact, thought Nell, looking at her watch, they'd better not be waiting to see her man, for it was already five minutes into her appointment time. Cheek, really. Might as well save herself a bomb and stick to the NHS if she was going to sit around kicking her heels anyway. Dammit, she paid *not* to be kept waiting. Had he forgotten she was famous, that her time was money?

She grabbed her shoulder bag, opened it, felt for her cigarettes; then saw the 'no smoking' notice. Now she was in trouble – mad as hell and forbidden her usual method of cooling down.

Fortunately, her rage took a silent form. Headlines and pithy sentences leapt into her mind's eye ready-printed in day-glo. Enough of these clean-air prudes. What about the right to have a drag when you felt like it? She could sense a new mood in the ether, sense it in her tingling fingertips and toes: people were sick of being told what was good and bad for them, what they should and shouldn't do. They craved to see these nanny types dealt a good hard thwack. Step forward the woman to administer it: crusading columnist Monica Nelson. Mentally rolling up her sleeves, she leaned forward in her seat with her chin on her hand and her face gone all soft and dreamy. An observer might think she was just nodding off.

A white overall came in. 'Miss Nelson?'

Nell jumped and dropped her bag. By the time she'd gathered her scattered belongings, she was flushed and startled looking. Crossing the consulting room, she stumbled over the edge of the carpet, grabbed rather than shook the surgeon's outstretched hand.

Apprehensive, he concluded, and proceeded to couch his message in convoluted form, incorrectly ascribing a balming effect to an excess of words. He put her X-rays into the projector, pressed the switch. Obediently, Nell stared at her lungs illuminated on the screen, thinking that while she was at it she'd take a swipe at the medical profession. After all, who'd put up the 'no smoking' notice? None other than this smarmy blighter, she'd wager. And what the flipping heck was he driving at – 'round thing like a golf ball . . ., very suspicious looking . . ., *growth*?'

'Hang about,' she cut in. 'You telling me it's cancer?'

Silence. A pressing together of finger tips, a narrowing of eyes.

He bloody well is, she thought, frantically fumbling with her bag fastening.

'I'm afraid that is, er, a possibility; that is, we can't rule it out, Miss Nelson. Not at this stage. Of course, as I said, it may merely be an abscess. However, the position, the size, that cloudy area to the left, do leave one with unpleasant suspicions. Not to worry,' – he reached for a diary – 'we'll get you in straight away. First of all we'll do a biopsy . . . a simple procedure, some mild discomfort for the patient, nothing too terrible. We insert a needle . . .'

'No, no, you can't. I mean, it's not possible; I'm all tied up.'

He continued to peruse his appointments book. 'How about Tuesday?'

Jesus Christ. Her fingers sought and clasped her packet of Silk Cut.

He leaned forward, gently reproving. 'And I most strongly urge you, Miss Nelson, to desist from smoking. There's some material here you might like to read . . .' He reached into a drawer. 'And try this chewing gum; several of my patients have found it helpful. You can take

113

this box to be going on with.' He pushed it with some leaflets across the desk; she stuffed them quickly into her bag. 'If it doesn't do the trick, there are other things we can try. Now, shall I mark you in for Tuesday?'

'Certainly not,' she snapped. 'I'm a very busy person. Next week's right out.' Hadn't she absolutely promised next week to Liz? Chrissy'd kill her, they'd neither of them speak to her ever again, if she let them down now after promising. 'Out of the question,' she insisted.

He turned a page. 'The following week? I think, you know, we'd be well advised to get on with it.'

'I suppose so. If you really think it's . . .'

'A week on Tuesday,' he concluded, pencilling it in. 'Come at nine o'clock. My secretary has the details and will take down your particulars if you call in her office before you go.' He rose and offered his hand.

The bastard. She tried to conjure a few headlines in self-defence, but they wouldn't oblige. She felt cornered, frisked, denuded of weapons; and her feet had acquired lead-weights. Ignoring his hand she tottered over the hideous pink and blue Axminster to the door.

He had the taste not to wish her a good afternoon.

'Liz', Nell began, then lifted her pen and looked at the word. Three letters only to bring a world flooding back. And such swamping feelings – some deadly like you were being throttled, others easeful like sitting in a jacuzzi. She wrote a comma then the name again. Funny how her letters to Liz were always handwritten. Not to anyone else. Usually, a typewriter on the coffee table was as informal as she got. But writing to Liz she needed a pen in her hand. Funny that. She wrote a second comma, followed by 'Liz duckie dear,'; took a drag on her cigarette, then settled her rump more firmly into the cushions and went on in earnest.

'I've been thinking about you today – well, I was kept hanging about this afternoon so I had to think of something, and you happened to pop up. I started remembering things I used to imagine about you at school – that you were encased in hard polished veneer, impermeable, so no grubbiness or damage could get at you.

'Of course, I don't see you like that any more. Well, you're not, are you? I mean, you're the antithesis of glitzy. People have to look twice to notice you're beautiful. Chrissy and I are the eye-catching ones. Blow me if I'm not running you down. Isn't that typical? Didn't mean to when I started out. But then I'm essentially negative, don't you think?'

This last comment amused her. She reached for her cigarette, drew in, and as she began to write again gave the letter a lingering smoke-bath.

'What hit me, wham, today was the thought that you really *are* hard and shiny – but inside, not out. You're hard-centred. Right at the core there's something indestructible – I picture it as a diamond. Perhaps it's integrity. Maybe it's self-belief . . . Whatever, it's definitely a strength, and because of it you'll beat whatever it is that's bugging you at the moment. That's my rock solid conviction. And you know my convictions always come true.

'Of course, I'm dying to hear all about it next week. It's just that I've a hunch you're really going through it at the moment and could do with something to hang on to in the meantime.'

At this point, she paused, hindered by fat tears in her eyes (whether for Liz or herself she couldn't say). She rubbed at them irritably (she hated having her flow interrupted), forgetting that she was not the schoolgirl Nell of her present mental image confiding her latest thoughts to close pal Liz, but Monica Nelson, famous for, among other things, her spectacular eyelashes. As she rubbed, a string of them peeled off, dropped into her tumbler of gin. Bugger, she thought, looking at it. She fished it out and laid it on a tissue to dry. Feeling lop-sided, she ripped off the other set, dipped it in the gin to even things up and laid it beside its partner. (Might be quite a discovery, gin; might gloss them up a bit.) Now, where was she?

Ah yes: 'something to hang on to in the meantime.' Oh dear, she'd run out of steam. 'Hope this will serve,' she scribbled. 'Keep smiling, flower – Nell.'

Liz would never guess a calamity had befallen the writer, she thought, reading the letter through carefully to make sure. And next week when they met at Chrissy's she must keep mum about it, because think how small and foolish Liz would feel if one of the friends she was confiding her woes to suddenly confessed to very likely having lung cancer.

An empty feeling, as if her stomach were a shrivelled balloon, suddenly assailed Chrissy. It knocked every other matter out of her head, forced her to focus on it. She endured it for as long as she could, then sat up with a great swirl of the bath water and pulled out the plug. Hastily she dried herself, then in dressing gown and slippers, her hand on the carved mahogany banister rail, pelted down the broad right-angled staircase.

The sitting room door was open. She fixed her eyes on the kitchen door across the hall, hurried towards it in a determined diagonal.

'Mum,' came Joy's complaining wail from the sitting room. 'Have you seen my new tape? I only put it down for a minute. It's not fair. Someone's always . . .'

She closed the kitchen door on her daughter's woe, went into the larder. A swift perusal of the shelves, and she decided on the cake tin; snatched it, wrenched off its lid; couldn't wait to go back for a knife, just plunged straight in, broke off a hefty wedge and stood where she was, one hand on the tin, the other stuffing chunk after chunk into her tireless mouth. Down it went, painfully, to grunts and moans, as she worked without pause to achieve a satisfying full feeling. When the

116

wedge was eaten, she stood motionless for a moment clasping her stomach, waiting for a kindly belch to rise and dispel the congestion. Phew, that was better. She was all set now: wouldn't get too panicky if the Rotarians were slow putting food in front of her. At a more leisurely pace, she rinsed her hands under the kitchen tap and went into the hall.

In the sitting room doorway she paused. 'Right. What was that?'

'Found it,' sang out Joy carelessly.

'Hmm,' said Chrissy and climbed the stairs. At the top, she crossed the landing towards the back part of the house and took hold of a door knob; turned it, pushed open the door, and was just in time to glimpse three schoolgirls fleeing in terror from a dead rook in the room on the right. Chrissy, Liz and Nell. They were always flying down the corridor when she opened this door abruptly, and were gone in a flash, so she could never decide whether they were the work of spirits or her imagination. Right now, there was a distinctly unghostly atmosphere. Overhead, shouts and clicks rang out – Clare and Neil, with cronies from the village, having a high old time at the new pool table in the games room. And from the room on the right where the dead rook had once lain, came the whoo-hoo-hoo of a pop song. Chrissy went in and was confronted by a whole series of Amandas in long mirrors round the walls; legs stiff and astride like a series of scissors; heads, arms, upper torsos flopping, going rhythmically this way and that. How Tony spoils her, she thought (not for the first time), taking in the specially laid flooring, the *barre*, the sounds system.

Amanda spied her upside down in a mirror. She straightened, went cheerfully to turn down the volume. 'Ready for me to do your hair?'

'I'm about to wash it. I say, love, do you think it's good for you to be always exercising? It's your evening off. Perhaps it'd be healthier to relax for once.'

117

This tickled Amanda. 'You are *quaint*, Mummy. No, no. I'm just making up a routine to this fantastic new tape. Not working out or anything.'

That was all right then, she supposed. 'About ten minutes?'

'OK. And Mummy: put your dress on and do your face when you've washed your hair, otherwise you'll mess up all my brilliant work, like last time.'

'Right,' said Chrissy, and departed to her bathroom to do as she was bid, waddling and clicking her fingers – not to Amanda's tune, but to a number remembered from when she was Amanda's age, the days of the university jazz club, of the brief love of her life. '*Uh-huh, this joint is jumpin'*, she sang in her head, which made her think it was a shame she had to go out tonight and leave it. Things she might do if she were not going out passed through her mind like out-of-reach treats – join in the pool game upstairs, get Joy (who liked doing bits of cooking) to help her bottle the plums, gossip with Amanda, nip over to the pub and say hello to Irene and George who were usually in the bar on a Saturday night (without Tony, of course; Tony hated the village pub; but this didn't stop Chrissy who dropped in whenever she felt like it, alone, with a friend, or with one of the elder children). Yes, it was a shame, all right. She rubbed shampoo into her hair and thought there was no fate more deserving of pity than to be going to a formal dinner – any formal dinner, the Freemasons' Ladies' Night, the Chamber of Commerce Christmas beano, Tony's Old Boys' dinner dance, a Dining In at the local police college, the Rotarian President's Evening; heart-sinkers all, especially when, as would happen tonight, she and Tony were guests of honour at the top table. Oh, that cringe-making business of introducing top-table diners to the rest of the room. Not that any of the ladies ever got more than a cursory mention: 'And next to Tony we have his charming wife, Chrissy.' – this after five

118

solid minutes devoted to the life and works of Tony Duckenfield. God, remember the time when she was caught cramming three chocolate mints into her mouth just as the spotlight fastened on her? Trouble was, the food came so slowly on these occasions, that by the time the last course arrived you'd forgotten you'd had the first two. Then sitting through those terrible speeches with nothing to take your mind off them but dregs of wine and any morsels your neighbours had left lying about. And those speeches . . . How could men stand heaping praise on one another, so fulsomely, blatantly, *seriously*. Never a titter. Never a squirm. With her own eyes she'd seen the subject of a eulogy gravely nodding agreement and at the end madly applauding with the rest. No doubt about it, men loved this sort of thing – glassy-eyed wife tricked out as a nod and a wink to a pretty deep wallet, cronies taking turns to praise a chap's unstinting effort for charity, for the community, for the blessed organization (not to mention doing quite nicely by yours truly). Really lapped it up, did men . . .

Now listen here, she commanded herself (she was by this time staring sternly into the bathroom mirror, having towel-dried her hair): don't for heaven's sake start being anti. Tony's been very fair – hasn't asked you to attend a function for weeks – forked out for a pool table without a murmur. So get into the bedroom and turn yourself into an *asset*.

She went to the chest-of-drawers, took out and put on her underwear, withdrew her dress from its plastic wrapper, wriggled into it. The dress (long-sleeved tight-fitting black velvet bodice attached to shortish, very full dark green taffeta skirt) she then swathed at shoulder level in a protective plastic wrap.

Amanda came in as she was applying her make up. She watched intently, making helpful comments. 'Oo, gorgeous eye-shadow, Mummy. You need a bronzey sort of lipstick. Yes, perfect.' When the face could not

119

be further improved, Amanda brushed out her mother's wet locks and started up the hand dryer.

'Don't go too mad,' urged Chrissy, later, when her daughter applied curling tongs. Her auburn curls were already exuberant, without further encouragement.

'You need masses of body to balance the skirt. See? Now stand up and give us a twirl. Oh, terrif.'

'You don't think the skirt's a bit short?'

'No, honestly, Mummy. It's perfect – really. You've got such super long legs. Thank goodness,' she added in heart-felt tone, checking herself in the wardrobe mirror, 'I take after you and not Daddy.'

Chrissy nudged her out of the way and studied her own image. At least the skirt's fullness hid the little round bump of her stomach – the only part of her ever to betray her insatiable appetite.

'Daddy's eyes'll go pop,' promised Amanda, gathering up her equipment, going to the door.

'Thanks for doing my hair, darling. Don't forget you're in charge tonight; though we won't be back late.'

'Don't worry. *Ciao.*'

When Tony arrived to change into his dinner suit, she was sitting scowling into the dressing-table mirror, thanking her lucky stars that Liz hadn't taken up her invitation to come earlier. Thank God Liz wouldn't see her looking like this; most of all, thank God Liz wouldn't see her and then tell Nell.

Tony, appraising her through his thick spectacle lenses, soon spotted a deficiency. 'What about the emerald necklace?' (Having laid out good money, he expected value.)

'Gosh,' – she scrabbled guiltily in her jewellery box – 'I nearly forgot it.'

He shook his head wonderingly.

'Fasten it on for me, then.'

'You're looking very lovely,' he conceded when the necklace was in place.

She got up and showed him the full effect. 'Skirt not on the short side?'

'Absolutely not. It's fine – on you. Shouldn't like to see some wives we could mention showing that amount of leg. But they're not all so nice and slim.'

'Thin,' she automatically corrected him, having always thought of herself as scraggy like Auntie Julie. Her little hummock of a tummy was her favourite feature, she often patted it for consolation. The best moments of her life were the months of late pregnancy when she could kid herself she was fat, voluptuous, a fertility goddess. 'I was worried in case it was a bit too young-looking.'

'Rubbish,' he retorted, holding his sleeves out for her to insert cuff-links. 'I read somewhere recently . . . Or did I hear it on the radio? Anyway, apparently Joan Collins is fifty-three.'

She stepped back. Enquired coldly, 'So?'

'Well, I mean – if she can get away with it . . .'

'I'm only forty-eight, you twerp.'

'I know.'

'So what are you driving at?'

He backed away, unable to recall. 'Well, it's not age, is it? And it's like, well, it's like, it's a sort of challenge.'

'*Joan Collins*?'

'She's a very good-looking woman.'

Spinning round, marching on the wardrobe drawer to rummage for her evening bag, she snarled at him in Auntie Julie's voice, 'Go shove a brick in yer cakehole, lad,' (a favourite riposte of Auntie Julie's); and as she bent over the drawer a harsh cackle (silent these twenty odd years) rang in her head. Joan who? rasped Auntie Julie. Never heard of her.

Liz's weekend was going rather well. She was awakened on Saturday morning by Nathan creeping around collecting things to stow in his overnight bag. Coming to, she remembered he was going to Brendan's to discuss forming a partnership. 'Don't forget your spray,' she called sleepily.

'Shan't bother. No need. Haven't had a twinge for weeks.'

'Take it,' she insisted. 'Just in case.' It was a spray prescribed for emergencies, a method of setting medication to work quickly.

'OK.' He took it from a drawer, tossed it into his bag. 'Cup of tea?'

'Mm, if you've time.'

She lay on her back watching splotches of sun fade and grow on the ceiling. 'Haven't you really?' she asked thoughtfully.

In the middle of choosing a sweater for the evening, he had to think back over what had been said. 'Had a twinge? No, not for ages. In fact, I've been feeling so good I'm beginning to wonder whether the condition's righted itself – if that's possible.'

'Oh, I'm sure it is,' she said, and sat up eagerly against the pillows.

'Basically, I try not to think about it. The consultant said keep busy, so I do.'

When he came to kiss her goodbye, he brought the promised cup of tea. Soon, she heard his car go up the lane. She sipped the tea and slid down between the sheets, watched the sun show up the knots in the pinewood chest-of-drawers, felt she'd been given a present. Which she had. She'd been given a delicious wafty feeling of weightlessness and peace. A conviction that Nathan was going to be all right.

Optimism carried her through the day. She spent most of it in the garden, weeding and dead-heading. Generally, she quite enjoyed gardening, certainly enjoyed the results of her labour, although sometimes the activity sprang a trap on her, locked her into an uncongenial train of thought. She knew why this happened: it was because she associated her mother with gardening; but understanding did not always save her from being caught off guard as she forked out the dandelions, pulled the chickweed, traced back to the spot from where the bindweed sprang. Her natural weeding stance was to crouch on her haunches. She could spend hours comfortably in this position like a peasant woman grinding meal or waiting for time to pass. On occasion, though, without her being conscious of it, her protesting knees would straighten, thrusting her bottom up into the air. Then, as her hands worked on, a feeling would steal over her that she had become her mother with a rump swollen to prodigious proportions and her feet become the stolidly planted platform of an obstinate woman, devoid – for all her delight in stuffing food into people – of charity or tolerance. To shrug off Mrs Stockdale, it was necessary to straighten up, walk about, go and sit for a while on the seat by the apple tree. Guilt took over then, the guilt of a child who dislikes her parent and knows she has turned out disappointingly.

Happily, this particular afternoon her body remained her own. Furthermore, her optimism about Nathan made it seem a very easy task to follow Chrissy's advice and keep off the subject of Rosie's affair.

Rosie came and went; with passable civility asked to borrow Liz's car, said 'Thanks,' when she came in at about half past six. Liz, who had been careful to stifle any curiosity about Rosie's expedition, merely nodded and went on leaning against the kitchen stove looking thoughtful. She'd realized it was a big mistake working so hard in the garden with no Nathan around, for here she was, utterly shot, and no grateful husband prepared to get her an evening meal.

'Something up?' Rosie asked cautiously, returning the car keys to the hook on the side of the dresser.

'Uh? Just wondering what we can eat. I suppose you don't fancy going to the pub?'

Rosie hesitated. 'Yeah, all right.'

Now, if she'd planned this expedition, it wouldn't have come off, Liz told herself later in the lounge of the Bluebell Inn. The haddock and chips arrived. Rosie picked up a chip with her fingers, held it aloft, let it curve into her open mouth. Liz pierced the crisp gold batter with the point of her knife, parted the gleaming flesh. Excellent nosh, they agreed.

Several people they knew were in tonight, and soon news of Rosie's A-level triumph went round; there was genuine pleasure, much teasing congratulation. Liz watched her daughter turn pink, laugh, protest, even look to her mother with a grin. She was careful to treat this casually, to remind herself that though tonight was going fine, tomorrow might well be a downer.

As they were leaving, they bumped into their good friends, Penny and Phillip Jarrow. Learning that Nathan was away this weekend, the Jarrows invited Liz and Rosie for Sunday lunch. Rosie declined, though pleasantly. Liz gladly accepted.

'All right if I borrow the car tomorrow seeing as you'll be at the Jarrows'?' Rosie asked on the way home.

'Sure,' replied Liz steadily, and changed the subject.

Sunday lunch at the Jarrows' did not proceed altogether smoothly. They were eating summer pudding when the telephone rang. It was the matron of a Hexham nursing home ringing to say Penny's mother had suffered a stroke. The meal was more or less abandoned, the Jarrows left soon afterwards in the car, Liz remained to clear up.

Staring through the window over the sink, Liz thought guiltily of her own mother. I ought to go and see her more often, she thought. I bank too much on Chrissy. When Mother writes and says 'Chrissy came the other day,' or Chrissy says 'Your mum's looking well,' I think, well that let's me off for a bit. Of course, Mrs Stockdale might be better suited by a visit from Chrissy (local prominent person's wife, regularly featured in the *Evening Telegraph*) than by a visit from

124

her unsatisfactory daughter. But you really don't give a toss, not at bottom, she told herself impatiently, drying her hands on the Jarrows' roller towel.

She checked the locks at the back of the house, lowered the catch on the front door, slammed it behind her.

At home, her car was in the yard. Not parked neatly, but abandoned by the kitchen door; also the driver's door was wide open, the keys still in the ignition. The house, too, was open to all-comers. Softly in her trainers she sped through the house, discovered no-one in kitchen or sitting room; came to a stop. A sound was coming from the study at the end of the hall passage, a long drawn-out mewing which finally exploded – 'But you *promised* me, Simon, you bloody well promised. Yes you did, you sod. I don't care, I don't care if she does hear, bloody good job . . .' It was a voice she'd never heard before, crazy sounding. Several seconds elapsed before she accepted it as Rosie's.

'What? Well don't *I* count? I'm sick of you always whining on about *her*. Meet me tonight, then. You must; you owe me that, surely. Because I've got to. Please, please, please, please, *please*. I'll do something terrible, then, I'll kill myself. Simon? Did you hear? I said "kill myself". *Si-mon*.' No further words, only sobbing with savage interjections. Crouched in the hall, Liz felt the house rock to the sound, like a boat pitching at sea. Unsteadily, she returned to the kitchen, stood just inside the door.

She didn't know what to do, she admitted, when three or four possible courses of action and their probable outcomes had chased through her mind like headless chickens; only listen and keep watch.

Suddenly, the study door opened. Rosie barged upstairs, slammed her bedroom door.

The house grew chill. It was ridiculous standing here in the shadowy end of the kitchen shivering in a T-shirt, yet she couldn't move for fear of missing some

125

faint indication of what Rosie might be doing. Her ears seemed to have enlarged with so much listening; the hummings and buzzings and clickings they reported made her doubt she had ever truly experienced silence.

Thank goodness Nathan would soon be home. Hang on, though; maybe she wouldn't involve Nathan, not unless things really got out of hand. If his angina flared up as a result of all this she'd never forgive herself, or Rosie. Another thing: while the maternal part of her was alarmed, another more sensible part was pretty sure the girl's threat was just that, issued to get her own way. Prompted by misery and desperation, no doubt, but without serious intent. Worrying Nathan with it would mean she couldn't handle what was probably an irrational dread. Which, with angina lurking in the background, just wasn't on. So that was that.

The decision left her lonely and dismal. Her head lolled back against the wall. She wondered what Chrissy and Nell were doing. Chrissy, she decided, was having tea in The Old Rectory kitchen surrounded by happy uncomplicated children. Nell? Probably staying with smart friends for the weekend. Or holed up in her flat with a lover. The images sparked an unpleasant 'left out' feeling, childish, petty; and a scary dread of being cast aside. A vivid memory flooded back of when she had originally experienced such feelings. It was when Nell and Chrissy got summer holiday jobs at the café at the end of the sea front. Barred by her parents from taking a 'common' job, she was reduced to meeting her friends at the end of their shift or going inside to sit at a table making a cup of tea last all afternoon. How jealously she had watched when the grammar school boys started coming to the café and she couldn't get the hang of the chit chat, the heavy looks, the charged silences. Nell and Chrissy seemed to be slipping away. Heavens – could that have been when she started enlarging Mr Poole? (This angle hadn't occurred to her before.) Had she made much of Mr Poole in order to recover her friends' attention? It was hard to remember any more, her brain seemed to have clogged.

Grown impatient with herself, she went out to the car and parked it in its proper place, returned indoors and walked to the foot of the stairs, where aiming to sound newly returned from a pleasant lunch, she called, 'You might have put the car away. What happened – got caught short or something? Rosie? I'm making a pot of tea.'

Long silence. Then a door handle rattled.

Rosie's voice sounded timid. 'Sorry. Yeah, I was desperate for the lav. Be down soon.'

'Right-oh,' she called lightly, and went to put the kettle on.

3
SOMEONE TO SWOON OVER

i

In her dream, Liz was chasing Ellie Goodridge. She'd been sitting in her car outside the Goodridge house when Ellie came out of the front door in her print maternity frock and her strappy sandals, a bag swinging from her shoulder, sun-glasses masking her eyes. Suddenly Ellie went berserk – cast off the bag, threw away the sun-glasses, screamed 'I'll do something terrible, I'll kill myself,' and went charging down the hill.

He's told her, thought Liz, springing out of her car, setting off in pursuit; Simon's confessed about Rosie. Got to catch her, got to stop her – 'Wait,' – running fit to burst her heart.

Along the path by the nursery school, into a different sort of road in a different kind of area, a bit grimier, a bit seedier, faintly familiar: rows of little houses with tiny gardens, a corner shop, a sad, fishy smell in the air. And there ahead, flying down the subway slope, went Ellie. Liz's feet after her barely skimmed the ground: down, down, under the railway, then up the long slope – going heavily now, her chest hurting – to the corner with Town Hall Square.

The number nine bus was waiting. As Ellie approached, its engine sprang to life, its bell pinged. 'Ellie, wait . . .'

Ellie leapt into the road, at the last moment turned her head – and Liz saw it was not Ellie she'd been chasing after all.

It was Mrs Poole.

*   *   *

Rosie came down early for once. She rushed to pick up the mail, sorted through the envelopes, without comment chucked the whole lot on to the table.

Liz, her hands full of breakfast things, yawning her head off after a restless night, leaned over the pile of letters. Nell's letter jumped at her, the yellowy-buff envelope, the small firm round handwriting in bright blue ink. Down went the butter dish and honey pot. It was as if Nell herself had arrived, for in her letters, Liz found a truer Nell than the one she encountered in the flesh, an essence of Nell with most of the extraneous matter – the up-to-the-minute gossipy worldliness, the cynical triviality – extracted. Liz kept everything Nell had ever written to her in a shoe-box hidden at the back of a shelf in her bedroom cupboard, important evidence that the friend she'd cared about since childhood still existed, was still linked to her. (Chrissy, of course, didn't need these bits of proof. 'Oh, you know Nell,' she would say when Liz rang to express horror over one of Nell's beastlier tabloid outbursts. 'She's only playing, she doesn't mean it.')

'Letter from Nell,' remarked Liz, taking a knife from the table drawer, slitting open the envelope. She raised her eyes to Rosie, who said nothing. Liz sighed: she had hoped the letter would spark some interest, for both her children were fond of Nell; both had enjoyed giddy holidays with her in London, doing the theatres, the second-hand bookshops, the street markets.

She found a much shorter letter than usual, read it through quickly, then sat down to re-read it. And to think she'd felt aggrieved yesterday, imagining her difficulties the last thing on Nell's mind. Full of contrition, she touched the letter lightly to her face and caught a bar-room niff of cigarette smoke. Nell and her ciggies, she thought indulgently. Mad for them since the age of fifteen. 'Any fags?' she'd mouth across the desks during registration. And if both Liz and Chrissy shook their heads, she'd look so crestfallen, Liz would hasten to reassure her. 'Got some lolly, though,' she'd murmur as they formed up for Prayers, 'we'll buy some at dinner.' And Nell would blink and smile as if settling herself to survive the morning. Only fifteen and puffing like chimneys, she recalled, looking across at her daughter, thinking, at least she doesn't smoke.

She returned the letter to its envelope and put it in her pocket, ready to be transferred to the shoe-box when she went upstairs.

ii

At home time, boys hang around the school gates. The boys' grammar school lies further up the road; most of the boys have to pass the girls' grammar on their way home. Liz, Nell and Chrissy have always been aware of these boys, also of the sort of girls who rush out to meet them, perch on the crossbar of a boy's bicycle, scream, lark about; but until they enter the fourth year and girls in their own class start behaving like this, they don't take much heed. Of course, some girls have always been boy mad. One or two have even been labelled 'dirty minded' for taking boy madness too far and becoming sex mad. The 'dirty minded' girls are pretty widely shunned. One such girl, Cheryl Lester, in the class a year higher than Liz, Nell and Chrissy, has such a fearful reputation she's rumoured to 'go on the docks'. Going on the docks is about the worst thing you can do. Females get had up before the court for it and fined; their names are printed in the *Evening Telegraph*. Just what they do on the docks is not clear. Sometimes the phrase *a nuisance to seamen* crops up in the newspaper reports, which conjures a picture of sex-crazed women vaulting the dock gates and hurling themselves on sea-weary home-bound trawlermen. It's such a detestable image, utterly shaming; Liz, Nell and Chrissy find even looking at Cheryl Lester brings them out in prickly heat. When Cheryl isn't seen in school any more, there are conflicting stories – she's stowed away on a Russian trawler, she's travelling with a man who worked the dodgem cars last summer. Then one day, down the corridor outside the classroom, comes Cheryl pushing a pram. The girls gape. When the bell goes they keep their distance as though babies are a disease you can catch. Only soft-hearted Mrs Evans, the geography teacher (and one of only two married members of staff), delays on her way to the staff room to peek inside the pram and say a few kind words.

Girls who are boy mad are by no means in the same category as those few who are dirty minded. In fact, during the fourth year, more and more girls develop boy madness until, when they enter the fifth, such girls form a majority. Liz, Nell and Chrissy are not among them. They know there are ideal men out there somewhere in the world, brilliant, handsome, sensitive creatures, qualified by these very virtues to be properly appreciative. Noisy bike-riding grammar-school boys are just a pain.

Chrissy lands in trouble with Liz and Nell when some of these boys call after her. 'Chrissy,' they shout, 'Hiya Chrissy,' as they pedal furiously past, clapping and waving to show off their no-handed bike riding. Liz and Nell turn on her with pained astonishment.

'It's not my fault. They were in my class at junior school. It's all right for you, they don't know your names.'

Their forgiveness is withdrawn when one boy actually dismounts, pushes his machine on to the pavement and walks along behind in his bicycle clips trying to engage Chrissy in conversation. This boy isn't raucous like the others, but is somehow more repulsive – small and dark with heavy spectacles and protruding wet lips. 'Weird,' says Liz. 'A creep,' says Nell.

'Yeah, he was always a bit peculiar,' Chrissy recalls. 'But ever so brainy; always came top of the class.'

He starts waiting at the gate at four o'clock. Chrissy

gives him no encouragement. 'I'm with my friends.'

'Shall I carry your bag, then?' asks this irrepressible nuisance whose name is Tony Duckenfield though his friends call him 'Quacker'. ('Whorr, Quacker, get in there, man,' and 'Nice work, Quacker,' are the cries coming from lads flying past on bicycles.)

'I'm not even going home yet.' (They're on their way to the cemetery for a smoke.)

'I could wait about for you if you like.'

'I don't like. Please go away.'

'See you tomorrow, then.'

'Don't bother.'

Such an exchange is conducted behind her friends' backs. Nell and Liz press on with their noses in the air while Chrissy, hindered by the need to repeatedly turn and repulse her follower, struggles to keep up. 'I don't know how you can,' says Nell when they finally shake him off.

'But I can't. It's not my fault.'

'Then don't even speak to him,' Liz advises. 'It's incredible cheek, following after us like that.'

'I know,' wails Chrissy miserably. 'Let's try slipping out of the canteen gate tomorrow.'

The main thoroughfares of the cemetery are broad unlined pathways. There are also narrow sheltered paths running along the sides of tall hedges which divide the cemetery into sections. They keep to these paths beside the covering hedges to avoid being spotted by the keeper whom they have cast, on the basis of no evidence whatever, as a villain of darkly violent disposition, a cross between Don John and Caliban. The grave diggers work in the newer sections of the cemetery. Nell, Liz and Chrissy stick to the old part where high Victorian memorials and lofty trees provide tasteful privacy. One grave in particular is their favourite. It has broad low slabs like steps at the foot of a guardian angel. They sit on these steps and loll back against the angel's skirt. Today, when they have

132

discarded their satchels, Liz and Nell look expectantly at Chrissy whose turn it is to supply cigarettes.

'I thought,' says she, bending down to unbuckle her satchel, 'we'd have a change.'

A sudden tensing of the atmosphere undermines Chrissy's confidence. She's been so much in their bad books lately (thanks to Tony 'Quacker' Duckenfield) that instead of helping herself as usual to three of Auntie Julie's Players Navy Cut she helped herself to some of the money set aside for milkman and paperboy with a view to buying a more sophisticated brand and thereby earning their gratitude and respect.

'What?' demands Nell.

'These.' She lays a slim square orange box on the slab beside her.

From a distance, they look at it.

'Du Maurier,' reads Liz, waiting for a lead from Nell before committing herself.

Nell puts her head in her hands. 'About as feeble a fag as you can get.'

'Honestly, Chrissy,' says Liz.

'I thought a change'd be good. I thought we were getting into a bit of a rut. You said we should experiment.'

'In future,' says Nell, 'stick to Players or Senior Service; or, if you're hard up, get Woodies.'

'Woodbines,' Liz translates, to demonstrate she's as up in these matters as Nell, and continues daringly, 'Or I suppose, if you're specially flush, you could go mad and get Balkan Sobranie.' She waits hopefully for confirmation.

'Mm-yes. Or Passing Cloud. But never, never Du Maurier.'

'Or Craven A,' Liz adds.

'But we always used to get Craven A,' Chrissy objects. 'They're the ones we got first.'

'Precisely. Because we lacked experience.'

'The other afternoon while you were at games, we

133

realized they were pretty sick, didn't we, Nell?'

'Yes. We think it's to do with the woman's red nail varnish in the adverts.'

'And her horrible hat.'

'So from now on they're out.'

Their reference to her being at games while they were demonstrating their independence is the last straw. Fed up with being in the wrong, she snaps craftily, 'Well, do you want one or not?'

They consider the small orange box, the sun winking on the unbroken cellophane casing.

'Might as well,' Nell says. After a few deep pulls, she feels they've been hard on Chrissy. 'It was good you tried to experiment, though. And nice to have a full box.'

Liz tilts her head back and blows a perfect smoke ring, watches it float past the angel's chipped nose. 'Mr Poole says,' she begins – and immediately captures them, for Mr Poole says things that other men of their acquaintance never say; things that make him an unusually interesting person. 'Mr Poole says *pavement* is the most beautiful word in the English language. The way he says it, it sounds like *pavvvement*.'

'Pavvvement,' they echo, trying it out. 'Gosh,' says Nell, 'I see what he means.'

'He must be quite poetic, Mr Poole,' Chrissy suggests. (*Poetic* denotes the highest order of human being.)

'I suppose he is rather,' Liz says.

'You are lucky, knowing him,' says Chrissy.

'Isn't she,' agrees Nell.

'Mm, yes. I suppose I am.'

At the start of the summer holiday following O levels, Nell and Chrissy get jobs at the Sea Gull Café, a black wooden hut at the quiet end of the sea front near the boating lake. They wash up and cut sandwiches in full view of the customers who are separated from the working area only by a short counter. Liz isn't allowed to have a holiday job. She fills the gap between getting up and meeting her friends after their shift with extra piano practice. It's not that she's become more keen on piano playing, but that she enjoys winning praise from Mr Poole. During the first year and a half of being his pupil the best he ever said to her was, 'Better; it's coming.' She performed well enough, otherwise he wouldn't have kept her on. Then something about music suddenly fell into place; it was like pouncing on the right bit of a jigsaw knowing it was going to fit – the idea of interpretation, that she could add something to mere correctness. 'Very good, you're getting there,' Mr Poole told her one day. He sounded surprised. Since then she's put more and more time in at the piano and is disappointed if a lesson doesn't elicit a morsel of praise and some discussion. It's these discussions – of a piece's shape and its contrasts, of climaxes, echoes and dyings away – that reveal Mr Poole's stunning sensitivity. She hoards up his sayings to show off later to Chrissy and Nell.

Mr Poole says, as it's the school holidays she can come for her lessons at three o'clock on Wednesday afternoons rather than her usual time of half past four.

It's her sixteenth birthday. All the other girls in her class are sixteen already: Nell was sixteen last December, Chrissy a few weeks back at the end of June; only Liz, the youngest girl in the class, has an August birthday. Mr Poole, when she let slip last week that next Wednesday would be her birthday, thought she wouldn't want to interrupt the celebration with a piano lesson; she protested that of course she would, she was long past making a thing out of birthdays. He seemed pleased to hear it and sort of mock-amused.

Just before three in the afternoon, in her pink and white candy-striped crisp cotton dress (*A Line*, the latest fashion: shawl collar, cap sleeves, skirt gathered on to a dropped waistline), she rings the doorbell. The door opens abruptly, and there is Mr Poole looking strangely sporty – not in his light-grey music-lesson suit but in grey flannel trousers and an open-neck shirt with a cravat instead of a tie. His changed appearance is disconcerting; faintly disappointing, too. She likes him the way he's become fixed in her mind, soberly dressed with nothing to distract from certain fascinating and memorable characteristics such as a brusque manner, a stern authority, and a sparing way with quips and smiles and personal remarks which makes you feel you've really earned them. However, she quickly adapts to his new look. What he is trying to do is give the occasion a festive touch in honour of her birthday. This touching fact becomes apparent when, with a twinkle in his eye and a lecture on never overlooking the over-riding importance of the great J. S. Bach, he presents her with volume one of *The Well-Tempered Clavier*. Inside it he's written, *from R. H. Poole, with best wishes* and the date. She's overcome. Perhaps for this reason he starts the lesson with a demonstration; takes the book out of her hands, opens it, plonks it on the music ledge, sits down, starts up a fugue. She stands by his side following the score.

There is a tiny pause when the piece ends, then up he leaps. 'Your turn,' he says, and the lesson goes on as usual.

'Good. That'll do. Concentrate on the Bartók for next week. Watch the phrasing of that middle passage. And if I may say so,' (gathering music books into her case, she looks up with a small frown, for he sounds suddenly severe) 'you've emerged as a very charming young lady, a great credit to your parents. Sweet sixteen indeed.' This last phrase is accompanied by one of his rare smiles which always come out crooked as if his lips aren't comfortable making them.

With a feeling of unreality she goes past the door he holds open for her. Down the path she doesn't let her breath out until she hears the door close.

Out in the street everything looks magnificent. The rows of small houses with fluted-glass front doors, the trimmed privet hedges bordering tiny front gardens, the stained yellowy pavements, green lamp-posts, corner shop, are all sharply defined and somehow endearing. Inside her there's an acrobat turning somersaults, flipping over and over. Her mind has filleted out the bit about being a credit to her parents, it's 'charming young lady' and 'sweet sixteen' shooting over and over to the top of her tingling scalp like bubbles in a bottle of Vimto. The doubts which have always lurked under the optimistic talk and starry-eyed day-dreaming she and Nell and Chrissy practise to bolster one another up (imprecise and unformed, but to do with the question: am I equipped to make a credible impact one day on the world beyond school?) have been answered emphatically. Mr Poole has applauded her sixteen years and a sterner judge would be pretty hard to find. She can't wait to repeat the accolade to Chrissy and Nell. It's a vote of confidence in all three of them, for what she is, they are, and vice versa. This goes without saying.

On the top of the bus to the sea front, she opens her case and takes out *The Well-Tempered Clavier*. The inscription is still there (it may be a miracle but it hasn't vanished). She dwells on it, fingers it, turns her head to look out of the window then tries to recapture the joyful amazement she felt when her eyes first fell on it. The R stands for Ronald. She wonders what the H stands for.

The ride terminates at the bathing pool where the bus idles for ten minutes while driver and conductress enjoy a smoke in the sun before starting the return trip. Everyone piles off. Swinging by her hand on the rail, Liz's feet down the stairs are weightless, flying. She bounds from the deck on to the pavement thronged with holiday-makers: people queuing with rolled towels underarm at the pool turnstile, people making for the beach or the amusement arcade; laden mums, kids on the want, lost-looking dads half missing the pit or the steel works. Liz turns away from the mainstream towards the more staid and decorous area surrounding the boating lake, where undulating paths lead through rockery gardens and a series of hump-backed bridges cross over the lake, where scooped out platforms sheltered by shrubberies provide convenient seating for pensioners and necking couples. At the end of the boating lake, in a gravelly car park surrounded by scrubby dunes the Sea Gull Café stands on stilts.

Liz is thinking about Chrissy and Nell. How pleased they're going to be with her. Besides the stuff about Mr Poole, there's the news that her parents have given her twenty pounds as a birthday present (together with the dress she's wearing and a hideous rope of pearls immediately repossessed by Alderman Stockdale for safekeeping). It's a small fortune. Certainly it'll keep them in cigarettes, lipstick and other essentials for the foreseeable future, which means Chrissy and Nell can buy *A line* dresses similar to Liz's all the sooner with their wages from the café. She imagines them exclaiming enviously over how she looks. They've already seen the dress; it was on display for a week in the window of M and B Modes. In fact, it was at Nell's instigation that she persuaded her mother to buy the dress for her birthday. Nell's mad about the *A line*. She says it's *the* look. Up the café's wooden steps and through the rough wooden doorway. 'Cherry pink and apple blossom white' blasts chirpily from the juke box, and here she is, right on cue, in her pink and white candy-stripes. It's the sort of thing that just would happen on a day like today when everything's going brilliantly; it's a tremendous joke, corny, like being in the pictures. The manageress is nowhere in sight. Nell and Chrissy are setting out cups and saucers on the counter. Halfway down the central aisle, Liz dumps her music case on a chair, holds her arms up crooked at the elbow, turns her head over a shoulder, sticks out her bum, completes the rest of the journey 'Come Dancing' style. 'Cha cha cha,' she cries wittily, arriving at the counter and spreading her arms over the cups and saucers. She's a terrific mimic of crummy telly programmes. Nell and Chrissy always fall about.

Not now. They stare at her hard-faced as if she's made a crass remark or showed them up. For a moment she can't take this in, thinks they're having her on, but Nell growls through her teeth and turns to the sink. She doesn't catch what Nell says, doesn't need to; Nell's back looks as stony as her face just did. Chrissy softens a fraction. 'Want some tea?' But her tone implies that Liz doesn't deserve this consideration. Somehow tea arrives in Liz's hand, and she carries it, concentrating hard (because suddenly she's in a dream and the ground might slip away), to where she left her music case.

What has she done wrong? Her ears are on fire and her head's roaring. She wonders whether Marge, the manageress, somehow got to hear about Liz making fun of her last Saturday and as a result Nell and Chrissy are in trouble. Even so, it seems unlikely that her friends would blame her, because they'd enjoyed it so much – Liz smoothing her hips, saying, 'Now girls, Mr Parton's taking me to the ware'ouse to pick up some fancies. No flickin' ash in the sink, Nell, and Chrissy keep your 'ands off them sarnies.' They'd had a good laugh, knowing Mr Parton (the Sea Gull's owner) was really taking Marge half a mile up the track behind the dunes, where they'd park the camper and climb into the back and close the frilly polka dot curtains over the van's windows. Everyone knows what Marge and Mr Parton get up to; old hands enlightened Nell and Chrissy on their first day.

The music's stopped, but there's a lot of noise coming from the other side of the room near the juke box. Liz looks over to where six or seven boys are crowded at one table. They fall quiet with their heads together, then break out in creaky laughter, punch one another's arms, pelt one another with balled up biscuit wrappers. Grammar-school boys, she guesses, otherwise they'd be working or playing the machines in the amusement arcade. One boy is slightly apart from the group. She recognizes him as the ugly one who dogs Chrissy's footsteps. A couple of boys get up and saunter to the counter. A hush develops as the others watch.

Something's going on.

Whatever it is, it's taking a roundabout route. Liz's eyes flick to and fro between the boys at the table and the foursome near the counter. Chrissy's pouring out tea. One of the boys passes over money, and he and Chrissy start talking. The other boy keeps his back to the counter, but he's not looking at his friends in the room; Liz can tell he's not seeing anything at all, just listening self-consciously. Suddenly his head lurches to one side and he says something in his companion's ear. A moment later, Chrissy goes to Nell at the sink and says something in her ear. The boys at the table snicker. There's a hiatus, then Nell wipes her hands and sidles to the counter and the boy with his back to it half turns round. A roar breaks out from the watching boys: 'Whorr, Mogsy.' They tip back in their chairs to fling forward, crashing their fists on the table.

Nell's cheeks are unusually pink. She's half smiling, not speaking. Chrissy is animated, laughing, tossing her curls, arguing. When two customers come in and go to the counter, Chrissy shoots a look of irritation to her companions before slouching over to serve them.

The boy they call Quacker gets up now and saunters to the counter. He says, unnecessarily loudly, 'Hiya, Chrissy.' Chrissy frowns, asks what he wants. Evidently, Quacker wants a wrapped chocolate wafer, for that's what he gets: that's all he gets; Chrissy moves away and turns her back on him. Quacker edges closer to the other two boys, places his arm on the counter, leans on it – a mime-show of bar-room nonchalance.

Marge bustles in and breaks it all up. 'Now then, you lads, d'you want summat? And you, take your arm off the counter – if you please. Chrissy, what are all them dirties doing lying on the tables? Get round with a tray. By heck, you can't turn your back five minutes with you lasses. Yes, duck?' – this to a customer who has gone to the counter. 'Two teas, Nell, and when you've seen to 'em, get butterin' them scones.'

Should she go or should she stay, Liz wonders. When Chrissy comes by she tries to find out. 'Are we, er, doing anything after?'

'Spect so,' Chrissy says, and hurries past with her tray.

Still considering the matter, Liz remains on her bentwood chair staring into her half-empty teacup. She begins to sense other people – the boys and Nell and Chrissy, even the other customers and Marge – looking at her critically. The feeling grows stronger and stronger so that soon she daren't raise her eyes. After a time she stops seeing the teacup and the smeary table, instead, as though spying on the scene from the rafters, she sees a girl in a stupidly jaunty dress sitting alone with her head bowed; she sees a music case propped against a chair leg looking ridiculously childish and out of place; she sees everyone staring at this girl, shares their contempt.

'Do you have to?' It's Nell at her side, hissing furiously.

'Have to what?'

'You know perfectly well.' Nell snatches her cup and makes off with it.

At least it's broken the spell and she can look round. Two girls have arrived to relieve Nell and Chrissy. There's a scraping of chairs; all the boys are getting to their feet. Chrissy comes to Liz's table. 'We're off. You coming?'

What a stupid question. Why on earth would she

stay? She grabs her music case and follows after them. Now the shock's worn off, she's begun to feel indignant.

The route taken through the boating lake gardens is the most complicated imaginable. Up the little hillocks, down and round they go, back and forth over the hump-back bridges, all at a snail's pace. Nell and Chrissy lead with Liz close behind, and the boys following after – all seven of them. When one boy starts hurling stones into the lake they all stop to watch as if it's a most interesting sight. 'What're we waiting for?' grumbles Liz, earning withering looks.

She's tired, her limbs feel heavy, her mind's gone numb. She wonders how long this futile wandering will continue; it's so aimless she can't imagine anyone summoning the wit to call a halt.

On a seat on one of the sheltered platforms, Nell daringly sits down. Chrissy joins her. Nell puts a cigarette in her mouth then looks round. They all know she's got matches in her pocket, but the boy called Mogsy dutifully comes forward and gives her a light. This seems to change things. They actually start talking.

'Ever go to the bathing pool?'

'Yeah, quite a lot,' lies Nell, and Chrissy almost nods her head off.

'Same here.'

'We're probably going Friday, aren't we Chrissy?'

'Yes, because it's our day off on Friday and tomorrow we get paid.'

'That's when we're going, isn't it, Dave?'

'Yeah. Friday afternoon.'

Liz sits down leaving a large gap between herself and her friends so that Mogsy and Dave can sit next to them if they want to. This, she guesses, is what Chrissy and Nell desire. However, all boys remain standing. The boy who chucked stones into the lake is staring at her. 'Will she be coming?' he asks.

Nell draws on her cigarette and stares ahead. Chrissy

looks across nervously. 'I spect you will, won't you, Liz?'

'Oh, *Liz*, is it? You coming, then, Liz? With your cossie and towel in your music case?'

This cracks them up.

Liz stands. 'Goodbye,' she says shortly to Nell and Chrissy, and with the despised case clutched to her breast, sets off at a good brisk pace.

The bus is waiting at the bathing pool. She breaks into a run when she sees it, fearing it may leave without her. But there's plenty of time, the driver hasn't got back into his cab yet. She climbs the stairs and sits among the tired families, impatient now for the bus to go.

Three dead people save Liz during the following hours. As directed by Mr Poole, she attends to the piece by Béla Bartók until she is note and timing perfect. Over and above the call of duty, she tackles the very difficult Bach fugue played to her yesterday by Mr Poole. When her fingers can take no more she lies on her bed reading Charlotte Brontë. It's as though Chrissy and Nell have gone away – which might be a frightening notion if she allowed herself to dwell on it; but she doesn't. They've gone away and so will she; ordinary life is temporarily suspended. When lapses occur in her concentration on works by the three great B's, she reminds herself, citing several examples, that people who go away usually come back.

It's a quarter to midnight on Thursday. She's nearing the end of *Jane Eyre* when, outside her bedroom window, a night creature screams. She holds the book to her chest, listening dispassionately and staring beyond the illumination thrown by her bedside lamp into the unseeable part of her room where nothing is definite, only suggested. In her mind an incident surfaces, rather as the wardrobe surfaces the longer she stares at its shadowy bulk, an incident she'd forgotten till now

143

which happened when she was having a piano lesson at Mr Poole's. Ordinarily, the house is quiet, but on this afternoon someone came in through the front door and went to the rear of the house, banged about, made a lot of disgruntled noise. Mr Poole, who was seated at the piano demonstrating how a passage in a Mozart sonata should go, stopped playing; got up and left the room. Though he closed the door behind him, sounds reached her – not constantly, but abruptly and incongruously, like sudden punches into the homely hush. Sharp howls – 'Ow', 'No' – and staccato words – 'Liar', 'Bastard'. She sat down hurriedly and began to try out the Mozart in order to be able to pretend when he returned not to have heard anything.

Her playing trailed away when he reappeared; she stood up, half embarrassed. Mr Poole played for ages, not just the bit she was learning but the whole movement. At the finish he sat for some seconds holding his brow with his fingertips. She'd been glad when the lesson ended a few minutes later, glad to run through the streets and under the subway into Town Hall Square to catch the bus. Now, though, she's reluctant to leave Mr Poole shutting his front door. Her mind reinstates him as he was a minute or two earlier on the piano stool. The longer she dwells on his attitude (revelations concerning poor Mr Rochester's difficulties as revealed in *Jane Eyre* fresh in her mind), the more clearly Mr Poole dawns as tragic hero.

She reaches over, turns off the lamp, slides down in the bed. She looks forward to Nell and Chrissy becoming themselves again when she'll regale them with this further evidence of Mr Poole's poetic nature.

It seems quite prosaic to get a phone call next morning from Chrissy.

'Elizabeth,' yells Mrs Stockdale up the stairs: 'Telephone. How are you Chrissy love? I hope that job isn't making you pasty. You need lots of fresh air and good food at your age – got to look after that schoolgirl complexion. Oh, here she is.'

Liz takes the phone, says 'Yes?' uninterestedly.

'Oh, hiya. Me and Nell are going up town to get new cossies. Mine's too tight in the bust, and Nell's is that horrible one. Yours isn't bad, but it'd be good to get sexy ones like Angie's and Val's. Nell's seen some with wires under the cups in that ever so nice shiny material. We got paid yesterday. Your mum's bound to give you some lolly, so are you coming?'

'I thought you were going to get *A-line* dresses.'

'We are. But cossies are urgent. We don't want to look laughing stocks this afto. Val and Angie'll be there, flaunting themselves. You are coming to the pool?'

'I'm not sure.'

'Oh, Liz.'

'If you and Nell are going to be foul again . . .'

'We weren't.'

'You were.'

'Nell just thought you were trying to draw attention to yourself.'

'That's stupid.'

'She said you won't fit in properly. And that does sort of show us up,' she added, giving her own opinion. 'Anyway, Nell's in a state at the moment over Mogsy. She's really mad on him, gone all swoony.'

'Crikey. I thought she couldn't stand that sort of thing. She said Valerie Dove made her sick.'

'I know. So it's serious. We've got to be considerate, tactful.'

'Flipping heck. Well, I hope *you*'re not swooning over anybody.'

'N-no . . .'

'Chrissy?'

'Not *swooning*. Not like Nell. But Dave's nice. And he's ever so good looking don't you think?'

'I suppose so.'

'And Timmo quite likes you.'

145

'Who?'

'Timmo. The one who asked if you were coming.'

'Then I'm definitely not.'

A pause. Then, 'P'raps Nell's right.'

'What d'you mean?'

'She says you're infantile. You only want us to do things you like doing and you want us to go on doing them for ever.'

Further silence – while Liz wonders if perhaps she ought to go with them; for she wouldn't like it, it'd be terrible if they cut her out. 'All right, then; I'll come.'

'Shopping too?'

'OK. What time?'

'Half ten at Nell's.'

'Wait for me if the bus is late. See you later.'

'See you later. And Liz, don't forget: be *tactful*.'

The journey to Nell's involves two buses and first of all a taxi. For over a year now, since she was fifteen, her parents have allowed her to overcome the disadvantage of living in the country beyond the reach of a corporation bus by running an account with the village taxi service. She takes a taxi to Bilsby, three miles nearer to town and the last village on the bus route. The bus from Bilsby takes her as far as Town Hall Square where she catches the bus which terminates at the bathing pool. Usually, she gets off this second bus at the stop outside school, or at one stop further on outside the Robinson Rec if she's going to Chrissy's, or at the next stop by the junction with the main road running past the docks if she's going to Nell's. This morning, she's five minutes late by the time she turns off the main road into Maud Street.

There's a row going on at the Nelson's. It's Chrissy who opens the front door to her, pulls a warning grimace, hangs on to her arm in the dim hallway, puts her mouth to Liz's ear.

'They've pinched her money.'

146

'Who has?'

'Her mum and dad. They say she's got to pay her way.'

'Pay her way?' Liz has never heard of such a thing.

'If she's earning, they say she's got to contribute.'

'How mean.'

'Nell's furious. She says it's stealing.'

'So what's going on?' (Apart from Nell's voice.)

'She says she needs the money for a new cossie but her mum says she's already got one,' reports Chrissy, who's been following the argument for the past ten minutes.

'Not that horrible one? It's out of the ark; it was her Auntie Jean's.'

'I know.'

'Mr Nelson isn't at home, is he?'

'He's at work.'

This, Liz supposes, is something. 'I wonder what we should do?'

Before they can do anything, Nell comes running out of the dining room and straight upstairs. Mrs Nelson, crying 'Monica,' lurches into the hallway, stops when she sees the two girls and slumps her shoulders as if all the stuffing's gone out of her. 'Oh, hello girls. Don't just stand there, come in and wait. She shouldn't be long.' She leads the way back into the dining room. 'Sit down; make yourself at home.'

They sit on the edges of two hard chairs. One of the younger Nelson boys is sitting in his father's armchair, absorbed in his reading, blind to all else. Mrs Nelson lays her arms over a chair back and leans on them. 'I don't know,' she sighs. 'You lasses.'

Thunder breaks out on the stairs, then Nell charges into the room. She's brandishing a fistful of battleship-grey-coloured rag, also a pair of cutting-out scissors. 'I've cut it up,' she cries, eyes blazing.

Mrs Nelson walks carefully round her chair, sits down. 'You've what?'

147

Nell flings the rag (formerly her bathing costume) on to the table, tosses the scissors on top. 'I've cut it up, the disgusting article. It was unspeakable of you to expect me to wear it; you just don't care if I'm a laughing stock. So now I need a new one. So hand over the money.'

Mrs Nelson has difficulty finding the words. 'You ... wicked ... What's your dad going to ...'

'Who cares what that loser thinks? He doesn't scare me, the pathetic pig. I demand you hand over what's rightfully mine. I earned it, so hand it over.' She thrusts out her hand.

Mrs Nelson's hand creeps into her overall pocket. Her face has gone greasy-damp, tinged green. She passes over some notes. 'This'll have to do you. But what I'm going to do, dear only knows, cos your dad took your bit into account.'

'Thanks,' snarls Nell sarcastically, stuffing the money into her skirt pocket. 'Come on,' she commands her friends, 'let's scram. They're beneath contempt, this lot.' She stalks from the room, Chrissy pressing after her.

Liz lingers. There's sickly fear in Mrs Nelson's eyes. She longs to say something, do something. 'Um, good, er, goodbye, Mrs Nelson. It was really nice. Thank you for having us.' The crassness of this makes her sweat so with shame that her eyelids stick open; she can't blink properly when she stumbles over the front door step and gets clouted by sunlight.

They catch a bus to the top end of town, run up the stairs, grab the two front seats. Chrissy and Liz sit on one side of the gangway, Nell on the other with her feet up. When there's something worth seeing down below, they all crowd to the same window and pass comment. 'Get her – really fancies herself.' 'Oh, they must be fond of a treat.' They leap off when the bus slows down to turn into the High Street. The conductor bawls after them, 'Hey, you: wait for the stop.' They saunter along the pavement, gazing in shop windows, conscious of money in their pockets. Eventually they go into the department store, help themselves to quick squirts of scent at the make-up counter, ('Ugh, what a pong.' 'God, smell mine,') make for the escalator and Swimwear.

For a start, they're not sure of their sizes. This necessitates experimentation, a lot of darting into one another's cubicle half-naked, imploring someone to put on some clothes and go back to the rail for 34's instead of 32's. Now and then there's a production: curtains held together while a head pops through demanding 'Ready for it?'; then the drapes thrown back, sometimes to reveal just a joke – a frankly hideous garment or something too daring – sometimes a real possibility, whereupon opinions are invited. They're at it for ages. They can't remember a more enjoyable time.

At last, with the saleswoman on the brink of getting really shirty, each decides they've picked a winner. They sober up, crowd in front of the mirror in Nell's cubicle and consider the combined effect. It's rather awesome. They wonder if they'll dare. So ravishing they look, they may send shock waves through the bathing pool, crack up the concrete, steam off the water. Another thing – as Chrissy puts it: 'It's a pity we haven't got time to get used to them.' For though the mirror shows three curvy sophisticates, inside they feel pretty much the same.

A cough interrupts them. 'Are you taking those?'

They agree that they are. Soon, clutching carrier-bags and holdalls, they're rushing to catch the bus to the bathing pool.

When they get there it's too early to go in, so they buy bags of chips and sit in a bus shelter. Nell thinks of Mogsy and loses her appetite, so Chrissy finishes her own then eats Nell's. They stroll up and down the promenade watching the bathing pool clock creep round. At two o'clock they decide to go in. Rather nervously, they undress in the changing room, put

149

on their new swimsuits, cover them up with towels, tiptoe outside.

The place is packed with holiday-makers. Nell starts worrying in case Mogsy never finds her. Chrissy spots Angie Hutchings and friends lounging on the concrete steps above the deep end. They lay out their towels on the steps nearby, not for the sake of Angie's company but because the deep end is the smart end, furthest from the families with kids. They sit down and lard their bodies with Nivea. Angie calls, 'Hiya,' and kicks Valerie Dove who's lying on her stomach. Valerie looks round. Lacking Angie's aplomb, she fails to hide her amazement. 'Crikey. Smashing cossies. Where'd you get 'em?'

'What, these old things?' drawls Nell.

'They're here,' breathes Chrissy, and Nell flops down and closes her eyes.

The boys are scarcely recognizable with their naked stick-like arms and concave chests; only the towels hanging round their necks slightly lessen an appearance of vulnerability. They perch on the steps between the two groups of girls, Angie and Co. to their right, Nell, Chrissy and Liz to their left.

From that moment on, everything goes boring and stupid in Liz's estimation; there's the same tense manoeuvring she observed at the Sea Gull Café, the same pointless tedium of the walk by the boating lake. But Chrissy and Nell seem content: Chrissy's reclining propped on her arms, wriggling her toes, chatting happily to everyone at once; Nell's gone pink and silent, but is smiling. After a time, the boys give the lie to their apparent frailty; become boisterous, chuck someone's towel into the water, flick things, chase about, lunge at girls, tickle their feet.

Liz is apprehensive. Making it abundantly clear that her feet aren't for tickling, she tucks them under her and looks studiously elsewhere. Mogsy and Dave go into a huddle. Suddenly, without warning, they grab

Nell by the shoulders and legs, carry her to the water, toss her in. Chrissy yelps and darts to the poolside. Dave comes after her, but she's too fly for him; as he goes to push her, she steps aside and trips him into the water. She looks to see where Nell has surfaced, then dives in cleanly and comes up beside her. Cheers go up. Everyone's excited – except Liz, who's terrified. She sees Timmo looking at her. Her fingers seek and grip the wooden railing by the side of the steps. As well as dread for herself, she's consumed with fear for her friend; she can't imagine how Nell will put a brave face on such stunning mortification.

Strangely, when Nell emerges from the water, she appears not the least bit mortified. Mogsy goes up to her with a towel – his own towel – and wraps it round her. She allows him to feed her a cigarette. It dawns on Liz that there's more to this business of chucking people into the water than mere tomfoolery. Angie and Co. are desperate to contrive a similar fate; they're standing by the water's edge, shivering and squawking, flapping their hands at passing boys, positively inviting a shove.

Meanwhile, Nell languorously combs out her hair.

'Fancy going to the flicks tomorrow after work?' Mogsy asks her.

Nell picks up her cigarette, takes a long drag. 'I might,' she says, blowing smoke in his face.

'Do you fancy it?' Dave asks Chrissy.

'Yes, it'd be good.'

A chilly breeze cuts through the compound, lifts paper, raises goose pimples.

'I think I'll go now,' says Liz, getting up and wrapping her towel round her.

Her friends take this calmly. 'Right.' 'OK.'

'Shall I call for you after work next week?'

Nell and Chrissy look at one another. They're wondering whether Liz possesses enough sense to shove off should she arrive and discover Mogsy and Dave there waiting. It's hard to frame this in words.

Nell says nothing, just narrows her eyes. Chrissy says doubtfully, 'Could do.'

'See you then,' Liz says.

'Yeah, see you.'

Timmo screws up a paper wrapper and tosses it at Liz's departing shoulder blades.

When it strikes her, she doesn't look round.

iii

At ten to four on Monday afternoon, in the corridor at the rear of The Old Rectory, Fenby-cum-Laithby, the *Evening Telegraph* plopped on to the mat. By half past four, Chrissy was roaring up the drive of the Fairfields Nursing Home in her red Scimitar. Two elderly gents stepped rapidly on to the grass. Abashed, she braked; breathed out, calmed down; pulled up in front of the pillared portico, opened the car door, swung out her long bare legs. Just in time, she remembered the box of chocolates on the passenger seat.

'Mrs Duckenfield to see Mrs Stockdale,' she called cheerfully to the girl on the desk.

'Of course, Mrs Duckenfield,' said the girl, who had recognized her. 'I think Mrs Stockdale may be having tea. I'll just find out. Will you join her?'

'That'd be nice.'

A few minutes later, Chrissy and Mrs Stockdale were cosily ensconced in easy chairs by a low table in one of the sitting-room bays.

'Oo, choccies. You are a bad girl, you know my weakness. Nasty matron keeps threatening me with a diet. What rubbish – at my age. Dear me, I'm long past fretting over my figure.'

Chrissy's eyes fell to the straining skirt barely covering two gigantic knees; she noted that there was now no margin between the outsides of Mrs Stockdale's thighs and the chair-arms; the past ten years had marked steady fleshy encroachment.

'Oh, it *is* nice to see you. Me and Mrs Garth were just saying . . . There's such a lovely photo of you and Tony in tonight's *Telegraph*. I don't suppose you've had time to see it.'

'As a matter of fact—' began Chrissy.

But Mrs Stockdale cut her off, leaned forward, hissed confidingly, 'By the way, dear, Mrs Garth's gone into the dining room with the others. I thought it'd be best. We'll tell her you're here later, otherwise we'll never get a word in and we do enjoy our little confabs. She's not as sharp as she was, she can't – how shall I put it? – take a hint. Don't get me wrong, she's my oldest friend and I won't hear a word said against her. I'm just putting you in the picture, so you won't be surprised or anything, 'cos she does – I have to say it – she does tend to monopolize. Now where were we? Oh, yes, you were telling me about the President's evening. Good dinner was it? Any surprises?'

This was the usual pattern. Mrs Stockdale had three objectives: firstly, to extract as much gossip as Chrissy was good for; secondly, to flaunt the quality of her visitor before admiring inmates; thirdly, when Chrissy had gone, to revel in the pleasure of doling out with helpful embellishment any titbits she'd managed to glean. As it happened, the Rotarian President's Evening, or at least its photographic record as published in the local press, had precipitated Chrissy's unplanned and impulsive visit. She and Tony were caught turning and smiling down from the Grand's staircase (even so, the photographer had surely had to grovel in order to catch her at that particular angle). As portrayed in the *Telegraph* her skirt was not modishly short but blatantly diminutive; her legs seemed to go on for ever. Tony would love it, of course, and all the envious joshing he'd get from his associates. Chrissy's reaction was a vision of Mrs Stockdale in her Fairfields bedroom busily snipping out the photo to post to Liz. Which was what she was here to forestall.

'As a matter of fact,' she repeated, 'the *Telegraph* arrived just as I was setting out. That's why I've come a bit later than usual. You see, I'd written a letter to Liz and when I saw the photo I couldn't resist cutting it out and slipping it in the envelope. So don't you bother, Mrs Stockdale; I've already sent her one.'

'Oh, good,' said Liz's mother, brightening. 'It might buck her ideas up.' She closed her mouth and waited as the maid, who had just come in, set down the tea tray. 'Thank you. Hm, rock cakes again. Never mind. Will you be mother, Chrissy love? I find leaning forward in these low chairs very hard work. No, dear, I'm glad *you* sent the photo to Elizabeth; she's got it into her head that I'm getting at her when I send her cuttings. But I ask you: weren't we right, her daddy and I, when we begged her to come home and find a nice job around here? Then she'd have done as you did – married a promising local boy, someone we could have taken to. Alderman Stockdale thought very highly of Tony. Dearie me, Elizabeth's life could have been so different. (Yes, do help yourself. I think they're salmon.) I don't have to tell you, Chrissy. I mean, look at you and Tony and those lovely kiddies and that beautiful house. No, sometimes I despair over Elizabeth. And you know me, I'm the last one to get down hearted. I suppose you've heard the latest? She's told you about Jonathan?'

'Um?'

'He's only going to marry that Indian girl.'

'Oh, Sushma,' cried Chrissy, trying to sound encouraging.

'*Marry* her. (Another one, dear? Do eat up.) Playing with fire. I warned Elizabeth. I said, "Do something about it before it gets serious; these things are easier nipped in the bud," I said. Don't get me wrong, Chrissy love, I've nothing against these people – *in their own country*. No-oo, I've nothing against them as such. But people should marry their own kind. Why, I remember the Hawtin girl – you must have known her, her father

154

was the dentist in Barton Street – yes well, she married a frenchy and look what that led to. And he wasn't even coloured. (Do try the Bakewell. I don't advise the rock cakes.) No, I warned Elizabeth; I said . . .'

God, she's terrible, thought Chrissy, cramming a quarter portion of Bakewell tart into her mouth at once. No wonder Liz gets upset; no wonder she keeps putting off visiting her. She wondered why she came so often herself. True, she was here today on an urgent mission, but this wasn't usually the case. She liked to kid herself that she was doing Liz a favour, and so she was, up to a point. Might as well admit it, though; Mrs Stockdale satisfied a craving. It was a physical thing, like the relief she got from eating: in some mysterious way she derived animal satisfaction from this appalling woman. Sometimes, breaking off from a shopping expedition for a bite to eat in some department store restaurant or high street café, Chrissy was struck by the mothers and daughters lunching together, daughters middle-aged like herself with their well-preserved mothers. Under cover of eating she studied these women, traced the sharper features of the younger woman in the less-defined face of the elder, observed how their gestures matched as they ate, talked, paused, smiled, frowned, turned their heads. The satisfaction they derived from their shared company was often so palpable that Chrissy felt it catch against her like warm breath. Mother, where are you? she'd silently mourn; look what we're missing, we could have such lovely times. Fun though it was going shopping with Amanda, it couldn't appease a sense of loss. These visits to Mrs Stockdale were the nearest she ever got to that.

'More tea, Mrs Stockdale? Several people you'd remember were there on Saturday night. The Shaws . . .'

'Thank you, dear. Jack and Nellie? Oh yes. Tell me, has she got over that nasty fall?'

Phew. Back on comfortable ground. She scoured her

155

memory for trivialities, and when it failed her, invented some.

After tea, Mrs Stockdale beckoned Mrs Garth and a few other inmates. Chrissy did her stuff, played pretty young wife (young, at least, to these dowagers) with charm and grace. Wowed them, carried them back to their own days of matronly glory, each one drinking in Chrissy and fondly imagining they'd been just like her.

When it was time to go, just to be sure, Chrissy reiterated her main point. 'Don't forget: there's no need to spoil your copy of the *Telegraph*; I've already sent Liz the photo.'

'Yes dear, I know. And it's been lovely seeing you. Sometimes I have to pinch myself to think you're not my own daughter. We're so alike, it's uncanny. I don't know how long it'll be before Elizabeth gets round to coming.'

'Oh, some time, I'm afraid.' (No point in sabotaging Liz's forthcoming visit by landing her with a visit to Fairfields.) 'I happen to know she's snowed under with work at the moment, so I shouldn't think it'll be much before Christmas. Never mind; I'll keep popping in.'

'You're such a thoughtful girl. Give my love to Tony. And tell him,' (here, tears stood in her eyes) 'tell him Alderman Stockdale would've been very proud. And of you, Chrissy love.'

Brr-rum-*rum*, roared the Scimitar down the drive, pretty accurately expressing its mistress's feelings.

iv

After all, Liz decides not to bother.

She dreads going to the Sea Gull Café; even the name startles her. The other night she dreamt she was standing in a bare landscape – sandy earth, lowering indigo sky; its only visible feature the black wooden-slatted hut on stilts a few feet in front of her. Without her moving a muscle, as though she were made of paper, some force propelled her to the foot of the hut's steps. Above her, the door opened. Music racketted out, grew in intensity until the hut quaked and the steps juddered. Impelled to continue up into the hut, she knew that when she entered it she'd implode with terror. Mercifully, before this could happen she woke. Only a dream: nevertheless, she can't shake off bad feelings for the place. Anyway, Mogsy and Dave probably meet Nell and Chrissy there most days now. She'd be in the way. Really and truly, she'd rather get on with her piano practice, not just the pieces set for her lessons, but new work explored on her own initiative, such as the preludes and fugues in *The Well Tempered Clavier*.

Mr Poole says she's coming on in leaps and bounds.

One Sunday at teatime the telephone rings. Alderman Stockdale wipes his mouth on his napkin then goes to answer it. He's gone some minutes, returns looking like he's landed a nice deal. 'It's for you, princess,' he says slyly. 'Mr Poole wants a word.'

Mr Poole? It's unreal. She's joyful, yet seized with trepidation. Matters are made worse by her father hovering in the doorway, distracting her with asides: 'You can do it. Go on, say yes.'

Mr Poole is not only the town's best-known music teacher, he also directs and conducts the town's best-known choir. The St John's Choir (named after the church in whose hall they rehearse) is esteemed for its yearly concerts in the Winter Gardens and for numerous contributions throughout the year to the district's musical events. Apparently, the choir is in difficulties; the accompanist has fallen ill, a substitute is required. Mr Poole thinks Liz could do the job; furthermore, the experience gained would be invaluable to her. Would she care to come along to the Wednesday evening rehearsal?

Her father nudges her. She's thrilled, nervous, she

157

can hardly think. 'If you . . . I mean, if you're sure I could . . .'

'I'd hardly have asked if I didn't. But it's entirely up to you.'

'Oh, all right. I mean, I'd like to.'

Her father snatches the receiver. 'She'll be very pleased to do it, Mr Poole. It's an honour. What? No, look: I'm coming into town tonight – blasted council business – so I'll call on you and pick it up. Really? Very kind of you, I'm sure. Yes, see you about seven. Excellent. Goodbye.'

He crashes down the phone, seizes his daughter's forearms, gives her a shake. 'Well done, princess. Let's go and tell your mother. By the way, I've arranged to pick up the music tonight, so you can get on and practise it. And Mr Poole says he'll run over it with you after your lesson on Wednesday, then you can stay on and have tea, and he'll take you to St John's in the evening. I say, Mummy, what do you think?'

By the time she comes to and discovers herself back at the tea table, her parents have jumped ahead; permanently incapacitated the regular accompanist and awarded the position to their daughter. Individually and privately, they picture a similar scenario: Alderman and Mrs Stockdale in the front row of the Winter Gardens, people they know all around, their daughter taking her seat at the piano and earning extra applause for her extreme youth; the notice in the *Telegraph* singling her out (they're confident about this because the editor happens to be a Rotarian; he and Alderman Stockdale attend the weekly luncheon together at the Grand).

Liz is thinking about Mr Poole's other pupils; the boy who won first prize at the music festival, the girl whose lesson comes before hers on Wednesdays who's already passed Grade Seven, and several talented adult pupils . . . She feels singled out, specially approved of, desperate to prove this is merited.

Because it's turned cooler, she's wearing her black
drain-pipe trousers; over these, a double breasted,
button-to-the-neck blazer in cream wool with black
edging, knitted by Mrs Garth for her birthday. Mrs
Garth always knits her birthday and Christmas presents.
Once, this didn't bother her; clothes were just clothes.
During the past two years, however, strong feelings
about what she wears have led to rows. 'If you don't
wear it Mrs Garth'll be hurt,' has been her mother's
battle cry, with Liz forever dragging on pastel coloured
cardigans to be discarded when out of eyeshot. Once
she left a pink one embroidered with rabbits under a
seat on the number nine bus. Now, older and wiser,
bowing to the inevitable, she strikes first. Last April,
when the spring patterns came out, she bought the
knitting instructions for the smart blazer she's now
wearing and presented it to Mrs Garth. Her mother
was scandalized. 'She doesn't mind,' wheedled Liz,
hanging on to Mrs Garth's arm and kissing her win-
ningly. 'Clever Mrs Garth's the only person I know
who can make it for me, and it's such a lovely
blazer.' Mrs Garth has already asked her to pick out
something she'd fancy for Christmas.

Mr Poole pretends to be taken aback by her outfit
when he opens the door. She knows it's pretence.
He's more used to seeing her arrive after school in
her uniform, so all her holiday outfits must cause him
mild surprise. No, he's acting startled-appreciative today to signal a subtle change in their relationship:
that she's no longer just another pupil, but a pupil
who is also the substitute accompanist of the St John's
Choir. They're colleagues (though she's very much the
apprentice): this is what his manner hints at. So she
grins and steps lightly past him with a little flick of
her head, as if conceding that she knows she's a knock-
out. But of course, as they both appreciate, this is a
joke.

The lesson begins – no joking now. For precisely half an hour (Mr Poole is a meticulous time keeper) they work on scales, arpeggios and set pieces.

'Well done. Now, we'll take a ten-minute breather and a cup of tea.' He opens the sitting-room door and goes into the hall, calling, 'Alison.'

Alison is his ten-year-old daughter who will soon sit the entrance examination for the grammar school. These are among the meagre personal details he's let fall over the past few months. Liz also knows his wife works for Burnett's, the big furnishings, fittings and china store in town, but she only knows this because her parents mentioned it.

They drink their tea in the dining room. Alison is shy, breathless and exuberant, all at once. She falls backwards off a chair-arm on to the seat, showing her knickers. 'Alison,' snaps Mr Poole, frowning, 'pass Elizabeth the sugar.' Mostly, Alison keeps her eyes unwaveringly on Liz, listens in silence to the conversation and passes things according to instructions.

'Just think,' she suddenly interjects. 'If I pass the eleven plus, I'll be in the first form and Elizabeth'll be in the sixth.'

'Lower third,' Liz corrects her kindly. 'The first year's called lower third for some reason. Then it's upper third, then lower and upper fourth, then fifth, then lower and upper sixth.'

'Gosh,' breathes Alison. 'I bet, if I go there, the other girls won't even believe I know you.'

'I trust there'll be no "if" about it,' says her father. 'But you'll have to be discreet: Elizabeth won't want to be pestered by a silly little girl.'

Liz laughs.

'Elizabeth,' begins Alison shyly.

'Oh, call me Liz. All the girls do.'

'Really?' asks Mr Poole. 'Your parents always refer to you as Elizabeth.'

'Friends call me Liz.'

160

'Well then,' says Mr Poole with pointed joviality. 'Time we got back to work, Liz.'

'But she is staying for tea?'

'*She*?'

'Liz.'

'Certainly. And when your mother comes home you can lay the table.'

He remains jovial for the next half hour – which is a relief because she really is rather nervous about this accompanying business. He explains to her what it's about. 'When you're practising, *hear* the voices. For instance: when you begin, "ta *tum*", hear the voices come in after you, "ta *tum*", before you go on. Then keep their line in your head. Think of it,' he lifts his hands, makes synchronizing movements, 'think of it as two people – a man and a woman – coming together to create a whole. Give and take. Ebb and flow. Following one another, complementing . . .' (Wow, she thinks, as a feather flicks in her stomach. Imagine telling this to Chrissy and Nell.)

At five o'clock a pupil arrives for a lesson. Liz goes to sit in the dining room with a handful of books he selects for her from the bookcase. Alison seems to have disappeared. She opens *Decline and Fall*, settles down to read.

Mrs Poole comes in at a quarter to six and effects an immediate transformation; changes the house from a building focused on the piano (someone playing, others listening, perhaps chatting and drinking tea but always with a sense of the piano waiting in the front room), changes it from this faintly holy place into an extension of the secular world outside. She breezes in with a basket over an arm, cursing the corporation for the rough state of its buses which she holds responsible for her laddered stocking; kicks off her shoes (literally: one, two, up in the air; Mr Poole's foot shooting forward to scoot them out of the way), bangs down her basket, turns and appraises the visitor. 'Mm,' she says, 'Alderman Stockdale's daughter.' Her eyes go mischievous. 'Your father called round the other night. I think he's a dish.' She pauses to see how this goes down, then, chuckling, removes lettuce and other green stuff from her basket, throws them into the sink and turns on the tap full blast. Mr Poole hovers round as if she were an over-boiling saucepan and he desperate to keep her lid on.

'The jacket's gorgeous,' she comments without looking round.

It takes Liz a few moments to understand she means her blazer. 'Oh, really?'

'It's terrific with the trousers. Where'd you get it?'

'Um, I chose the pattern for it, then my mother's friend made it up.'

'Ah, same dodge as me. Ever go into Jennifer Last?'

'Well, no. But I love looking in the window.'

'Exactly. Her prices are too steep. But there's no harm in looking. Gives you ideas, then you can go and hunt through the pattern books.'

'Elizabeth is a serious young lady. There's more in her head than the price of clothes.'

'Her name's Liz, apparently,' Mrs Poole coolly reminds him (for this is how Liz introduced herself). 'Oh my goodness.' She dashes to the towel ring and dries her hands, grabs Liz's arm, leads her to the stairs. 'Bet he hasn't shown you where anything is, and you've been stuck here all afternoon, poor girl.' They run upstairs together. 'Bathroom,' Mrs Poole announces, kicking the first door on the landing, and swivels to point to a door at the front of the house. 'My room. Hang on,' – she opens a cupboard door – 'clean towel. And if you feel like ten minutes' peace and quiet before coming downstairs, go into my room and close the door. You won't be disturbed.' Then she runs back downstairs calling for her daughter.

Liz closes the bathroom door feeling stunned. Mrs

Poole is a whirlwind. And extremely pretty – a thing, for some reason, she finds surprising. She mulls over Mrs Poole's final instruction. 'My room,' she'd said, as though it's her room only. Well maybe it is, but Liz is too shy to do as she was bid and go and see. Instead, she perches on the side of the bath looking to see what toiletries the Pooles use by reading the labels on all the tins, packets, tubes and bottles along the window sill.

After a time she goes back downstairs.

Over the meal, Mrs Poole wants to know what Liz's home is like, what it's like living in Wold Enderby, how her mother spends her time, whether she and Liz get on; and she specially wants to know as much as possible about Alderman Stockdale. 'He came into Burnett's recently to order fittings for the show house on that new estate he's building out on Wealsby Drive. He's got lovely taste, you can tell he's used to the best. It must be wonderful living in one of those new houses. I expect you've been over them, Liz, have you? Does your mother help him? What fun, choosing all the curtains and carpets and furniture, I'd love that. Your father's very photogenic, I always think, when I see him in the paper; he's like Jack Hawkins only with straight hair instead of crinkly . . .'

All the time Mr Poole looks crosser and acts jumpier.

Liz feels sorry for him, but at the same time, can't resist Mrs Poole. Like a child being read a fairy tale and conjuring her own pictures, Mrs Poole's eyes gleam and widen. These eyes are very dark brown. Her mouth is wide and lipsticked bright red. Her brown wavy hair is quite short and has gold lights in it. Liz can't stop looking at her.

'Dad's going to buy me a bike if I pass the eleven plus,' Alison confides to Liz suddenly out of the blue.

'And he's never going to speak to you again if you don't,' adds her father.

He must be teasing, thinks Liz. But his words,

unmitigated, hang in the air. Alison looks squashed, drops her head.

When Mrs Poole responds it's as if her husband hadn't spoken.

'And your mum's going to buy you a bike if you fail because she knows you'll have worked very hard and deserve one anyway.'

Alison tilts her face and smiles up at her mother; and Mrs Poole starts gathering the plates. 'It's tinned peaches and evaporated for afters.'

'You mean for *dessert*,' frowns Mr Poole.

They walk through the park to St John's. When they reach the end of the street where the Pooles live they're in a better area; the houses become taller and deeper, the spaces they occupy wider and leafier. There are plenty of people in the park this summer evening, despite a nippy breeze. Elderly people, stout and solid in white, are enjoying a game of bowls. Youngsters, standing astride their bikes, argue the toss near the duck pond. Around the flower beds and the band-stand, couples stroll, teenagers lurk; boys and dogs chase balls across the grass.

Mr Poole walks briskly with long strides, one hand in his trouser pocket, the other swinging his briefcase. Liz hurries to keep up, clasping her music case tight to her side. There's a feeling of stillness inside her, like the calm before an outburst. It's momentous to be walking chummily beside the austere and much speculated upon Mr Poole; she wouldn't be anywhere else or with anyone else in the whole world. All the same, ahead of her looms an ordeal. She might let him down, make a fool of herself. It seems to go in life that to have wonderful things happen you have to risk a penalty.

Yet, in the end, it's a minor triumph. Accompanying, Liz discovers, is much easier when the singers are present and actually singing, rather than needing to be imagined in the mind's ear. It's relatively effortless, particularly with Mr Poole conducting. Afterwards, she's exhilarated. Everyone's pleased with her and friendly. Mr Poole walks round smiling as though he's been vindicated. When he comes over to the piano he puts a hand on her shoulder and gives it a squeeze. Quite a hard squeeze. She feels like she did on the night school broke up when she and Nell hid at Chrissy's and each drank a miniature of green chartreuse.

Mr Poole walks with her to the bus-stop. He told her father he'd see her on to the bus and then phone the village taxi service. Usually, she phones ahead herself before getting on the bus, but Mr Poole says he'll ring from The White Lion where he's going for a pint.

'Going for a pint' gives her a jolt. She can't imagine it. It's amazing all the things she's learnt about him today – lots of disjointed detail. She hopes the bus will come soon and speed her away so she can start piecing it all together.

The number nine bus hoves in sight. When it stops, he puts a hand under her elbow and elevates her on to the deck. She sprints up the stairs on to a seat and looks down from the window. He's striding away, not looking back, going towards the pub.

On the telephone, Chrissy sounds cross. 'Where've you been? Why haven't you rung? It's been ages. I don't know how you could.'

'I'm sorry.'

'You just didn't care. And something terrible's happened to Nell.'

'What?'

'Mogsy's chucked her.'

'Chucked her?'

'Yeah. He's going out with Angie Hutchings. She's been after him for ages.'

'But what about you and Dave?'

'Oh him,' cries Chrissy scornfully. 'I was sick to death of him, only put up with him cos Mogsy wouldn't

165

go anywhere without him. It was pathetic really, but Nell couldn't see it, she was so mad on Mogsy.'

'Poor Nell.'

'It's been agony at work. We've been terrified in case Mogsy and them came into the café with Angie and Val. Imagine. Nell says she'd go out and drown herself. She says she'd quite like to die, anyway.'

'Crikey.'

'So you'd better come round quick, 'cos she needs us. My place. Nell'll be here soon.'

Liz stops herself saying that she'll come as soon as she's finished her piano practice, which is her first thought, and promises to come at once.

'Right,' says Chrissy, as though it's a matter of course.

V

Nell went round her office with a large bag, collecting bits and pieces from desk tops and drawers. You couldn't trust anyone in this business; three weeks' leave, anything could happen. The three weeks had been decided on with great reluctance. After totting everything up, trying to peer into the future (which was like squinting through pebble glass – she could dimly perceive something on the other side, but exactly what was another matter), she'd decided to play safe – ring up the office from a hospital bed and the obituary's half written before you put the phone down. Over a cleared-off desk top she'd spread out a stand-by column kept back for this sort of emergency. The remainder of her leave would have to be covered by the team, an arrangement she loathed – it provoked her latent paranoia, gave her the idea that trusted assistants were conspiring rivals, an arrangement, generally speaking, she went to great lengths to forestall. This time, however, there was no alternative.

One of the team, Belinda, had come in just now and was leaning over the desk reading the stand-by copy.

166

Any minute now, she'd start giving out in her high pitched twenty-something voice. Nell braced herself; nothing, she found, jarred worse on the nerves than a twenty-something voice giving out enthusiasm. The young these days were ludicrously prone to it, presumably because enthusiasm was thought keen and energetic-sounding and an overweening display of it would help them get on. Funny then, that she'd done OK. This wasn't to deny the odd helping hand on her route to the top (one in particular came to mind), but she could certainly swear, hand on heart, that enthusiasm had had nothing to do with it. Cynicism had been her twenty-something style, she was glad to recall.

'Oh, super. Terrif . . .'

'Well, don't mess it up, flower, that's all. And don't forget there's the stuff on the Blundel case, begging to be worked up into something useful. Right,' – she looked round – 'what've I forgotten?'

'Nothing. Stop worrying. Put everything here out of your mind. Just concentrate on having a well-earned holiday.'

'Actually, I'm not going away immediately. Tell Julian I may phone in with something in a day or two. Be seeing you.' She stomped out of the room and along the corridor, lugging her bag.

'Bye-ee' – the calls followed after her like doves' cooings. She stepped into the lift. Vultures, she thought.

She'd had an idea for a story bashing the medical profession, if only she could lay her hands on the right cuttings: something along the lines that 50 per cent of illness was actually caused by doctors. Or was it dentists ruining teeth? Her fingers rifled fruitlessly through the contents of her bedroom filing cabinet.

It was no good, her mind kept flipping; it was like a bird hopping from one stone to another, thinking the stone ahead concealed the juicier insect, never stopping long enough to find out. She closed the drawers and sat down, put her head in her hands and thought how it was all the consultant's fault – her foul temper, her inability to concentrate, her sheer bloody panic.

It wasn't the idea of something nasty in her lungs, nor that he it was who'd discovered and reported it; her pitiful state was down to a sure conviction that the man was out to humiliate her. A pointer to this was the way he'd immediately started bossing her around, as if finding something amiss gave him *carte blanche* to forbid her to smoke, summon her to bed, cut her up, submit her to any indignity he'd a mind to practise. She could envisage the scene now: she prone and helpless in bed, Mr Consultant, together with assorted acolytes, peering down and pretending sorrow while describing the limitations of her future life, watching to see how she liked it. Humiliation was the only word. And what a word – the most terrifying in the English language. Her whole life seemed to have been spent running from, saving herself from, some form of humiliation. Examples were too numerous to dredge up, though two – Fred leaving her, the bastard, just days before she planned to do it to him, and her father roaring drunk in the street dragging her by the hair into the house because the stupid sot thought she was her mother, all the neighbours gawping – figured pretty prominently. Looking back these days, specific details escaped her; but humiliation was there, all right; be-hind her was a whole well of it.

Bugger the work, she thought. I need to get away. Why not go to Chrissy's a day early? A cheering idea; she jumped up and went to the phone. Only as she was tapping out Chrissy's number did it hit her, what she was up to. God, you make me sick, she told herself wearily, tossing down the receiver. You know damn well you'd start blubbing to Chrissy about this lung business the moment you got there: what you're doing is trying to steal a march on Liz. Depressed, she went into the bathroom and turned on the taps.

168

Hot fragrant water was always so soothing, a never-fail medium for releasing ideas. A bright one came to her now. She could still go 'home' if she felt like it. There was no law saying she had to stay with Chrissy. She could spend a night at the Grand in town and go out to Fenby-cum-Laithby on Thursday as planned, all the calmer for having had twenty-four hours to herself. Good thinking, girl. She stood up and started being vigorous with the loofah.

vi

Liz goes to the Sea Gull Café quite often now; in the mornings she practises her piano playing, most afternoons (not Wednesdays) she sits in the café with a cooling cup of tea lending moral support to her friends, helping them out when Marge's back is turned, keeping watch through the windows. Nell says, if Mogsy and Angie come in flaunting their togetherness, she'll die, it'll be too humiliating. They try reasoning with her. Be aloof, Liz advises, think to yourself they're not worth it and then they won't be. Chrissy says if they do come in she'll accidentally on purpose spill tea in Angie's lap which could be quite a hoot. None of this convinces Nell, she says they don't understand and the best thing they can do is tip her off, allowing her enough time to dash out the back. It makes for rather edgy afternoons at the Sea Gull Café.

One warm afternoon the dreaded event occurs. Liz has become so used to peering through the window anticipating this arrival that at first she thinks she's hallucinating. So there's an unfortunate delay before she goes racing to the counter. As Chrissy breaks the news to Nell, the door bursts open.

'What's eating her?' asks Marge, when Liz's suspicious behaviour is topped by Nell's flight past her into the storeroom (where there is also a service entrance and a basic lavatory); but she's forced to abandon the enquiry by the bevy of lads at the counter wanting service. 'All right, all right, one at a time.'

Liz recognizes Mogsy, Dave and Timmo among these half dozen boys. She doesn't count Quacker Duckenfield who's been here all afternoon, sitting alone at the table nearest the washing-up sink. (He's here most days; for the past four, Chrissy's ignored him. When he wants something, she asks Nell to serve him; when Marge told her off for this and insisted Chrissy pour his tea, she did it sloppily, snatched his money, gave him change, all in silence. Tony Quacker Duckenfield made a huge miscalculation four days ago when, running a nervous finger through the sugar spill on the counter, he let it be known that of all the grammar school girls, Chrissy's rated the prettiest. 'So?' she demanded furiously, staring him out, for people are always saying this, she doesn't need a squirt like Tony Duckenfield rubbing it in. 'Pretty' is not what Chrissy aspires to. She hankers for gravely beautiful like Liz, or for one of the adjectives increasingly applied to Nell: 'interesting', 'moody', or best of all, 'sexy'. Since that outraged 'So?' she hasn't vouchsafed him another word.) Liz stares across the room at Angie, Val, Gilly and Beryl, who are flopped on chairs at a table near the juke box. They stare back at Liz. When the boys troop to the table with cups of tea, the girls spark up, go giggly, make remarks behind their hands while looking at Liz or at Chrissy. The boys catch their mood. 'Hiya, Liz. Where's your music case?' calls Timmo. 'Where's Nell, then?' asks Dave. 'Rolling her own?' They crack up with laughter.

'Nell, how long you going to be in that toilet?' yells Marge. At which Angie and Co, and especially the boys, lose all control – hoot, rock, slap, aim punches.

Two women customers, looking askance, scrape back their chairs and go towards the store area.

'Nell? There's folk out here wanting to use that toilet.' (Screams at this from Angie's crowd, chairs up-ended, people sprawled on the floor.) 'Flamin hell, what's got into you kids today? You hear me, Nell? Come out of that toilet. What's she doing, Chrissy, what's up with her?'

'It's you, shouting "toilet". Why don't you shut up?'

'Don't you speak to me like that, monkey. Now, listen here, Nell,' – Marge marches upon the lavatory – 'come out that toilet this minute.'

'Leave it,' cries Chrissy, as Marge attacks the door handle.

Singing starts up in the café, of that old favourite, 'Oh dear what can the matter be?'

'If this doesn't stop,' threatens Marge, storming back into the café, 'I'll fetch Mr Parton; he's only outside fixing his van. What the blummin heck . . .?'

Bedlam's broken out. Angie's killing herself on Mogsy's knee; Beryl and Val are screaming and trying to repossess some article pinched by two lads who are playing toss with it.

'Right, you lot, out,' yells Marge, marching on them, pointing the way. She waits, arms akimbo, until they've staggered through the doorway. But they don't leave the vicinity, they go running to the back of the café where they gather and yell under the smallest window, 'Run out of paper?', 'Go on, Nell, flush it,' and similar comments.

A short distance away, Mr Parton withdraws his head from the van's engine, listens, runs towards the café, yells that he'll call the coppers if they don't disperse. They amble away, calling parting shots.

'What the heck's going on?' Mr Parton demands, ascending the café's rear steps, wiping his hands on an oily rag.

'Don't ask me,' calls Marge, running between counter and storeroom. 'These girls have gone haywire.'

'It was you shouting "toilet",' cries a distraught Chrissy. 'I told you to stop.'

'Now listen here, you . . .'

171

'Nell, they've gone, you can come out now. Oh, Liz,' (for Liz comes creeping into the storeroom) 'what're we going to do?'

'And who the heck's she?' demands Mr Parton.

'Another of 'em,' says Marge. 'Always hanging about.'

'Well, she can clear off, too.'

'Shut *up*,' screams Chrissy, 'we're trying to help Nell. If anything's happened to her it'll be your fault, with your "toilet, toilet" you stupid woman.'

'That's it, you're fired,' roars Mr Parton. 'Beat it, the lot of you. Damn kids; more trouble than they're worth.' And as Marge dashes back into the café calling 'Yes, love?' to a customer, Mr Parton attacks the lavatory door.

'She won't come out while you're here,' Liz points out reasonably.

'Right. Then you've got two minutes to get her out yourselves and clear off the premises. You can call round Thursday for owt you're owed. Two minutes, mind.'

In the sudden peace, Chrissy and Liz look at one another. They go to the lavatory door, lay their heads against it. 'It's just us,' Chrissy calls in a small voice. And Liz urges softly, 'Let's go, Nell.'

There's a sound on the other side; the bolt slides back, the door opens.

She comes forward slowly like a sleepwalker. They each take an arm, help her through the doorway and down the steps very carefully, keeping their bodies in contact and their eyes on Nell's feet, as if at any moment she might disintegrate.

At least there's no sign of the gang. There's only Tony Quacker Duckenfield; he's collected his bike and is standing in his bicycle clips holding the handlebars. 'You won't be coming here tomorrow then, Chrissy,' he observes, blinking at them through his thick spectacles.

172

'Push off, four eyes,' snarls Chrissy, putting heart and soul into it. After a moment, he goes.

They take the long way round to avoid the boating lake gardens; eventually arrive at the main road.

'Where now?' wonders Chrissy.

'The cemetery?' suggests Liz.

Nell's still locked in her stupor.

Fifteen minutes later they're in their favourite spot. Chrissy feels for Nell's ciggies. Liz finds the matches, applies the flame. They don't talk, just sit clasping their knees, smoking, staring ahead, side by side under the guardian angel.

Time passes. It's Nell who finally breaks the silence. She says – and it's the first thing she's said for hours, since before Mogsy and Angie came into the café: what she says is, 'I'll never forgive myself.'

'It wasn't your fault,' soothes Liz.

'No, it was them. It was her,' Chrissy cries.

She doesn't hear them. 'I'll never forgive my appalling taste. How could I have felt like that, when he was so, when they're all so, so *pathetic*?'

What can they say?

Footsteps sound on the other side of the hedge. They listen (they're too low down to see anything) as someone draws slowly closer then goes slowly by; it's a marked tread, evenly spaced, somehow resigned. Bird-squabbling breaks out in a nearby tree; leaves drift down. This summer, thinks Liz, is nearly over.

'Mr Poole says,' she ventures in an attempt to lift Nell's spirits, 'that a man and a woman coming together create a whole, he says they complement one another, and he puts his hands out and moves them about like this saying, "give and take, ebb and flow . . ."'

'Go-osh,' shudders Nell, stunned. 'That's marvellous.'

Liz and Chrissy watch her face going dreamy, her smile coming. It feels hopeful, like the day brightening after a squall.

On Tuesday evening, Liz and Nathan were sitting over an uncleared kitchen table, the last of the food swallowed nearly an hour ago, the last half inch of coffee gone cold in their mugs. They sat in the gloom, holding hands across the table top, planning their future. Nathan had more or less decided to leave the firm and join forces with Brendan. Facts, figures, enquiries, projections had been studied over the weekend: he'd liked what he'd learned. Only this angina business had stayed him from making a firm commitment, but now, talking things over with Liz, he saw there was no cause for delay: either he'd need an operation at some time in the future or he wouldn't; if it fell out that he did, a brief interruption was all it signified. And they'd pay off the mortgage, Liz decided, with the bit of money she'd had from her father. Jon was launched on his career and soon to marry Sushma. They must assume Rosie would require funding for a few more years, despite her protestations about not going to university. But the season of always putting the children first was drawing to a close; a new era beckoned, the time of Nathan and Liz. Once Rosie was off their hands, why, they'd feel positively rich on Liz's salary alone, which was pretty good these days now she was a senior clinician. They were as excited as newly weds.

'Come here,' said Nathan, tugging on her hand, pulling her on to his lap where she landed with a bump, feet shooting upwards, face falling on his shoulder. 'I could end up glad I married you.'

She laughed so hard at this that if it hadn't been for his arms holding her she'd have ended up on the floor. She'd phone Jon in a minute to report this gem, for Jon was a connoisseur of his father's sayings; he filed them in his memory under the title 'Dad' to lovingly bring out like any collector of oddities. His all-time favourite was a remark uttered on the occasion of his engagement, when, with an arm round Jon's shoulder, pints of bitter to hand, his father had helpfully advised, 'One thing, son – don't have kids; kids finish a man.'

She had her arms round him, one round his neck, the other round his waist and her nose snuffling him, thinking what a deep pleasure it was, this close contact with a body as familiar as her own, satisfying in a peculiarly elemental way, when the back door opened and Rosie stepped in and put the light on.

'Christ,' she muttered, startled by the unexpectedness of two faces springing at her from semi-darkness, maddened by the stupid way they were blinking at her, by their closeness. Mauling each other in the dark, she thought. At their age. Disdainfully, she made to walk past.

Nathan shot out an arm. 'Hey, Rosie, where've you been? How'd you get back?' For no car had turned in the yard or stopped in the lane.

'Jenny's,' she said shortly.

'Did Jenny drive you back?'

'Yeah,' said Rosie after a small hesitation.

'Why the hell didn't she drive you to the house, then? Rosie? Oh, blast the girl.'

Rosie had flung off. Enough to make you vomit, she thought, stomping upstairs, they're not normal, always pawing each other.

Nathan had gone tense. Liz climbed off his lap and started to clear away the supper things. They washed up in silence, each nursing the thought that Rosie's man had dropped her off in the village. Why the hell couldn't he bring her to the door, wondered Nathan resentfully. Can't have much about him – that, or he's got something to hide.

Liz, who had a clearer picture of the homecoming, concluded that Simon was still seeing Rosie despite the difficulties, and despite Rosie's threats.

Nathan went off to watch *News at Ten*. Liz said she'd join him in a minute, but remained standing at the

175

sink, staring at her reflection in the night-blackened window. She heard herself saying to Rosie, 'When I was a girl, younger than you, only sixteen in fact, a rather similar thing happened to me. So I do know . . .' She'd begun like this in her head many times, always trailing off into self-dismissal. The young, as she very well knew, don't want to hear about their elders' youthful mistakes, especially when offered as harbingers of their own. The young are passionately insulted by the idea of not being unique but merely part of an age-old pattern; they must make these mistakes for themselves, otherwise how were they ever to truly learn? Telling Rosie about the past would be worse than useless; it would be alienating. All the same, she would say one thing to Rosie before she went to Chrissy's, just the one thing, she promised her reflection in the window glass. So she might as well say it now and get it over with. She went upstairs and tapped on Rosie's door.

Rosie grunted.

Liz pushed the door open, didn't go in, but stood leaning back against the door frame. 'I'm not sure whether you know this: Ellie Goodridge is pregnant, about six months, I'd guess. Also, they've got a four-year-old boy who has the manner of a child from a loving and stable home. As you had, and Jon. That's all.'

She went back downstairs to join Nathan.

Rosie hurled the door closed. Liz told herself not to mind, it had needed to be said, she was relieved to have said it.

This time in her dream their roles were reversed: Liz fleeing, Ellie chasing. It was the same route they took, down the alley between garden fencing and playground wire netting. When she drew near to the nursery school the boys on bikes were waiting. One boy was holding an apple, weighing it. He'd throw it at her as soon as she was past him. She knew this, braced herself for the blow; even so, the shock of it against her shoulder blade sent her tumbling, and the effort to right herself and keep going – for Ellie was still pounding after her – almost tore her heart open. Ellie was pitiless, she'd drive her into the ground, Liz knew, sobbing brokenly at the thought of herself so mercilessly pursued.

The sky darkened as they shot into older territory; rows of little houses with tiny front gardens sped by; there went the corner shop, now came the subway. Down she plunged as a train roared overhead, up, up, straining towards the corner with Town Hall Square. If only the bus would be waiting. She'd be safe on the bus.

The bus was there indeed. She leapt on to the deck, stood looking into the conductor's face willing him to ring the bell. He stared back blankly. And Ellie was coming, she was drawing alongside. Liz struggled to get out the words, to tell him 'Press the bell'; but her tongue cleaved to the roof of her mouth. As Ellie sprang, she hurled herself up the stairs. The bell pinged, the bus lurched; Liz went flying.

She was free, airborne.

viii

Sixth-formers. For at least three weeks the title pleases. Being in the sixth doesn't suddenly convert them into conforming good types, rather it seems to confer more leeway to be the rebels they are and render any attempts to inhibit them that bit harder for authority. Their manner of entering the sixth is a further boost, for they are not here merely to re-take failed O levels or add one or two more and leave at the end of the year to go into a bank or nursing; no, no, they're three of a mere sixteen girls studying A levels for university or college entrance. Furthermore, their O-level results were among the best; Nell's were supremely *the* best, in fact the best for years. During the last days of the summer holiday, Nell was actively courted, summoned to school by teachers desperate for her to take their subject at A level. She has been persuaded to take four subjects rather than the customary three, for, as the Head pointed out, one of her chosen subjects, Art, is a mere 'frill'. Liz is also taking one of these 'frill' subjects (music), though no-one has suggested she attempt an extra one. English Literature is the only course Liz, Nell and Chrissy share in common and for this reason, and because they are the only English Literature A-level students, they consider it their most important subject.

Nell's brilliance, indeed, their triple success, has confounded certain teachers' prognoses. It's a spit in the teeth to those hard-faced looks, sarky comments, dire warnings. For the first few weeks they swank around the place. Then the novelty wears off, there's work piling up, plenty to seize their interest, new dreams to conjure – and one old one woefully under-exploited by their innocent fifth-former selves which they now perceive as having breathtaking possibilities: Liz's relationship with Mr Poole.

Nell can't get over how mature Liz has proved to be. It's a thing she constantly marvels over, how, when she and Chrissy were fooled by the hateful grammar-school boys, seeing charm in their skinny bodies and wit in their thick-head humour (where none at all existed), Liz remained impervious, stayed constant to an ideal. Maddeningly, this ideal was carved out months earlier by the three of them; he's a joint effort. 'Poetic,' recalls Chrissy. 'Lycidas,' murmurs Nell. So how, Nell wonders, did she and Chrissy get side-tracked? There's a lot of catching up to do. Things have moved on.

Liz is flattered, also nervous. ('Mr Poole's not specially good looking and he's quite old. It's more what he's like *inside*.' 'Yeah,' they breathe. 'Absolutely.') She's unwilling to misrepresent her hero, to claim more than the facts merit, to paint him falsely in vital particulars; at the same time she's reluctant to put them off, the opportunity to dwell on him and linger over enthralling detail is too tempting. Luckily, her scruples only serve to enhance their respect for a friend who can spot quality even when it lacks the customary indicators. They want to hear every detail they missed while their attention was distracted. They want to hear every detail several times.

On the gravestone steps under the guardian angel, huddled against the autumn chill, they listen, prompt, speculate. Chrissy holds her cigarette between gloved fingers, but Liz, who takes her pleasure from the feel of the cigarette rather than smoking it, and Nell, whose attitude to the business is deadly serious, both strip their cigarette-holding fingers bare. As Liz speaks, Mr Poole strides again through the park swinging his brief-case, or stands gazing thoughtfully (and probably with inner sadness) out of his sitting-room window before turning round to make some pertinent or revealing remark; once more his hands coax passion from the St John's Choir and his eyes convey messages to the accompanist. Particular weight is given to Mr Poole gripping Liz's shoulder after the first rehearsal. They ask her to demonstrate. Also, his assisting her on to the bus afterwards is found significant. Under cross-examination, Liz cannot say she has noticed in him a habit of old-fashioned courtesy; ergo, they reason, his hand under her elbow reveals a compulsion to touch her. This also accounts for the fierceness of his grip on her shoulder. The more they analyse, the more certain they become of Mr Poole's secret passion, a passion he manfully endeavours to hide though cannot help betraying now and then in tiny manifestations.

All very alluring, but Liz knows there's a drawback. In her heart of hearts she can't think of a single reason why Mr Poole should hanker for her in preference to the spirited and attractive Mrs Poole. She tries to convey something of Mrs Poole's flavour; the French

179

phrase *jolie madame* springs aptly to mind. At this, Nell sucks in her breath and Chrissy knits her brows. They don't care to hear praise for Mrs Poole. Kicking her shoes off and going on about new clothes and luxurious modern housing is indicative, opines Nell, of a shallow personality. ('Shallow,' echoes Chrissy, approving the word.) Someone truly worthy of Mr Poole would have the taste not to work in a shop; they'd do something artistic, or failing that, something fairly intellectual like working in a library. ('A library'd be all right,' agrees Chrissy.) Working in a shop and going on about film stars like ghastly Jack Hawkins betrays lack of taste and a frivolous nature. ('Frivolous, mm.') Nell draws deeply on her Players Navy Cut and postulates how grating to the nerves all this shallowness and frivolity must be to someone of Mr Poole's sensibility.

Come to think of it, Liz recalls, Mr Poole does get rather jumpy in Mrs Poole's presence, frowning at her remarks, even contradicting them.

'There you are,' they say.

'It must be agony for him,' thinks Chrissy, 'a person of taste forced to live with someone so, well, *basic*.' Rather like her own hardship in having to share a home with Auntie Julie, she privately imagines.

'Absolute hell,' agrees Nell, 'particularly now he knows Liz. Meeting someone sensitive, someone artistic, must make his position feel all the more poignant.'

Chrissy falls on the word – '*Poignant*.'

The feeling grows in Liz that she owes it to herself as well as her piano teacher and her friends to try and appreciate Mrs Poole rather less.

By October, Mrs Hilary Dowling, accompanist of the St John's Choir, has recovered sufficiently to resume her duties. This is a mixed blessing. Preparations are underway for the Winter Gardens concert, there is now a Sunday morning rehearsal as well as the usual one on Wednesday evenings, and Mrs Dowling, though a thoroughly competent musician, is ignorant of all the little performance details so far settled upon during September. Mr Poole diplomatically combines joy at her return with anxiety for her sciatica recurring. He proposes that Liz should continue to attend rehearsals as Mrs Dowling's understudy, just in case.

On the first Sunday morning in October, Alderman Stockdale drops Liz off at St John's on his way to pick up his secretary who has kindly agreed to go over some urgent accounts. ('I don't know why Carol puts up with it,' Mrs Stockdale remarked, lavishly buttering her breakfast toast. 'You exploit that girl, expect her to drop everything at a moment's notice – Ideal Home Exhibition one minute, chasing up plumbers or sorting accounts the next. I'm glad *I*'m not your secretary.' 'So'm I, my dear, otherwise things wouldn't be so comfortable here. I'm a fortunate man. I was only saying to Councillor Turner the other night, where would we be without the ladies? Ready, princess? I'm going to get the car out.')

Liz anticipates a disappointing morning; she's apprehensive lest Mrs Dowling resents her presence, she expects to feel out of the swing, cast aside. What she's looking forward to is afterwards, walking through the park beside Mr Poole, having lunch with the Poole family. (For Mrs Poole insisted on this last Wednesday. 'If the poor girl's got to give up her Sundays, too, for the blummin old choir, the least we can do is give her some lunch. You will come, won't you, Liz? You brighten us up, doesn't she, Alison? And if it's nice in the afternoon maybe we could have a run out somewhere. Is the car up to it, Ronnie? Hasn't seized up or anything while I've been hauling the groceries home on the bus and standing in the rush-hour queue getting soaked to the skin? It does still *go*?')

As happens so often when her path crosses Mr Poole's, things turn out to be unexpectedly, magically, wonderful. That Mrs Dowling is not *au fait* with the performance as so far developed soon becomes apparent. Mr Poole, looking grim, tries to quickly explain matters while the choir listens in tense and uncharacteristic silence. He actually sends Liz a beseeching look before suggesting she take over and give Mrs Dowling a rest. It's a heady compliment, she knows he hopes Mrs Dowling will take her cue from the understudy's performance. She doesn't let him down. Afterwards, his look of gratitude makes her bones melt. 'You do play nicely, dear,' whispers Mrs Dowling generously. 'I see what he was getting at now about those *staccato* bits.'

Leaves litter the park. Mr Poole, striding, swinging his briefcase, sniffs decay in the air. Some people, he observes, are excited by the smell of autumn; he, on the other hand, is made sombre, the word 'elegy' springs to mind. 'El-e-gy,' he intones, looking at her sideways. When her heart stops turning over, she repeats these observations several times in her head – like learning a quote for an essay – to be sure they're remembered for Chrissy and Nell.

Drawing near to the house, an intermittent clacking is discovered to be the noise of Mrs Poole's shears clipping the hedge. 'Giving it its last tidy of the year,' she tells them. She is watched by her next-door neighbour to whom Mr Poole nods curtly as he strides indoors. Liz hesitates on the garden path because Mrs Poole is introducing her, in a roundabout sort of way, to the neighbour. 'This is Liz. Alderman Stockdale's daughter.'

'I know. I've seen her going in. Cooped up with him all afternoon, she was, some days last summer.'

'That's because she helps Ronnie with the choir. He thinks the world of her.'

Her ears burning pleasantly, Liz is turning to go into the house when Alison charging out forestalls her. 'Hello, Liz. Dad said you were here. Would you like to read my composition what I got "ten out of ten

182

excellent" for?' Her thin face gleams with excitement; she's holding out an exercise book.

Liz takes it, half-expecting Mrs Poole to urge them inside. Instead, a low groan comes from the hedge and the neighbour launches into a soft diatribe.

'It's that pain again, isn't it? Leave off that clipping, Sheila – John'll finish it for you later when he comes out to do the grass. I can't think why you keep killing yourself. It's a pity *somebody else* doesn't pull his weight, wouldn't hurt him to do a hand's turn in the garden. I caught him paying the milkman on Friday – still in his dressing gown at ten o'clock in the morning. Go on, Sheila; leave it for John.'

'Whoo,' gasps Mrs Poole, arching her back. 'OK. If you're sure he won't mind.'

'Course he won't. John's not frightened of a bit of work.'

'Right. Thanks. Really, Alison; fancy keeping Liz standing about out here; she can read that indoors. See you, Pam.'

A smell of roasting meat comes from the kitchen. 'Like a sherry, Liz?' Mrs Poole calls.

'Well, I . . . All right, thank you.'

'Pour us two sherries, Ronnie.'

They go into the dining room. Mr Poole hands his wife and his pupil each a small glass of brown liquid. 'Vile stuff,' he opines, and Liz wants to kick herself for having fallen in with Mrs Poole's suggestion.

'Here's looking at you, kid,' says Mrs Poole, winking at Liz over her glass.

The meal is roast pork with sage and onion stuffing, roast potatoes and parsnips and tinned processed peas. She suspects it would find little favour on the Stockdale table, nevertheless, perhaps because of this, she rather enjoys it. Apple pie and custard follow.

'Coffee, Liz?' asks Mr Poole.

'Coffee?' cries Mrs Poole as if he's gone mad. 'What do you want coffee for?'

'It's usual, I believe.'

'Rubbish. Let's get out while it's still fine. And when we come back we'll have a nice cuppa tea. That's the ticket, isn't it, Alison? Come and help Mum side the dishes, and Dad can go and collect the car, and Liz can talk to us or go and sit in the front room.'

'Where're we going?' joyfully asks Alison, springing to her feet and inadvertently farting.

'Alison,' roars her father.

'Sorry, it was the peas.'

'Don't be stupid.'

'Yes it was. You said peas make you . . .'

'I did not. Get out, you rude girl. We'd better leave you behind.'

'Of course we won't,' Mrs Poole says calmly. 'And you did say that, Ronnie, last time we had peas and you . . .'

'*Si-lence.*'

In the prescribed hush, Mrs Poole and Alison clear the table, while Mr Poole stands jingling change in his trouser pocket. Suddenly, he turns on his heel and charges from the room. Almost at once a Bach prelude pours out, notes ring and dazzle, chords resound, the little house is filled with fiery brilliance. Nell's right, thinks Liz, listening to his performance; this cramped house, this mundane domesticity, must be simply crippling. At the music's close he doesn't hang about; the front door slams almost before the last chord dies.

'We keep the car in a lock-up,' explains Mrs Poole. 'It's just round the block, so he won't be long. How about Bealby? Have you been there, Liz? It's lovely, isn't it? Really sweet.'

'Dad, Dad,' cries Alison, skipping to the gate when a smoke-trailing Hillman Minx draws up, 'we want to go to Bealby.'

Bealby is a rarity in their part of the world – a conventionally pretty village. Charming stone dwellings are clustered between tussocky hills; there are little rills, rocky pools, a hump-backed bridge, even waterfalls. The pub does teas in the summer, trippers' cars clog the lanes. The Stockdales and their friends often motor out to pause for a few minutes' gaze through the car windscreen at the surrounding countryside; then they repair to the pub, and before going home buy cut flowers and eggs from one of the cottages. Liz has always connected Bealby with boredom. It's a draw for people who haven't an idea what to do when they get there, ennui sets in as they step out of the car.

Mrs Poole, it transpires, has a very clear idea. 'Draw up just before the bridge, Ronnie.' She turns to the girls in the back. 'The path to Barnes Manor is one of the prettiest – takes you over the stream; and the Manor's really interesting, don't you think?'

'Spooky,' says Alison.

'I don't really know. I've never been there.'

Mrs Poole is surprised, but Mr Poole is deprecating. 'It's only a folly, built by the Barnes family at the end of the last century. That's why no-one bothered much when it fell into ruin. I don't suppose Liz's parents consider it merits attention.'

'What're you talking about Ronnie? It's fascinating poking around. You'll think so, Liz, you'll see.'

The weather's not over warm, but it's dry and sunny. They stride out along the path in a buffeting wind, clamber up and round a hillside where it's more sheltered, then drop down towards the stream. In the distance, what appears to be a crumbling Elizabethan manor house looms.

'Airmen lived in it during the war,' says Alison. 'Some of their stuff's still lying about, letters and combs and fag packets.'

'Cigarette packets,' Mr Poole corrects her.

'What I always think of is all those young men flying off into the night. Lots never came back. Their letters

185

are still lying about in the very rooms they were sleeping in before they set out,' says Mrs Poole, shivering slightly.

As they scramble towards it, Barnes Manor becomes less a romantic ruin, more a broken building. The roof's half gone, birds call in the rafters; doors lie open – will never close again – as though inviting wanderers. The inside walls have tatters of old paper hanging, like unshorn locks on a balding head. Floorboards are broken and dusty. Letters lie heaped in corners. Liz thinks it strange that no-one's returned to gather them; it's as if a postman weighed down with mail called here one morning and finding the place deserted, emptied out his bags in disgust. They finger some of the letters, sadly read out bits of them to one another.

'Got lots of boyfriends, Liz?' asks Mrs Poole as they return outside into the bracing air. Mr Poole and Alison wait for her answer.

'No I haven't,' she declares, and they laugh at her vehemence.

'Why – don't you like boys?'

'We think they're pathetic. Nell says . . .'

'Nell?' asks Mr Poole.

They pick their way over the rocky path, and Liz tells them about Nell and Chrissy. They jump the stream, lift bramble branches for one another to pass under. To satisfy Mrs Poole's particular interest, Liz describes the desultory walk through the boating lake gardens with the grammar-school boys. Encouraged by their enjoyment, she goes on to describe the Sea Gull Café incident. Alison is impatient with this talk of boys, she wants to hear more about Chrissy and Nell. Daringly, for she feels safe with these people, Liz confesses how she and Nell sometimes stow away at Chrissy's, though she holds back on the really wicked stuff, such as trespassing in the rectory and staying overnight in school. By the time they arrive back at the car, she's high on the pleasure of making people laugh. Their

186

wide smiles, raised colour, the animation charging the journey home, are an accomplishment. She revels in it.

They have tea, then Mr Poole prepares to drive her to Town Hall Square to catch the bus, with Alison coming along for the ride. Mrs Poole, who has been paddling about in her stocking feet because her feet are killing her, reaches for her slippers in the cupboard under the stairs, then comes flopping down the path to watch them go. At the last minute, Liz winds down the car window. 'I've had a smashing day,' she yells.

'Me too. It was grand,' calls Mrs Poole, laughing, waving.

ix

Liz rose early. It was Wednesday (after all she hadn't managed to get off a day earlier) and this would be her last appearance at work for a few days. There was much to do. First things first, however. Still in her dressing gown, unwashed, no tea inside her (though the kettle was on) she took note pad and biro from a drawer of the dresser, sat at the table and wrote, 'Dear Rosie, as you may recall, I'm going away for a few days . . .'

Hang on, did 'as you may recall' sound snide? How about 'You remember me telling you' instead? Still sounds like I'm getting at her, implying she's too wrapped up in herself to notice what anyone else is doing – which she is, of course, though it won't help matters to point it out. My goodness, she's got you in a tizz. Stop dithering girl, barge straight in.

On a fresh sheet of paper, she began again.

'Dear Rosie, tomorrow I'm off to Chrissy's for a few days. Afraid that means one less car about the place for you to call on, so use the enclosed for taxis. Dad and I are going to eat at The Fox at Laithwick tonight. Fancy joining us? Love Mum.'

She opened her purse, took out two twenty pound notes and sealed them with the letter in an envelope. Misgivings about the money, of course, faint stirrings of resentment: Jon, as a student, had always found holiday work – stacker of supermarket shelves, factory sweeper-up, loader of garage doors on to lorries (rather dangerous, this, in high winds: she'd worried) and later, having won a firm's trust and respect, temporary storeman doling out valuable parts and equipment to workers on the shop floor. It's not Rosie's fault, she told herself for the umpteenth time, it's the present job situation. Though would Rosie, so wrapped up in her affair with Simon, actually take a job were one offered her? Ah well, she remembered well enough from her own girlhood the bind of being stuck in the country when most of your friends lived in town. She wrote 'Rosie' on the envelope, ran softly upstairs and pushed it under her daughter's door.

At seven thirty, Nell's alarm clock sprang her from a vivid dream. It was a moment before she came to, for the dream was disturbingly realistic with no clues – odd incongruities, strange abstract features – to allow a part of her mind to know that she was in fact dreaming, as sometimes happened. Details of the consultant's room were correct, his manner proper, his message clear: she had terminal cancer; there was nothing he or anyone else could do to save her. So impressive was this that the first two or three bleats of the alarm clock she took for his bleeper. Oh, the relief of realization, of thrusting out a silencing hand. Phew, just a dream.

Then it hit her. Returning to consciousness had by no means put her in the clear. She was indeed sick and might be doomed. The terror was all the worse for following so hard on relief. She began to whimper, half expected her mother to come rushing in, so large was her fear, so shrunken and infantilized was she beside it.

She sat up and reached for the familiar packet topped by the familiar lighter on the familiar ashtray. Not there, of course. Last night she'd thrust them away in the bottom of the drinks cabinet, determined to begin a new life minus cigarettes in the morning, with the journey home to distract her from withdrawal pangs. Well, she needed one, couldn't think straight without one. She got out of bed, almost immediately became tangled in a heap of clothes, then tripped over a pile of papers. Half blind (minus her contact lenses at this time of the morning and heaven only knew where she'd dumped her spectacles), she felt her way through the perils of her bedroom. Tidiness had never come to her naturally, neither was any living space ever sufficiently capacious to accommodate her habit of collecting and hoarding printed matter. The sitting room and dining alcove where she entertained people were kept bare and clean, but for many years now her bedroom had been more of a lumber room, betraying her expectation of no-one entering it other than herself. ('Don't expect me to do no good in that bedroom, Miss Nelson,' read the cleaner's regular note, 'not till you've had a good clear out.')

In the sitting room, Nell's hand groped into the cupboard for the familiar stack of smoking things. The little pyramid secured, she made off with it back to bed. After a draw or two, her mind began to function sensibly (it was just an exploratory business at the moment, and if the worst was found to be the case there'd be treatments), but her heart remained unconvinced. She was still shaky, still in peril . . . Right, she admonished, then attend to something else. She pressed the button on her transistor. Get mad with the *Today* team – infuriating bastards usually managed to stir up the old 'go out and bash 'em' instinct. But all she got was *Thought for the Day*, some creepy voiced holy joe droning on about justice. 'That,' announced one of the early morning know-alls, 'was the Right Reverend Richard . . .'

'Oh, bog off,' she snarled, hitting the switch.

189

In her kitchen, Chrissy was getting tough. 'No argument, just do it,' she ordered, jabbing towards her daughters with a bread knife.

'But why can't they both have the spare room? It's big enough, it's enormous.'

'I can't ask them to share.'

'Well, one could have it and the other could have Clare's,' said Joy comfortably. 'That's fair cos she's the youngest. You don't ask Amanda to move.'

'Because Amanda's on the other side of the house, you pillock. I want your two rooms because they're more or less equal. I can't give one of my friends a huge room and the other a much smaller one.'

'They're always coming,' grumbled Clare.

'No they're not. It's been ages.'

'Yes they are. You should let 'em take in turns to have the best room.'

'Why the hell am I arguing?' She chucked down the knife, spread her arms in wonderment. 'Not another word. Finish your breakfasts, then go and clear up. I want an empty drawer, a half empty wardrobe, a cleared dressing table top from both of you. And don't go flinging your things all over the spare room, put them away neatly.' She cut some bread and put it in the toaster.

After a minute's thought, Joy hit back. 'It's sexist. You don't ask the boys to move.'

'And it was pretty sexist of you two bagging those nice rooms in the first place. Shut up about it, or . . .' But they were so smothered in treats and good fortune it was difficult to focus on just one item for withdrawal. 'You'll be sorry,' she ended lamely as the toast popped up.

'What's going on?' asked Tony coming in in his business suit. No-one answered. He stood watching as she swung into action with the frying pan. She was wearing a baggy T shirt and shorts; her hair, or as much of it as would be caught and subdued, was held back by a stretchy velvet ring she'd borrowed from Amanda; no make-up dulled her shiny freckles, she looked exactly as she had all those years ago performing similar tasks in the Sea Gull Café.

'And I hope *you*'re not going to make difficulties or ask me to do things,' she told him. 'You owe me, don't forget – begging me to go on the Inner Wheel Committee – you know those women get on my nerves.'

'I'll be good as gold,' he promised. 'Meek as a lamb.' There was no need for all this totting up, he'd give her anything within reason.

'Right.' But her eyes were still bright with battle fever. 'So long as everyone here understands: the next few days are *mine*.'

'Can't think why you're so aerated. I like you having your chums to stay.'

So he did, up to a point. It was very satisfactory ramming home to his erstwhile enemies how well Chrissy had done by marrying him. Mind you, he thought, they'd only got to look at her and then in the mirror. Despite the make-up and the classy clothes and her obvious belief in the contrary, Nell looked older than her years, her face gone saggy and lined from continually squinting over cigarettes and her bottom spread from too much sitting over typewriters. Liz was still a looker in a quiet sort of way, but she'd certainly let herself down by marrying that engineer. It was a nice little cottage, the Learmans', in a beautiful spot, but it hardly compared with the Fenby-cum-Laithby Rectory. No wonder her dad was dead set against the marriage. Bloke in a million, Alderman Stockdale; put a nice bit of work the Duckenfield way. Knew what he was doing by it, though; probably wished it was Liz who'd become Mrs Duckenfield instead of Chrissy. Fat chance, thought Tony, watching his wife load a plate and bring it towards him. He'd determined on Chrissy at primary school, and she was still the prettiest, liveliest, sparkiest girl in town. And no mean cook, he reflected as an omelette was set in front of him. 'Thanks, pet.'

'Sorry there's no bacon. I'll get some more in today.'

'It's fine,' he insisted, slicing off a piece with his fork; it broke tenderly, moistly. 'Mm, beautiful.'

Liz was between patients when the receptionist put her head round the door. 'Your daughter phoned. I told her you were tied up. She asked if you'd ring back.'

'Thanks, Molly.' Heart thumping, she raised the receiver.

'Oh, Mum,' cried Rosie, sounding breathless. 'Thanks ever so for the money. It's really nice of you.'

Gladness flooded, and relief. 'That's OK. I know it's a problem for you, getting about.'

'Yeah, thanks. Um, I don't think I'll manage tonight, by the way. But you and Dad have a nice time; enjoy yourselves.'

'We will,' promised Liz lightly. 'Perhaps see you afterwards? I expect I'll leave early in the morning.'

'Yeah, see you afterwards,' she said. Then added, 'Love you, Mum.'

'Love you too, darling,' said Liz, and Rosie rang off.

Liz replaced the receiver slowly, then sat looking at it, anxious in case she'd sounded surprised saying 'Love you too'. Lord, she was an idiot, always needing something to worry about. Impatiently, she thrust back her chair, rose, went to the door. A patient was waiting in the corridor. 'Mrs Hanslope,' she invited warmly. 'Do come in. Sorry to have kept you.'

South of Sheffield, Nell turned the hired car off the motorway into the service station car park. It was almost full; she drove through the rows looking not for a space but for the entrance to the eating area. Several free places here, due to rationing 'disabled' signs. Into one of these Nell unhesitatingly drove; sprang out, locked the car door – smiling vaguely (to convey short-sightedness) at a man who was watching – and made a beeline for the concrete steps leading to the ladies'.

Made comfortable again, she proceeded to the eating area, passing a darkened hall full of grunting, flashing machines and screen-struck wordless youth. Beyond wide open doors there was a shop and a self-service restaurant. The shop window display made her think of taking something to Chrissy. She went through the turnstile, her resolve turning to doubt when she met pastel china ornaments, cut-glass vases, ribboned chocolate boxes, country scene toiletries. 'Brontë Biscuits' announced a tasteful package. She imagined Charlotte frowning down, pouting her fleshy lips. Oh, go on then – after all, there were half a dozen junior Duckenfields, and Chrissy would eat anything. She took down a box and made for the check-out where a line of people waited, listlessly clutching newspapers and sandwiches and sweets – and ice cream and cold drinks likely to become runny cream and warm drinks by the time they were paid for. Leaving one foot in the queue to reserve her place, she strained over to reach copies of her own newspaper and two others.

In the restaurant she bought a cup of coffee and carried it to the smoking area. She lit up absently, deliberately not noticing what her hands and mouth were up to as she scanned the newspapers. After a time she raised her head and met the gaze of a man a few tables away. Unflinchingly, she stared back, made a point of doing so; it made her mad the way men indulged their curiosity as of right but it was somehow instilled into women to deny themselves a similar freedom unless chaperoned by a man. Soon the man looked away. Nell's attention wandered. These terrible places, she thought as she usually did, no attempt made to screen off the roaring road, no real possibility of five minutes' peace. Stubbing out her cigarette, she rose, gathered bag and Brontë biscuits and went to find her car.

193

A few miles further north, she turned east on the M18. Easy driving now; miles of uncluttered road. Barely an hour later she caught her first glimpse of the dock tower. Home, she thought, and then told herself roughly that it wasn't her home, her parents being dead and her siblings scattered, that she wasn't even born in the place, that she hadn't lived in it for nearly thirty years. New developments appeared on both sides of the road, factories and sky-soaring pipes of the processed food industry. Once, the town had exuded a fishy saltiness; you could tell which bus route you were travelling on simply by the smell's strength, for the clothes of everyone connected with the docks, from porters to smartly suited office workers, were imbued with the familiar odour. Now, it was oven-ready chips and onion-laced beefburgers coming at her through the car's air vents. She snapped them shut; jumped on the brake – what the hell? Oh, a new roundabout, and – good Lord – a fly-over. But where was the Victorian tram shed? Where *was* it? She scanned the view with the indignation of a returning native fearing developers have been on the loose. *There* it was, almost hidden by a ghastly new shopping complex – all the usual horrors, names made famous in TV jingles stamped luridly on hangar-like buildings of painted metal, black glass. Everywhere the same these days, she thought savagely, moving into the lane marked 'town centre'.

She'd been back several times before, of course, but had always made straight for Chrissy's, cutting out the town, driving the last twenty miles of the journey via a country route. Today, she drove cautiously down a new wide route bordered by multi-storey car parks, wracking her brains to recall what had been here before, startled by sudden glimpses of the familiar.

The Grand, she found, had a modern bit stuck on the back, in fact, the modern bit probably formed the greater part and was built over the car park. She stowed the car, pulled out her bags, made for the nearest door.

Down anonymous corridors, through silently swinging fire doors, into the old part, the Grand proper. On her right she glimpsed the dining room. A memory pounced – Bertie had brought her here, her first meal in a posh restaurant. She checked in at reception using her real name without a qualm – they were too slow in this neck of the woods to make connections, too humble to envisage visits from the famous. Her meagre unpacking accomplished, she set off on foot to stretch her legs and discover what was left of the old place.

Not a lot. The town had been comprehensively 're-developed'. It had apparently not occurred to its inhabitants that razing to the ground all the quaint unique buildings and erecting in their place the ubiquitous shopping mall and office block might be neither inevitable or desirable. Local businessmen and professional advisors like Mr Tony Duckenfield had enriched themselves in the process. The Old Butter Market had been obliterated, ditto the Bull Ring. Only the parish church still stood – but in a sea of concrete bounded by shops hawking cheap jewellery, furry furniture, second-hand clothes, the latest sounds – and one or two isolated trees encased in paving slabs reprieved from the former churchyard. The old church was as ill at ease as a beached whale. She averted her gaze from it, looked over the road and spied to her surprise a window full of press photographs. Of course – the *Telegraph*'s uptown office. She crossed over impatiently, smiled in at the window. Just think: from this crummy little outfit sprang her amazing career. Jeff Hutchings, editor, gave her her first proper assignment (as a favour to his chum and fellow Rotarian, Alderman Bertie Stockdale, no doubt. But why quibble? Didn't she do a fantastic job?)

Her dreamy smile vanished, her eyes came almost wide. There in front of her in glossy black and white (on the Grand's staircase if she wasn't mistaken) stood Chrissy: Chrissy as never before viewed and certainly never imagined, Chrissy as in an ad for hairspray, or possibly one for tights or leg-hair depilatory, or for toothpaste – fair do's, it was a brilliant smile; a faintly *passé* image of bouffant glamour, what this town really goes for, Nell guessed. Well, well, well. And little Tony with his paw on her arm. Nice one, Quacker. She squinted through the glass to note the photograph's number, went inside.

Two men stood at the far end of the room looking at something on the counter, discussing it. Local hacks, she thought, or possibly hack plus photographer. She cleared her throat, drew herself up. Would they salute her? Would they heck-as-like. Their eyes glancing over her prompted no halt in their conversation. This isn't London, she reminded herself, it's not Manchester, not even Leeds; just a bloody backwater.

The girl on the desk, who had been taking down a customer's ad for the classified section, now turned her attention to Nell.

'Um, a photograph in the window, number 19. It's a friend of mine. I'd like to surprise her.'

'Number 19,' echoed the girl, looking through a drawer. 'Oh yes, the Rotarian dinner. Why, it's Mrs Duckenfield.'

'You know her?'

'Not *know* her,' said the girl, slipping the photograph into an envelope, taking Nell's money, 'not as such. But her photo's often in the *Telegraph*. She's one of those you can't help noticing.'

Mm, thought Nell, know what you mean. We're all Pavlov's dogs: stick a pretty face on a page and our eyes zoom to it, never mind the headlines alongside of earthquakes and disasters.

'I always think,' the girl said, handing Nell her change, 'Mrs Duckenfield looks like somebody.'

'Herself, possibly?'

'Oh, yeah,' she chuckled. 'But you know what I mean – *somebody*.'

Nell closed her bag and went out into the street.

She was hungry. Where to eat? There used to be a good place over the river behind the shops, she remembered, also a decent pub in Bartholomew Street. But suddenly she was too weary to go in search and turned back to the hotel. In the lounge she ate a smoked salmon sandwich, drank a glass of mineral water and glanced through last night's *Telegraph*. After a coffee and a cigarette she felt strong again, decided to drive around, look up old haunts – usually she didn't bother, so it would make a change which might prove interesting.

It came to her during a purposeful drive towards the other end of town along the old bus route to the bathing pool (after initial hesitation and accidentally driving twice round the one-way system), that she was searching for something, for the nub of her feeling that here was 'home'. Well, the top end of town certainly wasn't home, the Grand and the shops and the newspaper office and the poor jettisoned parish church; she hadn't even bothered to cross the little bridge over the river to examine once more the former granaries and warehouses which had become bars and night spots and the one good restaurant. Ten minutes' drive brought her to the dock area and the backstreets where she'd walked as a girl. Maud Street almost went by without her noticing; just in time she swung off the main road and parked outside her former home. Nothing changed here (other than the addition of a few parked, clapped-out looking cars), the dock wall at the end of the road, the broken bits and pieces littering tiny front gardens, the rickety looking front doors, the window surrounds shedding plaster; no 'redevelopment', certainly no improvement. She remembered her father staggering drunkenly over the road and the night he'd yanked her inside by the hair, remembered her sister Marion gracefully sauntering up to the house as if about to enter a bijou residence; remembered bringing Chrissy and Liz here, inveigling them inside with her drawing ability, holding their attention with her skill, for

197

the house had little else to offer. With an uneasy rush of irritation, she also thought of her mother and how, because her father had made a practice of bullying her, she, Nell, had somehow needed to follow suit. Allying myself with the strong, she diagnosed now with some disgust – not disgust for her younger self, but for the father who'd been unworthy of the alliance and for the mother whose weakness had prompted her into it. One thing – she could look at the house and state truthfully, hand on heart, that here was not 'home'. It was empty to her, meant nothing. She made a five-point turn cursing the street's narrowness, turned back on to the main road.

Soon she turned into a better quality area, avenues of tall semis, eventually Lister Avenue, and drew up outside number 142. Poor Auntie Julie, she thought, hoping to conjure up the lady by staring at the bay windows. But these were quite the wrong windows, for Auntie Julie had dwelt at the back; up there was Chrissy's room where she and Liz would sometimes hide for the night. She began to feel, not at home exactly, but warmer, on firmer ground. Gently she drove on, at the traffic lights turned left towards the sea front.

Slow going here, crowds of holiday-makers wandering in the road, eating, fooling, spilling out of shops selling sticks of rock, rude postcards, fish and chips. The bathing pool was gone, as Chrissy had explained it was now a leisure centre; no doubt young Amanda was somewhere inside cavorting in front of an exercise class. Depressing idea. She pressed the accelerator neglecting to glance right to check whether there was still a Winter Gardens. The boating lake went by, then, as had always happened at this point, the sea front began to peter out, a pathetic little miniature railway the only sign of progress between the dunes. But, oh golly, that black shack – wasn't it . . .? Yes, for there was the name painted roughly in white: the blessed

Sea Gull Café. She pulled on to the rough parking ground in front and sat shaking her head, then switched off the engine and lit a cigarette; after a time found 'Cherry pink and apple blossom white' unaccountably playing in her head. Frowning she flicked ash out of the window, decided to move on.

Where now? Wold Enderby, of course. She chose the route carefully so as to avoid going through Fenby-cum-Laithby by mistake and encountering any roaming Duckenfields.

The village was even more attractive than she remembered, there was a new housing estate on its edge, but the village proper was unspoilt, spruced up if anything, particularly the smaller cottages. Of course, The Mount was not an ancient house; built in the thirties, she supposed. She left the car outside the church and went to find it.

Oh, but it was lovely: roses round the tall windows, creeper on the gable end, long smooth lawns, deep flower beds, and an orchard, still, beyond. Memories came in waves making her giddy. She leaned against the wall and peered at the steps to the front door across the drive. 'Hurry up, mustn't keep Daddy waiting,' she heard Mrs Stockdale say, and saw three girls ushered forward by a stout matron. On the top steps Bertie waited (Alderman Stockdale as she had known him then), mind-blowingly handsome in his dinner suit (handsome like Jack Hawkins hadn't somebody said?), waiting to drive her and Chrissy home. Then jumping into the enormous car, watching out of the back window as Liz performed a mime show to give them an uproarious send-off.

Phew, how she'd lusted after this place. Her heart was going like the clappers. Was this it? Was chez Stockdale 'home'? She was stuffed to the gills with fond remembrance. But no, she decided, it was more the house of dear close relatives. Heigh-ho – perhaps 'home' couldn't be pinned down, was diffuse.

Thoughtfully, she drove back, but instead of returning to the top end of town and the Grand, steered once more in the direction of the sea front area. This time, she drove past the schools, first by what used to be the boys' grammar school and was now a comprehensive, then by the former girls' grammar. Here, she turned into a tree-lined side road and parked beside the hockey field. She got out, walked to the front of the school, stood gazing at the windows of the various classrooms she'd sat in. No emotion stirred until she raised her eyes to the windows at the top of the building. The library. Good Lord – even as a schoolgirl she'd been looking for some sort of 'home'. Or was it just that she and Liz and Chrissy had spent a lot of time trying to stow away together?

At the top of the road where she had left the car were the gates to the cemetery. Her steps, as she went towards them, began to quicken.

They've got children, she thought, as she went along the path between the graves, and husbands; people who really care about them. Leaves in the beech hedge were already turning colour, birds darted urgently in overhanging branches. She took a wrong turning, felt foolish, for she had only the vaguest memory of the grave she sought. It had a figure over it, didn't it? Maybe an angel. She set off down another path, feeling conspicuous though there was no-one about. On the point of giving up, the grave suddenly loomed before her. The years vanished in a flash; it was only yesterday that she and Liz and Chrissy had squatted on these steps under – yes, she remembered now – the guardian angel.

She longed to go and crouch there now, but wouldn't allow it. Instead, she lit a cigarette, folded arms over chest, studied the memorial. I'm not the odd one out, she thought. When something threatens them they don't go running to their husbands or their children; they do as I do, summon the other two. We're the same; we may not seem so, but inside we're still the old firm, the triangle. She inhaled deeply and wondered, is this 'home', this place where we hatched plots and schemed the future and tried to make sense of life? I do believe it is.

4
VIRGINITY – GETTING SHOT OF IT

i

I don't have to go, Liz thought, with difficulty eating toast at seven fifteen in the morning. Departing members of her family she could wave off with a light heart – it was their decision to go; if as a consequence they got smashed up on the motorway she would be devastated, but it would not be *her fault.* Setting off on her own initiative, deliberately leaving Nathan, abandoning Rosie, reckless without Jon given an opportunity to stay her, was a different matter – wilful, one might even say wicked, chancing the family well-being for her own gratification. These were her pre-journey feelings (too involuntary to be called 'thoughts') as she sat glumly pushing toast down her too-dry throat.

She rose, took her plate to the waste bin, emptied it of toast. Holding a mug of tea, she stood staring out of the window, telling herself that once on the road these unreasonable feelings would dissipate, as usual.

Goodbyes had been said last night: Nathan had no need to be up before eight and she'd decided on an early start, having in a weak moment telephoned the Fairfields Nursing Home to say that as she would be passing by the town today she'd drop in for lunch with Mrs Stockdale – though what destination could possibly take her near such an out of the way place she had not yet applied her mind to. Might as well see her before you go to Chrissy's, she'd told herself, then you won't have to make a special trip till Christmas.

She carried her bags out to the car, hesitated. It was no good, the chances were overwhelmingly against crashing, but just in case . . . Through the kitchen she ran, up the stairs, into the bedroom. Nathan was sitting on the edge of the bed in his pyjamas, scratching and yawning his head off. 'Love you,' she said, giving him a hug.

'You came all the way up here to say that? Very nice of you, not everyone bothers.'

'Fool,' she laughed, punching him, and was able, after all, to drive off grinning broadly.

'Telephone,' cried Chrissy, raising her head to the rafters. Surely one of them would answer. But no – as usual they were all waiting for some other member of the family to shift themselves. Her fat-and-flour larded fingers hesitated over the pastry bowl. She'd ignore it; bound to be for one of the kids. But what if . . . Oh no, not with all this food prepared, she thought, grimly and inadequately scraping the fingers of her right hand against the bowl's rim. Gingerly she raised the receiver between tips of thumb and middle finger. 'Yes?'

'Chrissy,' began Nell, confirming her friend's fears.

'Don't say you're not coming.'

'Calm down, petal, I'm virtually on your doorstep. Just wondered what time you expect Liz.'

'I see.' One annoyance assuaged, another materialized – she hadn't bargained on a lunch guest today.

'Don't worry, shan't embarrass you by turning up early. Thought I'd aim to be there to welcome her, that's all.'

'I suppose you could come for lunch, as you're so nearly here.'

'Wouldn't hear of it.'

'Well, if you're sure. Liz is lunching with Mrs S at the nursing home.'

'That's nice.'

'Getting it over with, is how she put it. A bit awkward for me – I swore blind Liz wouldn't be coming here for ages – you know, trying to let her off the hook.'

'Can't think why Liz makes such a song and dance.'

'Yes you can. You weren't exactly keen on yours. Anyway, she said she'll be here sometime after three.'

'Then shall I arrive sometime after two?'

'Fine. That'll be great.'

'See you, chum.'

'See you,' replied Chrissy, dropping the receiver, viewing with dismay how fatty crumbs were everywhere.

'Mum?' Clare cried, running in.

'Huh,' said Chrissy. 'Typical.'

'Hello, Mummy.'

Mrs Stockdale watched her daughter walking towards her across the Axminster and wondered where she'd gone wrong. The girl looked like one of those women you saw on Channel Four if you weren't careful, the sort who burn their bra. No effort made – jeans, T-shirt, hanging hair. She recalled Chrissy the other afternoon – her pretty print skirt, buoyant curls, bright lips – a sight for sore eyes (as Mr Hartington had commented afterwards). 'Hello, Elizabeth, you do look pasty. Are you sure you're eating properly?' A finicky attitude to food was half the trouble, of course; always faddy as a child, not like Chrissy who'd relished a bit of home cooking, poor lass. It might have done madam a service to have swapped places with her little friend for a while, see how she fared with that awful aunt.

'It's lovely to see you, dear,' Mrs Garth was saying tearfully.

(Mrs Garth was becoming a bit of an embarrassment, liable to dampness in more than one department, as Mrs Stockdale had confided to Mrs Entwhistle.) 'Sit down,' she urged.

'I'll pop along – leave you to talk to Mummy . . .'

'No, stay, Ada,' Mrs Stockdale commanded generously. 'I dare say you'll be interested in Elizabeth's news.' For herself, she had no great hopes, her daughter had an irritating habit of removing the shine from even creditable information. 'How did Rosie do?'

'Um, well, thank you; she was quite pleased with herself.'

'Neil Duckenfield got two Bs and a C in his mocks, Chrissy said. By golly that Chrissy's a good little mother – and if it's old fashioned of me to say so, I'm sorry but I stand by it. Well, what did Rosie *get*?'

'Um, three As. She was quite surprised. So were we.'

'Why didn't you say so in the first place?' cried Mrs Stockdale, torn between exasperation and pride. 'Did you hear that Ada? – Rosie got three As. Mrs Entwhistle's grandson got one A and two Bs; from the way she was going on at breakfast the other day, you'd think he was a genius. That *is* good news. I shall have to send Rosie a little present. I hope she's going to make something of herself, use her talents sensibly.' And not in some faintly disreputable and financially unrewarding occupation like her mother's, she had no need to add.

'It's early days.'

'But she'll go to Durham like Jon?'

'Perhaps. She's thinking of taking some time off first. You heard,' she asked, turning to Mrs Garth, 'about Jon and Sushma getting engaged? They hope to marry in the spring.'

'Oh – lovely,' nervously quavered Mrs Garth.

'And how are you both? I must say, they seem to look after you here; it feels very comfortable.'

'How we feel,' answered Mrs Stockdale, 'depends very much on Cook. She has her off-days. I said to Matron, braised lamb's all very fine and good, but not twice in one week; dumplings tend to lie very heavy. Variety's the spice of life, I said, never mind being too handy with the pepper pot. You'll be all right today, though,' she confided, parting her elephantine knees in order to lean forward, 'it's a roast.'

A sated feeling came over Liz, panic that she would be unable to swallow a thing. 'Let's take a stroll in the garden; it's such a lovely day.'

'After lunch,' Mrs Stockdale said firmly. 'We like a turn in the afternoon, weather permitting, don't we, Ada? Otherwise we've no appetite for tea.'

Liz opened her bag and began hunting in it. 'Some photos to show you – in here somewhere – of when Jon and Sushma came. Oh yes, here we are: taken on Bewick Moor – Sushma fooling with Nathan, and one of me on a stile with Jon.'

'Very nice,' said Mrs Stockdale politely, keeping the photographs at arm's length.

ii

Virginity's a subject they've begun to think about a lot. On the whole, despite recommendations from Milton, Shakespeare and Edmund Spenser, it's not an attractive notion. They watch Miss Cummings go starry-eyed as, hand pressed to breast-bone, she stoutly intones,

> No savage fierce, bandit or mountaineer,
> Will dare to soil her virgin purity.
> Yea, there where very desolation dwells,
> By grots and caverns shagged with horrid shells,
> She may pass on with unblenched majesty . . .
> No goblin or swart faery of the mine
> Hath hurtful power o'er true virginity.

and fierce desire nags their guts to dissociate from any such sentiments.

'Do you not think,' asks Miss Cummings one day, peering mistily and kindly over her spectacles, 'that all women possess a degree of beauty; that womanhood is of itself beautiful?'

Gosh, no, they gasp, squirming at the very images

conjured by 'womanhood' – features buried in fleshiness, waddling ungainliness, lack of spirit, lack of fun, domesticity. They think of mothers and aunts, neighbours and spinster teachers. Definitely not.

Miss Cummings looks disappointed.

After school, dodging the caretaker, they sneak into the library, sit whispering in one of the bays between the bookshelves, staring out of the window. Sometimes, looking down, they spy those elderly virgins, Miss Cummings and Miss Henry, crossing over the road hugging piles of books to their bosoms before disappearing down a side-street towards the little terraced house they share. Miss Cummings is the less repellent of the two (visually speaking), her hair worn in a soft bun, her face smooth; it's her friend, Miss Henry (head of Science), who's the real frightener (shouldn't like to meet her in the cut on a dark night, drawls Nell), with mannish cropped hair, ginger moustache and a shape, give or take some lumpy undulations, that's more or less cuboid. Miss Cummings and Miss Henry are two of half a dozen older members of staff, all single, who are graduates of Bedford or Westfield Colleges. Stored up virginity is enough to give you the creeps, think the watching girls. Fatal to delay too long before getting shot of it.

They spend hours in one another's bedrooms, in the cemetery, in the library, debating the optimum moment for disposal – also with whom and in what manner. Some girls are obviously too precipitate (Cheryl Lester is cited as an example), some make a right mess of it (Cheryl again), and loads of women, probably the majority, squander themselves on undeserving men; though when they really get down to it, a deserving man is hard to name. Only one male of their acquaintance can they nominate with confidence and enthusiasm. 'You're so lucky,' sighs Nell, waving her cigarette over Liz like a holy water sprinkler. 'God, I wish it were me.'

'But,' begins Liz.

'Not just "lucky",' objects loyal Chrissy, 'after all, Liz found him, it's her he wants.'

'But we don't actually know he . . .'

'Oh, it's Liz he wants out of all the women in the world. She must be really something.' Head tilted back, eyelids lowered, Nell considers her.

'And it doesn't really matter which one of us it is, because we all sort of share him, you know, through talking and getting to understand and appreciate him.'

'Absolutely.'

Liz's mouth has gone dry. 'But we don't *know* he wants me, not for certain.'

'Of course he does.'

'It's obvious.'

'Is it?' she asks, encouraging them to dispel her doubts, to reiterate all over again how she possesses those special attributes vital as daily bread to a man of Mr Poole's sensibilities.

They duly oblige. Furthermore, thinks Nell, it probably seems a miracle to Mr Poole that he's managed to find her, for there are very few females around of their high quality. Chrissy bets he can hardly believe his luck.

Liz is never sure whether this is a delicious game or something more in earnest. As with all good fantasies, it's important to hang on to a thread of credibility. So she half believes, and bolsters her faith by recalling how he's taken to smiling at her as though they share secrets, how he says specially nice things about her playing and appearance, how he always endorses his wife's invitations to Sunday dinner or Wednesday tea, how on the way to the bus-stop afterwards he confides snippets of information about his history, making her feel she alone is their repository. Even so, her imagination can't take the final leap, can't have him declare himself; it's too enormous, like the world ending in a rainbow-flashing ecstasy-building thunderclap.

Nell foresees the day when Mr Poole will be so overcome that he'll just blurt it out.

'You really really think so?' asks Liz hoarsely.

'Certainly.'

Chrissy nods like a prophet. 'And Nell's almost always right.'

Towards the end of March, high winds stir up the North Sea. Bulging waves break over the shore wall. An ice-cream kiosk is swept away, the amusement arcade is smashed to pieces, seaweed lies strewn in the gutters of side-streets. When the wind dies back, the temperature plummets; snow falls on iced-over pavements.

Mrs Hilary Dowling, hurrying for a number four bus, takes a tumble which re-ignites her sciatica. This is cheering news to Alderman and Mrs Stockdale (who were most put out by Mrs Dowling's recovery, particularly when it was she and not their daughter who accompanied the choir at the Winter Garden concert), and their joy is vindicated when Mr Poole asks Liz to step into the breach for the St John's Thanksgiving Concert. This event, a one-off affair to celebrate the belated completion of a restoration programme following war-time bomb damage, does not have the same prestige as the annual Winter Garden concert; nevertheless, the Stockdales eagerly broadcast the coming event to friends and acquaintances and make certain the *Evening Telegraph* is thoroughly briefed on their daughter's role.

The publicity pleases Mr Poole. 'A charming photograph of you in the *Telegraph* the other night,' he says, giving Liz his skewed-mouth smile. Liz, who had winced at the photograph (and at the article singling her out) is immediately reconciled to having appeared in print.

'What are you going to wear? Have you thought?' asks Mrs Poole during the washing-up after tea before Wednesday evening choir practice. Mr Poole is in the

209

front room giving a piano lesson, Alison in the dining room doing her homework. Putting her head on one side, looking mischievous, Mrs Poole adds, 'Has your mum thought?' (Lately, Liz and Mrs Stockdale have exchanged harsh words. 'Mum's got no idea,' Liz has confided to Mrs Poole, whose trim figure and smart clothes have brought this fact home to her. Not all mothers are frumps.)

Polishing a plate with a teacloth, Liz frowns, for Mrs Stockdale's mind is lodged in the party dress groove – pastel satin, full skirt, bows, puff sleeves, something to emphasize an accomplished daughter's tender youth. 'We've had a row about it. I want something smart that'll fade into the background. I mean, the choir wears black and white, so I think I ought to. Mum says I'm too young for black. Her friend Mrs Garth offered to knit me a white angora jumper – it'll make me itch, I said, put me off my playing. So now Mum's threatening to get her dressmaker to run up a white dress. I've told her I won't wear it. It'll probably have a sash and a princess neck-line. She wants me to look childish to impress her friends, which is showing off, really, it makes me sick. I'm sixteen and a half, and I've a good mind to go out and buy something myself; I could put it on in the ladies just before the concert.'

'Oh dear, poor Liz. Would you like me to have a word with my friend who works in Binns – ask her what she's got, if she'd look out for something?'

'Oh, would you? That'd be great. Anything *you* spot would be perfect.'

Mrs Poole laughs and tips away the washing-up water.

'No, I really mean it.' Of course she does. Mrs Poole, smart in an unflashy sort of way, bright and modern and young looking, couldn't help picking a winner. Even her father's noticed, often makes favourable remarks after calling to pick Liz up from the house or if he's happened to bump into Mrs Poole in town. 'An attractive woman, Mrs Poole. Smart dresser, trim figure, knows how to make the best of herself.' – are some of the things he's said. Because Mrs Poole is laughing at her, she cites her father's opinions as evidence. 'So if I tell him *you*'ve seen just the thing, he's sure to be on my side and back me up against Mum.'

Mrs Poole has stopped wiping down the draining board and is listening intently. The door to the front room opens; Mr Poole ushers out his pupil. 'Ronnie,' she calls, 'come here.'

Mr Poole enters the kitchen, looks from one to the other.

'Tell him what you said, Liz. Go on.'

Liz's heart sinks, she'd much rather not. 'I was only saying how it'd be great if Mrs Poole spotted the right dress for me.'

'Yes, yes, but tell him why. It's because Alderman Stockdale's an admirer of mine. Liz thinks a recommendation from me would go down very well with her father. He thinks I'm attractive, Ronnie. Smart, he said, didn't he, Liz? Trim. Was it just "trim", or "trim figure"?'

'Is it necessary for you to be so vulgar?' sneers Mr Poole, before turning on his heel to hurry upstairs.

'He doesn't like it when it's me getting the compliments,' Mrs Poole tells Liz. 'Must say, though, it's nice to be noticed once in a while.'

Liz, while regretting Mr Poole being drawn into the affair, still regards his wife as her best bet for securing a decent outfit. 'Thank you very much for taking an interest.'

'What? Oh, you mean in your dress. Of course, love, don't worry; I'll pop over to see Shirley tomorrow lunch hour.'

On Sunday after choir practice, as has become the rule, Liz goes to the Poole's for lunch. Mr Poole closes the front door and indicates the sitting room, but Mrs Poole calls her into the kitchen where she's leaning down over the oven basting the roast, her face shiny with heat, her Goray skirt and brown jumper swathed in a white wrap-around apron. The neighbour is lolling back against the door, watching.

'There's something for you to try on upstairs,' says Mrs Poole, closing the oven door. 'You've met Liz Stockdale, haven't you, Pam?'

'Yes,' says Pam, eyeing Liz with disapproval.

'Ronnie's star pupil,' says Mrs Poole. She crinkles her eyes up at Liz. 'In my bedroom. Go on up, there's a full length mirror.'

'Thanks,' says Liz, turning, running upstairs with 'Ronnie's star pupil' ringing in her ears.

She goes gingerly into the room Mrs Poole calls 'my bedroom'. There's a dress lying on the bedspread, in soft grey wool with white linen collar and cuffs. She holds it up. It's perfectly plain, perfectly straight, but around the bottom, starting just above the knees, it's ringed with a circle of fine knife-edged pleating. She sheds skirt and jumper in record time, pulls the dress on over her head. Standing in front of the mirror she knows nothing she's ever worn has suited her better.

A tap on the door. 'Only me,' calls Mrs Poole.

'Oh, come in,' cries Liz, rushing to open it. 'Thank you, thank you.' She spreads out her arms, twirls.

'Suits you – thought it would. It's the new French look.'

'It's gorgeous, perfect, it's really me.'

'Let's hope your mum and dad think so. If they don't, it doesn't matter. Shirley let me have it on appro. Just bring it back on Wednesday.'

'Never,' cries Liz, crossing her arms, hugging the dress to her chest.

Mrs Poole laughs. 'You're so like me at your age – knew just what I wanted, wouldn't be dissuaded. But you're right, it's just the job.'

'Can I phone Daddy to come and pick me up later? Then I can show him and we can fix it up today.'

'Fine by me.'

Later on, when Alderman Stockdale arrives, Liz shoots upstairs and Mrs Poole suggests a drink. 'Cup of tea, or something stronger? I warn you, you may need it, your daughter's got something to show you.'

'In that case . . .'

'Get out the Scotch, Ronnie. Or is it gin, Alderman Stockdale?'

'No, no, right first time.'

'Soda?'

'Just a smidgin.'

'Thought you'd be a Scotch man. Cheers. Well, Li – Elizabeth' (just in time Mrs Poole corrects herself) 'was a bit anxious about what to wear for this concert, and I happened to see this little number in Binns the other day when I popped in to see my friend who works in the dress department.'

'I'm quite sure anything chosen by you, Mrs Poole . . .'

'Hang on, wait till you see it. And if it doesn't suit there's no harm done; I can take it back in the morning.'

'Daddy,' calls Liz from the landing. 'Daddy, are you there?'

Mrs Poole leaps to her feet. The two men and Alison follow her into the hall.

Liz is coming slowly down the stairs.

'My, my, princess, very smart, very tasteful. Got to hand it to you, Mrs Poole, it suits her down to the ground. Your wife has an excellent eye, if I'm permitted to say so, Mr Poole.'

'In this case I must agree,' Mr Poole says heartily.

'Come along, dear lady, I'll write you a cheque.' Alderman Stockdale places a courteous hand on Mrs Poole's waist and ushers her back into the dining room. Evidently he has done with his daughter, who cries out, 'I'll bring down the price ticket,' and chases back upstairs to fetch it from the carrier bag.

When she arrives in the dining room and puts the

213

ticket on the table, Mrs Poole and her father are getting along famously.

'You look smashing, Liz,' whispers Alison. 'Doesn't she, Daddy?'

Where is Mr Poole? She turns, sees him hovering in the hall, goes to join him. 'You, er, do think it's suitable for the concert?'

'It's charming. On you, it's distinguished. You're sure it'll be comfortable to play in?'

Her face falls, goes serious. She hurries into the front room, sits down at the piano, plays through the introduction to one of the concert pieces. 'Yes,' she says, lifting her hands from the piano and smiling with relief. 'It feels fine.'

'When you sit,' reports Alison eagerly, 'all the little pleats fan out . . .'

'Out you go when Liz is practising,' cries Mr Poole, shooing his daughter into the hall; he shuts the door. Looking stern, he comes to stand behind the piano stool. 'Try an arpeggio using the full extent of your arms.'

She flashes through G major, G minor, B flat major, A sharp minor. 'Really, it feels . . .'

His hands come forward, clasp her forearms, draw slowly upwards gaining pressure, pulling her back. When they reach her shoulders, his fingers dig in. 'No tightness anywhere?' he asks, his voice gone strangely thin. 'Important to be perfectly relaxed in the shoulders.'

'No, no tightness,' she chokes. Where it lies against his chest, the back of her head's on fire.

'Good,' he says, setting her abruptly upright; and goes briskly out of the room.

In a moment she hears his rather boisterous laugh ring out, mingling with her father's.

They're frowning at one another in the gloomy passage outside the Head's study, straining to hear what's being

214

said on the other side of the door, hindered in this by the noisy satchel-packing crowd in the sixth-form cloakroom. Losing patience, Chrissy leaps upstairs to remonstrate. 'Can't you shuddup,' she yells, and when they pause and stare, 'Nell's on the carpet; we're trying to listen.' The girls quieten, but giggle and make sarky comments; they think if Monica Nelson's getting carpetted it's no more than she deserves.

Chrissy has rejoined Liz. They can hear something now, all right, but not Nell telling the Head where she gets off (her expressed intention); what they hear is the Head screaming, 'In my entire teaching career . . . such a stubborn, difficult, and, yes, *insolent* . . .'

Liz whispers that she's a good mind to barge in, but Chrissy hangs on to her. Nell would be furious, better to go and wait for her in the library as they promised.

Tossing their heads as they pass the first-floor cloakroom, they continue on up to the second floor. The library is deserted. They sit on opposite sides of a table in their usual bay, staring out of the rain-washed window. Some minutes later, Nell's footsteps sound on the stairs. They brace themselves, suspect that things may become tricky.

Nell flops down beside Chrissy, slaps sheets of paper on to the table, doesn't speak.

'Did she, er, see the point, Nell?'

'Don't say she's insisting on you taking it out.'

Nell looks grim, shakes her head. 'I tried,' she sighs, 'I mean *really tried.*'

Teachers, their sympathetic moans convey – simply hopeless.

'Trouble is,' Nell shrugs, 'she's a hypocrite. Likes to pretend sympathy for the *avant-garde*, reality is, she's as hide-bound as the rest. Began by trying to get round me, put on that smarmy voice, said what a *marvellously* witty and elegant piece of writing it was, unfortunately marred by one small blemish which she

215

was quite confident I would remove, me being a mature sort of gel and having had my little joke on poor Miss Cummings. Then sat waiting with this daft smile on her gob, eyes hard as steel. Wouldn't dream of it, I said. Wouldn't dream of removing a single word. She goes pink, starts on about how such a sharply offensive word leaps at you from the page, distorts the balance. Absolutely, I said, glad you noticed, exactly the effect I was after; quite simply, it's the only possible word at that juncture. I explained how I'd tried 'em all out – the softer swear words and the merely blasphemous. I thought she was getting the point when she completely lost her rag. Bawled her head off, eyes popping – I mean, really went screwy. Screamed that if I didn't remove *that word* she wouldn't print the article. Right-oh, I said, give it us. She flung, I snatched, and I must have just sodded off – can't remember exactly, there was such a din, my head went funny.'

'Crikey, Nell.'

'I could tell from the gleam in her eyes she knew I was right. But there it is. She'd rather sacrifice artistic integrity than face up to a few old fogies. I find that despicable.'

'The school governors might make trouble,' suggests Chrissy.

'And parents,' adds Liz. 'Mine, for instance. If Daddy saw it he'd get straight on the phone.'

'Pathetic,' snarls Nell.

Soothingly, they agree.

'It'll be a useless magazine without your contribution,' says Chrissy. 'Yours is always the best.'

'The only bit with laughs,' sighs Liz. 'God, it'll be all hockey match reports and how the history soc had beans on toast in the Cosy Caf on an outing to Crowland.'

'And poems about the first snowdrop. I suppose,' Chrissy ventures, 'you could cut out the whole of the paragraph – which would still make your point – that you can't allow that section to be ruined. But the rest is so good, it'd be a pity to lose everything.'

Nell looks at her with contempt. Then winces, cups her cheek with a hand.

Toothache, they deduce, averting their eyes. Nell has been bothered by a wisdom tooth coming up in the wrong place for some weeks; tomorrow she has an appointment with the dentist who proposes to dig the tooth out. She's terrified, has had nightmares, has even written a poem about the agony of fear. It suddenly occurs to Liz that Nell's stand over the magazine article may be less a matter of principle, more a diversionary tactic. She *needs* this row, thinks Liz; she's engineered it.

'I need a fag,' says Nell belligerently.

But it's pouring outside, not a day for the cemetery. From the way Chrissy darts a look at her and suggests going to see the X-certificate film at the Regal tonight, Liz knows she's drawn the same conclusion.

'No money,' says Nell. 'Anyway, I've got to finish that essay for Cummings.'

Liz wonders whether now is the moment to give them her news. She's been keeping quiet about it all day in deference to the crisis over Nell's article; now she thinks it might be just the thing to buck Nell up. 'I say, something happened yesterday. Could be significant.'

'You mean with Mr Poole?' Chrissy encourages.

'Don't say you've actually made progress?' sneers Nell, but not without interest.

'You remember I told you Mrs Poole was going to look out a dress for me?'

'Yes?'

'Well, she found a brilliant one – dead straight to just above the knee, then a circle of little pleats. In plain grey, with white collar and cuffs.'

'Mm?'

'Really brilliant. Gosh, she's got flair. Even Daddy

217

says so. Whatever you say, Mrs Poole's got terrific taste.'

Nell brushes this aside. 'Well, she would have, wouldn't she? Otherwise he'd never have married her. The point is, does her taste go far enough?'

'And we know it doesn't,' Chrissy remembers. 'Those awful things she says about the choir and music.'

This is true. Often Liz has been shocked.

'And she only reads *Woman's Own.*'

'Well anyway, Mr Poole liked the dress, too. He said it was distinguished.'

'Er?'

'And charming.'

'Ah.'

'But he wondered whether it'd be comfortable to play in, allow me to move my arms about freely. I thought, crikey, and dashed to the piano. The funny thing was, he shoved Alison out of the room. So then we were alone, see? Anyway, I had a bit of a play and told him it was fine. Then, then . . .'

'Yes?'

'Well, he's standing behind me, when, suddenly, his two hands take hold of my arms, then slowly, slowly, start creeping up; and when they get to my shoulders, his fingers dig in like talons. *Squeeze.*' Nell bites a knuckle, Chrissy gasps. 'And he pulls me right back till my head's jammed into him.'

They fall, groaning, over the table.

'Come and show us,' demands Nell, recovering.

Liz goes to stand behind Nell, gives her a demonstration. Chrissy demands similar treatment.

'Hang on a mo,' says Nell when Chrissy's head is resting on Liz's breast bone. 'Chrissy's too tall and you're too small. Change places.'

They do as they're told. 'Right, when he'd got your head back like that, what did you do?'

'Nothing,' says Liz, surprised.

'Nothing? My God, if you'd just looked up, you twit,'

(she jabs a hand under Liz's chin and hoicks up her head) 'he'd probably have leaned over and kissed you.'

Chrissy springs away. Liz rushes back to her chair.

'Should she have done?' wonders Chrissy, sitting down.

'Not *necessarily*,' decides Nell (and Liz lets out a sigh of relief). 'What did happen next?'

'He let go of me and went out of the room. Then I heard him laughing with the others. It made me feel sort of awful, that.'

'P'raps he couldn't stand the disappointment. Next time,' Nell warns, 'be ready for him.'

'I'll try,' promises Liz, knowing she never will. After a moment's silence, she has a bright idea. 'Why don't you two come to the concert?'

'Great thinking,' says Chrissy. 'We could study him.'

'I can get you tickets, or you could come with my parents.'

'We'll come on our own,' decides Nell. 'We don't want to be distracted.'

St John's hall is the largest, best appointed church hall in the district, twice the size and with better facilities than the hall belonging to the parish church in the town centre. This is because St John's hall was rebuilt from scratch after the war, large enough to be used for worship during the more prolonged restoration of the church next door, comfortable enough to attract bookings for entertainments and functions. Tonight's audience contains music lovers, supporters of the choir, parishioners, civic dignitaries, members of the clergy, and representatives of town organizations. Alderman and Mrs Stockdale are in their element – so many people to nod and wave to, and, of course, they have seats in the specially reserved section which consists of the four front rows. It's first come first served in the rest of the hall. Chrissy and Nell were here early to claim seats bagged by Liz with her music case and

219

a volume of Milton's *Poetical Works*. She's chosen seats at the side of the hall so her friends will see Mr Poole's profile when he signals to the choir's extremities and not just his back, which would be the case if they sat more centrally. And she's chosen seats on her side of the hall so they can watch his special gestures to her at the piano. Chrissy and Nell have been sitting here quietly, not speaking, for over twenty minutes. With expressionless faces they've watched scores of entrances, including the Stockdales'. So far they haven't managed to identify Mrs Poole and Alison, largely due to their reluctance to turn round. 'Have you seen her yet?' growls Nell at intervals, and Chrissy turns her head briefly. 'No,' she whispers. Perhaps they won't recognize her, they've only got Liz's description to go on. In any case, they're here to study Mr Poole.

The choir files in. Liz slips to the piano stool. Then, to polite applause, a not very tall, not at all handsome man sweeps in. 'Sweeps' is what he does, decides Nell, who has always mentally reserved this word for women in evening dresses; she's never seen a man move so briskly, firmly, seamlessly. They stare at his dark suited back with crushing disappointment. However, certain facets emerge, glimmers of what Liz might be getting at. For instance, a commanding power. The smallest movements of his hands produce stunning results: the choir rises as one person, draws one breath, belts out a chord; a look to Liz and there's a fair old racket from the piano, too; some rousing singing, then quietness and a sweet sounding solo from a woman whose looks don't live up to her voice; then he motions the choral voices back in, softly, stealthily, and there's a passage of heart-rending harmony during which Nell and Chrissy catch him in pained ecstasy with his eyes shut. They dig their elbows into one another. 'Crikey,' breathes Nell.

During the interval, people stand about and chat, buy coffee from the hatchway at the side of the hall.

Chrissy and Nell remain seated. Mrs Stockdale stays put but swivels about a great deal as people come up to kiss her cheek and chat. 'You know that's our little girl at the piano?' they hear her ask more than once. Alderman Stockdale stands talking with a group of men in the aisle. Chrissy wonders whether a woman squeezing past holding the hand of a pale girl with thin plaits might be Mrs Poole. 'You remember what Liz said about *jolie madame*?' she says, nudging Nell, indicating. They study her – her shapely rust-brown suit, her short wavy hair with auburn lights, her shiny red mouth – looking for points to scoff at. It's not easy. 'Probably isn't her,' Nell says.

But it is. A voice they recognize confirms it. Alderman Stockdale's effusions are peppered with 'dear lady', his hand finds frequent occasion to touch her arm and back, he stoops gallantly to exchange words with Alison. It's all rather depressing.

At the concert's close they're pounced on by Mrs Stockdale.

'Why, you two girls. Elizabeth didn't say you were coming. You could've sat with us. I'm afraid they're having a little do afterwards, just the singers and Elizabeth and Mr Poole, so it's no use waiting. But Elizabeth's daddy could run you home.'

'It's all right, we're getting the bus,' says Chrissy quickly.

'Are you, dear? Where *is* Alderman Stockdale?'

'Over there with Mrs Poole,' says Nell.

'Oh, yes. Well, goodbye girls.'

The crowd thins. Liz comes running, grabs their arms, leads them to an empty corner. 'Well, what did you think? It's *him*, isn't it – Lycidas?'

'A bit old for Lycidas,' objects Nell. 'His hair's grey.'

'But Liz told us about that and you said it didn't matter,' Chrissy points out. 'It's what he's like inside that counts, his poetic soul.'

'Mm, I suppose bits of it fit: *Who would not sing for*

221

Lycidas?' Nell quotes thoughtfully. 'They sang for him like stink.'

'But did you see his face?' asks Liz. 'The passion he puts into it?'

'Oh, we did. And I liked the way he swept on and off, no messing.'

'And when they clapped he didn't smirk – not like that awful singer – just looked grave . . .'

'Spent . . .'

'Exhausted but dignified.'

'Then cleared off. That was rather fine, I thought.'

'I knew you'd feel it,' cries Liz with shining eyes. 'I'm so glad you've seen him at last.'

'We've seen *her*, too,' says Chrissy. 'She doesn't look at all artistic.'

'But she may have sex appeal,' thinks Nell – ominously to Liz and Chrissy, 'if your dad fawning over her is anything to go by.'

'Oh, that's just Daddy.'

'And Mr Poole wouldn't fall for anything so cheap,' declares Chrissy.

'Heavens, no,' agrees Liz. 'He needs to be inspired. He needs . . .'

'A soul mate.'

Liz stares at them, thrilled.

'See you. We've got to go for the bus.'

'Hope it's a good party.'

'Ring us tomorrow if there's any news.'

'If there's any progress at all.'

'Oh, I will,' vows Liz. 'I will.'

Liz is high on universal love. She's like a puff-ball cloud in an azure sky, wafted, shone on. These people, the St John's Singers adore her, she adores them, they adore one another. There's lots of well-laced fruit punch being drunk, though Liz is sticking to lemonade. Everyone in the room has congratulated her, petted her, teased and joshed her. Also, the choir's leader made a pretty speech praising Mr Poole and everyone drank his health. Never was there more friendly, jovial company. She's still exuberant when Mr Poole escorts her through the moonlit park on the way to his house where her parents are being entertained by Mrs Poole while they wait to take her home.

'This is the happiest day of my life,' she cries, gambolling along the main route through the park, swinging her music case in high, over-arm circles.

He laughs, grabs her free hand as though to calm her down, but hangs on to it. After a few seconds, still clasping her hand, he bends his arm upwards squeezing her forearm into his side. They continue along the path, linked fast together.

Really, it's a very awkward linking. Initially, she's stunned by it, remembers to be thrilled by it – won't Nell and Chrissy go wild? At the same time she can't dispel a sneaky feeling of embarrassment. The trouble with it is, it's ungainly, pulls her over, gives her a touch of Hop-Along Cassidy. To cover her embarrassment and protect him from the idea that he may have ever so slightly bungled, she prattles on gaily about the concert and how everyone loved it and what super marvellous people the St John's Singers are. He laughs a bit, says little. Just hangs on to her.

Suddenly, without warning, he steps off the main route on to a narrow tributary path, and from there to a path screened by tall conifers encircling a huge ornamental flower bed.

She falls silent. Nell's prophesy is about to come true: he's going to kiss her; he's marching her round and round this deserted garden looking for a likely spot. Her heart bangs in her chest as she waits for him to do it. Here's where it'll happen, she thinks more than once, but still he marches her on. When they arrive back at the entrance to the circular garden she's relieved as well as let down. Then she's confused as he begins a second tour. Sometimes they speak, mostly they proceed in silence. She can't imagine what's holding him up; there's no-one about.

Halfway round a third circling, he stops and swings her round to face him, takes her music case, drops it, clamps his mouth on to hers. The kiss goes on and on; she wonders whether it's bad form to breathe, wishes she'd checked this point with Nell who did a lot of kissing with Mogsy. Also, the kiss is disappointing, not at all the melting fusion she'd imagined, more of a dental clash and soon (to her horror) an oral probe. When it ends, he stands back, seems uncertain. She waits for his declaration, the words to make everything fine and wonderful and banish her reservations. When he says nothing at all, she's so mortified by the omission, she rushes to save him from it by saying it herself. 'I love you.'

He gives a laugh, more disbelieving than amused.

'I do, I do,' she cries, full of indignation and fright.

'Come here, then.' This time the kiss nearly breaks her head off. She's bent over backwards, her body rammed into his. Unbelievably, his hand comes under her coat, under her demure little dress even, finds and clasps her buttocks.

'What's the matter?' (She's gone rigid with shock.)

Not liking to draw attention to what his hand is doing, she says nothing, goes limp.

A grinding of his pelvis against her stomach goes on and on. She stares up at the moon riding high above; it's winking nursery-book face looks lop-sided tonight as though preoccupied with far more important matters than anything happening to Liz Stockdale. Part of her is crying babyishly, another part is determined to exact some positive outcome from all this to report to Chrissy and Nell. When he at last relaxes his hold, she asks – almost like establishing the price of something: 'You do love me too?'

'Yes,' he answers after only a small hesitation (taken in order to get his breath back, she convinces herself).

'Because I love you.'

'Do you?'

'Surely you know? Surely when I've, when . . .' Her crying part is threatening a take over.

'Then promise you'll get out of school one afternoon next week and come to the house.'

'All right, then. Monday if you like, when I've got free periods.'

'Good girl.' He kisses her gently and she feels rather better.

Completing the walk through the park, he holds her hand in a pleasantly relaxed fashion, sometimes giving it a squeeze, swinging their arms between their bodies. His voice to her is tender. Her spirits rise, she starts to correct her impression of what has gone before. Under a street lamp he looks her critically up and down. 'Taking a last lingering look before we go indoors to face the others,' is how she will account for this to Nell and Chrissy.

'Don't forget your promise. Two o'clock, Monday?'

'I won't forget,' she vows.

The light in the Pooles' hall is like a search light. She shies from it, finds the only eyes she can meet with ease are those of the over-excited Alison.

'That child should be in bed,' snaps Mr Poole.

'And bed's where my little girl ought to be,' says Mrs Stockdale, 'from the look of her.'

'Come along, princess.' Her father's arm round her shoulders guides her out to the car.

On the journey home she can't recall saying 'good night' to Mr Poole, can't remember where he was when they left, can't remember seeing him.

iii

The Old Rectory was just as Nell remembered it – well, it would be, wouldn't it? – with Chrissy vetoing every fashionable fad and property enhancer (Spanish-style

225

patio, mock-Victorian conservatory, Hollywood swimming pool) for which eager little Tony had been keen to whip out his cheque book; the kids could have any amount of expensive indulgences so long as they were erected in the back of the house or the outbuildings or discreetly in the paddock; for Chrissy, the rectory must remain as she first clapped eyes on it as a thirteen-year-old hiding in the shrubbery.

She parked in the drive in front of the house, got out of the car. Chrissy in her sandals came running across the lawn, clopping over the gravel – 'Hi . . .ya,' – Nell waited – 'Oh, Nell,' – and was roundly hugged.

'Greetings,' said Nell coolly, smoothing herself down, and Chrissy laughed and grabbed a case.

'Come on. Same room as before, OK?'

'Anywhere.' She followed her on to the lawn, a bemused look on her face, thinking, I still can't believe this is legit. 'Do you ever half expect someone to come and throw you out?' she asked, stepping through the sitting-room french windows, then, not waiting for a reply, exclaimed, 'Oh, this deep, cool room. So clever of you to have kept the look and the atmosphere.'

'It was lucky I had prior knowledge,' said Chrissy, leading out of the room, across the hall to the wide stairs. 'You remember the lay-out?' she asked, when they got to the top. Opening one door, she indicated another. 'Your bathroom, yours and Liz's. The kids won't bother you, they're all in the back, and we've got our own. This is your bedroom. Want to unpack in peace?'

'Of course not. Hang around.'

Chrissy pointed out the vacant cupboard and drawer space, then sat on the bed beside Nell's suitcase. Nell threw back the lid – Chrissy stared in frankly – and started unpacking.

'Which kid have I discommoded?'

'Clare. And you haven't, really. She didn't mind a bit.'

'Must find her a little present.'

'No, don't, Nell. Liz won't have got Joy anything. It's not necessary, they get far too much.'

Nell shrugged and shook out a shirt-waister dress in cerise silk. It always narked her when Chrissy and Liz put her right about the kids. Made not having any seem clumsy, like a handicap. She'd never forgotten the first time the three of them got together, Chrissy and Liz as mothers. Both bloody breast feeding. Never mind Lady Macbeth's ravings about nipples plucked from boneless gums, this lady had to sit on her hands she was so seething with jealousy – not of their blasted babies, but of their sharing something which she couldn't. Since then, she'd had her own chance at motherhood and decided not to bother.

'Gorgeous colour,' Chrissy was saying. 'Bet it looks knock-out.'

Nell held the dress under her chin. 'Yes?'

'Terrific.'

She looks awful, Chrissy thought, wonder what's gone wrong? It was usually man trouble when Nell looked seedy; she thrived on pressure at work, new projects, TV, a book, a commission to travel somewhere; no, it had to be a man making her look so rotten. There was something odd about her make-up, too, it was sort of detached-looking. Shouldn't like to see her without it, Chrissy suddenly thought. Once – it didn't seem so long ago – Nell's eyelashes and face-moulding seemed enormous fun. In those days, when they could still remember what the naked Nell looked like, these frankly false embellishments were just that, clever, witty bits of sophistication. Now she'd got used to the artificiality, Chrissy felt peeking underneath might be scary. Luckily, Nell always came down to breakfast in her war-paint. As for the other end of the day, she'd make good and sure she and Tony were tucked up in bed before Nell emerged from the bathroom.

'You'd never guess what I've been doing.'

'Oh?'

'Looking up old haunts.'

'In London?'

'Here.'

Certainly I wouldn't have guessed, thought Chrissy. Not like Nell to get nostalgic.

'Arrived yesterday, went everywhere – school, your home, my home, Liz's, the blessed Sea Gull Café, the cemetery – remember the guardian angel?'

'What on earth for? And why didn't you stay here?'

'Because I wanted to stay at the Grand. I had my reasons. That reminds me. Let's have a swanky night out, the three of us – Tony won't mind, will he? I'll take us to dinner at Court's Hotel. I've always wanted to eat there. Remember how we used to slope past on the prom, staring in at the posh visitors at their candle-lit tables thinking they were creatures from another planet? We'll get a window table so we can look out and gloat.'

'All right,' said Chrissy, thinking she could always freeze the salmon. 'If it's OK with Liz.'

'Surely dinner at Court's won't upset her plans?'

'Shouldn't think so.'

'Right.'

An overnight bag had been dumped on a chair. Nell opened it, took out a cigarette packet which she laid on the dressing table, then sensed tenseness. 'Don't worry, shan't smoke in the house, but I suppose it's OK to smoke in the garden if I pick up my fag ends?'

'Of course,' said Chrissy, firmness of voice conveying agreement with the restriction as well as the concession.

'Present for you.' She drew out a small flat package.

'Thanks. Hope it's nothing expensive. Oh.' Chrissy, having peeled back the wrapping, was looking down at a photograph, the one of her and Tony at the Rotarian dinner.

'Aren't you pleased? Thought you'd be tickled pink.

It was in the *Telegraph*'s window. Bought the frame at Gunthorpe's – great match, isn't it?'

'It looks a rather expensive frame.'

'Well, it wasn't very. It's not real. I mean, the silver's real, but it's not original art nouveau, just repro; thought it suited the photo. What's the matter? Honestly, I do believe you think I only bought it to show Liz up. The truth is,' – she scrabbled in the bag – 'here's what I got you originally.' She produced the packet of Brontë biscuits, tossed it on the bed. 'Modest enough to complement Liz's bottle of plonk, eh? I just happened on the photo when I was exploring yesterday, thought I'd surprise you out of – out of sheer affection, you ungrateful wretch. And as a matter of fact, when I was mooching about in Gunthorpe's a little something caught my eye for Liz, too.'

'Oh, Nell, I'm sorry. Actually, Tony'll be thrilled, he loved this when he saw it in the paper. I'll put it in our room.'

'Suit yourself. Never quite sure about my motives, are you, petal?'

'I said sorry.' She carried the photograph across the landing to her bedroom where she stood it on a chest of drawers, thinking that it was a very nice frame and when Nell had gone she'd put a photo of Amanda in it and stand it on the chest in the hall.

Nell had followed her. 'OK if I come in? I always think the view from this window's magnificent.'

'Yes,' Chrissy agreed, joining her. They gazed out over the rolling countryside, a soft breeze billowing the curtains. Nell, resting her hands on the sash-window frame, confided, 'I've got that fluttery feeling. Always get it when it's going to be us three again.'

'Do you?' said Chrissy, surprised. She'd always assumed it was she who set most store on their get-togethers, that the threesome was more necessary to her because she'd been a sort of orphan and the other two her adopted family. At least Liz and Nell had had proper families.

'It's the prospect of a bit of alchemy, I think,' Nell went on. 'Do you know how I picture us? – three gypsies with our heads together over a single crystal ball, determining fate. I've been party to a good many conferences in my time but none of them could touch ours for making schemes come true.'

'Funny you should say that. I was only thinking the other day – probably because of Liz being so desperate to consult us: I don't think we've ever individually taken a major decision or embarked on anything truly significant without getting the OK from the other two.'

'Mm,' said Nell, vaguely. To change the subject, she looked at her watch. 'Liz'll be here soon. Hadn't we better go down?'

iv

It's very late on Sunday night. Perhaps it's the early hours of Monday morning – could be, they've been lying here for hours (she in the middle of the bed between Nell and Chrissy) talking in whispers, holding their breath when Auntie Julie thumped to the bathroom, yelled some admonition to Chrissy's dad like 'Swallowed your brew, have yer?' or had a coughing fit. Since Nell turned over and they all fell quiet, she's lain staring into the dark for ages. Sometimes a car goes by, making the line of street lamplight above the pelmet wobble. She can't sleep but she's glad she's here with Chrissy and Nell and not alone in her narrow bed at home. Her friends give her strength: 'A triangle is a strr-ong shape,' she thinks to herself in Miss MacBride's voice, to bolster her spirits.

Immediately they heard Liz on the phone this morning they knew this was it, that they must get together instantly. She's told them all about yesterday evening in the park; they've talked it over several times. Now she understands that any little doubts she experienced were due to inexperience and shock. 'Because it must have come as a shock,' reasoned Chrissy, 'however much we've talked about it. You know how it is, you hope something'll happen but secretly, in your heart of hearts, you don't believe it will, because it's too wonderful.' And Nell agreed, adding, 'You're brilliant Liz, you actually brought it off.'

It was delicious basking in their praise, reassuring to have things explained so neatly. For instance, though disconcerted to hear Mr Poole had not in fact declared undying love, Nell and Chrissy soon deduced that this was down to Liz jumping the gun. 'You should've waited, let him judge the moment,' Nell decided.

'I suppose I couldn't stand the suspense.'

This was understandable, Chrissy said, but a shame. Liz promised to try and hold her tongue in future and take her tip from her lover – though in point of fact it was Nell who used the word 'lover', making the others gasp at the importance it cast.

About what happens tomorrow Liz is less sanguine. It's rather taken her breath away how her friends calmly anticipate the relinquishing of her virginity (perhaps not 'calmly'; more 'confidently', like speculating on a birthday treat or some other good thing which by its very nature is bound to come to pass). She demurred a little, wondered wasn't it rushing things a bit, surely he'd hold back, and was she really ready?

'Crikey, Liz, the poor man's been in a ferment over you for months. He's killed himself trying to hold back.'

'Nell's right, Liz. You've got to be fair.'

As for her not being ready, hadn't they all agreed to get shot of their virginity at the first worthy opportunity? Remember Miss Cummings, remember Miss Henry.

'God, you're so lucky,' sighed Nell. 'I wish it were me.'

'Or me – only it couldn't be, I'm not interesting enough,' Chrissy added modestly.

Lying on her back, listening to their untroubled breathing and her own stomach bubbling, Liz wishes her fate were indeed transferable. At least Nell's had some experience. And Chrissy's so athletic (a quality which, after last night's performance, Liz suspects might come in handy). She, on the other hand, will be half dead by morning if she doesn't soon catch some sleep, able for nothing but flopping about with her eyes drooping, sighing and yawning . . .

It's the dead part of the dinner hour, girls who go home not yet returned, those who've dined at school hanging about outside or sitting in the sixth-form room. So with luck they'll have the cloakroom to themselves for a while. Chrissy and Liz are standing in front of the mirror, Chrissy combing Liz's hair, Liz spitting on to a block of mascara prior to touching up her eyelashes. Nell's watching from the doorway where she's ready to prevent interlopers, offering advice like 'Not too much in case it smudges.'

Wouldn't you know? – here comes Valerie Dove.

'Push off,' says Nell.

'Do you mind? I want to use the toilet.'

'Scram,' barks Chrissy as Nell bars Valerie's way, and Liz, applying mascara, mimics, 'Want to use the toi-let'.

'What's up, Val?' Now Angie Hutchings arrives, tries to peer in.

'Nothing to interest you, Hutchings,' says Chrissy, moving aggressively to support Nell.

'They won't let us in.'

'Cheek, honestly.'

'Use the bogs downstairs,' Nell advises.

'You heard,' says Chrissy, criss-crossing the doorway with arms and legs.

Grumbling – 'Who do they think they are?' –

Valerie and Angie nevertheless depart. Chrissy resumes fiddling with Liz's hair and Nell suggests a smearing of lipstick.

Liz, obediently applying *Italian Pink*, wonders how they get away with it. What makes them seem so tough? It must be something to do with being a three, people are more used to dealing with pairs of friends or a gang. Also, there's the feeling they get when they're together of being powerful; maybe power is like a smell, people can sniff it. It only works when they're together; on their own they're nothing special, as vulnerable as anyone else . . . But this is not a helpful thought. 'Gut rot,' she gasps, bending over, clutching her waist. 'I wish you two were coming with me this afto, or at least riding with me on the bus.'

'If we all three go missing it'll be noticed. No point in asking for trouble.'

Chrissy's right. But at least there's time before the bell goes to accompany her to the bus-stop.

And time while they wait for a final spot of morale boosting.

'Remember, in a way, you're doing this for *us*,' Nell admonishes. 'It'll be broadening. I think I'll make a start on my novel.'

Chrissy's hopes are more mundanely focused. 'It should help us appreciate things more in English. I mean, we've always said Cummings is hopeless because she doesn't know what the poets are on about half the time. We're bound to gain valuable insights.'

'Maybe,' says Liz, with a worrying lack of enthusiasm.

'Just think, you'll be different after this, more mature.'

'It'll be the saving of her,' predicts Nell.

'What do you mean?' demands Chrissy.

'You know how we've always dreaded turning out like our mothers or Auntie Julie? Well, this'll put Liz absolutely in the clear. Can you imagine Mrs Stockdale bunking off school to go and meet her lover?'

233

'Just a minute, dear, while I unhook me corsets,' suggests Chrissy.

'I 'ope this won't play havoc with me bowels, young man,' offers Liz as Auntie Julie.

They laugh so hard, Nell falls off the pavement. A passing car swerves, hoots angrily. Nell catches hold of the bus-stop pole, swings to safety on an outstretched arm. 'I can imagine my mum getting jumped on in the cut, but never in a million years having a mar-vellous lover like Mr Poole.'

'Mr Poole,' drools Chrissy, and in spite of her nerves an enjoyable thrill jolts Liz's stomach.

When the bus arrives, they watch her jump on board and her legs vanish round the turn of the stairs. As the bus moves off, they back up against a garden fence to squint upwards.

'I hope she remembers everything,' says Chrissy, as Liz's black curtain of hair is spotted and her white hand shimmering to and fro like a fish swimming close to the surface, 'the atmosphere, the subtle nuances.'

'And the mechanics. Not being absolutely *au fait* with those is where my writing falls down, I have to filch from other people's. This should be a tremendous help – if she doesn't let us down.'

'Of course she won't. Liz wouldn't.'

They wave vigorously till only the bus's rear is visible.

On top of the bus, no longer waving or craning her head, Liz finds the larky feeling, which had built up in her at the bus-stop, subsiding. At the same time, half her brain goes numb. She looks out of the window, at gardens and the fronts of houses, at the tops of people's heads, at trees and telephone wires; all so familiar, and so near she could touch them, yet strange-seeming, remote. The conductor comes whistling up the stairs. In a dream she pays him. When the bus turns into Town Hall Square, she stands up and finds her limbs gone sleepy as her brain, it's an effort to move. She walks through the underpass on legs that feel like sausages. Where they're taking her seems too unreal to be true. But it *is* true, her enfeebled brain warns, what she needs is to sit down somewhere and think about it. Her stupid legs plod on, and in any case, no suitable seating presents itself. When she gets within two blocks of Legget Road where the Pooles live, her legs go slower while her heart quickens. What if she turned into the road next before Legget, then turned right again and went back to Town Hall Square? She could catch a bus home and pretend to be ill – wouldn't have to pretend very hard, not if her heart carries on like this, as if it's going to burst or something. She could be ill again tomorrow to avoid Chrissy and Nell, and be too ill to speak to them on the telephone if they ring up asking to speak to her. She'd have to be ill on Wednesday, too, to get out of her piano lesson. God, she'd never be able to go to piano lessons again, it'd be too stupendously embarrassing. But how could she explain that to her parents? They'd be mystified. Her father would ring up Mr Poole. Mr Poole might be shocked and let something slip. Crikey, then what? In any case, she'd never see Mr Poole again. Never. The end.

Her feet inch almost to stop. How, she wonders, will she ever get to sleep again? She's been getting to sleep on fantasies of Mr Poole for ages and ages. And what about everything they've built up around him, she and Nell and Chrissy? It'll all go for nothing. Will they forgive her? More likely pretend to and secretly despise her. She'll despise herself. She's beginning to already.

There's an emptiness inside her, getting bigger and bigger. Deliberately, she shuts her mind and lumbers forward, in a few seconds, turns the corner into Legget Road, pushes the gate open of number five.

Registration over, Chrissy and Nell gather their books, go up to the library. They sit in their usual bay, staring out of the window. Neither speaks. Chrissy's excitement has waned. In its place, a tiny hunch, weak as a tendril peeping through soil, has grown to fearful proportions; she's sick with apprehension lest, just half an hour ago, they dispatched poor Liz to a horrible doom. Perhaps she won't go, thinks Chrissy, putting herself in her friend's shoes. Perhaps, instead of going to Mr Poole's, she'll catch the next bus home.

This outcome hasn't yet occurred to Nell. She's too busy stoking the excitement inside her. It's Liz, she reminds and hugs herself, immaculate little china-doll Liz, all gleaming and delicate like in the secret image she invented for her when they first made friends and she could never feel entirely comfortable with Liz's classy speaking voice, her pretty manners, and all the other subtle polishings that come with a well to-do home; it's Liz, the china figurine of her private imaginings gone to get herself dirty with a married man – thereby unexpectedly fulfilling Nell's wickedly subversive day-dream. (She can remember her precise whereabouts when the idea came to her: she was turning into Maud Street on her way home from Chrissy's, brooding about Liz being so shiny and neat, when the thought just popped into her head: how delicious to see this shiny neatness get all smudged up.) It was a premonition, she thinks, now, awed by her perspicacity. Almost frightening. Perhaps she's got special powers.

'What're you looking so pleased about?' frowns Chrissy.

'Mm?'

'There's no need to sit there slavering.' Setting an example, she opens her history text book with due and proper seriousness.

Mr Poole must have been watching out for her and fairly leaped to the door; for there's no time to press the bell even, before it opens and he's urging softly, 'Come in.'

It's a double shock. On top of this startling abruptness, there's also his strange appearance. No pin-striped piano teacher's suit on today; in its place a shiny Paisley dressing gown. Horrible. She can't believe it, after one amazed stare, tries to keep her eyes off it.

He closes the door, explaining how important it is to enter and exit swiftly because Pam next door is a nosy parker always checking up on him, also, it's important to keep their voices down, bearing in mind Pam's sharp ears. Would she like some coffee?

'Yes, please,' she whispers.

'Not as quiet as all that,' he says kindly, though obviously pleased she's taken the message to heart.

She waits in the kitchen doorway as he busies himself with the coffee things. He's looking pleased, obviously doesn't dream how unlike himself the dressing gown makes him. He's smiling his usual skewed smile, but she's never seen it last so long before. He's talking about his coffee-making prowess. 'Has to be treated with respect, never boiled, allowed to stand for precisely four minutes.' Four minutes, oh dear. Now he's stopped moving things about and is just standing there smiling – she could almost say grinning – at her.

'Aromatic,' he suggests, lingering on the word, speaking, it takes her a few moments to grasp, of the coffee.

'Oh, yes. Ever so.'

'Nervous?'

'No, of course not. Well, a bit.' A horrid little laugh escapes her, making her blush, and the worst of it is, he never takes his eyes off her for a second. She doesn't know where to put her own.

'Because there's no need to be, darling.'

Darling – crikey. She straightens up, tries to look nonchalantly adult. 'I've always admired those coffee cups.'

'Have you? They were my mother's.' He tips up a saucer and squints at the maker's name. 'Mm, Minton.

I hadn't noticed. Better take good care of them. You've very good taste for one so young.'

The praise relaxes her. For the first time she registers the coffee smell, looks forward to her drink.

'We'll take it into the dining room, but remember – walls have ears.'

She follows him, sits in one of the two easy chairs. When she's taken a few sips, he wants to know what she thinks of it.

'Gorgeous.'

'It's a Viennese blend, with figs.'

'Gosh.' Already something to impress Nell and Chrissy.

They drink in silence. 'Come here,' he whispers when she puts her cup down.

Where? she wonders, getting up. He's still in his chair. She goes towards it. He pulls her down, spreadeagled on top of him.

'Darling, darling,' he's saying in her ear while fondling, squeezing and rearranging her; 'darling, darling,' between kisses. The 'darling, darling' makes these other things more acceptable, persuades her to reciprocate a bit – though not too much in case she's not supposed to. Her overriding feeling – more of a worry, really – is for the unattractiveness of sprawling about with her skirt half up showing her suspenders and her bra unhooked beneath her blouse. Far better, she can't help thinking, to take everything off and be done with it; but she doesn't like to indicate this, doesn't like to indicate anything at all, being so entirely new to the situation.

'Shall we go to bed?' he asks suddenly on hot breath in her ear.

She dares only to nod.

'Very quietly, now.' He takes her hand, draws her up the stairs, into a room at the back of the house (over the dining room, she calculates; so this must be *his* bedroom). He throws back the bedclothes, turns his back, unties and lets fall the dressing gown. She wonders why he put it on in the first place since he's wearing shirt and trousers. Now he's unfastening buttons. It's an opportunity to strip off her own clothes unobserved. This done, she scrambles into bed, pulls the sheet right up to her chin.

Without looking at him directly, she glimpses pimply bottom with faint redness in the crease. This bottom can have nothing to do with the Mr Poole she knows and loves, or even the Mr Poole she's explored in fantasy; it's a bottom on it's own, disembodied; furthermore, it's unlike any bottom of her experience, being flattish and bulgy rather than smooth and round; perhaps all men's bottoms are like this, she wouldn't know. Men, she remembers, aren't called upon to be beautiful, which is just as well.

He's collected up all his clothes and is laying them in calculated order on a chair. What will he think of her untidy heap on the floor? Before she has time to get really worried on this score, he's slipping under the sheet beside her. 'Darling,' he's saying. 'Darling, dar . . .'

He must have forgotten something. He's jumped out of bed and looking through his clothes. Back again now, slipping what he's retrieved under his pillow.

'You've never done this before, have you?'

'Of course not.' She's indignant, hurt.

Now he's all over her, poking at bits she'd rather he didn't. Isn't he supposed to put his thing into her? This handling feels rude. Oh God, he's even taking a look. If only he'd just hold her nicely further up, look into her eyes, murmur to her, make her feel it's her unique magic moving him, instead of like she's a telly having her knobs twiddled while he hunts rather heatedly for better reception. (In her vague imaginings, they two would lie in one another's arms, stare trance-like into one another's eyes, while everything down below happened deliciously of its own volition prompted by

the power of romantic love.) At last his head comes
up and he heaves on top of her. Thank goodness,
she thinks, bracing herself.

But he's paused to scrabble under the pillow.
Suddenly she knows what he's reaching for – the
contraceptive – one of those horrible balloon things
she and Nell and Chrissy stared at under a bench in
the Robinson Rec.

'Do you know what this is?'

Help, he wants her to look at it. Reluctantly turning her head, she sees it's not long and dangly after
all, but a neat round thing.

'Never, never do it without one of these,' he says,
sounding fierce like he does when he's talking about
Bach. She's used to agreeing with this tone of voice. It
takes her a second or two to digest his implication and
feel outrage.

'When? What do you mean? I'll only be doing it with
you . . .'

'All right, all right. I just wouldn't want you to
think . . .'

'So why did you say it?'

'Shh. Come here.'

He's smothered her protests with kissing. Now he's
saying really nice things like 'You're lovely, do you
know that? Exquisite,' but she can't get the contraceptive remark out of her mind. What he said didn't make
sense, because after today they'll belong to each other,
she to him, he to her. So what did he *mean*? And fancy
saying it at this moment. It's made what they're doing
seem cheap somehow, sort of mucky.

Worrying away, she hardly registers what's happening, except that he's heavy and their skin keeps sticking
and dragging. When he comes into her it's a shock. How
can anyone call this love and hurt someone so much?
Luckily, it stops pretty soon. Another minute and she'd
have screamed, Pam or no Pam.

He rolls off, lies puffing beside her, then flings over

a damp arm, gives her a pat. 'Next time you'll enjoy it, you'll see.'

Next time. She's fighting back tears, she feels so sorry for herself. 'Shall I get dressed now?'

'Already? Oh, all right – it'll give me plenty of time to clear up. Use the bathroom, if you like.'

Thankfully, she crawls out of bed, gathers her heap of clothes and hurries to lock herself in with the blue porcelain, and Mrs Poole's talcum powder, bath salts, jar of cold cream, tissues, shampoo, tube of Veet, lined up and observing her on the windowsill.

Eventually, she creeps downstairs. There's a great lump in her chest, she aches for some loving person to come and comfort her.

And he does. Mr Poole is himself again, suited, combed, immaculate. And he's beaming at her, holding his arms out. She hurls on to his chest.

He tips up her chin. 'You still love me, then?'

'Oh, yes,' she chokes, clinging to him.

He rocks her, strokes her. 'My darling. My sweet little angel.'

In heaven at last. She wants this moment to go on and on.

Unfortunately, there's Pam to consider. Primary school will be out soon; she'll be looking out of the window for her brat of a son. Better skip out, now, while the coast's clear. Hang on a second, he'll just peep through the net curtains in the bay window, see if he can spot her.

She's left feeling bereft.

He's back, looking satisfied, opening the front door, squeezing her shoulder, saying, 'See you on Wednesday, leave the gate.'

That's it, then. His eyes, though twinkling, manage to indicate an impatience to be seeing her disappear through the gateway.

'Goodbye,' she whispers.

Almost at once the door closes behind her. She

241

guesses that he's dashed to the sitting-room window to check she's safely gone and determine whether Pam's started her vigil yet.

Out of sight of the house, her pace slows down – it has to – there's sandpaper lodged between her legs. Ouch, crikey, hell. Town Hall Square seems a cruelly long haul.

After all, she will have to feign illness, she decides on the bus going home. Straight upstairs into her own cool fresh bed is the only future she can contemplate. The thought of Chrissy and Nell pouncing on her tomorrow is too much; she needs time to recover.

'Elizabeth, duckie, whatever's the matter?'

Wisely, Liz doesn't stagger past, but delays in the kitchen in order to secure maternal co-operation. It's quite easy. 'Been sick, Mummy. Rissoles for dinner, too fatty, kept repeating.'

'Rissoles,' cries Mrs Stockdale wrathfully. 'Wouldn't touch one with a bargepole. Hide a multitude of sins, do rissoles. You poor lamb. What can Mummy get you?'

'It's made me so weak and wobbly throwing up like that, I think I'd better go to bed.'

'Quite right, dear. Up you go, and Mummy'll bring you a nice cup of tea.'

'Just water to sip. I still don't feel easy.'

Mrs Stockdale turns on the tap and lets the water run cold and fresh. As it runs, she plans her daughter's recovery. 'Only me,' she calls softly, coming up with the water.

Liz, lying in bed, smiles wanly.

'Here we are, duckie, take a few sips. It's vital to keep up the liquids.'

'All right, Mummy,' says Liz. She sips dutifully, lifting her eyes over the tumbler to her mother's face, fastening on it with the obsessive gaze of a suckling baby. Which moves Mrs Stockdale. She senses their rather prickly relationship taking a turn for the better.

242

('She's been through her difficult patch,' she mentally rehearses to her friend, Mrs Garth, 'and now she's coming up on the other side, emerging into womanhood you might say, and she feels the need of her Mummy's friendship . . .')

'Tomorrow, lovie, I think you should stay at home. Get your strength back. After all, we'll have to coax your tummy with some nice wholesome food. I thought Marmite soldiers for brekky, then milk pudding for lunch, take a breather, a little stroll in the afternoon and your appetite should be good as new so you can do yourself justice at tea.'

'I'm sure you're right, Mummy. Perhaps I'll just sleep now.'

'Of course, pet,' whispers Mrs Stockdale, tiptoeing out, closing the door behind her ever so quietly.

Over their evening meal, Mrs Stockdale runs through tomorrow's itinerary with her husband. She wonders whether a milk-based soup would be preferable to milk pudding. On the other hand, Elizabeth will need extra sugar to restore her energy. Alderman Stockdale just grunts and turns the pages of the *Evening Telegraph*, so Mrs Stockdale excuses herself and goes to the phone to talk it over with her best friend.

Mrs Garth approves the plan, especially kicking off with Marmite soldiers. 'Marmite couldn't turn anyone's stomach, it's the opposite of sickly. What's she having now?'

'Nothing,' cries Mrs Stockdale, her heart shooting to her mouth. 'Just water. That's all she feels she can take.'

'What about a fizzy drink? I always swear by ice-cream soda.'

Mrs Stockdale knows, knows with a doom-laden thud, that her larder is entirely deficient in ice-cream soda, and for that matter any other fizzy drink. There's tonic in the drinks cupboard of course, and bitter lemon . . .

'Oo, no. Not the same thing at all,' vetoes Mrs Garth.

'The pub,' shrieks Mrs Stockdale, spying salvation. 'I'll get back to you later, Ada. Daddy, Daddy,' she yells, running into the dining room. 'Our little girl needs a fizzy drink. Go to the pub for a bottle of pop. Ice-cream soda if they've got it, but any sort's better than nothing.'

'Are you sure she wants it, or is this one of Ada Garth's daft ideas?'

'Hurry. It's dangerous for girls of Elizabeth's age to get run down.'

'Oh, good Lord, all right,' mutters Alderman Stockdale, feeling into his trouser pocket for change. Not for the first time he wishes he were at work rather than home; in the office it's no trouble at all to secure out-of-the-way comestibles via the simple expediency of dispatching a minion to fetch them. Resenting the faintly demeaning errand, he sets off, scowling, down the gravel drive.

'But not dandelion and burdock,' his wife yells from the doorstep. 'Elizabeth can't abide it.'

Nell and Chrissy feel Liz's absence like a punch in the diaphragm. 'Knew it,' hisses Nell, during registration. Skipping Prayers, they dive into the cloakroom, lock doors, perch on lavatory rims, until the noise of feet descending the stone staircase fades. Then they slip up to the library, alternately sitting on and hugging a radiator, for there's a keen wind coming off the North Sea which at least keeps away the rain, though scurrying black clouds seem to reflect their sense of life speeding by with nothing gained.

'She *may* have gone to him,' Chrissy says. 'She may just be ill this morning. Or she may have got ill on the way to his house, in which case we can't really blame her.'

'She's not ill, she's chicken,' sneers Nell, scowling at the books in rows, her hands itching to snatch and tear them, so violent is her disappointment. 'Let's face it, we're talking about the Stockdale baby. That's what she is, essentially; years of that Mummy and Daddy stuff have had their effect.'

'I do think,' says Chrissy, daring to be fair, 'that if she got cold feet, it'd be understandable. Actually, I think I might have.'

Which does not one whit impress Nell. The chances of Chrissy attracting a mature male, as opposed to the adolescents who whistle after her, are too remote, in her estimation, to waste time on. 'Always knew she was a booby at heart, though I did hope our influence had put guts into her.'

'You can't say she hasn't got guts. Remember when she crawled across the parapet at Wraithby Grange? Admit it – you and I were shit scared. And she's fantastic standing up to the Head, better than you, you just antagonize her.'

'Because she's posh and the Head's a snob. Upbringing again.'

They fall silent, stare out of the window. Faint strains of hymn singing rise from the hall.

'Anyway, whatever happened or didn't happen, she's still our friend.'

'I suppose so,' Nell says grudgingly. 'But it'll never be quite the same.' After a while, she brightens. 'You know, maybe she hasn't loused things up entirely. We'll ring her at dinner, find out what she's got to say for herself.'

Liz has finished her Marmite soldiers, she has drunk a second cup of tea; she's calculating what time they'll ring her – bell goes at twelve twenty-five, first sitting for dinner is twelve thirty, they'll bolt their meal, be in the phone box by twelve forty-five, twelve fifty at the latest. 'That was lovely, Mummy. I can feel it doing me good. Better give it loads of time to settle, though, shan't want to eat again before one.'

'All right, dear. A nice semolina pudding at one o'clock. Or would you rather have rice?'

245

'Um, rice, I think. I expect the girls'll phone me during the dinner hour, wondering where I've got to. So I'll answer if the phone rings.'

('She's such a popular girl,' says Mrs Stockdale silently to the absent Mrs Garth.)

At twelve forty-five she's lurking in the hall, confident of her mother being unable to tear herself from the oven. (She'll be watching the pudding through the smeary glass door, willing it to brown nicely, to retain every scrap of nourishment.) When the phone rings, Liz gets to the receiver on the second brr. 'Hello?'

'Hi, Liz,' calls Chrissy, striving for cheeriness. 'What's up?'

From the shuffling and breathing coming down the line, Liz can tell two heads are pressed to the receiver. 'Up? Nothing.'

'Ask her,' hisses Nell.

'Did you, er, go?'

'Go?'

'You know, to Mr Poole's?'

Liz gives a little laugh. 'Of course. You didn't think I wouldn't?'

'She says, "of course".'

It takes Nell a moment to adjust. 'Ask her how it went.'

'Er, how did it go?'

'Oh, fine,' says Liz, condescension coating her voice.

'Ask why she's stopped off school, then.'

'Just tired,' Liz continues languorously, 'absolutely bloody shattered. And school – well,' she gives a little laugh, 'I couldn't be bothered.'

'She says 'cos she couldn't be bothered.'

'I know, I heard.'

'So you're quite OK, then, Liz?'

'Will she be in tomorrow?'

'I'm perfectly fine. And of course I'll be in tomorrow, I'm seeing *him* after school.'

This, if they needed it, is final and complete proof.

'Got to go and eat lunch now.'

Nell snatches the receiver. 'You're brilliant, kiddo.'

Chrissy snatches it back. 'Oh, Liz . . .'

'By-ee.'

She's rung off. They spill out of the phone box, stunned as night creatures suddenly hitting daylight.

'God, I wonder what it was like . . .'

But Nell's mind is on another tack. 'She sounded different, did you notice? It's changed her already. No more porcelain doll.'

Chrissy halts in her tracks. 'What do you mean?'

'You know – polished little Liz. Life's roughed her up a bit.'

'Roughed her up?' She grabs Nell's elbow, pulls her round.

'I only meant it'll have made her more interesting,' says Nell, backtracking fast in face of Chrissy's aggression. 'Bound to have.'

Chrissy lets her go. 'I think this proves what I said. In some ways Liz is the bravest, most advanced of the three of us.'

'Absolutely, I agree,' promises Nell. She punches the air. 'Yippee, it's amazing.'

Nell's agreement is the ultimate accolade; celebrating, Chrissy breaks into a run. 'The most stupendous thing we've achieved so far,' she yells back over her shoulder, as though describing a stunt they've pulled off by combined effort. Which maybe it is.

It's the same pattern next day, she doesn't have to go into details, something's preventing them questioning her closely, they're content to hang on to her every word, grateful for every snippet, reading volumes into the turn of her head, sudden smiles, silences.

At break they amble round the hockey field. 'Oh, Liz,' sighs Chrissy from time to time, as relief at her friend's return from the great adventure is replaced by wordless, pleasurable speculation as to the adventure's course. Nell says nothing, just smiles to herself.

After dinner, they go to the cemetery. It's nippy, but the sun's out. Nell offers round her packet of Players. Chrissy takes one, Liz declines. Nell and Chrissy exchange glances.

Emboldened by nicotine, Nell gabbles the question. 'You did actually go to bed together?'

'Of course,' says Liz, raising pitying eyebrows.

'Of course they did,' snaps Chrissy, glad to be sure, mad with Nell for asking.

'Sorry. It's just I can't quite take it in.' She pulls on her cigarette – 'You're so' – breathes out smoke – 'nonchalant about the whole thing.'

'Really?' Liz tips up her head, smiles at the guardian angel, clasps her hands behind her head. 'Is that how I seem? Interesting.'

They gape, know they'll have to make do with gleanings for the time being.

After school, when Liz has dashed off to her piano lesson after a careful session in front of the cloakroom mirror, Chrissy and Nell dawdle through the Robinson Rec.

'Preoccupied,' pronounces Chrissy of Liz.

'You can say that again.'

'Only to be expected, when you come to think about it.'

'Absolutely.'

'Expect she'll be more forthcoming when she's got used to it.'

'Yeah. Wonder if he's actually going to teach her piano today, or something more interesting.'

'Oh, God,' shudders Chrissy. 'Don't.'

Beethoven's *Sonata Pathétique* (first movement) is not going well. Maintaining the fingers of her left hand at full stretch for the fast arpeggios is killing her. She stops playing, clasps the fiery pain in her knuckles and wrist, bends her head over it. 'This piece is too hard. My left hand's not strong enough.'

'Nonsense,' he says. 'It was coming along beautifully last week. You've tensed up, that's the trouble.' He grasps her left arm, straightens it, runs his hand up and down. 'Relax.'

Now her stomach goes taut as well. She looks away from what he's doing to her arm, whispers, 'Do we have to have a lesson?'

There's a pause.

'Of course we do,' he says, not in the hurtful piano teacher's voice he's been using ever since she arrived, but softly, intimately. 'Your father's paying me to give you one.'

This reference to commerce appals her. She can't think of a suitable reply. 'Not this piece,' she pleads.

'All right, the Bach. Jump up. I'll play it to you.'

His performance is so beautiful, so clean, she's taken up by it.

'Now you.'

She responds with as near a copy of his rendition as she can muster.

'Good. All right, we'll leave it at that for today. But don't give up on the Beethoven, will you?' His hands grasp and press down on her shoulders. 'Work on it – for me.'

She nods.

'How about Saturday evening?' he asks in a low voice. 'Can you get out without causing comment?'

'Oh yes. I often stay at Chrissy's on a Saturday. That'd be OK.'

'Have to be latish, I'm teaching till seven. Then there's tea and so forth. I usually go for a pint around nine. Shall we say a quarter to nine outside the White Lion? You can pretend to be waiting for a bus, I'll drive along and pick you up.'

She's impressed. Obviously he's put thought into this. 'Fine.' She jumps up and starts packing her music case.

He takes her hand as far as the sitting-room door,

249

squeezing very hard, then drops it and calls for the next pupil who is waiting in the dining room. 'Good-bye,' he says loudly, holding open the front door. She steps past him without replying.

Pam's near her front gate picking up litter; she straightens up and looks across. Liz, closing the Pooles' gate, affects not to notice her.

The Saturday pick-up is accomplished so smoothly it might have been rehearsed. The car draws up, the back door opens, he calls, 'Jump in, keep your head down,' drives on. Now and then he turns to glance at her and smile. Mostly, he looks straight ahead. He asks questions, 'Everything all right? No problems?' Also, he wants to know what story she told Chrissy – she didn't mention him, did she? (his voice sharp at this, so she hurriedly denies it), and won't Chrissy's aunt think it odd? She does most of the chatting, explaining Auntie Julie's funny peculiarities and how completely uninterested she is in the doings of teenage girls, and how she and Chrissy and Nell make a practice of misleading their families over their whereabouts. He's very interested, prompts her, chuckles a lot.

When he pulls off the road, the car starts bumping. She raises her head to take a peep. They're on a rough track, coming to rest in a tree-shrouded clearing – clever of him to have found this place; obviously, taken a lot of care. He switches off the engine. It's dead quiet.

'Well?' He turns and looks at her – she smiles nervously – then clambers over the front seat to join her in the back.

It's much better in a car, she decides. Being so cramped, he can't dive up and down, he's more or less forced to keep his head near hers and an arm round her shoulders. It's more spontaneous, less arranged. Best of all, he's making love to her in his piano teacher's suit, he's the real Mr Poole. One disappointment: though unquestionably the real Mr Poole, she discovers a side to him she's never guessed at, a less-refined side, given to saying things that secretly make her flinch. Just the same, while he's touching her she gets a hiccup of pleasure – nothing momentous, nothing important, just it takes her by surprise. And when he enters her it doesn't hurt so much, which is a relief.

'Did you come?' he asks, when he subsides.

'Where? Come where?'

He sighs. 'Never mind.'

Another mystifying use of a simple word which, for some reason, she finds off-putting.

But now the love-making's over, she gets down to what *is* important – making sure his understanding of why they're doing it corresponds to her own. It's hard to get going on the subject, but loyalty to the scenario she, Chrissy and Nell have so carefully crafted spurs her on. In the end, she just blurts it out: 'This means we're together now for ever and ever, doesn't it? I mean, the fact we've made love is a commitment.'

'Oh, darling.'

'But it is, isn't it?'

'Of course. But I'm so much older. You've got your whole life ahead of you.'

'Don't say that. It's done, now. You did feel we absolutely had to?'

'Oh, I did. Broke the eleventh commandment for the first time in my life – *Never mix business with pleasure.*'

Not a remark to treasure for Chrissy and Nell. The cheapness of it scares her, tells her she's got it wrong, this man isn't as she thought he was. But it's much too late for such an idea, she pushes it away, lays her anxieties on a single word. 'Pleasure?' she objects, her voice gone quavery.

'Darling, it will be, I promise.'

'But I'm not talking about pleasure, I'm talking about you and me coming together irrevocably.'

251

'I know you are.' He starts kissing her again.

She holds him off. 'So you do agree – we're *pledged* to one another?'

'If that's what you want, my love . . .'

'I do, I do.'

'Then so do I. Now give me a kiss.'

She's wild with relief. ('He says we're pledged to one another,' she reports joyously in her head to her friends. 'For ever and ever. It's a commitment.' 'Oh Liz,' they breathe, enraptured.)

Then she notices he's having a second go.

V

Liz drove away from Fairfields fed-up with herself; she could have shown more interest in the menu, instead of clamming up as she always did when her mother mentioned food (so childish, that, like a baby clenching its mouth when it sees a spoon coming); she could have made more of Rosie's results – which were fantastic, after all – rather than coming over all goody-two-shoes (it's not nice to boast); and she could have worn a pretty dress, or at least some decent trousers with a crisp shirt, something to please her mother instead of just picking out things to be comfortable in on the journey. She was a selfish bitch, really, as well as a slob; she'd come to regret today. And so on. All true to her eternal habit of finding personal fault. Sometimes, like a dog chasing its tail, she'd have a go at herself on this score, too: 'so self-obsessed, it's sickening, boring,' she'd rant, viciously glowering in the driving mirror as like as not, for her worst moments of self-disgust usually occurred when she was caught in heavy traffic. This afternoon, the driving smooth, the lanes peaceful, she was merely glum.

She'd taken not the direct route to Fenby-cum-Laithby, but a minor road to Wold Enderby, through which she drove slowly, pausing a while outside her old home. Now, she was driving along the lane she and Chrissy and Nell had walked up one morning, looking for mischief, no doubt, some innocent building to break into, some orchard to rob. Driving between the steep banks, a memory came to her of a quarrel; she couldn't recall what about, just the awful feeling of falling out, like teetering on the edge of a precipice hoping somebody would have the presence of mind to pull you back. One of us must have, she supposed, seeing that we survived.

Oh my goodness, Fenby-cum-Laithby village green. Where we made an exhibition of ourselves, falling off the seat (still here), shrieking and laughing and showing our knickers. Probably to the amazement of half the village. She vividly remembered the shame of entering the village shop afterwards. Then how they'd walked down this road taking swigs from a bottle of pop, until they arrived at this very gateway. She swung in, light-hearted now, memories having buoyed her up. Nippily, she covered the drive, braked, switched off the engine, unbelted, was so swiftly out of the car and over the gravel, she almost caught them by surprise.

They heaved out of their deck-chairs, started across the lawn. At this distance it could have been the teenage Liz flying towards them in her plimsolls, the same trim body, same haircut; not quite the same face, but in pretty good nick, thought Nell, who hadn't seen Liz for ages; she looks a bit tired, thought Chrissy, who had.

There were three deck-chairs set out, also a table. 'I'll get your bags, you stay here,' said Chrissy, giving the other two time to get used to one another.

A small package lay on the table. 'A pressy,' said Nell, passing it. 'And don't frown, I had enough of Chrissy's disapproval earlier over her present. What it is — I arrived yesterday — not here, at the Grand. I've been having a private wallow, all the old haunts. Going round the shops, I saw that in Gunthorpe's.'

'I haven't got you anything,' Liz began, before the

wrapping came off and delight got the better of her –
'Oh, Nell . . .'

'Of course not. We're not into gift exchange, no dodgy
in-laws to propitiate, none of that stuff. Well, Tony,
maybe – I've brought him a bottle of Scotch, from the
two of us. Chrissy said not to treat the kids.'

'Oh, good thinking,' cried Liz, referring to Tony's gift,
unable to take her eyes off her own. 'I've only brought
them a bottle of plonk.' She tried it on various fingers,
found it fitted the middle one of her right hand, held
it out, turned it in the sunlight – a Victorian rose-gold
ring set with a garnet and tiny seed pearls.

'Knew it was you.'

'Can I show it to Chrissy?'

'Of course.'

'Show me what?' asked Chrissy, coming by with Liz's
bag. 'Oh, Nell, how sweet. And so perfectly Liz. In fact,
so Liz, you couldn't have spotted it and not bought it
for her.' She slipped an arm round Nell's shoulders,
taking more pleasure in this gift from Nell to Liz than
in any she could have received herself. It demonstrated
Nell's wholeheartedness towards their present project
(that of helping Liz). It's going to be all right, she
thought.

When Tony came home from the office, they were
still sprawled in the garden.

(In point of fact, they'd been out of the deck-chairs
and were now back in them; earlier, they'd helped Liz
to unpack. 'I want to go in through the back way,'
she'd insisted, '*sneak* in. God, can you believe it?'
They stood in silence for a moment by the shadowy
back stairs. 'We'd have been branded juvenile delin-
quents if we'd ever been caught.'

'We were too smart,' said Nell.

'And we didn't do any real harm,' said Chrissy.

'Breaking and entering, the odd spot of larceny – no
real harm, your honour, not as such . . .'

'Shh,' warned Chrissy, remembering her children who might be listening.)

Tony saw them through the french windows and backed away – not before noting their wine glasses, the almost empty bottle of Vouvray.

'They've been drinking out there all afternoon,' Joy exaggerated, sensing her father's perturbation, playing on it like a cat with a mouse. 'I only hope we get something to eat tonight.'

The kids feel it, too, he thought, pouring himself a Scotch. Taken a couple at a time they weren't too bad, but there was something horribly daunting about the three of them together.

He downed his drink, put the empty tumbler on the coffee table, stepped through the open french windows. Better get it over with. 'Hello there,' he called, striding over the lawn.

They turned to look.

His courage dipped, he longed wildly for the phone to ring. It was a single gaze turned on him, it seemed, only in triplicate.

vi

They're fiercely protective of Liz. They have to be, she's in lots of trouble. For one thing, the other girls are getting at her. Funny how they've sensed what Liz is up to, not the details, of course, not that she's doing it with an older man, a married man. At least, Nell and Chrissy don't *think* they've guessed this much: 'They're too limited, their imaginations wouldn't stretch that far,' is Nell's opinion. Even so, they seem confident that she's carrying on with somebody. 'It's because of changes in her, physically,' says Nell. 'They're a dead give-away.' Chrissy, who hasn't noticed any, makes a point of looking out for them. Sure enough, she finds subtle differences, for instance, in the way Liz moves: no more nipping about on fast neat feet, now

255

she slouches her weight from foot to foot, rolls her hips, scrapes her heels, never hurries. Also, she's taken to leaving the top buttons of her shirt undone, often her shirt hangs out over her skirt, and her skirt sometimes has concertina wrinkles in it, especially after she's come back from seeing him in the dinner hour.

This is another thing – she takes terrible risks. If a certain time of day suits Ronnie (as she now calls him), she'll just go, walk out. So she's in trouble with the teachers. She's been caught sneaking back into school twice, and once the Head caught her bunking off. The Head believed her plea of sudden illness, but some members of staff, notably Cummings and Henry, look at Liz like she's a bad smell. Also, her work's suffering. Nell and Chrissy are killing themselves doing Liz's work as well as their own. Nell covers for her in English, Chrissy in History; they write up notes for her, even write essays for her to copy, racking their brains to make them different to their own. They can't help her with Music. Music's gone right down the pan. Miss Tulty's reported her to the Head. 'Think I'll give up Music,' sulks Liz. 'Anyway, it's only a frill.'

'Better try and flannel the Head,' Chrissy says anxiously. 'You don't want her ringing up your dad.' She combs Liz's hair, then spits on a tissue and rubs at the traces of last night's mascara under Liz's eyes.

'Say you've got trouble at home, and it's putting you off your work,' is what Nell suggests, but Liz doesn't think the Head would swallow it. The Stockdales aren't those sort of parents (unlike the Nelsons).

'You'll have to fall back on illness, then. Might be wearing a bit thin.'

'How about tiredness?' wonders Chrissy. 'There was this case in Auntie Julie's magazine about a woman who was so tired she stopped washing and eating even.'

'All right,' sighs Liz. 'I'll give it a go.'

In the event, her prep-school upbringing comes to her

rescue, all those nice manners and polite phrases and diffident smiles demonstrated and encouraged by Miss Millicent rise in this time of crisis to the rather murky surface. 'I get so tired,' she smiles apologetically. 'I can't think why.'

The Head is relieved. The Miss Cummings, Miss Henrys and Miss Tultys of this world are far too ready, in her opinion, to blame every slip in performance on a girl's discovery of the opposite sex. She's going to enjoy putting the silly duffers right. 'Anaemic,' she imagines telling them. 'Knew it soon as I got a close look at her – white as a sheet, dark under the eyes.' She lets Liz go after extracting her promise to visit a doctor. 'Would you like me to write to your mother?'

'Oh, no – thank you very much. Mummy will take me when I've told her about our talk.'

These mothers, thinks the Head wearily.

'And I'll try and make up Miss Tulty's work,' promises Liz, 'when I'm feeling a bit better.'

'That's the spirit.'

Liz closes the door of the Head's study, almost collapses into the arms of her friends. They lead her upstairs.

In the sixth-form cloakroom, the girls see them coming and fall quiet. Angie Hutchings mutters something, the others turn away and snort into their satchels. It's the sort of occurrence Chrissy and Nell have to contend with regularly. Liz doesn't seem to notice – if she does, she doesn't care – but Nell and Chrissy know this sort of challenge can't be ignored. Otherwise, people will say things openly, Liz's affair will be accepted as fact, she'll be in big trouble, maybe asked to leave. So they stamp on it. Hard. Even when, as in this case, they didn't catch what was actually said.

'There's a pair of your knickers doing the rounds of the boys' sixth, did you know, Hutchings?' Nell enquires loudly.

The girls know it's invention; just the same, Angie

Hutchings gets funny looks. She's furious, flame red. 'I'm going to report you for telling lies.'

'I don't think so,' murmurs Nell.

Angie flounces off. She'll be more careful in future about slandering Liz, at least for a while.

Nell's terrifically good at this type of tactic – making up outrageous stories on the spur of the moment. 'They just come to me,' she says modestly. They're effective precisely because they *are* outrageous; people don't want the slur repeated so they swallow their objections.

Chrissy's forte is physical intimidation. Not that she actually does anything, she doesn't have to, suggesting what she might do is sufficiently menacing. When someone needs their mouth fixing, Chrissy bides her time (but not for too long) then gets them alone on the stairs or in the cloakroom. 'Oh, excuse *me*,' she'll say, flattening her victim against the wall merely by towering with her eyes flashing and her shoulders jutting. It works, helps make the gossip-mongers wary, helps keep the lid on the pot.

Jolly hard work, though. By the summer term, they're feeling the strain. It's a good job there are compensations.

Like the thrill they get from watching her and listening. Liz has not, after all, given them the details once hoped for, never enlarged on the mechanics, as Nell once put it. And they've accepted this. They know she's gone somewhere they can't quite reach, that they'll only discover these things when they go there, too. All the same, little bits of information get dropped. They seize on these, speculate. And they've acquired a sort of sensual understanding simply by observing her. It's this that gives them the thrill, makes their throats go dry, their stomachs clench. They'll be lolling about – on the grass at the back of the hockey field, for instance – and Liz will suddenly go dreamy as if forgetting they're there; she'll sigh and luxuriously stretch her limbs out, arch her back, raise her breasts, smooth a hand slowly down the length of a thigh. 'Ah,' she'll sigh, smiling lazily, then roll over on to her stomach, flopping her head on a crooked arm. 'Ahh.'

They don't move, don't speak; their fingers dig into the ground. When the conversation starts up again, Nell and Chrissy have voices like hinges needing oil.

She's lying beneath an oak in the deserted grounds of Barnes Manor. Under her, Ronnie's old mac; on top of her, Ronnie. When they move, the bruised grasses send out waves of woozy-making hay and clover fumes. Directly overhead, through leaves and branches, there are patches of blue – very intense, almost navy. Beyond the tree's shade there's no colour, just light melting. She is melting, with Ronnie, into the earth, falling.

Love-making out of doors is like swooning. It's great indoors, too, but different; her mood alters with the place. Languor is what she feels right now, and oneness – she, Ronnie, the sky, this deep pasture, insects buzzing, birds calling, soft wind sighing.

She doesn't often see Mrs Poole these days; in fact, tries hard not to. When Mr Poole insisted on her calling him 'Ronnie', she was afraid of saying it by mistake in front of his wife. So one day during tea, he said – speaking far too loudly – 'By the way, I've told Liz it's time she called us by our Christian names.'

Mrs Poole looked surprised. Liz looked down at her plate.

He's told her how he came to marry Mrs Poole. They met at a tennis club. She was lively, energetic, vivacious. Imagine his disappointment when her true nature came through, for within months it was clear she was no more than an empty-headed woman entirely wrapped up in cleaning the house, tidying the garden, shopping, cooking, gossiping, and working in flashy shops.

'See? Told you,' say Chrissy and Nell, as if what he's said only goes to vindicate their early intuition of Mrs Poole's unworthiness. None of them think it's a good job one of the Pooles is bothered about the family upkeep, despite Ronnie's confession that piano teaching is pretty unrewarding, financially speaking.

'Money,' they scoff, as if anyone could be material-istic with Mr Poole to love and cherish. 'No sense of what's really important,' pronounces Chrissy of Mrs Poole.

Pam next door is still a source of worry. Ronnie's right about her, she's always spying. It's amazing how many times, when Liz is entering or leaving the Pooles' house, the woman pops up from behind a curtain or out of her gate, even once, as Liz turned into Legget Road, out of the corner shop. Liz has stopped reporting these sightings to Ronnie; they only make him edgy; then he says she'd better not come to the house for a while.

The extent of Mrs Poole's materialism is brought home to Liz by Ronnie's account of how he came to lose his share in the house – the story prompted by Liz having one of her chivvying sessions. (She's always trying to pin him down. 'We will be together soon, Ronnie? When? Two years or three?' Ronnie says they must wait till Alison's old enough to understand, and Liz spends a lot of time privately calculating when this might be.) On this particular occasion, Ronnie raises difficulties as to *where* he and Liz can be together. They'll have to start from scratch, he says bitterly, because number five Legget Road belongs to Sheila, has done ever since she made him sign it over to her.

'How? Why?' an indignant Liz demands to know – and it all comes out about Natalie Tate.

Ronnie had an affair with this woman. ('Oh, ages ago – yes, yes, *years* ago – oh, two or three – look, maybe it was three or four. Do you want to hear about it, or not?') Sheila found them out, said she'd tell

Natalie's husband, divorce Ronnie, take Alison away, unless Ronnie made over the house, thus relieving her new-born sense of insecurity.

Liz doesn't give a damn about the house. 'He's had an affair with another woman,' she cries to Chrissy and Nell utterly beside herself, blind with tears, clutching their hands.

They do their best, tell her it's because Mrs Poole wasn't up to him, didn't understand him, that he had to look elsewhere. Liz needn't worry. Now he's got her, he'll be happy and safe for ever. She can put Natalie Tate right out of her mind.

'But she only lives across the park. In Torrington Avenue. He could still see her.'

'He wouldn't.'

'By accident, then.'

'So? It wouldn't mean a thing to him.'

She needs them to tell her again and again. Endlessly concerned and patient, they oblige.

She calms down, persuades herself that she's come to terms with it; but it's shaken her to the core. It's as though she's forgotten it wasn't *her* he was unfaithful to, but his wife. The world seems full of older women, vindictive, out to rob her, spying on her secretly from behind their curtains, bent on luring him into their homes. She's vulnerable, weak, up against it; against their wily machinations, she feels, she hardly stands a chance.

She's waiting by the cloakroom door. At the first clack of the bell, before the peal gets going properly, she's off – down the stairs two at a time, along the verandah (heads turning as she flies past), down the drive, into the road. She doesn't care if she's seen; so what? Ronnie'll be picking her up in a minute. She hasn't looked any further than this; the world can end once she's reached him, if it wants.

Turning into Brian Avenue, she slows down. He'll drive up any minute, she doesn't look round. Sometimes he's late and she has to keep walking up and down hateful Brian Avenue with her stomach churning and a feeling growing that everything hangs on his turning up, that if he doesn't, she's dead. Today, his car draws alongside her almost immediately. Oh, top-hole day – she had a feeling it was going to be wonderful, she was right. They don't speak, don't need to. She pulls the rear door shut, flops back along the seat. Smoothly, Ronnie drives on.

He looks at her in the driving mirror a couple of times, grinning. Light-heartedness bubbles up in her. She can't sit up and chat, as she'd like to (you never know who's car might come alongside at the traffic lights – in Ronnie's worst scenario it's the aldermanic Stockdale Humber – and you never know who might be standing on the pavement's edge waiting to cross – in hers, it's Mrs Poole), so she takes off her shoes, tosses one after the other, up and over on to the passenger's seat. It's a small venting of her desire to be wicked, to have a bit of fun.

He's still grinning, so she takes her socks off, rolls them into a ball, chucks. Next, she wriggles out of her skirt, makes it into a sausage, sends it over like a dart. 'Hey,' he says, 'what're you doing?' But his grin's gone really wide, he's craning his neck to glimpse a larger portion of her in the driving mirror. She slumps her back flat along the seat, her bent knees lolling open, and starts unbuttoning her shirt. Soon this, too, lands on the passenger's seat. 'Careful, whatever are you up to?' But his cautious words are belied by chuckles and swift head-turnings. She rips off her bra and pants; he fairly jumps in his seat as they land beside him. 'Oh-ho,' he chortles, 'you naughty girl, you'll get me locked up,' and puts his foot down.

When they turn on to the track, she doesn't sit up as usual, just lies there, doll-like, getting jolted. He doesn't waste time, he's over into the back almost as the engine dies.

Nothing languorous about today's love-making. It's fast, punchy.

'You haven't practised this, have you?' he asks sadly, when her fingers abandon the effort.

No answer.

He sighs. 'You mustn't let it go, darling.'

'Why?' She sounds indignant, yobbish even, but she's nearly crying.

'I should be very disappointed if you did.'

Bugger Beethoven, she thinks.

He rests his hands on her shoulders. 'If I'm to continue taking your father's money – and obviously, I must – then you'd better keep on learning. Understand?'

She bites her lip, holds her breath.

'And how's the school work coming? Have you caught up in Music yet?'

She shakes her head.

'Oh – Liz. You'll never get to university if you go on like this.'

'I don't want to.'

Now he's mad with her. 'Of course you do,' he snaps, removing his hands. 'You're going to university, my girl, and that's that.' He might have been talking to Alison.

'I'll decide what I'm going to do, thank you very much.'

'If you talk like that, I'll begin to change my opinion of you. I thought you were bright, an intelligent, cultured young lady.'

'Balls.'

Sucking in breath, he swings away. 'If there's one thing I can't stand, it's a woman swearing.'

She glances at him. He's gone to stare out of the window.

'Perhaps it's been a mistake,' he says.

'What has? What do you mean?' He won't like her raising her voice – there's a pupil waiting in the dining room – but she's past caring.

'Shh.' He's by her side at once, grabbing her arm to quieten her – with force if necessary.

'Well, don't say things like that,' she whispers. 'I can't bear it.'

'I can't let you throw your whole life away. I'm not worth it.'

'Oh, Ronnie.'

He hands her his handkerchief.

'Look, it's nearly the summer holidays. Things won't be so hectic, we'll have more time, more opportunity. Alison's going camping with the Guides as soon as school breaks up, she'll be gone for ten days; with Sheila at work, you and I can be together here as often as we like.'

'That'll be terrific, Ronnie.'

'So will you promise me to pull your socks up– get on top of your school work, try harder with the Beethoven?'

'Oh, yes, I promise.'

'Good. Better, now? Jump up, then, and I'll show you how it ought to sound.'

This is how it will be, she thinks, once we're together. She's in the cake shop, secretly playing housewife. What shall I get him for elevenses? she wonders, looking up and down the counter – sugared doughnuts, Danish pastries, currant buns – and underneath at the refrigerated display – éclairs, cream slices, meringues. If they were living together now, he'd have been up and working from quite early on this morning. Composing, probably, because living with her is bound to get his creativity flowing. She's got a picture in her head of her cranking a starter handle – like on an old car – and Ronnie roaring into life. Nell and Chrissy agree: with Liz inspiring him every day, all his latent talents

264

will blossom, he'll be energized. Having been hard at it from early on this morning, about now he'd be ready for a break – a cup of coffee and a bite to eat, a chat about how his work's going. Then I'd do a bit of tidying up, then make us some lunch . . .

'Er, two meringues, please.'

She watches the assistant manoeuvre the cakes into a box and tie the parcel with string; hands over the money, goes out. In the street, she makes for the phone box against the wall of the parish church; flinches at the sour smell as she pulls the door open, puts in the coins, dials his number.

'Yes?'

'It's me. Everything all right?'

'Yes, all clear. Next door's putting her washing out, should keep her occupied for a bit.'

'I'm in the Old Market.'

'What are you doing there?'

'Getting some cakes – meringues.'

He chuckles, meringues are his favourites. 'I'll put the kettle on. Hurry.'

Eight minutes later, she's flitting up the path. He's left the door on the snib; she pushes it open and steps in. He hurries to close the door himself to make sure it's done quietly, takes the cake box from her, returns to the kitchen.

From where there's a great smell of coffee – she draws it into her lungs, hangs on to it and wanders into the sunny dining room before breathing it out. Time stretches ahead like wanton luxury, they've hours and hours ahead of them.

'Keep away from the window. I told you she was hanging out her washing.'

'Oh, sorry.'

He's holding a tray, and relaxes his fierce expression to suggest taking it upstairs.

She darts out through the hall, makes to go scampering up, but restrains herself in time to avoid a second

265

telling off. Step, step, she climbs stealthily in the approved noiseless manner. The prospect of their third day together in less than a week must be going to her head, she keeps forgetting about Pam.

They remove all their clothing and get into bed. He pulls the tray on to his knees, pours the coffee. She doles out the cakes. Stifled giggles, sugar dust puffing with every bite, crumbs gathering in their skin creases. He leans over, licks up a chunk from her smooth abdomen. She squawks under her breath, grabs his hand, bites from his meringue; cream messes her face. They fall back laughing, finish eating, lick one another clean. Now sip their coffee. No need to rush; they've so much time, they can waste it. Not that they aren't already thinking about what comes next – probing with toes, slowly and thoughtfully sliding shin against shin. They put their coffee cups down. Still, they let the time go by. 'Mm, funny, isn't it?' she muses. 'How people are never what you think they are, once you get to know them.'

'Aren't they? Not talking about me, by any chance?'

'In a way. I used to dream about Mr Poole. It seemed impossible I'd ever, you know, really get him.'

'And then you did.'

'No, I didn't. I got Ronnie. Mr Poole vanished. I can only just remember him if I concentrate hard.'

'You're not trying to tell me you're disappointed?'

She lifts her head to look down on him earnestly – 'Of course I'm not. I'm just saying . . .' – flops back. 'Oh, I don't know what I'm saying. Just, wasn't I a daft kid? I couldn't be disappointed in you, Ronnie.'

'No? Really?' Now he leans over her, puts a hand on her breast. Suddenly, it's serious . . .

At first, Liz thinks it's Pam's front door slamming. The sound reaches her through his thrusting and strenuous breathing. She's more startled by Ronnie jerking up his head and propping his torso on stiff arms either side of her head, than by the distant thud.

'What?'

266

He clamps a hand over her mouth. Now she knows it wasn't Pam's door slamming.

They're utterly still.

'Ronnie?' calls Mrs Poole from downstairs.

'Shit.' Ronnie's flying – bottom, arms, trousers; bits of him flash and fling, he's a whirlwind. 'Don't move,' he hisses, 'don't make a sound.' Very quietly, very stealthily, he creeps to the door, presses it tight shut and turns the key.

Liz's eyes are hooked on him, he seems to have forgotten her existence. Buttoning his shirt, he goes to the dressing table mirror to smooth his hair. All the time Mrs Poole's voice comes closer and closer. At first sounding quite normal. 'I'm not very well. Mr Wilkowski's been ever so kind, drove me home. Will you phone the surgery, try and get me an appointment? I'll have a lie down . . . Where the heck *are* you?' A pause, then the door handle rattling. Now she sounds annoyed. 'What're you playing at? Open up.'

For Liz, who hasn't moved a muscle and stopped breathing some moments ago, the room starts swimming.

'In a minute. I'm just getting dressed.'

'Well, open the door,' she demands reasonably. 'I've seen you in the buff before.' She agitates the handle. 'Open it, you idiot.'

Ronnie just stands there. Liz prays he'll do no such thing.

'Open it, Ronnie, I want to see you.'

'Why don't you go downstairs and put the kettle on?' he suggests in a tight voice.

Another pause, very lengthy, before hell breaks out. 'Open it, open it now. You hear me, Ronnie? Damn well open this door.' She abandons the handle to pound the door; kicks it, too.

Then stops. Goes quiet. There's a long tense hush. When she speaks again, her voice has gone hollow, very deep, like a voice coming from the bottom of a well. 'You've got a woman in there.'

This loosens Ronnie up, starts him gabbling. 'Of course I haven't, you know I wouldn't, you know perfectly well . . . Just go downstairs like a sensible person and I'll come and join you. Make us some tea, for heaven's sake, I've had a migraine, taken some tablets. Go on, Sheila, I shan't be a second; let me hear you going downstairs and I'll be straight out.'

'You *have* got a woman in there,' she cries, her new deep voice gathering frightening power. 'After all you promised. *In my home.* It'll be the last time, Ronnie, you'll see. God, I'm sick of it. Why couldn't you do it in *her* house, you pig, mess up her home, see how her husband likes it? I want to kill you, you bastard. And you, whoever you are, do you know you're about his twentieth? That's right, isn't it, Ronnie, or haven't I kept up? Bastard, rotten bastard . . .'

Liz is making scant sense of all this. Frozen in her jackknife recoil from love, it's not the words that rivet her, but their passionate delivery. It's the real Mrs Poole out there on the landing, the one she first got to know, the one who was her friend, who was fun. All this time as Ronnie's lover she's thought of Mrs Poole as Ronnie paints her, as Nell and Chrissy want her to be, as she, Liz, has needed her to be . . . The banging and yelling, seem lodged right inside her head. It's like being shaken and Mrs Poole screaming, 'How dare you pretend I'm not me.'

Ronnie comes and leans over the bed. 'In a minute,' he says in her ear, 'I'm going to open the door . . .'

'No, please . . .'

'Listen. I'll turn the key and rush out, push her back and grab her. You keep behind the door, then lock it as I rush out. Whatever happens, she mustn't see it's you.'

'No, she mustn't,' Liz agrees fervently. 'But who does she think it is?'

'No-one. She doesn't know. She's off her head. Ready? I'll count to three.'

She nods, shuffles off the bed.

'One, two, three.'

He's so quick, even Liz is shaken. Mrs Poole is taken quite unawares. The horrid surprise in her voice as Ronnie grabs her and Liz turns the key makes Liz's blood run cold; it's one of those fearsome night-time screeches you try to block out with a blanket. Plainly, he's manhandling her, but Liz doesn't care, she just hopes he'll get rid of her quickly and she can escape without betraying her identity.

Shivering, standing on the carpet, listening to the struggle on the stairs, she decides to increase her safety by shoving the wardrobe up against the door. This is easier thought than done, but she summons the strength from somewhere. When she's finished heaving and shoving, she finds the house gone quiet, then detects a quiet discussion going on – near the front door, she thinks. Then, from right underneath her in the dining room, Mrs Poole cries out, 'It's all right, Pam, he hasn't killed me, he's got a woman upstairs, that's all. I'm not going to budge till I've seen who it is. I'll come round and talk to you later.' Further murmuring follows, then the front door closes – evidently Ronnie seeing off Pam.

Now Liz hears Ronnie's voice in the dining room, sometimes low, sometimes sharp, coming from a spot near the doorway. Mrs Poole must be pacing about, her voice rises clearly, but in swings and swoops. Their voices go on and on.

Has he forgotten her up here? Why doesn't he do something to get her out of this fix? Not just keep talking and talking. What are they talking *about*? Stark naked, for it hasn't occurred to her to put her clothes on, freezing cold, she kneels on the thin carpet and presses an ear to the floor.

Natalie Tate – the name, uttered no more loudly than

269

other words, leaps at her through the floorboards, pings like a tennis ball between the Pooles: 'Natalie Tate.' 'No, not Natalie.' 'Natalie bloody Tate.' 'I tell you it's not Natalie.'

'Who then? That woman in the choir? You told me she moved to Lincoln.'

'She did, I haven't seen her for years.'

'Janet Rowse. Is it her?'

'No, it's not.'

'Don't say it's that woman from Shenley Street.'

'Of course it isn't – what do you take me for?'

'Then tell me who, for God's sake. You'll have to in the end, so you may as well have done with it. I know – it's Bella. Oh, you bastard, you mean bastard . . .'

Liz's eyes feel full of grit. All these women. Why doesn't Ronnie deny them properly, tell her he doesn't know a single one of them? Because he does, whispers a voice in her head. No, no – her fists strike the floor; but yes, yes, comes the whisper. 'Bastard,' she yells with Mrs Poole, 'bastard!' – her fists drumming.

Next thing she knows, someone's tapping on the bed-room door. 'It's me,' says Ronnie shortly. 'Open up.'

She doesn't know whether she dare. Anyway, the wardrobe's blocking it. 'I can't.'

'Oh, don't be *stupid*.' Sounds like he's sneering.

She goes and places her hands on the wall, her rump to the wardrobe and gives a heave. When the wardrobe's shifted a bit, she opens the door.

'What the dickens?' he asks, squeezing in. 'What got into you? There I am trying to persuade her to be reasonable, and *you* start throwing tantrums.'

'Who are they?'

'Er?'

'All those women.'

'No-one. Figments of her . . .'

'They must be someone. She wouldn't ask if they weren't anyone.'

'Let's keep to the point.'

'Tell me the truth. Have you had other women be-sides Natalie Tate? Oh, Ronnie . . .' Her breathing has gone so rapid and shallow, she can't keep up with it.

'Listen, will you? And for Pete's sake get dressed. I'm going to tell her it *is* Natalie Tate in here. Might be dodgy getting out of it later, but anything's better than her knowing the truth. Christ, if she told your father . . . She'll wear it being Natalie. She knows Natalie's terri-fied of her husband, which will explain us not wanting to give away the name. Once she thinks she knows, she might calm down. Which would give us a chance to think of something. But for heaven's sake, behave yourself; no more noise. Lock the door after me.'

She gets dressed when he's gone. She doesn't be-lieve him about the women. It takes a while for her to understand this. When she does, she's not horri-fied, just empty. Also very cold, she wants a pee. They've started talking again, but she's not listening. All she wants is to be out of this house and never come near it again. In her whole life.

Then it's like a shaft piercing her. It starts hurting with Mrs Poole's cry of 'Oh no', which grabs her at-tention for the next bit — 'I've had the most terrible thought,' and an awful inevitability comes over her, and the pain gets sharper, and she knows how it's going to end . . . 'Ronnie,' wails Mrs Poole, 'I hope you'll tell me I'm wrong. It couldn't be, could it? You couldn't be so wicked. Tell me it's not, it's not *Liz*?'

There's a huge hole of silence after this. Then Ronnie shouts and Mrs Poole shouts and Liz whirls round. The window. Oh God, she's got to get out of here somehow.

She opens it, leans out. Directly below her is the roof of a lean-to shed. She could jump down on to this, and then on to the ground. Might hurt herself, but it'd be better than staying locked up in here. She hitches her bottom on to the sill, swings her legs through the opening; is easing out her body when a movement makes her look across into next-door's garden. It's Pam at the washing line, looking up at her. Right up at her. Looking and looking.

When she tumbles back into the room, she's like a dog jerking from an electrified fence. That's it, then, she thinks. Mrs Poole is going to know.

Time passes. She considers peeing into the coffee pot, decides there'd be too much. Perhaps just wet on the floor, who cares? She'll never set eyes on the Pooles again.

There's no time. He's rapping on the door again. 'It's me.'

She opens it, stands back, not looking at him.

'Right, here's the plan. I've persuaded her you *are* Natalie Tate.' (She doesn't say anything.) 'For a moment back there I thought she'd rumbled us. Did you hear?' (She nods.) 'So I laid it on thick about how terrified you are – Natalie is, I mean, of her husband finding out. I told her, if she stays calm I'll try and persuade you – Natalie – to come down and talk to her. Now, what we're actually going to do is this: you're coming out too, keep behind me down the stairs, then when I go into the dining room pretending you're on your way, you dash into the kitchen and out through the back. If she guesses what we're up to, I'll hang on to her for as long as possible. So it's up to you to be quick. Better not go out the front way, the whole street'll be watching by now.' (She doesn't mention Pam; he'd go mad if he knew, it might delay her escape.) 'Ready? Go.'

Her legs are like jelly trying to match his on the stairs. She's halfway down when he reaches the bottom. He doesn't look back, just keeps going straight on into the dining room and closes the door. 'Right,' she hears him announce, 'she'll be down in a minute. She's just paying a visit to the bathroom.' Mrs Poole must have smelt a rat: as Liz scurries to the back door, there's the sound of a scuffle, then a howl of rage which makes Liz's fingers go useless trying to turn the back-door key. Will it ever turn? Ages go by. Finally, she manages it, goes stumbling and running down the garden path. Now the latch sticks on the back garden gate – 'Open, *open*,' – gives suddenly, spilling her into the alley where she runs smack into someone. Pam, of course. Pam staggering back and hitting the wall.

Liz is the first to recover; picks herself up, turns to flee for her life . . . Then can't. 'Please,' she pants, leaning briefly against the wall to get her breath. 'Oh, please – tell Mrs Poole I'm sorry.'

Now she's off: stumbling, skidding in gravel, clutching at railings as she flies round corners, feet running away with her down the slope of the subway where sounds loom close and hollow and large – train banging, whistle piercing, Mrs Poole shrieking 'Not *Liz*?' – and her bladder gives way, there's a trail behind her as she pants up the incline, her hopes pinned on turning the corner into Town Hall Square and finding (please God, I'll be good for ever, only let one be there) a bus waiting.

Twelve years on, they're helping Nell move house; out of the home she's been sharing with Fred during their brief marriage, into a flat she doesn't intend sharing with anybody. Chrissy and Liz are kneeling on the floor wrapping and packing pieces of china. In theory, Nell is also doing this, though most of the time she sits with an ashtray between her outstretched legs, ruminating. 'He was hardly the answer to a maiden's prayer,' she reflects, 'in the bed department.'

They don't encourage her. They already know more than they wish to know of Fred's shortcomings. Nell goes on musing in silence, until her mind lands on a fresh aspect. 'I suppose the first one always spoils you for the rest.'

'First what?'

'Man. Fling. Affair.'

273

'Oh?'

'Well, yes. Inevitably, when you come to think about it. The draw of the unknown, the terror, the magic . . . You can never recapture all that.'

Chrissy and Liz glance at one another, both thinking the same thing – how, when Nell was a student in London and they two were undergraduates at the more lowly university across the river, she never breathed a word of any affair, never mind a brilliant introductory one spoiling her subsequently for all else.

'You never told us about your first,' Chrissy says accusingly. 'We always supposed it couldn't have been up to much.'

'Not worth reporting,' says Liz. 'You were a bit cagey in those days, we thought.'

Nell narrows her eyes, smokes intensely down to the last half inch of her cigarette, takes her time stubbing it out. 'What I mean is, you dolts,' – she's already shaking the cigarette packet, checking her supply – '*our* first affair. You know, with Mr Poetic Poole. God, the energy we expended on that, imagining, scheming, longing, *thrilling*; it was bound to be downhill ever after.'

There's a stunned silence while they gape at her.

Chrissy, who wishes always for harmony between them and can sense a fight coming from the way Liz grabs the edge of the tea chest, decides to give Nell the benefit of the doubt and encourage Liz to do the same. 'That *is* how we thought about it then,' she appeals, 'I do remember us agreeing that you were doing it for all three of us.'

'Bollocks,' says Liz, springing to her feet. 'I don't believe a word of it. And if it *were* true, if she really has been carting that episode round in her head as an ideal first encounter, all I can say is, I'm sorry for her. Because I don't even count it as *mine*. It was a sham, a con, making love with someone who wasn't real. And if you don't mind, I'd rather it wasn't mentioned again. *Ever*. Coffee?'

'Oh – yeah.'

'Please.'

'Can she mean it?' hisses Nell, when Liz is safely out of the way. 'That we can't ever talk about it?' It's not as if they do very often, in fact Nell can't recall the last time the subject arose. It's a bit thick, though, Liz slapping on an embargo.

'*Shh*,' commands Chrissy. 'Go and make a start on the books.'

vii

'Mu-um,' said Clare, getting fidgety towards the end of dinner, which was being taken at the vast kitchen table and had gone on rather long. She slid out of her chair and went over to Chrissy, leant against her, swaying backwards and forwards on her toes so that her stomach kept butting Chrissy's arm.

'Well, what is it?' Chrissy went on nibbling at her piece of cheese, but slipped her free hand round Clare's hips. 'I can't say if you don't ask.'

Clare fell still, dropped her head on to her mother's shoulder.

Nell and Liz looked on while Chrissy, pretending matter-of-factness, took plain and tactless pleasure from her daughter's attentions – laying her cheek against Clare's head, her hand giving little pats. Liz dropped her eyes and thought of Rosie. Nell felt gooseflesh rise on her arm where no child nudged her, and wondered whether it would have been like this for her and thingy – must be nice having your own rub up against you like that, natural as a puppy; it was possibly therapeutic, too. Maybe, if she'd gone along with Nature she'd be healthier now, wouldn't have been forced to smoke all those blessed cigarettes, nor drain so many bottles down her throat. There again, would motherhood have jelled with fearless journalism? She guessed not.

'Oh, Mum.'

'Why don't you just come out with it?'

'She wants to go to the kids' disco,' said Joy in superior tone.

'It's not kids'. It's the youth club.'

'Under sixteens,' scoffed Neil.

'Cathy's going. Her mum says it's OK.'

'Who's running it?'

'Mr Beasley.'

'Can she, Tony? If she's back by half ten?'

'I suppose that means I'm expected to fetch her,' said Tony, sounding long-suffering.

Clare's head had jerked up. 'Half ten?' she repeated aghast.

'Half ten, take it or leave it.'

'OK,' she conceded placidly; popped a kiss on her mother's cheek, yanked herself off.

'Thanks, darling,' said Chrissy to her husband, 'kind of you to offer, because we three are going for an evening stroll.'

It was the first Liz and Nell had heard of it.

Good-oh, Liz thought. She'd already put them in the picture about Rosie and had been wondering how to broach the Poole connection – was feeling mildly embarrassed about this, since it was she, after all, who'd said they weren't ever to discuss it: might be easier to do while strolling along, more casual.

Nell looked anxiously towards the window. Wasn't it nearly dusk? Didn't bats and things come out when it got dark in the country? Was it true they got tangled in people's hair or was that just an invention of the horror movies? Better wear a scarf.

'Cold?' asked Chrissy, ten minutes later, puzzled by Nell stumping downstairs swathed in scarf and light-weight trench coat.

'No, but it does feel rather late in the day to be setting off for a walk.'

'We lazed about all afternoon. Won't sleep soundly

if we don't get a bit of exercise. Specially Liz, after her journey.'

New to the idea of exercise as one of the day's vital ingredients, Nell made no comment.

Liz came running downstairs. 'Where are we going?'

'Follow our noses.'

So, with nothing planned, and no-one paying particular attention to where nose-following was leading, they entered the lane between two steep banks that links Fenby-cum-Laithby with Wold Enderby.

5
PERCEPTION

i

Chrissy held the door open, Liz helped Nell inside. They lowered her into one of the plastic-covered easy chairs. 'Orrh, that's more like it,' she gasped of the bar-room fug. 'That raw air outside was killing me.'

'Fresh air,' Chrissy corrected her.

'Whatever, I don't go for it.'

'Drink?'

'Scotch. Neat.'

Liz said she'd have an orange juice. Chrissy went to the bar to negotiate for drinks on tick, none of them having brought any money, also for a phone call to Tony.

'Are you OK, Nell?' asked Liz, taking and chafing her hand. Nell didn't look OK. She was wheezing before they got to Wold Enderby, almost collapsing when they arrived at the village green.

'You two walk so darn fast.' Her eyes filled; Liz's concern was tempting.

'Maybe you're starting a cold.'

Chrissy brought their drinks over. Nell snatched hers, gulped half of it down.

'Is she all right, do you think?' Chrissy wondered.

'She's fine and perfectly able to speak for herself,' snapped Nell, looking round – at plastic and Formica everywhere, horse brasses, facetious notices. 'What a grotty little pub.'

'Shush, do you mind? They were very nice about our drinks. Luckily, I know the landlady from when I was on the school committee.'

278

'Saved your bacon, anyway,' Liz reminded Nell.

'Was it always like this?'

'We never came in here, did we?'

'Perhaps not.'

Their flap over, Nell had interrupted Liz's flow, Chrissy recalled; she'd been going into the Poole fiasco, all sorts of details she hadn't let on about at the time. 'You were saying – Mrs Poole yelling *Not Liz*? has gone on haunting you. Has it really?'

Liz stared at them (fanatically, her friends rather uneasily thought). She was thinking that it didn't sound right the way Chrissy said it, and was hunting for words to describe the true quality of Mrs Poole's memorable shriek. 'Her voice leapt *up*,' she explained at length, 'like eyebrows shooting, like horror striking.'

'Gosh,' said Chrissy, pacifyingly. Nell tried to imagine it, narrowing her eyes.

'I remember exactly because all the time I was running away it kept on in my head, under the subway with a train banging overhead, her shriek like a whistle piercing (and, oh God yes, I wet myself), over and over on the bus going home, then up the lane . . . I remember streaking past the Rector's wife, she called out, must have thought I was mad, but I couldn't stop because I could still hear her – "*Not Liz*?" – like an accusing Fury.'

Nell and Chrissy took up their glasses.

Liz picked up a beer mat, flipped it over a few times, put it down. 'That's it, you see, that's what I dread for Rosie more than anything else; something like that hanging over her for ever, someone's pain that she knows she's caused.'

'Mm, but *accusing*?' wondered Chrissy, gently. 'Obviously, you've remembered her exact tone of voice, but are you sure you've interpreted it correctly? Put yourself in her place. You suddenly suspect that the female your husband's got locked up in the bedroom isn't some mature married woman, but a sixteen-year-old kid he's been entrusted with; furthermore, a kid

279

you've actively encouraged to visit the house. What do you do? Scream your head off, I dare say. But not to accuse the kid; in sheer horror at your husband, hoping to God it's not true.'

'Of *course*,' agreed Nell. 'She'd be terrified of the consequences – not entirely without cause as things turned out.'

Liz was dumbfounded. 'Why on earth haven't I ever worked that out for myself?'

'Because you'd got into the habit of hearing her with the ears of a guilty sixteen year old.'

It was true. It made her shake with relief and regret. If only she'd gone to visit Mrs Poole, not immediately afterwards, but a few years later, as she'd once considered doing but never summoned the necessary nerve. She'd even caught a glimpse of her once. She was shopping with her mother, they'd got the children with them. Coming down the escalator in Binns, she'd glanced over the rail into the eyes of a surprised yet intently watching Mrs Poole. Luckily, Mrs Poole was attending to a customer – Liz, of course, had had no idea she was working there. Three-year-old Rosie was playing up, so it was easy pretending not to have seen her. Then she'd hurried her protesting mother and children out of the shop. What a waste of a chance, she thought now; a few words introducing her children, a smile, some little gesture to show that her behaving all those years ago as if Mrs Poole didn't count had been an aberration, that in the end Mrs Poole had got through to her. Sadly, all she'd ever managed by way of paltry acknowledgement was that gabbled apology via the next-door neighbour.

'Will Tony be long, do you think?' asked Nell, regretting very heartily having set out minus cigarettes. She wondered whether she dare ask for some on tick, whether the landlady's good nature would extend so far.

'He's got to collect Clare first then drop her off at home.'

'I never told you, I suppose, what I blurted to the neighbour when we collided in the back alley afterwards?'

Chrissy frowned, Nell blinked.

'Oh, you mean when you were making off? I didn't know you said anything, did you, Nell?'

'Can't say I did. I say, Chrissy . . .'

'I said *Tell Mrs Poole I'm sorry*. Makes me squirm, now, to think of it.'

'Mm – I suppose it was a trifle inadequate. Chrissy, flower . . .'

Groaning, Liz put her head in her hands. 'It'd have been better to say nothing. Trouble was, I'd just realized that everything I'd experienced in that house was a sham – except for Mrs Poole's friendship. If only . . . I suppose it is too late, now, I couldn't . . .'

'Er, Liz,' said Chrissy, breaking in, fearing where this might lead (and something in her voice made Nell decide against pestering for cigarettes right now). 'Liz, dear, I didn't tell you before because I wasn't sure you'd want to know. She's dead. They both are. He died, oh, three or four years ago; there was quite a splash about it in the paper – local musician and so forth. She died a few months later – just a few lines in the obits column, widow of the late Ronnie Poole.'

'Oh,' said Liz, and after a time returned to fiddling with the beer-mat.

Little else was said by anyone until Tony breezed in.

Tony was not unhappy to have been called out on this mission. 'Nell's in a state of collapse,' his wife had reported over the phone, which had prompted the memory of another occasion – standing with his bicycle outside the Sea Gull Café hoping as ever for a word with Chrissy, the back door opening, Nell staggering out, Chrissy and Liz supporting her like escapees from a battle zone, one of them snarling (his beloved, probably), 'What do you think you're staring at? Push off, four-eyes.'

Tonight, thick-lensed spectacles agleam with his expectations, lips wet with readiness to impart the gems he'd rehearsed, he bustled up to them with total confidence. 'Couldn't make it home, eh, Nell? Anno Domini catching up? Poor old duck, I thought you were looking more than usually haggard. Never mind, Tony to the rescue, give us your arm.'

'We'll manage, thanks,' Chrissy told him through gritted teeth. 'Go and settle up at the bar.' And from her look might just as well have added, 'Then drop dead, four-eyes.'

Nell seemed reluctant to go to bed. They told her she ought to, she looked tired, was possibly breeding a cold. She squinted at them suspiciously, then dropped her eyes to the magazine on her lap, whose pages she was turning too regularly to allow proper perusal. Maybe, thought Liz, she thinks we're only waiting for her back to be turned before starting on about how old she's looking. Chrissy feared she was trying to out-sit them so that she could light up and stink out the sitting room. Liz yawned and excused herself. 'Honestly, Nell, I'm dead beat,' she heard Chrissy complain as she went upstairs.

She used the bathroom, got ready for bed, then went to the window and pulled back the curtain. Hours after sunset, it was still not completely dark; shadowy rosiness hung over the garden, the sun's afterglow. Almost too nice to be indoors, she thought, her eyes going to the cloud of shrubbery at the base of the lawn where she'd once hidden to stare up at the house, full of delicious fear and a craving for the three of them to get inside and inhabit a corner. What incredibly good fortune to be installed here by right, as if their childhood dreams of stowing away had actually come true – trust Chrissy to have wangled it, always the practical one, their anchor, the one most determined to keep them from drifting apart.

Well anchored was how Liz was feeling right at this minute – calm, steady, enjoying a peace of mind she hadn't known for weeks. All down to her friends making her think again about Mrs Poole's reaction. In one sense it made no difference to her, she couldn't divorce herself from how she'd been at sixteen; how she'd felt then and what she'd been capable of were still part of her. But everything grafted on during her life since gave her a new view of the episode (very likely, as Chrissy had pointed out, a view closely aligned with Mrs Poole's). It had taken Chrissy's words to make her look; she'd got into a habit of *not* looking, of cutting off her memories because they felt too uncomfortable.

Murmurs on the landing, a door closing – Nell and Chrissy retiring. She closed the curtain, felt her way to bed, thinking what a good job it was for her that they'd managed this get-together. Between them, they could always sort out a crisis. Already she was feeling slightly detached from Rosie's affair. Not sorry she'd had a go at persuading her to consider Ellie and the children. But that she'd done enough. It was up to Rosie, now.

She fell suddenly and deeply asleep. When a noise woke her, it seemed hours had gone by, not minutes. She got up, opened her door, looked out. Light showed under Nell's door. 'It's me,' she whispered, softly tapping. 'Anything the matter?'

'Don't come in. I've, um, dropped one of my lenses. You'll only tread on it. Go back to bed.'

'If I'm careful can't I help?'

No answer.

In the master bedroom across the landing, Chrissy gripped her husband, held him still. 'Just a minute.'

'What's the matter?'

'Shh.'

He held himself rigid for what seemed a cruelly long moment, then cautiously reclaimed his privileges. Chrissy, who was now certain of something going on outside on the landing, clambered off him and scrambled out of bed, inadvertently sticking the point of her elbow into slack skin on the inside of his arm. He lay stunned, unable to decide on the area of his greater discomfort.

Chrissy slipped on her dressing gown, silently opened her door.

'*Found* the little rascal,' came Nell's stage whisper. 'Panic over. Night, night, Liz love.'

'Night, Nell,' whispered Liz, and, on seeing Chrissy, shrugged and shook her head.

A wave, and Chrissy withdrew, closed her door, stood pondering for a moment in the dark.

'What's the matter?'

'I don't think Nell's very good, you know.'

'Looks well past her sell by, if you want my opinion.'

'Nobody does. And it was lucky for you I didn't kick you in the goolies, the way you spoke to her in the pub.'

'Oh, Chrissy,' he groaned.

She snorted, but halfway through the exhalation, turned its impatience into a sigh. Better get it over with, she thought, dropping her gown, sliding into bed, otherwise he'll only pester in the morning. Or worse still, sulk. If there was one thing guaranteed to spoil a visit from friends it was a disobliging husband casting edginess about. Pathetic, though, the way he always wanted to be doing her whenever Nell and Liz came to stay. She wriggled close and put an arm over him. 'Sorry, love,' leaned over, kissed his nose. 'I was worried about her that's all. Now,' – she dragged parted lips over his ear, cheek, mouth – 'I'm all yours.' For it was only fair, as well as prudent, not to upset little Tony.

284

Back in bed, Liz was finding falling asleep for a second time hard to do, disturbed by a growing conviction of something badly amiss with Nell. Their getting together had already worked powerfully for her; time now, to get Nell sorted.

ii

Mrs Stockdale thinks Liz is looking peaky. Which is no wonder when you consider all the meals she's skipped lately, and how even when she does come to the table she just picks at her food. 'Look at that plate, Daddy. Now, aren't I right?'

'Dockers on strike again,' growls Alderman Stockdale into his *Evening Telegraph*. 'They'll have the country on its knees before they're finished. Finish your tea, princess, and do us all a favour. I suppose your pal Nell's father's one of these perishers. A red, isn't he? I'd give 'em red . . .'

Fortunately, Mrs Stockdale has another matter on her mind, of more tangible and urgent concern than a daughter's peakiness. Couch grass has appeared in the rockery. Its origins are a mystery, its seeds are never permitted to hatch out on Stockdale land. Mrs Stockdale is inclined to blame the people in the new house over the way; it's not good enough, buying a prime village plot, spending pots of money building a fancy house, and then neglecting to tend the garden. People have a duty to their neighbours, but what can you expect from the sort of folk with money to burn nowadays? Couch grass is the very devil. Every tiny plant, every heavy stone will have to come out, then the ground cleaned and re-cleaned. There's Stan, of course, (garden help) but would he be sufficiently thorough? Mrs Stockdale doubts it, knows she won't rest easy till she's personally turned, raked, inspected, every square inch. It's going to be a mammoth task.

'I'll help, if you like,' offers Liz, who has no plans to

go anywhere or see anyone beyond the narrow boundaries of her home for the foreseeable future. Lying low is her current occupation. A spot of vigorous digging might relieve the tedium.

'Oh no, duckie, Mummy wouldn't dream of it, not with your pianist's hands. No, you get on with your practice, I don't seem to hear you doing much lately. I was saying to Mrs Garth only the other day, wouldn't it be nice, I said, if our Elizabeth got her Grade Eight before going to university, round her piano lessons off nicely . . .?'

Liz scrapes back her chair, leaves the room.

A tap on the office door, then Josie puts her head round. 'Sorry to bother you, Alderman Stockdale, but there's a woman on the line. Wants to speak to you, says it's something to do with your daughter.'

'Huh? Better put her on, then. Hello, Alderman Stockdale speaking. What's this all about?'

'Oh hello. You won't know me. I'm a friend of Sheila Poole, wife of Mr Poole, the music teacher.'

'Oh yes?' – brightening.

'Sheila's in hospital. Heart spasm, the doctor says. They're keeping her in for observation.'

'I'm very sorry to hear that.'

'Yes, well, it's your daughter's caused it, Alderman Stockdale – her and Mr Poole. Sheila caught them at it. No surprise to me, she was always coming round to the house when Sheila was out. If she were mine she'd get a good bottom smacking.'

'Would you mind giving me your name, madam?'

'Like I said, I'm a friend of Mrs Poole's. I don't want Sheila lying there in hospital worrying what your daughter's getting up to with her husband. You people who get on the council, setting yourselves up as examples . . .'

'I repeat, your name, madam?'

'Just keep that girl under control.'

'Josie?' yells Alderman Stockdale, crashing down the receiver. 'Put Jack Greenaway off, tell him I'll see him tomorrow at his convenience. Get Carol to hold the fort. I'm going out.'

Nell and Chrissy have been job-hunting along the sea front, giving wide berths to the bathing pool, the boating lake and the Sea Gull Café. They've canvassed the amusement arcade and the fun fair, the souvenir shops, the booths selling candy floss and ices, the fish-and-chip cafés. It's 'Sheffield fortnight'; the town's full to bursting with steel workers and miners, their wives, their offspring. You'd think someone would've offered them work. Maybe they haven't tried hard enough. Maybe they've failed to disguise how superior it all makes them feel, the tatty goods on sale, the pathetic games of chance, the flimsy shooting ranges, the greasy-looking stall-holders with only a glitter of avarice in their eyes to tell you they're not walking waxworks; and the Sheffies themselves, poor duffers. Maybe they should try looking keen; but maybe not, after all they're aiming to blend in with the scene. A man at the Jolly Fisherman offers them washing-up, but at less per hour than they made last year at the Sea Gull. They say they'll take it, though. 'How old do you have to be to get on the line at Frigid Fruits?' Nell wonders as they trudge off down the road. 'Seventeen and a half,' sighs Chrissy, 'and you've got to be nimble, they can pick and choose.' 'Next summer, then,' says Nell; but she's not over-confident, the burgeoning frozen food industry represents the summit of every local student's vacation ambition.

They're on their way to Chrissy's, now, to scrutinize Mrs Atkinson-next-door's fashion and beauty magazines which Mrs Atkinson passes on to Auntie Julie when she's done with them. Auntie Julie sometimes turns a page or two, cackling and scoffing; mostly, she just tosses them aside. 'Flaming useless, even for the cludgy,' she says (the shiny paper lacking the absorbency of newsprint). At the traffic lights, they turn into Lister Avenue, go slouching down towards number 142.

There's a small car parked outside. There's a man sitting in it. He's watching them through the driving mirror. As Chrissy puts a hand on her gate, he springs out, runs round the bonnet, calling softly, urgently, 'Chrissy Thomas? Liz Stockdale's friend?'

Chrissy looks at Nell.

So does the man. 'Are you Nell, by any chance?'

It's Mr Poole, they suddenly see.

'Look, would you mind getting into the car? There's something I need you to do for me – and, er, Liz: I must get a message to her. Please?' He opens both front and rear passenger doors. Nell shoves Chrissy towards the front, herself gets into the back of the car. Mr Poole runs round, jumps in, turns on the engine. The gears grate, the car gives a lurch, Mr Poole's hands shake when he pulls on the steering wheel. The car goes two blocks down Lister Avenue then turns left. Nell settles back. Perhaps they're being abducted. She feels mildly cheated when Mr Poole draws into the curb. The engine dies; it's very quiet.

Mr Poole clears his throat. 'Uhum. Allow me to introduce myself: I'm Ronald Poole. Have you been in touch with Liz recently? In the last two days at all?'

'No we haven't, have we, Nell?'

'You know about, um, Liz and me?'

'We know *some* things,' says Chrissy cagily.

'I thought so,' says Mr Poole, who had continually emphasized the need for perfect secrecy to his young lover. 'She mentioned you to me. That's how I tracked you down. Looked up Thomas, Lister Avenue in the phone book, got the house number, waited outside.'

'Why?' asks Chrissy. She can't manage a more polite, less bald enquiry.

Nell can. 'Is it because something's happened?' she

288

asks, shuffling to the edge of her seat so as not to miss anything.

'I'm afraid, yes, um, a rather unfortunate occurrence. Liz and I were together when my wife came home unexpectedly.'

'Flipping heck. You mean she caught you? Were you and Liz actually . . .?'

'Well, yes, in a manner of speaking. Though my wife didn't appreciate who it was – the person with me, I mean. Trouble is, our next-door neighbour saw Liz trying to effect a get-away. The silly girl panicked. I told her to keep her head down . . .'

As Chrissy detects that Mr Poole does not sound lovingly concerned for Liz but irritated and vengeful, emptiness fills her stomach, widens until skin, flesh and bone feel strained to contain it. She imagines plugging it with pacifying chocolate bars, bagfuls of smothering chips. Then, envisioning the ensuing belch, an image of her gaping mouth springs to mind – but instead of gas coming forth, sound blares – 'wah, wah, wah' – like an infant's bawling . . .

'Liz and I haven't been in touch since this, ah, incident. It's now impossible for me to speak to her in person, but somehow she must be warned. You see, this neighbour I was telling you about – it must have been her, I can't think of anyone else who would . . .'

'Would what?' prompts Nell, nudging close enough to see Mr Poole's pores sweating.

'She rang up Liz's father. Told him Liz and I are involved.'

'Crumbs.'

'He drove straight over to see me. Fortunately, I was alone in the house. It was unpleasant to put it mildly. Frightening. In point of fact he threatened me.'

'You mean, threatened to kill you?' gasps Nell.

'He threatened to harm my daughter, Alison.' But the name is too much for Mr Poole, his voice shakes on it; several moments elapse before he continues. 'He said if he discovers I've harmed his daughter, he'll personally harm mine. He'd got his arm across my throat at the time. I believed him, I don't mind telling you. That man, I believe, would be capable of anything.'

'Je-sus,' breathes Nell.

Mr Poole drops his head as a woman emerges from one of the houses. When she closes her gate they see she has a dog on a lead. She's coming their way. In silence, Mr Poole waits for her to pass.

Chrissy barely sees the woman. The significance of her urgent hunger has begun to dawn on her. It's a sensation she connects with childhood, and listening to this man beside her, she is feeling more and more infantile. This man isn't Mr Poole at all, not in the least little bit. Mr Poole doesn't exist, they dreamed him up, like kids playing a game. She wants to yell, 'We're not playing this stupid game anymore.' She wants to seize Nell and shake her till she rattles, put a stop to her constant prompting of this man which, in Chrissy's present state of mind, is coming over like a three-year-old's persistent demands of 'Why is it? What for?' She wants to find Liz this instant and comfort her – 'Don't worry, it's only a game, only pretend.' These men, though, Mr Poole and Alderman Stockdale, aren't pretend. They're horribly real. Worse, they are adults, and as such have secret motives and drives. Adults aren't for playing with.

The woman, having paused at a lamp-post to oblige her dog, at last goes past the car.

Mr Poole watches her recede in the driving mirror. 'In view of this threat,' he goes on, 'this threat against Alison, you understand, I swore to Alderman Stockdale that Liz and I hadn't ever, you know, really done anything. I admitted we'd become emotionally entangled, but said it had gone no further than a bit of kissing and cuddling.'

'You think he swallowed it?'

'Yes. Well, I suppose no man likes to believe his

daughter isn't . . . that she'd . . . Anyway, I'm sure he did. Of course, Liz and I are never to go near each other again; I gave her father my word.'

Suddenly Mr Poole smartens up and swivels round towards Nell, who is, after all, doing all the responding. (As he moves, Chrissy flinches, her hand seeks the door handle.) 'Look, it's absolutely vital for Liz to be put in the picture before her father gets home. Could you phone her, please? Tell her, if he questions her to deny everything – apart from a bit of cuddling and so forth – flatly deny anything else. Tell her he threatened to harm Alison. Tell her I'm begging her to co-operate for Alison's sake. You will, won't you?'

'All right,' says Nell.

'We'll walk back, thank you very much,' says Chrissy, opening the door, jumping out.

Mr Poole leans over for a parting shot. 'Impress upon her: nothing happened, nothing important.'

'All right. Goodbye.' She slams her door and opens Nell's – 'Come on' – and when Nell sits blinking in her usual dazed manner, yanks her out savagely. 'Will you get a move on? Hurry.'

Later, they go and wait at a bus-stop near the Robinson Rec (for Liz's reaction to their phone call was to flee from home that very minute). They sit on a bench, waiting for the bus to come, thinking their separate thoughts in silence.

After a while, Nell sighs deeply. 'Isn't he just fantastic? Don't you think he's the most fabulous man you ever heard of?'

Chrissy can't believe it. 'Mr Poole?'

Nell blinks. 'Not him, idiot. Not that slimy weed. God, wasn't he pathetic? What on earth did Liz ever see in him . . .'

Chrissy wants to protest that it wasn't just Liz, but all three of them who saw something, but Nell goes rattling on.

291

'No, no. I'm talking about Liz's dad, of course. Alderman Stockdale. Doesn't it give you the shivers the way he'd stop at nothing? I always thought he was incredibly handsome and dashing and everything. But God, he's ruthless. Oozes power. It must be fantastic having someone like him for a father, someone you can really respect . . .'

Before Chrissy can gather her wits, the bus comes into view. They jump to their feet. Liz is on the deck, clutching a holdall. As the bus slows, she jumps, lands in their arms. Her eyes are huge and dark, her face chalk white. They lead her into the rec, find a quiet bench.

Though she can hardly speak, Liz is desperate to know something. 'What you said about Alison. It wasn't right, was it? Daddy didn't say he'd harm her?'

Nell and Chrissy look at one another. 'It was probably said in the heat of the moment,' soothes Chrissy.

'You mean he *did*?'

'That's why Mr Poole was wetting himself,' Nell explains.

'But it's wicked, horrible. Alison hasn't done anything. And what does he mean, *harm*? How harm her? How?'

She's shouting, now, crying. Nell searches for tissues. Chrissy puts an arm round her. She blows and cries and re-blows her nose; Nell has to look away, there's so much mucus everywhere, leaking from spent tissues, trailing between Liz's fingers.

'Can I stay at your place?' Liz asks Chrissy.

'Of course.'

'You can come to ours, too, when you like,' offers Nell. (There's a spare bed in her room; sister Marion is now training to be a nurse in Leeds.)

'Thanks,' says Liz. 'Because I can't ever go home again.'

So it's back to looking after Liz. Mostly, she stays at Chrissy's, sometimes at Nell's, sometimes all three crowd into Chrissy's room. They've got holiday jobs. Liz goes to the Gainsborough Hotel in the business end of town where she scrubs and polishes the tiled entrance hall, cleans the ladies and gents, shines the brass, vacs the stairs and landing. Nell and Chrissy wash-up and peel potatoes for chips at the Jolly Fisherman near the sea front. They have to be extra kind to her, specially considerate; she's nervous of shadows and innocuous sounds, always imagining someone's watching or following her. Sometimes, for no apparent reason, silent sobs shake her.

On the morning after her flight from home, Liz got up, drew back Chrissy's curtains, and discovered her father's big black Humber outside. Her heart hit her throat. In the end, she went down to face him. 'Get in,' he commanded. She considered taking to her heels, chucking herself under an approaching van, dashing back into the house and throwing herself on Auntie Julie's mercy. Then did as she was told. The car, silent and sinister, sped through the morning rush. He finally spoke when they were two miles from Wold Enderby. 'I'm going to ask you one question, and I want the truth, yes or no. Were you and Poole lovers in the full sense of the word? You know what I mean – did you have sexual relations?'

'No,' she almost shouted, going scarlet. 'No' would have been her answer with or without knowledge of the threat to Alison, it was a protest, her only means of warding off what felt very like indecency on the part of her father. It apparently satisfied him; he grunted, then said, 'I haven't told your mother. Best if we don't.' (Not out of consideration for his wife and daughter, she understood, but to save himself from prolonged earache.) When they arrived at The Mount and she made to get out of the car, he shot out an arm. '*Don't*,' he warned quietly, 'see, speak, or have anything at all to do with Poole again. If I ever hear you have, it'll be the worse for him. I've already spoken to Charlie

Spendlow, one of the governors of the Convent School. Poole takes singing classes there on Friday afternoons. Any day now, he'll be hearing they've dispensed with his services. Get the picture? I've got clout in this town. Step out of line, and he'll be the loser.'

She listened, said nothing. When he got out of the car, she too got out, then pelted into the house, straight up to her room.

Later, when the evening paper arrived, she scanned the classified ads and spotted the job at the Gainsborough; telephoned at once, was invited to present herself at the hotel that evening. Not wishing her father to suppose she was setting out to waylay Ronnie, she explained where she was going. Mrs Stockdale was aghast. 'Tell her, Daddy, tell her she'd be better off doing her piano practice. What about her Grade Eight?' Alderman Stockdale ignored her. Thinking it over, he decided a bit of hard work at this juncture wouldn't do his daughter any harm. And as one who frequently put business the Gainsborough's way, he'd make good and sure she was afforded no opportunity for mischief. 'Make sure Higgins, the manager, registers your name, understands who you are,' he advised. Perhaps the surname had an effect, for she was immediately offered the job. Afterwards, she rang home to explain that she'd be staying at Chrissy's because of the need to get to work early.

One morning, on her hands and knees with a scrubbing brush, her eyes meet a pair of highly polished, finely tooled, ox-blood shoes. Unmistakable. 'Hello, Daddy.'

'Good morning. Mr Higgins about?'

'Um, I'll, er . . .'

A door opens. The manager hurries forward with a jovial 'Good morning, Alderman.'

'Morning. My daughter behaving herself? Doesn't try flooding you out every morning, I trust?' (In her surprise and embarrassment, Liz has slopped the bucket.)

294

Mr Higgins laughs with exceeding heartiness and hopes he might be of service in some way.

'You might at that. Got a couple of Norwegian chappies coming over next month. They'll be here for three or four days. I'm looking for a comfortable billet for them.'

'Indeed, wonderful, sounds right up our street,' intones Mr Higgins, bowing and extending an arm towards his office.

Her father hasn't been back since, as far as she knows. But the thought that he might, and at any time, makes her jumpy. She's grown a physical fear of him. The only times she feels safe and secure are when she's with her friends; so long as she's with them, nothing really bad can happen (a triangle, she chants silently, is a *strong* shape).

They hate their jobs. Liz particularly loathes cleaning out the gents, scrubbing dried-on vomit from the tiles in the morning, trying to flush away the mess before she has to put her hands in it, or the house-keeper wants to know what's keeping her with the ladies still a disgrace. Nell and Chrissy feel jaded and nervy from hours spent in steam and grease and trying not to be caught against the sink by fat Al, the fish-fryer. They're going to pack them in as soon as they've earned enough money to see them through the coming term.

Tonight she's sleeping at Nell's, in the narrow bed that used to be Marion's. The back of her right hand is resting along the wall. If she put out her left hand she'd touch Nell's bed which lies against the opposite wall. She's not all that keen on staying at Nell's, but Chrissy says she ought to now and then, otherwise Nell's feelings might be hurt. Chrissy's always on the lookout for possible slights going between them. Liz prefers the greater privacy at Chrissy's. Auntie Julie is never sure whether she's staying there or not, and is largely indifferent. This house is full of Nelsons, mostly male, noisy, curious. However, Nell always seems pleased when Liz suggests staying with her. 'Oh good,' she says, and tonight added, 'I've got a terrific drawing of our Keith's to show you – of the cranes you can see at the end of the street. That kid's really brilliant.' Liz has admired the drawing, made herself pleasant to Mrs Nelson (to an unnecessary degree according to Nell) and is now lying in bed already dreading the morning alarm. From her steady breathing, Liz judges Nell to be well away. Then, suddenly, they're both wide awake and sitting up. Liz is petrified. 'What is it?'

'Dad,' says Nell. 'He's going through a bad patch at work.'

Sounds to Liz like a bad patch right outside their door. Tremendous shouting, crashing about, a stream of curses, threats. Then definitely the door under attack. Quick as a flash, Nell's shoving her bed against it.

'Oh God, no, help, help, please help,' chunters Liz through clacking teeth.

'Do shut up. He wouldn't come in here intentionally. It's not us he's after.'

There's a muffled wail as if uttered through a mouthful of blanket, a thud, then silence.

'I can't stop there again, I can't, I can't,' she jabbers to Chrissy next day after work.

And Chrissy lets her off – for the time being – till Mr Nelson's got over his bad patch. 'Then take in turns,' says Chrissy, firm as ever about being considerate to one another.

It's a week later. Chrissy and Liz are settling down for the night, when there's a sound like gravel hitting the window. Chrissy gets out of bed, cautiously looks out. Nell, who left them half an hour ago, is back again, standing below in the garden, preparing to chuck up another handful. Chrissy creeps downstairs and lets her in. Under the bedroom light they examine

296

her. One side of her forehead is red and puffy, her clothes are awry. She's angry.

'I was nearly home, just crossing our road, when Dad comes steaming round the corner. So I wait for him, speaking civilly as one does, specially with several neighbours looking on. But the stupid sot thinks I'm me mum. "Where've you been, you whore, soon as my back's turned?" – something like that, and me going, "No Dad, it's Monica, remember?" and smiling nicely 'cos of the neighbours. He doesn't get it, though, just comes at me, grabs me by the hair and yanks me indoors. Christ, the humiliation. I'm not staying under the same roof again. Not till he apologizes . . . What's the matter with her?' she demands, as Liz starts sobbing uncontrollably. 'Bloody hell, it was me who got it.'

'Oh Nell, how awful, I hope it's not bruised. We'll put cold water on it, I'll get a flannel. Please Liz, stop crying.' Chrissy doesn't know how best to divide herself. 'Tell you what, when I've got Nell the flannel, I'll sneak downstairs and make us all some cocoa.'

They've never returned to school more gladly. The holiday was a grind; most of what they earned frittered away in vain attempts to ease the job-misery. Also, living in dread of their fathers proved nerveracking for Liz and Nell. At least Chrissy doesn't have that worry. Her father barely exists, never exchanges a word, doesn't even look at them when they're there in the room. Nothing stirs him, not even Nell being rude. '*Can* he speak, do you suppose?' she wonders, head on one side, Mr Thomas barely five feet in front of her. Liz and Chrissy drag her away to remonstrate, but in the end only crease up laughing.

The exciting thing about returning to school this term is that they're now in the upper sixth. The top of the school. At the end of this year they'll leave, become university students. The prospect makes them feel quite elderly.

Another novelty about school this year for Liz is the presence of Alison Poole among the first-formers. It's a heart-stopping moment when she first notices her – small, skinny, pale, permanently anxious looking even when smiling and calling a shy 'Hello, Liz.' Liz returns the greeting but hurries past, mindful of the danger of causing unspecified harm. Harm – it's the darkest word Liz can think of; never fails to jump at her whenever she sees Alison. Prefect duty during morning assembly affords an opportunity to observe the girl at length. 'Let us pray,' says the Head, and the first formers (who don't yet know any better) press their hands together and close their eyes. Alison's still got her rat's tail plaits. There are veins on her forehead very close to the surface – violet set in ivory. This makes Liz think of yellow-hammer's eggs, frail, friable, terrifyingly prone to crack and splinter. The image incites a despairing urge to protect, mocked by the knowledge that it's she who has put Alison in danger.

Members of the upper sixth are often asked to supervise prep for the first and second years. One Friday afternoon, Liz is sent to Lower Three B. Her heart sinks. Alison's class. She goes in with a cold face. 'Just get on with it,' she warns, climbing on to the teacher's tall chair, looking at no-one in particular; 'the more work you get through now, the less you'll have to do at home.' Apart from a few whispers, the odd snigger (easily quelled by a sharp look), it's an uneventful half hour. Except when Miss Horton comes in with an armful of marked history essays. 'Right, here you are,' she says, then calls out names so that girls will come to the front and collect their exercise books. Sometimes she makes a comment, such as, 'Dear me, you'll have to do better than this,' or 'Good effort, promising.' When she calls for Alison Poole, her face lifts. 'Yes, Alison, an excellent piece of work. It's not often I award ten out of ten.' When the bell goes, Liz closes her book, climbs down, makes to leave. At the door, hesitates, turns and looks for Alison. Who is looking at her. 'Well done,' Liz says, risking a smile, then leaves quickly to prevent any exchange developing. Because, what if the girl mentioned it at home? She must never forget: harm could be lurking.

They've buckled down to work, the teachers notice. Miss Cummings observes that it takes the approach of final exams before some girls wake their ideas up. The more kindly Head doubts whether the famous three were ever as bad as painted, just more independent than your average girl and, who knows, possibly more enquiring?

There are three possible outcomes for pupils in the upper sixth: a teacher's training college, a northern provincial university, or the Bedford and Westfield Colleges of London University (with which, as old girls, the spinster squad have maintained their connections). This last option is available only for the best and brightest; is attained on average by one girl every two or three years. Generally speaking, it's down to option one or two. Clever Nell is being prepared for Bedford College (Miss Cumming's *alma mater*) to study English. She's also expected to win one of the scarce county scholarships. Chrissy and Liz are still trying to decide where to aim for, what to study. Chrissy supposes she'll settle for history. Liz only knows she will not, after all, be reading music. When the Head passes on an invitation to the nearest university's open day, they take it as a subtle nudge in this direction. Manchester might be pushing it.

Anyway, they tell one another, it'll be a day out.

They take the train; then cross the river on the ferry (the *Tattershall Castle*) on which they hang about in the first-class lounge (there doesn't seem to be any other class lounge) admiring the polished wood and shining brass, watching brown-grey water swipe the portholes;

until a ticket collector approaches, whereupon they nip upstairs and climb over the barrier on to the lower-class deck, taking shelter from the North Sea wind behind one of the fat funnels. There's a bus waiting at the pier. This takes them to the city bus station where they change on to a university-bound bus.

They enter the grounds. They're simply terrified. Yesterday they were sixth-form elders, today they're a couple of schoolkids trying not to stick out in a throng of real sophisticates. Liz reaches into her pocket for the type-written instructions, gives them another reading. 'The Porter's Lodge in the Arts Building.' But where? They'd rather die than ask. At last they home in on it, restored to their senses by the sight of a military-type uniform among all the jeans and turtle necks, crepe soles and stilettos, and undergraduate gowns worn in cunning sling-back style like stoles.

About twenty sixth-formers finally gather at the porter's lodge. Their student guides are reassuringly friendly. First they are taken on a general tour, then divided into groups to accommodate particular inter-ests. Liz makes a discovery: as well as school subjects, there are hitherto unknown subjects, such as philos-ophy, sociology, psychology. In the psychology lab she is pounced on by a student, pressed into becoming a guinea pig. 'It won't take more than fifteen minutes; afterwards I'll buy you a coffee.' So she goes into the booth, dons earplugs which transmit an assortment of sounds, watches a screen. Groups of figures flash by; she is to repeat what she can remember of each sequence into a tape recorder. Then she must take off the earphones and do it all over again without the noise in her ears. She never learns why exactly, except that Mike has to ask lots of different people to co-operate in order to test some hypothesis. He takes her into the union building and buys her a coffee, introduces her to other psychology students. She'd like to know what psychology *is*, but can't very well ask without showing herself up; anyway, earnestness wouldn't suit the mood which is relaxed, jokey. At some point, though, the answer dawns on her: this subject is about human behaviour, what makes us tick, our perceptions and how these can alter. There's a satisfying click of recognition inside her; it's as if psychology's a magnet and she's a pin – *zzzap*.

'How'd you get on?' she asks Chrissy when they meet up for tea.

'OK. Wouldn't mind coming here. Did you hear the jazz band in the Arts Club at lunch? Terrific.'

'No, but I had a good time. I wouldn't mind coming here, either. Think I'll do psychology.'

'Gosh. Wonder what old Cummings will make of that?'

'And the Head,' adds Liz. 'She'll probably call it a frill.'

They leave after tea, stand outside the gate waiting for a bus to the city centre. At the bus station they change on to a bus for the pier. On the ferry, they climb the shallow iron steps to the deck and stand looking over the rail at cars thumping over the gang plank and, at last, the rope being unwound, and brown-grey water churned white as the wheels move and the engine grates. Further out on the river, wind and spray send them scurrying below. They go into the first-class ladies where there's a comfortably upholstered bench as well as wash basins and lavatories, reasoning that in here the ticket collector can't catch them. When the ferry lurches and bangs during the docking operation, they hurry out to stand innocently in the corridor where everyone waits to disembark. Up the ramp to the train – it's one of those without a corridor. They get into a compartment and slam the door, spread themselves, feet planted apart on the seat opposite, to deter other passengers. The stratagem succeeds; when the train moves off they have the compartment to themselves.

They stopped talking sometime ago, they've a lot to

think about. Liz looks at the flat landscape of fields and dykes and scattered red-brick farmsteads half-hidden by dark tree-clumps. The ploughed earth is blackish-brown, the pasture dense. The cattle are Lincoln Reds, hides of rich wine velvet against the lush green grass.

After a time she stops noticing. She's back in the little booth in the psychology lab, wearing earphones, watching the screen with numbers flashing up. The numbers fade; Mrs Poole looms. She looks out as though from a TV screen, winks, raises her sherry glass: 'Here's looking at you, kid.' Next she appears at the table, looking gravely at Alison: 'And your mum's going to buy you a bike if you fail because you'll have worked very hard and deserve one anyway.' Then she's standing in her bedroom, smiling with her head on one side: 'Suits you, I thought it would.' Mrs Poole plays on against increasingly insistent background noise coming through the earphones. This noise is a clash of voices – her own, Nell's and Chrissy's, Ronnie's – and the sound of the piano playing. It's hard to make out what the voices say exactly, but their overall message is clear: never mind what you see on the screen, Mr Poole is the goal. Mr Poole, Mr Poole, Mr Poole. 'Trust *me*,' says Ronnie, and Mrs Poole's image starts wobbling. 'Damn interference,' she hears her father complain, as jigging lines roll over and over. Mrs Poole is submerged. There's just flicker and noise, a prickly blare.

Perception, she thinks, sitting up straight to cast off the daydream. Perception and how it can be altered. Quite definitely this is something to think about.

A man and a woman get in at one of the stations. Reluctantly, they gather in their legs. Meeting the bleak stare of the newcomers, Liz suddenly foresees that as well as doubtful teachers, she's going to encounter strenuously objecting parents. 'Psychology? What's that when it's at home? Who's been putting ideas in your head?' Her father will detect subversive undertones. Her mother will find nothing boast-worthy in

302

the word, unlike 'music' which betokens charming accomplishment and can only enhance social and marriage prospects.

Stick to your guns, she warns herself as the train judders over the points near the terminus. If you do, I may let you off. (She means, she may begin to feel better about herself; for ever since the Poole episode she has felt tainted.) If you chicken out, I'll despise you for ever. (She means, if she fails to follow her own impulse now, she'll be doomed to a shadowy, dull-spirited apology of a life spent imitating the Stockdale code.)

Crossing the station footbridge, she links arms with Chrissy. 'I'm definitely going to do psychology,' she says, not adding but managing to convey, 'Please back me.'

'Of course,' endorses Chrissy, catching her meaning. 'And we'll be together. Pity about Nell. But she needs London, don't you think? Anyway, there are the holidays.'

'And we can write.'

'That's true.'

'It'll be brilliant getting letters from Nell, they'll be more like Nell than in real life, if you know what I mean.'

'Her being in London will give us a broader perspective.'

'I suppose it will,' says Liz. 'In a way.'

iii

Liz sat with her cup of tea watching the Duckenfields take breakfast, only Chrissy lending permanence to this movable feast. It began with just Chrissy, Amanda and herself, a cosy twenty minutes, Chrissy taking her ease, for Amanda required nothing from her mother beyond a kiss and cheery conversation as she happily mixed grains, seeds, nuts, yoghurt and brewed a mug of rosehip tea. 'Make some for you?' she piped so abruptly that Liz had to repeat and decode in her head (and so early in the day) before thanking her and declining. 'Oo, but it's terribly good for you, tones you up, gives you bags of energy, mm, and so yummy.' Chrissy sent Liz a smile, which read 'Isn't she a pet?' then rose from her chair and began setting out her stall – loaf of bread, tray of eggs, bacon rashers, bowl of tomatoes.

Next came Tony in his business suit. 'Morning, Liz, Amanda pet.' Chrissy, under starter's orders, offered, 'bacon, egg, tomatoes, fried bread?' and was given the signal for off – 'Smashing.'

'Paper?' he asked Liz, offering his *Daily Telegraph*.

She shook her head – 'Still coming to.'

'Ahah, you slept well. That's the ticket.' – and shook out his paper.

The sun was pouring in through the window over the sink. Amanda had sprinted to open an outside door when fat first hit the frying pan (silently applauded by Liz); with the cool draught came the ripe smell of late summer, the rapturous throbbing of a thrush.

The others came down in turn, Joy, Neil, Clare. Chrissy kept order with the bread knife, rallying, cajoling, laughing, groaning. Dear Chrissy, thought Liz: pouring oil, jumping on any breach of the fairness code; in short, keeping the group together – always her great obsession.

From overhead sounds of coughing reach them, subdued at first, working to paroxysm. Chrissy and Liz looked at one another.

'Those ciggies,' sighed Liz.

'We shouldn't have encouraged her,' said Chrissy.

'Like hell we did. It was she who was mad for them.'

'But if we hadn't gone along with it, she might have given up eventually.'

'I doubt it. Anyway, what did we know then?'

'True,' sighed Chrissy. 'Sounds like bronchitis.'

Ten minutes later – Clare the only child remaining, her head over a book among the crumbs – Nell staggered in. 'Do you know, this stink you've set up in here came curling under my very door? Literally. I sat up in bed and watched it, horrid blue smoke. If there's one thing I loathe it's the smell of pig frying. Makes me heave. Nearly coughed my guts out.'

They eyed her sceptically, thinking of her nicotine-cured nasal passages.

'What're you going to have?' Chrissy asked, when the phone rang. 'Clare,' she commanded, without taking her eyes off Nell.

Clare rose and stomped away.

'Cup of tea'll do me.'

'Oh come on. Have a bit of toast.'

'Yes, go on, Nell. Chrissy's gooseberry jam is out of this world.'

Clare came back, sat down to her book. 'It's for Liz,' she reported casually.

Across the room Liz bounded, the vivid breakfast scene snuffed out in an instant by the thudding recall of her own domestic situation. Rosie? she wondered first, then more ominously, Nathan? All this in five seconds. Simultaneously, she pulled the kitchen door shut and reached for the receiver. 'Hello?'

'No sweat, love. Just thought I'd brighten your morning.'

'Oh, Nathan.'

'About Rosie. Things may be looking up.'

'Yes?'

'She was late in last night. Didn't want to play the heavy father, but I got a bit anxious.'

'Of course.'

'So I hung around. Soon after midnight a car came swinging into the yard, right up to the house, music thumping. Actually it was one of those jeep things – I went racing up to look out of the landing window; a young fellow in the driving seat, Rosie next to him, and three kids in the back – recognized one of them, the tall girl with specs and frizzy hair . . .'

'Jenny.'

'That's right, Jenny. They turned the noise off, then sat talking and laughing, trying to keep their voices down, you know how they are . . .'

'Yeah.'

'Then Rosie jumped out. "See you tomorrow," she called, merry as a bird. Then the chap in the front said he'd call for her sometime this afternoon.'

'Well, blow me,' said Liz, 'sounds just like life as it used to be.'

'Exactly. She was even singing to herself in the kitchen, making coffee and so forth. Hopeful, don't you think?'

'Oh, very.'

'I'll keep you posted. Thought you'd want to know.'

'Thanks, darling. But Nathan – don't, er, I mean, try and pretend not to notice anything. Act casual.'

'Casual – me? Listen, mate, I'm so laid back, people have been known to assume I'm asleep.'

'Huh.'

'Everything all right there? Chrissy and Nell OK?'

'Mm,' she replied, looking at the closed kitchen door, deciding this wasn't the moment to mention Nell's bronchitis. 'Nell's taking us out for a meal tonight. That smart hotel on the sea front.'

'Well, enjoy yourselves. Give them my love. 'Bye for now, Liz. Someone's coming in to see me.'

'OK. Ring me again.'

She returned to the kitchen to report the good omen.

iv

The day they leave school, Angie Hutchings cries. A full-throttle, flopping about on people's shoulders, sopping wet performance. Her friends sniff a bit, too, but don't give the full works; just droop around as though Angie's crying is sufficiently comprehensive to save them the whole hog. There's a reverence in their manner, implying that because it's lovely Angie bawling – the girl with the most cool, the most pull with the boys – leaving school is lent added poignancy.

Chrissy, Liz and Nell don't cry. They turn on the weepers their trademark 'no-comment' stare, the stare that makes them a trinity. Then get on with the day's business, that of making a polite round of the teachers to exchange largely insincere farewells.

The next day they clock on at Frigid Fruits.

They have Chrissy to thank for their jobs. Two weeks before the end of term she bluffed her way into the factory and hung about in the corridor until Mr Hutton, the floor manager, came out of his office. No good just leaving your name and particulars and dates of availability, she'd been advised by a seasoned vacation worker, an ex-grammar schoolgirl now at university; try and grab Hutton, look lively, impress him, it's your only hope. Chrissy was looking her liveliest (which is considerably livelier than most). When Mr Hutton came rushing to take a telephone call, she watched him through the open door, sprang the moment he put the receiver down. She came straight to the point, tossing her newly washed curls, keeping her bright eyes wide to look extra alert, her spanking white teeth smiling raring to go. Mr Hutton lingered even when the tannoy claimed him. ('Attention Mr 'Utton. Peas coming in.') 'You mean there are two more like you?' he asked, grinning. And when she promised that there were, 'Oh, go on then,' and reached for a sheet of paper and a biro. 'Stick your names and particulars on here. I'll put you down for Thursday the twentieth. First shift, clock on at seven.'

It's now seven fifteen on Thursday the twentieth. They were here at six forty-five, but have only just clocked on. This is because, when they arrived, no-one had heard of them. Lesser spirits might have mumbled and left, but Chrissy stood her ground. 'Mr Hutton told

307

us to come,' she insisted. 'Go and ask him.' Mr Hutton was duly sent for. His eyes brightened when he saw Chrissy, dulled with doubt as she dragged forward her companions. 'These your friends?' he asked, thinking that the little pale one would never stand eight hours at a conveyor belt, and the other one was dozey-looking.

'Nell and Liz,' confirmed Chrissy with enthusiasm. 'We were here really early. It's them in there who've made us late, they haven't got our cards.'

'Make 'em out, Pat,' called Mr Hutton. He looked again at Nell and Liz. 'It's a week's trial, mind. You'll be out if you're not up to it.'

Now they're in the main hall, a great metal-framed barn containing several conveyor belts tended by the female workforce. Men and lads work in the cold store and can be seen at the far end of the hall in their padded clothing with hoods and wellies and giant gloves, going and coming through swing doors pushing trolleys. Chrissy, Nell and Liz are wearing standard issue green overalls with green headscarfs tied turban-style. Nell and Liz hate these scarves which have immediately wiped out their personalities and turned them into anonymous factory hands. They are considerately keeping their eyes off one another. Chrissy has no patience with them. 'Think of the money,' she advises. 'I wonder if we should go up to her, or just wait?'

She's talking about Jackie, the supervisor, who, they have been told, will tell them where to go and what to do.

'Crumbs, she looks rough,' murmurs Nell. 'Worse than Marge at the Sea Gull, remember her?'

'Oh, don't,' moans Liz, whose stomach hurts.

Jackie is gaunt and flash. She wears the standard green overall, but unbuttoned, like a coat. Underneath, is a shocking-pink top showing scraggy cleavage and a tight white skirt slit up the front almost to crotch level. Her uncovered hair is bleached with dark roots. The two men she is talking with, Mr Hutton and a

308

younger fellow, are wearing suits. All three hold clipboards. Jackie's laugh belts out, harsh as sandpaper. Mr Hutton waves his clipboard towards the waiting three. 'Flaming 'ell,' says Jackie, 'who sent these?' Mr Hutton walks away.

'Right, come on, you.' She jerks her head and goes clacking away on her stilettos. They follow, end up at a conveyor belt covered in trembling strawberries. 'Strawberry 'eading,' Jackie explains, and shoves each girl bodily into a line of women at strategic points. 'Look after these,' she asks of the girls' neighbours, shooting her eyes up to heaven.

Seems easy enough, they think. You grab a strawberry, divest it of stalk and leafy crown, put it back on the belt. The green waste you drop into a bucket at your side, together with any damaged strawberries.

'Girls,' shrieks Jackie to the assorted females – which includes mothers and grandmothers – 'there's too many bad uns coming through. Ida and Joyce can't cope.' Ida and Joyce are experienced workers at the end of the conveyor belt who supervise the dropping of cleaned strawberries into waiting freezer trays. Another experienced worker stands at the head of the line emptying boxes of strawberries on to the belt. Jackie runs up and down the line. 'You lasses in the middle, get your fingers out.'

Their fingers are already out and hurting like mad. Strawberry seeds have jammed under their nails, strawberry juice burns in little cracks in their skin. There's no time to suck or in any other way soothe their wounds; Jackie comes clacking past at regular intervals to check their buckets.

Chrissy was glad when they were put on a strawberry belt, foreseeing opportunities for regular snacks. Now, after several stolen mouthfuls, she wishes she hadn't bothered; the reek and feel of strawberries are bad enough without tasting them, too. The 'girls' up and down the line chat amiably to one another. They work fairly fast, but not fanatically. This is in marked contrast to the behaviour of women at a neighbouring belt devoted to piece working who work grimly in silence, intent on their flying fingers.

Around half-past nine, the women grow edgy. 'What's the time?' they ask. 'I want to wet my whistle . . .' 'Hey, Jackie,' calls a bold spirit, 'Maeve here has got her legs crossed.'

At last Jackie stalks to the top of the belt. 'Ten minutes,' she yells, and presses a button.

The women run. Liz, Nell and Chrissy are left staring at the stationary belt. After a moment, they amble after the fleeing women. In the cloakroom, there's a queue for the lavatories. Women are squatting on the benches under the coat pegs, opening flasks, gulping tea. Liz, Nell and Chrissy haven't brought any. Through an open door a few women can be seen outside in the yard, pulling hard on cigarettes. Nell feels in her coat pocket for her packet of Players and goes to join them. Liz joins the lavatory queue. Chrissy puts her mouth under the cold tap and gulps water. Suddenly, the place clears. Nell and Chrissy, unable to believe it, check their watches.

'It's diabolical,' says Nell, stubbing out her cigarette.

'Come on, Liz,' calls Chrissy.

From behind a cubicle door, Liz wails that they'd better go back without her. When she comes out, the area's deserted. She feels weak and shaky, full of impotent rage. Ten miserly minutes.

'Good job Jackie didn't see you,' comments her neighbour as she squeezes back into line, for luckily, a couple of minutes ago, the tannoy summoned Jackie to the office.

At twelve o'clock, several conveyor belts halt at once. This break is for twenty minutes. There's an even longer queue for the lavatories. Sensible women who have brought lunch boxes, crouch on cloakroom benches or take them outside. Chrissy, Liz and Nell follow the imprudent few over the road to the corner shop. They buy chocolate bars and crisps and bottles of Tizer, take them to the yard where they sit on the sun-warmed concrete. Here they meet a couple of older girls, ex-grammar school pupils, now at college. Then four lads come in from the cold store, peeling off their padded clothing, which prompts the girls to rip off their headscarves and shake out their hair. The lads are ex-grammar-school boys; two of them recognize Chrissy from primary school days. Introductions follow. A pleasant lunchtime is just underway when a whistle blows. 'I don't believe it,' says Nell. 'I'm not bloody budging till I've finished my fag.' They leave her with the lads.

Five minutes later, Nell is bawled out by Jackie. 'What the flamin 'ell do you think this is – a sodding picnic? Try it on again, lass, and you'll be out of here before you can blink. Christ, where do they get 'em from? I'll have my eye on you, girl, so just think on.'

The next three days are spent picking over strawberries. On the fourth day, the tannoy conveys mounting despair at the too-frequent arrival of pea lorries. 'Attention Mr 'Utton, peas coming in.' 'There's more peas coming in, Mr 'Utton.' 'Attention Jackie. Mr 'Utton says better open another pea line, quick.' Nell, Chrissy and Liz are among the workers moved to a pea belt. The peas are fed into a noisy podding machine which spews them on to conveyor belts where bits of pod and stalk and, most crucially, poppy heads, must be removed before the peas reach the freezer trays. These poppy heads are a major concern. 'There's poppy 'eads coming through,' shrieks Jackie every few minutes. 'Girls, there's still poppy 'eads getting through.' The suited men come bustling up: 'Message from the management, girls,' bellows their intermediary, 'We've got to get out all these poppy 'eads.'

Chrissy, Nell and Liz stare at the swimming peas, their eyes straining for the tell-tale ridges of the green and remarkably pea-like seeds of *Papaver Rhoe'as*. An agitated Jackie patrols behind the lines, peering into waste buckets for evidence of industry. Evidently, this is a task at which the newcomers shine. Their buckets are held out as shining examples, older women exhorted to produce similar crops of poppy heads. At lunch time, Nell, Liz and Chrissy sense their popularity has taken a knock. They are ignored, backs are turned on them. Which doesn't matter a toss once the lads appear.

'Coming to the pub tonight?' asks John, a medical student at Newcastle.

'Can't afford it till pay day,' Chrissy sighs.

'On us,' cry the generous fellows. 'See you in the Blue Anchor at eight.'

'Oh yeah?' sneers Nell. The Blue Anchor is a popular place to take women on account of the landlord's refusal to serve the fairer sex with pint glasses (a not uncommon scruple in these parts); females must sip daintily from half-pint goblets.

But beggars can't be choosers. 'OK, see you,' they promise, getting to their feet as the whistle summons.

Most weekends they go to Liz's. Liz isn't keen to go home at all, but has accepted Chrissy's argument that it's best to forestall parental complaint: showing up at weekends will maintain the fiction that she still lives at home even though in spirit she's flitted. Liz is grateful to her friends for being so accommodating.

Chrissy's view as expressed to Nell is that it's only fair to Liz, who, after all, spends all the rest of the week with the Thomases or the Nelsons, thus saving Chrissy from taking Auntie Julie too personally and imposing some obligation on Nell's dad to behave himself. As they've learned over the years, tricky or oppressive domestic situations can be borne more easily as part of a three. Privately, Chrissy knows she loves going to Wold Enderby and can put up with any amount of Mrs Stockdale's awfulness so long as Mrs Stockdale is feeding and pampering her.

And Nell's view of the situation . . . Well, who knows what Nell's thinking, what's really going on behind those heavy-lidded eyes, those dreamy smiles, those odd sharp eccentric-seeming statements which come out of the blue like little eruptions from a complicated thought process? Sometimes it's a mystery even to Nell. 'Mm,' she says, in agreement with Chrissy. 'Don't worry, I enjoy going. Absolutely fascinating.'

A memory stirs in Chrissy. Suddenly suspicious, she warns, 'Don't ever let on to Liz what you once said to me – you know, about her dad. Liz wasn't thrilled by his threats. They upset her.'

'Gosh, yes, so they did.'

'And no flirting,' Chrissy says, surprising herself as well as her friend, for the observation was uttered without pre-thought, prompted by a flash recall of Nell batting her eyelids at Alderman Stockdale.

'Do I really flirt?' blinks Nell, looking pleasantly intrigued.

'Yes, you do a bit.'

'That's interesting. I hadn't realized.'

The day after A-level results come out, they arrive at work in a very cheerful frame of mind. The results arrived at their homes yesterday, posted on from school. Liz had to ring up her mother to learn what hers were. They've all done well, better than their teachers' forecasts. Their university places are safe; Nell is certain of a County scholarship. At Frigid Fruits, the news filters out. To their surprise their workmates on the line seem genuinely interested and pleased. 'Well done, love,' they say. 'You lasses have the right idea; wish I'd done better at school; you'll make something of yourselves, more than that Jackie,' – are frequently expressed sentiments, the last offered as a particular commendation.

At lunch break, they tell the other student-workers. There's great rejoicing. John, the medic from Newcastle,

313

puts forward the brilliant idea of celebrating on Friday night at the Gaiety ballroom, where Ken Colyer's Jazzmen will be the star attraction.

When they come off their shift, they are most displeased to discover Tony Duckenfield outside, evidently waiting for them − in bicycle clips, blazer and tie, as ever.

'God, what's that creep doing here?' Nell groans.

'Come to pester me, I expect,' says Chrissy.

And she's right. 'Hiya Chrissy. How've you been?'

'Hiya,' she mumbles, setting off at a brisk pace, Liz and Nell hurrying at her side; Tony, pushing his bike, maintains a two-pace distance.

'Had your results?' he calls.

'Yeah,' says Chrissy, not turning round.

'Pleased with them?'

'Yes, thanks.'

'Me too. I'm going to do Law at Manchester.'

'Really.' They turn the corner. Tony turns, too. Chrissy loses patience. 'Haven't you got somewhere to go? Something to do? We'd like a bit of peace if you don't mind, we've been working since seven.'

'I don't need to bother getting a holiday job,' Tony says smugly. 'My mother says, as long as I'm studying she'll look after me.'

'But you're not. You've left school.'

Tony frowns over his spectacles. 'But there's masses of reading to do for university. I'm not messing about. You need a good degree to make plenty of dough.'

They all slow down and look at him. Nell wonders whether the comment is a sign of unsuspected qualities lying deep within Quacker Duckenfield. To Liz, it serves to reinforce what she senses and dislikes about him from the greedy way he licks his lips, and the way no hint of how he's coming over to other people ever disturbs him or deflects the remorseless pursuit of his aims.

Chrissy just wants her dinner. 'Is that so? Like I

314

said, we're in a hurry, if you don't mind.' She jerks her head and nudges her friends. 'Come on, or they'll be shut.' She means the chip shop.

They're not the only ones celebrating at the Gaiety. Angie Hutchings is there, looking lovely in strapless black satin and stiletto sandals, partnered by a tall man in a suit. They've heard on the grapevine that Angie's results were disappointing, though good enough to confirm a job offer from a bank in town, where businessmen will jostle to be served by her and stare at the gold locket and chain dangling over her pert bosom while she counts their money, bracelets jangling, painted nails flashing, and feel, when she smiles and meets their eye, that maybe they're in with a chance. But how wrong they'll be, thinks Liz whose picture of Angie's future this is, for Angie's no fool and what she's celebrating here tonight is her engagement. 'Hiya, Angie,' they cry, greeting her like true friends. 'Congratulations, you look smashing.' She shows them the ring, a diamond solitaire. They coo over it, even Nell finds something nice to say – 'Cor, that must have cost a packet.' 'Yes, well Des has his own business,' she confides, 'he's Pattersons the bakers, used to be his dad's before he retired.' They let her see they're impressed, for it's amazing how generous and full of affection you can feel when you'll soon be moving on. (In their minds they've half left this town already, though where they've half gone *to* remains vague.) Gilly, Beryl and Val are with Angie and Des, plus their own young men – all twentyish in suits, strictly non-student types. They spot several newly ex-grammar-school boys at the bar, including Mogsy and Dave, all of whom they ignore, having far out-grown them.

The men they are with, all university students doing vacation work at Frigid Fruits, are wearing sloppy sweaters, open neck shirts, creased-looking trousers. Two of them have beards, all have longer hair than is currently acceptable in the world of jobs. Nell, Liz and Chrissy are wearing the circular skirts (great for jiving), flat shoes, scoop-neck tops they bought last Saturday when they went to Leeds on a fashion expedition (caught the seven-thirty train in the morning, back by nine at night). They grab a table, cram chairs round it, get in the beers; light up, chat, joke, watch the jivers on the floor. It's a local band playing at the moment, quite good, but they're saving themselves.

At ten o'clock, Ken Colyer brings on his team. They jump to their feet, clap and cheer, start jiving at once to 'Harlem Rag'. These university lads are terrific, they think, carefully imitating their jiving styles; and where they're going they'll be plenty more like them. No jazzmen in the world to match these, though, thinks Chrissy, aching with love for Monty Sunshine – or possibly for what he does with his clarinet, swooping, soaring, piercing, producing sound like flowing molten glass.

Ken Colyer puts his lips to the microphone: '*Goin' home* . . .' They sing along with him, high on the prospect of soon going in the opposite direction.

Later, Liz is so happy smooching to 'Early Hours' with John, she finds they're kissing, sort of accidentally, as if the kiss is part of the dance. When the music stops, they hug and grin, then part and join the others.

Afterwards, lying in bed at Chrissy's, she remembers the kiss, and thinks with a start that it was her first since Ronnie's last. She lies staring into the dark for some minutes, then turns on her side and closes her eyes. As if a ghost has left her.

At the beginning of September, the pea, bean, strawberry and raspberry harvests over, their jobs at Frigid Fruits come to an end. Their dismissals feel timely: they've made some money, they can use a few weeks' freedom before starting at university. One of the first things they plan is a clothes-buying trip to Leeds. During August, a great deal of effort was expended researching the sort of image they hope to present as freshers on campus. Most Saturday mornings found them in Smith's in town, where, to the hindrance of paying customers, they stood by the shelves studying all the high-class magazines and foreign journals before replacing them limp and dog-eared with all their goodness extracted. Liz and Chrissy can now clearly visualize their ideal look: shoes with highish heels, straight-cut skimpy skirts, over-sized crew-neck sweaters; for evenings they'd like up-to-the-minute sack dresses, but guess this phenomenon has yet to penetrate the north of England. Should be simple enough garments to run up, though, they reason: just two straight bits of material stitched together at the sides. 'Don't you reckon, Nell?' Nell looks as if she's giving the matter earnest thought but may take some considerable time reaching a conclusion. Liz and Chrissy are concerned for her. She's become distant, disinclined to share their enthusiasms. They wonder if this is because it's she who must strike out on her own. Liz thinks it wouldn't be so bad if they were all going to different places; as it is, Nell must feel it keenly that she's the odd one out. Chrissy says they must make a special effort to show poor Nell that the coming parting won't in any way hurt their friendship.

On the train to Leeds, they have the compartment to themselves. Liz and Chrissy are like moles digging for Nell's response. 'Oh, I don't know – what d'you think, Nell?' 'That'd be terrific, wouldn't it, Nell?' 'I can just see Nell in midnight blue, can't you Liz?' Never conceding more than the odd 'Uhuh,' Nell sits with her jaw slewed and her eyes half shut. While they enthuse, speculate, throw questions at her, they secretly wonder what she's thinking about. Towards the end of the journey, without changing her expression or moving her body in the least degree, Nell says in her off-hand gabble, 'Better if we split up when we get there. Easier to concentrate on our own.'

They gape at her. Her eyelids are like shutters. When she speaks again she sounds defiant as when she's talking to her mother. 'It was hard enough earning the cash; I want to make sure I spend it sensibly. It's impossible to think straight with you two prattling.'

The atmosphere in the compartment solidifies. Not a muscle moves as Liz and Chrissy stare at Nell, racking their brains for the true reason behind her wish to separate, having instantly discounted the one given.

'Surely,' tries Chrissy at last, 'if we take in turns to say where we want to go . . .'

Not a flicker from Nell.

Her voice thin and tired sounding, Chrissy makes another attempt. 'If we go about it quietly and thoughtfully . . .'

Enlightenment comes to Liz. She goes hot inside. 'Oh, leave her,' she snaps. 'Let her go off alone if that's what she wants.'

Nothing further is said till they're on the platform. 'See you at five twenty-five?' Chrissy calls after Nell, who mumbles agreement and stalks off. They let her get away, then they, too, hurry out of the station. Chrissy wants to know what prompted Liz's sudden warmth.

'She feels she's out-grown us. After all, *we*'re only going to a provincial university.'

'Oh surely not. Maybe she wants to discover what it feels like doing things without us; get herself used to it.'

'No. She's decided she's too good for us. Can't wait to cut loose.'

Gloominess fails to forestall some brilliant purchasing. On the market they discover straight skirts in black and grey which are virtually identical to much pricier ones in the shops. They find the perfect shoes in Saxone. After despairing that none of the women's sweaters in the stores are sufficiently voluminous they

318

have a brainwave: march brazenly into a mens' department and discover sweaters of the precise tweedy look
and bulky shape they desire. This last is such a feat of
perseverance they long to boast of it to Nell. Instead,
they go into a Wimpey bar, sit on tall stools with
their carrier bags propped round the legs, munching
hamburgers, slurping milkshakes through straws, discussing her like mourners at a wake. They tot up all
the things she's done for them. If it hadn't been for Nell
coming on the scene they'd probably have ended up just
ordinary chums like Angie and Val, like Beryl and Gilly
– predictable types, Liz accepting the sort of role her
parents planned for her, Chrissy endlessly hang-dog
over Auntie Julie's peculiarities. Nell showed them
things parents and school were determined to keep
hidden, stretched them, made them think, question,
dare to be different and not ashamed of it. Nell was the
yeast in what might have been a pretty flat mixture.

'Hope she doesn't go off us all together,' says Liz.
'It'd be terrible to lose Nell.'

'Like losing a part of your body,' agrees Chrissy,
squirting extra ketchup from a plastic tomato to make
her last chunk of hamburger go further.

They sigh, wipe their mouths, screw the paper ser-
viettes into balls; jump down, gather their carrier bags,
head off for the department store's make-up counter
where they'll dab free samples of perfume up and down
their arms, sniffing till their nostrils tingle.

'I need some mascara,' Chrissy remembers.

'I might get some eye shadow,' thinks Liz.

When they arrive back at the station, there's no sign
of Nell. 'She's going to miss the train,' frets Chrissy,
looking up and down the platform.

Then a woman in a close-fitting black suit and high-
heel shoes, with doe-eyed make-up and razor-cut hair
(jagged fringe, side wisps swept forward to the cheekbones), saunters towards them. Liz feels sick – it's
like a dream she used to have of running after her

319

mother, and her mother turning, but with the face of a stranger. Chrissy's brain is like a horse refusing a jump – it's *not* Nell, nothing like.

'Hello,' says Nell off-handedly.

'Hello,' they return feebly, feeling very young, very foolish.

The train comes in and puts an end to their tongue-tied gaping. From this moment, no train will ever arrive at a platform where Liz is standing without flicking an image of Nell to her mind's eye, Nell looking as she does now, seriously grown up. They clamber on board, search for seats. It's quite crowded, they're lucky to find a compartment with two free corners: Liz and Chrissy sit one side of the gangway, Nell sits opposite.

'Have you blown all your money on that?' asks Chrissy, hoping Nell hasn't because the outfit she's wearing will never serve as student garb. (Presumably, the clothes she set out in this morning are contained by the expensive looking carrier bag.)

'Most of it,' shrugs Nell, 'but the hair cut wasn't cheap. Had it done at Teazy Weazy's.'

'Gosh, Nell.' It must have cost her a fortune. But it does look terrific. 'It transforms you,' says Liz. 'Shows up your cheekbones. It's tremendously flattering.'

'Thanks.'

'The suit's very glamorous,' Chrissy concedes, at last getting round to mentioning it. 'But where would you wear it?'

'Oh, round and about,' says Nell airily, looking out of the window.

'At college?'

'Heavens, no. Any old thing'll do for there. I'm thinking of my career. If you want to *be* somebody you've got to *look* somebody.'

'You've certainly managed that,' says Liz. 'You look like someone in those glossy mags. Suits you, though. I wouldn't have thought it, but it does. You really carry it off.'

'It's a lovely shape, very sophisticated.'

'Thanks,' beams Nell. 'I'm glad you like it.'

They settle back, Liz and Chrissy made tranquil by knowing their opinions were not unimportant. Liz recalls her earlier indignation with scorn; she's insightful, now: naturally Nell had to go off and do her shopping alone, impelled by a need to discover her new self. And this new-look Nell, for which Liz already feels affectionate admiration, is just the first outward sign of something that's going to happen to all of them. They're going to do different things, develop different tastes. The thing is to welcome each other's ventures, not meet them with hostility like disapproving parents. They must hold fast to their first open-minded acceptance of one another, then, however far apart they end up on the outside, inside they'll stay friends.

Chrissy's having similar thoughts – Liz can tell from the way when their eyes meet there's no sense of intrusion or interruption. Over the gangway, Nell's looking relaxed, so maybe she's thinking along the same lines, too; though it's impossible to be sure because her face is half turned away, she's smiling at the slag heaps outside the window.

When they get off the train, Nell says she'd like to go with them to Chrissy's house to change; she doesn't want her brothers gawping and making comments. Of course she doesn't, they say, walking to the number six bus-stop.

They jump off at the traffic lights, Liz and Chrissy thoughtlessly, easily, Nell holding her breath in case she rips her new tight skirt or topples on her high heels. Down Lister Avenue they go, carrier bags swinging, along the side of the Robinson Rec, past all the red-brick semis with their net curtained bay windows and tidy front gardens. Tony Duckenfield is sitting astride his bicycle, one foot resting on the pavement, outside number 142.

'How did he *know*?' groans Chrissy. 'Has he got spies or something?'

'He's probably been here hours on the off chance,' Liz says.

'Don't think I can stand it.'

'Tell you what, why don't we all go and stay at my place for a bit?' Liz still avoids being at home as much as possible, still suffers uneasy darts of physical fear in her father's company, barely suppressed irritation in her mother's; but in the company of her friends, these feelings can be surmounted.

'That's a good idea. Shall we, Nell?'

Nell takes her time. 'You two go,' she says generously. 'You won't be seeing much of me either way because I've got an idea for my novel. I'll probably go and work in the library.'

'That's terrific, Nell.'

'Marvellous. And when you feel like a break just come out and join us.'

'Oh, thanks,' says Nell, blinking at the pavement.

'Hiya, Chrissy,' calls Tony Duckenfield.

'Hello,' says Chrissy coldly, unlatching her gate. She goes up the path, the others following.

'I say, Chrissy, you doing anything tonight?'

She opens the front door. 'What's it to you?' she says, waiting for Nell and Liz to step inside.

Before he can answer, the door thuds shut.

The waiting area in Hennage and Stockdale's chapel of rest is luxurious – thick carpets, thickly upholstered armchairs, a thick airless atmosphere faintly scented by flowers. At the reception desk just inside the plate glass entrance sits a pale-faced blonde. It's all very different from the reception area at A.J. Stockdale, Builders, from where she's just hurried, thinks Nell, sitting not too far back in one of the armchairs to save the back of her suit jacket from creasing, pressing her knees together under the hem of her tight skirt, keeping her ankles bonded and slanted to one side as shown in magazine photographs. Her breathing's calmed down, thank goodness; no-one would guess the pounding she's given the pavement dashing over here. 'Alderman Stockdale isn't in today,' the girl on the desk at A.J. Stockdale, Builders had told her.

'Will he be in tomorrow?'

'No, he'll be on site tomorrow – you know, the new executive estate we're building down Wealsby Drive,' said the girl looking hard at Nell as if it had suddenly crossed her mind that here stood a customer. Giving full credit to her smart new suit, Nell confidently demanded to know the whereabouts of the alderman today. 'Chapel of rest,' answered the girl, suitably lowering her voice.

An altogether classier type of female, and one not to be impressed by a sophisticated outfit, guards the desk here. Mind you, thinks Nell, smart black suits are every day occurrences in this sort of place, stands to reason. Nell was told she could wait if she wished, but Alderman Stockdale was in conference and really it would be better if she stated her business and made an appointment. Ignoring this advice, Nell trod with some difficulty over the deep pile carpet and lowered herself on to the chair where she now sits.

She's been waiting half an hour. Sometimes the receptionist glances across at her and sighs. Sometimes she speaks into a telephone. Ten minutes ago a red-eyed couple came in, were directed to chairs, where they sat aiming sympathetic comradely expressions at Nell. The receptionist spoke into the phone; a dark suited man appeared (silently – no doors clicked, no footsteps sounded) and led the couple away. Now, without warning and so stealthily Nell's heart leaps, another man appears. He looks across at her, goes to confer with the receptionist, who shrugs. 'Says she'll wait; may be after a job,' Nell's straining ears manage to catch.

The man, who is large and confident-looking, comes

strolling over, sort of prowls round her in a semi-circle, like a dog weighing up another. 'Can I help you, love?' he leers, coming to a halt at her side. He leans a hand against the wall, peers down the front of her jacket.

'No thanks.'

'Tell us what it's about,' he urges. 'I may be able to help. I'm the deputy director, Peter Rawlins. Pete to my friends.' Stepping back, he dips his head, stares frankly at her legs and as far under her skirt as her posture allows. 'After a job?' he suggests, straightening up. Fingering the knot of his tie, jutting his chin, he adds, 'Might be able to help you there. What's your name?'

'Miss Nelson, to you, lad,' says Alderman Stockdale. 'Friend of my daughter's. But I don't think we need detain you.'

It occurs to Nell, as Pete what-ever-his-name-is reddens and rapidly departs, that Alderman Stockdale has been watching for some moments.

'Come in,' he invites her, indicating an open doorway.

Nell goes through into a small room which has a little-used feeling – just two chairs and a desk, a bowl of roses, a photograph of Mrs Stockdale in evening dress, another of Alderman Stockdale and some mates standing about with a minor royal – the Duke of something.

'What a pleasant surprise. Didn't recognize you at first. That's a very charming outfit.'

'Thanks. I adored the way you did that, by the way.'

'Did what? Oh – dispatched mi-laddo with a flea in his ear?'

'Masterful,' she breathes, arranging her legs.

'And how can I assist such a lovely young lady?'

Endeavouring for the moment to overlook his devastatingly handsome features (which always send her fluttery weak), she takes a deep breath (which lifts her breasts prettily) and begins. 'You remember me telling you I want to be a journalist?' She breaks off, laughs self-deprecatingly. 'No, of course you don't . . .'

'I remember.'

'You do?' she beams – 'Gosh. Well, what I need is some experience of how newspapers work. I've been slaving away at Frigid Fruits for the past six weeks, earning the necessary; now I'd really appreciate a couple of weeks in a newspaper office – doing anything, odd jobs, you name it; I want to see all sides of the business. Then, for next long vac I've set my sights on a bit of reporting, instead of wasting time doing rubbish work in a factory.'

'Take your point, but why come to me? You want to see Ron Anderson, the editor.'

'Why ask the monkey when you know the organ grinder? I'm not daft, I know what feeds newspapers. Pick up any issue of the *Evening Telegraph*, ask yourself who's bought the most advertising space. If I wanted a job with the corporation transport, I'd still come to you. It's your name plastered all over the buses.'

Alderman Stockdale chuckles, crosses a crooked leg over a knee, starts tapping a toe against the desk top. 'Elizabeth know you've come to see me?' he throws at her suddenly.

'Certainly not.'

He nods – 'Smart girl.' His tapping foot falls still, his head lolls back; he studies her down the length of his long nose. Coolly, her mouth twisted up in a one-sided smile, she returns his gaze. Amusement grows on his craggy features. Suddenly, he sits up and consults his watch. 'Let's see, now, it's Wednesday; Ron Anderson will be lunching at the Grand. Ever been there for a meal?'

'Never.'

'No? It's a nice place, it'd do justice to that smart outfit you're wearing. Come and have lunch with me and I'll introduce you.'

'I'd adore to.'

He leans over the desk, picks up the phone. 'Tell Arthur to bring the car to the door. I'm taking a lady to lunch.'

Walking across the dense carpet, this time with no trouble at all, passing the receptionist, his hand proprietorially under her elbow, Nell knows she's cracked it. Smart girl, she makes him repeat in her head. Very smart.

Long grasses on the orchard's edge, flies buzzing, a distant mower whining; beyond the lawn, glimpsed under hanging greenery and between spikes of red-hot-poker, the house shimmering. It's a dream, thinks Chrissy, pushing spread fingers through daisy-speckled grass tufts; if it were mine I'd be happy for ever, wouldn't go anywhere, I'd just inhabit. Not like Mrs Stockdale, though, always fussing, making people dizzy with constant chat and trivial worries; I'd be more of a chatelaine floating about the place all gracious and content, casting wellbeing. It's so important *how* you inhabit a place, she thinks. Her parents have ruined her home for Liz; she lives here cautiously, as if it's an open prison with capricious warders who at any moment might clang the gates shut. What a waste. She turns her head and looks at her companion who is reading flat on her stomach at the far edge of the blanket – Liz, who is not here anyway in spirit, but with her heart in her mouth in Brighton, led on by Graham Greene.

'I hope Nell's getting on all right with her novel,' says Chrissy, watching Liz turn a page.

'Mm?'

'Nell. Hope she's getting on with her novel.'

Frowning, Liz looks up.

'Shall I get us a cup of tea?'

'If you like.'

Chrissy puts her hands under her shoulders and bounces to her feet. 'She certainly deserves it to be going well, sacrificing all this lovely peace and relaxation for it.'

Liz thinks hard. 'Oh, you mean Nell's novel. Bound

to be going well. Nell's brilliant.' And as Chrissy goes ambling over the lawn calling that she won't be long, Liz settles comfortably again to her book.

In the kitchen, Mrs Stockdale is preparing black-currants for jam, stringing glossy purple fruit into a yellow bowl with the prongs of a silver fork.

'Oh,' says Chrissy, entranced by the sight. 'Can I stay and watch?'

'You can help, Chrissy love. But put a pinny on; these don't half stain.'

Chrissy helps herself from a clutch of aprons hanging on the pantry door.

Tea is forgotten. Neither Liz nor Chrissy notice.

V

'Let's get the bus,' said Nell, gazing after one through the car window. 'Sit on top at the front like we used to – remember? – rubbishing everything.'

They'd decided to explore; look up old haunts, take a look at the town's recent developments. Liz, who was still feeling concerned about Nell's breathlessness last night, was prompted to indulge her. 'We could do the round trip,' she agreed. 'Take the number six to the bathing pool, come back via the docks on the number eleven.'

'If you like,' said Chrissy doubtfully, 'only it isn't the bathing pool any more, it's the leisure centre.' She drove up the ramp into the multi-storey car park. As a native and one no longer familiar with the corporation bus service, she joined their scrutiny of bus-stop notice-boards with some embarrassment; Liz and Nell were like pushy tourists, jumping aboard, chasing upstairs to grab the front seats.

The number six bus went through the best part of town, along a broad tree-lined road with houses big as mansions, each house vying for grandeur with the one next door – witch's hat turret on one, castellations on the next, Tudor-type timbers and mullioned windows embellishing a third. When the housing became less hysterical, giving way to solid semis with lawned gardens, garages, double gates, they anticipated the approach of the two former grammar schools. Liz asked Nell if she wanted to get off or ride on.

Nell looked at her, then at Chrissy across the gangway. They're humouring me, she thought. There could be only one reason. They'd guessed something was the matter with her. She turned her head to stare at the ranked houses of prim suburbia, which ought in the light of her present circumstances to appear depressingly lower-middle class, but could still, she discovered, impress the girl from Maud Street. How did she feel, she wondered, about Liz and Chrissy learning the full alarming truth? As ever, her emotions were difficult to disentangle. There was definitely an element of excitement – the cropping up of a matter of significance calling for their exclusive and combined attention had always been exciting; there was also fear, because Liz and Chrissy knowing about it would make the illness seem more real, less susceptible to being pushed to the back of one's mind; there was also relief, the simple relief of telling one's nearest and dearest – for if not Liz and Chrissy, who else was there?

'Shall we get off or go on?' Liz asked again as the former boys' grammar was passed and the girls' came into view. Chrissy, woman of action, had already leapt up, and now sat down again.

'Off,' said Nell suddenly, and they all rose and ran, revealing their lack of practice by crashing into seats along the gangway. By the time they made it downstairs, the bus had passed the school and was heading for the next stop.

This was the Robinson Rec. A leap from the bus brought Chrissy up against the pavement seat she and Nell had once sat upon, waiting for a distraught Liz. The memory hit her hard; she turned an anguished face to Liz; but Liz, untroubled by recollection, was lending a helping hand to Nell who was having difficulty dismounting. 'Lost the hang of this,' gasped Nell, as the bell pinged and the bus moved off too soon for her comfort. She stared hard at the recreation ground ahead of her. 'Bloody Robinson Rec,' she commented, as though affronted by its continued existence. 'The hours we spent gassing on those seats in there.'

'Yuk, and what we would find underneath them,' recalled Liz.

'What did we find?' asked Chrissy, looking blankly into the grounds. But the others had moved off up the road in the direction of school.

'It's so absolutely the same,' marvelled Liz when they reached the gates. Her eyes went to the top of the building. 'To think we spent an entire night up there. What on earth explanation would we have given if we'd been caught? I doubt we could have put one in words.'

'It was odd of us, when you come to think of it,' said Chrissy.

'We were eccentrics,' Nell said proudly, puffing rather as she proceeded up the road at the side of the school.

'Where's she going now?'

'Nell?' They hurried after her.

'If you had to select one place,' said Nell, 'one place out of all our old haunts, which would it be?'

'How do you mean, exactly?'

'One place that crystallizes how we were.'

They pondered for a while. Then Chrissy said, 'School, I suppose. That's where we started from.'

'School's too general.'

'The library, then, where we used to hold our confabs.'

'What do you think, Liz?'

'I'm not sure I can pinpoint one place.'

'I think,' said Nell eventually, passing between the cemetery gates, 'I think in here.'

Liz and Chrissy looked at one another. 'She would,' Chrissy said. 'The place where we came for a smoke.'

'Yeah. The be-all and end-all of Nell's day. "Anyone got a ciggy? Whose turn to bring the fags?"'

Ignoring them, Nell went stolidly down the path.

'She's going to that grave, the one with the angel.'

'Oh, Nell, you're not, are you? We'll never find it.'

'I found it the other day.'

'You mean you came here?'

'Yep.' She turned left. 'Down here. Remember those trees?'

They gave no answer, finding the expedition suddenly unsettling.

'There,' Nell said at last.

They remained on the path, surveying the memorial.

'We never even knew whose it was,' said Liz, making to walk over the grass. But Nell caught her arm. 'Let's *not* know.'

'All right,' she shrugged, and took a step back.

In silence, they imagined it decorated with their young selves: Liz on the steps with her head thrown back popping smoke rings and watching them drift past the angel's shoulders; Nell beside her, hunched over the cigarette she'd craved all morning, making a brilliant observation or setting them right about something; Chrissy perched on the ledge surrounding the grave, her legs stretched over the grass, listening intently, letting her cigarette burn itself to extinction between fingers held as far from her body as possible.

'The dear old guardian angel,' Liz said softly. 'Remember coming here after that scene at the Sea Gull?'

'I wanted to die,' Nell remembered, 'and came to the right place to do so.'

Chrissy linked arms with her, after a moment led her away.

They returned down the path. 'Perhaps,' suggested Nell as they rounded the corner, 'the inscription on it reads: *Here lie Chrissy, Liz and Nell.*'

'And perhaps it doesn't,' said Liz firmly, taking Nell's other arm. 'Don't be so Gothic.' She shot a look at Chrissy, signalling *what are we going to do with her*?

'Let's take the bus to the front. There's a very nice coffee shop in the leisure centre. It's time you two noticed how this place has brightened up since our young days. Come and have a look.'

'Sounds like a good idea,' Liz said.

And Nell detected that they'd stopped humouring her, were now determined to take her in hand. Either way, it was very gratifying.

Nell had forgotten the major drawback of bus travel – that it involves a great deal of physical activity, climbing on, jumping off, walking a great many steps in between. By the time they alighted from the second bus of the day she was practically speechless. Liz and Chrissy made briskly for the leisure centre, inviting her to recall this, marvel at that. 'Want to look round before or after coffee?' asked Chrissy ominously and, checking her watch, added a further heart-sinking thought: 'We may get a peek at Amanda if we're lucky.' Fortunately, Liz suggested coffee first, and in thankful silence Nell followed them to the escalator. Up they went to the top floor. Stepping off, her cough started. Hacking, gasping, she only just made it into the coffee shop before collapsing into the seat they manoeuvred under her. Chrissy gave the order. Liz made concerned noises and patted her back. She'd got a very nasty cough, they told her. Also, she seemed short of breath. These symptoms shouldn't be ignored: as soon as she got back she must go to her doctor. Nell nodded as and when she could, all her attention focused on breathing. The coffee arrived, also pastries. Nell slipped a pill into her mouth, sipped some coffee, flopped back in her chair. As her breath came more easily, a warm lax sense of relief stole over her, almost somnolence. They reported that she was looking better, at which she smiled dozily. Evidently satisfied, they stopped looking worried and gazed around.

Through a plate-glass wall could be viewed the not entirely alluring North Sea – light, they agreed, restful. The whole area was charming, very prettily done. Greenery grew everywhere in pots and hanging baskets, there were green slatted chairs and tables, pink cloths and cushions, pink and green plaster coiled round columns supporting the ceiling and moulded decoratively on the archway entrance. Liz said it was so attractive she couldn't believe they were in the same old town, and Chrissy, taking her point, explained how the whole complex (though a source of delight and remuneration to her children) was to Tony as a red rag to a bull; one of his clients had been faithfully promised the contract for its design and erection (a rewarding prospect for Tony, too, she implied), only to see his hopes dashed at the last minute when the council underwent a sinister change of mind and commissioned an outfit from somewhere down south. 'From London?' queried Liz; and Chrissy, to whom all places south of the Wash were much of a muchness and simply foreign, shrugged and tucked into her pastry. Liz followed suit, enquiring mid-mouthful about the various activities the building accommodated.

While they chatted thus, Nell was gripped by one of the internal inquisitions she often went in for during bouts of weakness and depression.

It would be fair enough, she argued with herself, *if* Liz had resolved her anxieties, to have a crack at setting out her own, which, under the cool calm exterior she believed she maintained with laconic remarks and an amiable expression, were churning inside her like a choppy sea. However, given her record, there was always a chance she was up to her tricks again. She'd caught herself out so often in the past trying to upstage the other two (like the awful way she behaved that time they went to the hospital where Chrissy was going to have her breast operation); sometimes *privately* upstaging them, hugging the knowledge to herself in secret, as in her capture of Bertie. She couldn't kid herself that that episode could be entirely explained by Bertie's powerful attraction and because he was able, as she had supposed, to be very helpful on her behalf: really, did she *have* to go after Liz's father? (Such a devious bitch, she even made herself suspicious.) On the other hand and in her favour was the plain fact of her illness. Certainly her chums would want to know about it, be given a chance to support her. So why the hesitation? Scruples over upstaging Liz? Or a secret wish to endure the ordeal alone, so that afterwards, dead or alive, they'd say, 'Gosh, wasn't Nell brave, sparing us? Didn't she have guts?' But the reality was that she didn't have guts; she was longing to spill the beans and would soon be whimpering over them like a baby. Perhaps it was this knowledge putting her off. Dammit, now she was going round in circles . . .

'You OK, Nell?'

Dazed, she managed a nod.

'Eat your pastry, then. They're scrumptious.'

Instead, she lit a cigarette. Trying to pin down one's motives, she reflected, was like running down the sort of endless tunnel you get trapped in in dreams, trying this door, the next door, finding, whichever door you open, just another tunnel. Take the Poole business. During all the talk last night, she'd suddenly remembered herself as an envious twelve year old mentally turning Liz into a spotless, delicate, china figurine, and thinking how tremendously thrilling it would be to see this spotlessness smudged. Was this ever in the back of her mind during those sessions when she and Chrissy encouraged Liz to act on her infatuation? She couldn't recall. Nevertheless, the idea had lain there somewhere, deep inside. Motives were such slippery customers, like those blobs of mercury she and Liz and Chrissy used to pursue over the laboratory bench-top during boring science lessons. You could go out of your mind trying to pin down motives. Right now, she couldn't work out whether she craved her friends' love and sympathy or preferred to suffer alone rather than see the horror of her situation mirrored in their eyes. Knowing herself to be a spineless so-and-so, this was probably the key dilemma, and all her nice feelings about holding back until Liz was ready to vacate the stage, mere sophistry. Feeling she'd at least settled that much, she pulled smoke into her lungs, extra deep. Then exploded with another coughing fit.

'Nell, for Pete's sake put out that horrible cigarette and take in *nourishment*,' cried an exasperated Chrissy, giving the remaining pastry a shove. 'I'll get us some more coffee.'

'Oh Nell, are you sure you're OK?' Liz asked, taking her hand.

Fortunately, the second cup of coffee restored calm swiftly. Chrissy was about to suggest moving on, when a plump matron came rushing over to claim her. 'Barbara,' exclaimed Chrissy, embracing the newcomer. She turned to Nell and Liz. 'You remember Barbara from school? Well, perhaps you won't; she was five years below us.'

Below us, thought a stunned Liz and Nell, searching the folds of Barbara's face for a glimpse of the little girl they might have remembered.

After an exchange of pleasantries, Barbara asked Chrissy to come over to her table and say hello to her mother.

'Fat's so ageing,' murmured Nell, watching them go.

'Chrissy looks a kid beside her,' Liz said.

'Ten years younger, at least.'

'We're not kidding ourselves, are we?'

'Certainly not. Wonder if Chrissy dyes her hair. It's still got that burnished brightness.'

'I happen to know she doesn't. She has got a bit of grey, but its finely spread – unlike mine.'

Nell studied her. 'Silver always shows up more in black,' she said kindly. 'Wouldn't know about mine, haven't seen its natural shade in years. I must say, Liz, you're looking a lot more relaxed than when you arrived. Are you feeling better now about the Rosie problem?'

'Much. Not that it's resolved, so far as I know, just that I've taken a step back from it. Couldn't manage that before. It's being here with you two that's done the trick. You know how it is. Whatever happens to us when we're out there on our own, at the back of our minds we know there's always this way of making ourselves safe and strong. Always works . . . Whatever's up?'

Nell was hunting for a tissue. 'Must have got grit on a lens,' she mumbled, dabbing her eyes, blowing her nose. 'Phew, that's got it. I'm looking forward to the ride back, are you? Going past Frigid Fruits, Maud Street. Remember getting the number eleven bus to set off on one of our Saturday morning shopping expeditions? Remember buying those swimming cossies?'

'And lying about in them at the bathing pool? Right below where we are now, come to think of it.'

'Gosh, yes,' said Nell, looking searchingly at the floor as if for traces.

'Sorry,' said Chrissy, coming back. 'Her brother was in my class at primary school. Used to go and play at their house. Her mum's a sweetie, she used to make knock-out cakes. All set? Shall we take a peep at Amanda before we go?'

'Of course.'

'Do we have to?' groaned Nell, as Chrissy went to pay the bill.

'Yes we do,' said Liz. 'Chrissy's super chick in action, remember, so mind and be properly admiring.'

'OK,' sighed Nell. 'But it might be tough.'

*   *   *

Clare, they discovered on their arrival back at The Old Rectory, still seated at the kitchen table, still engrossed in her book.

'Good Lord, haven't you moved since breakfast?' asked her mother.

Declining to look up, Clare went so far as to let fall the minimum information. 'Rosie rang for Liz.'

6
MOVING ON

i

'Well, thank you madam,' said Chrissy sarcastically. 'I suppose you couldn't tell us a bit more? Like, for instance, how long ago Rosie rang.'

'I dunno,' whined Clare, staring in stupefaction at the printed page whose message she could no longer decipher due to her mother's nagging. 'Just now, wasn't it?'

'You tell us. We weren't here. It would have been polite to have made a note of the time for Liz, also to have passed on any messages.'

'But there weren't any,' Clare objected – quite understandably, thought the watching Nell, in view of Liz not hanging around long enough to gather details, but careering into the hall to the nearest phone, pulling the door shut behind her. Though the more potent cause of Clare's petulance, Nell judged, was the pain of separation from a compelling read. She remembered it well. 'Good book?' she enquired, walking across to see. 'Ah yes: C.S.Lewis.' Animation sprang in Clare's face. 'Yes,' she answered, 'brilliant;' and with a finger inserted to keep her place, closed and clasped *The Lion, The Witch And The Wardrobe* to her chest, got to her feet. 'Actually,' she said to her mother, 'I was only reading down here waiting for you to come home so's I could tell you about Rosie. Actually,' (it seemed a favourite word and throbbed with misunderstood virtue) 'I was peacefully reading upstairs till I had to go and answer the phone. No-one else bothered.'

'Well, now you're here you can wash those mugs.'

'That's not fair, I didn't dirty them.'

Nell's heart went out to her. 'Go on, hop it. I'll see to the mugs.'

Seizing her chance, Clare shot away – up the back stairs, considerately avoiding the main hall and Liz.

'Honestly, Nell,' grumbled Chrissy, joining her at the sink. She sighed. 'Wretched child. Never mind, she'll grow out of it.'

'Oh, will she?' asked Nell, thinking this would be a shame.

'Of course. Even Amanda went through a surly stage. Not over books, over her pony. She wanted to live with the blessed animal, wouldn't be parted from it five minutes without a fuss. Talk about sulking. Yet see how she's turned out.'

'Indeed,' said Nell.

'Couldn't ask for a sunnier nature. And just think what terrors we were. Difference was, no-one ever twigged what we got up to. My lot didn't care, yours were too care-worn, Liz's, I suppose, were too complacent.'

'Something like that,' agreed Nell.

During this time, Liz and Rosie were enjoying their longest conversation in two months, the crux of it being, from Rosie's point of view, to discover whether or not her mother had enlightened Nathan about her affair with Simon Goodridge.

'No I didn't,' said Liz. 'He guessed there was some-one, but not the details, and certainly I didn't inform him.'

'Oh, Mum, thanks – I realize it was because you wanted to spare Dad the worry, but I'm so glad he doesn't know, so relieved. You see, it's finished.'

'Oh? Since when?'

'Since the night after you went to Chrissy's. You were right about him, Mum.'

'Was I?' asked Liz, sure she had never uttered an

opinion for or against the man personally.

Rosie evidently remembered differently. 'Oh yes, he's a complete bastard. He was using me. Apparently, eighteen months ago, their second kid died. Simon didn't want them to have any more because he couldn't stand the risk of ever again going through the same misery. When his wife got pregnant he was furious, wanted to punish her.'

'How do you know all this?'

'He told me. I rang him, said if he didn't come out and talk to me I'd bloody well turn up on the doorstep. So we met, and he gave it to me straight, hoping to get me off his back. Said he'd found me madly attractive and all that, but basically I was just his way of hurting her.'

'Oh dear.'

'Yeah.'

'Love, I'm so sorry.'

'Don't be, I'm well rid. Anyway, I've met this super guy, and guess what? – he's a second year at Durham. We're going up together in his jeep. What an entrance, eh?'

'So you're going to university after all?'

'Of course I am. I rang up the admissions tutor – it's all OK. And I've got a job at the cash-and-carry starting Monday – lousy money, but it'll help towards new jeans and things. I've decided to go for the country look. What do you think – Alistair screaming up the drive, me leaping out in Levi's and boots, check shirt, maybe a hat?'

'Alistair comes with the jeep, I take it?'

'Yep. You see, Mum, now everything's turned out OK, it'd be such a waste feeling bad and guilty for nothing – which is how I'd feel if Dad knew about it. I mean, I know *you* won't hold it against me. Well, Dad wouldn't intentionally, but fathers are weird.'

'Mm. Well, it's good to hear you sounding happy and friendly again.'

'Oh Mum, I'm sorry I've been so awful. But I was really wretched. Part of me never wanted it to happen in the first place, another part was flattered and excited, and sort of terrified you'd try and put obstacles in my way. I thought it meant he loved me. I truly did.'

'I know. We always do.'

'From now on I'm going to enjoy my life.'

No words of regret for Ellie, Liz noticed, putting down the receiver after chummy goodbyes; not that it was any business of hers; she should stop projecting her own hang-ups on to Rosie. Now to her own business. Her finger stabbed out the number, her ear marked the interminable clicks – hurry, hurry, please be there. A woman's voice answered. Trying not to plead, she asked to be put through. More clicks, more waiting, then at last, Nathan. 'Darling, it's me. Good news. Rosie's difficulty is over, and that's official.'

'You mean you've spoken to her?'

'She rang me. And she *is* going to Durham. I couldn't bear you to be worried for another second.'

'But I wasn't.'

'Well, just making sure. Honestly darling, that daughter of ours is tough as old boots. Where does she get it from? My father, probably.'

'Certainly not us. We're just a couple of softies. So you don't think whatever it was was serious?'

Did she detect a residue of concern? 'No,' she answered emphatically.

'And definitely no harm done?'

'Certainly not.' (She bit back the rider 'to Rosie.')

'Phew. Well I must say it's a relief. I was pretty sure last night things were on the mend – whatever they were. Did you find out exactly?'

'Not . . . *exactly*. Just that it's definitely over and life goes on as originally planned. Listen, love, from now on she can paddle her own canoe. No worries, eh?'

'You're the boss.'

'You're so precious to me, Nathan.'

'And you to me. 'Bye now, love.'

'See you soon.'

She went back to the kitchen in search of tea.

They stopped talking when she came in, watched as she went to the sink and put the kettle on. 'Panic over,' she told them. 'Rosie's already on to the next chapter – her dazzling arrival at university, jeep-owning bloke in tow. My goodness, the young of today are more resilient than we ever were.'

'Speak for yourself,' said Nell.

'Oh Liz, thank heaven; I'm so glad.'

'I sometimes think it's jolly fortunate for kids that mothers are programmed to love them.'

'Very.'

Nell went to the door. 'I think I'll go and lie down for a bit; make sure I'm fresh for tonight.'

'We don't have to go out if you're not up to it.'

'Of course I'm up to it. I'm anticipating it keenly. See you later.' With which she left them to their own devices.

ii

Like a conjurer's trick, Nell turns into her letters – between four and six sides of cramped neat handwriting arriving with steadfast regularity and alternation, this week's to Liz, next week's to Chrissy. Nell-in-the-flesh dims, they can barely picture her doing any of the things she mentions, doubtless because she mentions very few, and those she does are mundane, like trying out a new hair colour or losing a library book, things done by everybody. It's her witty commentary, her eccentric and hilarious point of view, that make live things of these pieces of paper, live like electricity or magnetism; so much so, that during their first three university terms they fail to notice how Nell herself has receded. There's never anything in her letters that can't be shared. They pass them over like treats; take

341

turns to reply, mourning that they can never hope to entertain Nell as she them. Which is strange, because Liz's and Chrissy's letters are packed full of doings, their lives are so full they barely have time to mention every memorable happening. But then, as they ruefully point out, they lack Nell's gifts – her sharp eye, her wicked way with a pen.

Though Liz and Chrissy often see each other, they by no means live in one another's pocket. They don't even reside in the same hall; Liz was allocated a room in Thornthwaite Hall, a large custom-built residence with a warden and a junior common room, Chrissy a room in Jameson Hall, a rambling Victorian house providing cosy accommodation for a mere eighteen women. Though initially dismayed, neither felt impelled to try and arrange a swap. Soon, Chrissy was enjoying visits to Thornthwaite as Liz's guest at Sunday high tea when Liz would point out personalities currently figuring in common-room gossip, and Liz was enjoying the informality of dropping into Jameson for coffee in the kitchen. On campus, they are known to be friends, but adjudged to be different types. Chrissy is one of the stars, a terrific looker, competed for by men wishing to date her, talked about, written about in the gossipy student newspaper. No party or dance has really happened without her. Everyone knows who Chrissy Thomas is, Chrissy knows everyone who matters. Liz is regarded as a serious type – attractive and therefore noticed, but a student who mostly sticks to her department. She spends most of her time in the psychology lab working on her own projects, taking an interest in other people's. Her favourite way to relax is over beer in the mixed common room with a gang of friends. She sometimes goes out with men from outside her circle, but by these has been designated 'cold'. This means they never get anywhere with her sexually. Men don't get far with Chrissy either, but she escapes this label. For one thing, men know she's a valuable commodity, they're grateful to be seen with her merely for the way this boosts their reputation (no serious stud can afford to be snubbed by Chrissy); for another, men keep quiet about not getting far with her for fear others are more successful, and they resist the temptation to lie in case Chrissy gets to hear of it and their chances are scuppered for ever.

Chrissy has an independent attitude to dates, often preferring to arrive on her own, particularly at Saturday night hops. Other than for big occasions – end-of-term dances, Union Ball, Freshers' Ball – dance music is provided by the university jazz band (jazz being the music of the moment, student musicians being available for free). Chrissy is a jazz fanatic, never missing the Friday lunchtime concert where she sits with her eyes closed, her shoulders rhythmically dipping forward like delicate wings caressing the beat; never missing the Saturday stomp, where she's choosy about who she dances with, being such a whizz on the floor herself. Men who move well jostle to partner her.

The star of the jazz band is its trumpeter, Joe Johnson, a large, bearded man, older than the average student, reputed to be in his late twenties or early thirties. The other members of the band range from mediocre to competent: Joe Johnson is the real thing. At some point in the evening, something can click between Chrissy and Joe – it's hard to say what starts it off, but, suddenly, the trumpet's growling intimately and Chrissy's on her own, hands in the air, body shimmering. Other dancers make space around her, keep their own movements small; watch, nod, grin. At the end of the number, Joe comes down from the stage; he and Chrissy hug; they stand drinking beer together, drape their arms along the other's shoulders.

'We're just good mates,' insists Chrissy, when Liz assumes a closer relationship. Liz accepts this. The next time she sees her, Chrissy's on top of a bus with a new bloke in tow. As for Joe Johnson, he's inscrutable: smiles at you in a lazy sort of way, doesn't say a lot, is popular as a campus personality, has no special girl (except Chrissy who says there's nothing in it). In Liz's mind, it's hard to separate Joe from his trumpet.

One evening after a late lecture, Liz and her friends pile into the mixed common room for snacks and drinks. She's walking over the floor balancing plates on top of beer mugs (this is her shout, she reminded Mike, he bought the drinks last time), when, pausing to look up and see where Mike's sitting, she notices a couple on a nearby settee – not necking, exactly, more cuddling: it's Chrissy and Joe Johnson. Liz's heart goes chill. Her friend's eyes are closed, there's a strange look on her face, a mixture of bliss and pain; her arms round Joe's chest are taut, like a child's desperately clinging to a comfort object. Steadying herself, Liz moves on. A few minutes later, when she's sitting down sipping her beer and ostensibly listening to the chat around her, Liz clearly sees the truth of the matter. Chrissy spoke honestly when she described Joe and herself as 'just good mates'; but this is not the state of affairs Chrissy desires. Chrissy's in love.

Towards the end of their first year, Liz and Chrissy apply for vacation work at Frigid Fruits. Nell writes to say she won't be joining them; she's landed a job on the local rag – nothing much, reporting weddings and local functions, that sort of thing; but at least it's a start. Thrilled, Liz and Chrissy write back at once. Congratulations, they say, it's bound to lead to more interesting assignments (once the editor's had a look at her stuff and appreciates what a genius he's employing); and anyway, then can all meet up in the evenings.

In the event, they see little of Nell. If she's not dashing off to cover council meetings, she's doing research for her novel. They don't object. They're working lots of overtime, trying to earn as much as possible before setting off on a hitch-hiking and camping holiday in France with a group of friends from university.

Liz stays at Chrissy's during the week, Chrissy goes to Liz's every weekend. On Friday evenings, they like to stroll up the lane towards Fenby-cum-Laithby, taking in the peace and quiet, the fresh air. On one of these strolls, Chrissy comes to a sudden halt, gasps as if a sharp pain has struck her, grabs Liz's hand. 'I love him,' she says, her voice cracking. 'It's no good, because he doesn't ever want to be serious about anybody. But I can't help it, Liz. It's killing me.'

Liz wraps both her hands tightly round Chrissy's.

It's getting dusk. After a moment, they drop hands, turn, start briskly back home.

Bats, like bomber aircraft, take flying swoops at their heads: they stand in the drive on the porch-light's fringe, watching and ducking. It's hard to believe the assault isn't directed at them personally.

'They can't see us.'

'They can sense us, though.'

Chrissy shivers.

She can't be cold, Liz thinks, it's too humid, and they've walked back at a cracking pace, she herself is quite clammy; it must be depression over Joe. 'Who's this?' she asks, to lift Chrissy's mood, and starts stomping about with an imaginary partner, arms stiff and outstretched, nose in the air, expression haughty – under her breath humming a syncopated tune.

'Oh God, Marie Jacobson,' laughs Chrissy, brightening up immediately.

At which, Liz changes her dancing style, goes neat and tiny, creeps round an absent partner.

'Brilliant – Philly and Mike exactly. Go on, do me.'

Liz's arms fling high, she twists and twirls with exaggerated sensuality. Screaming half in protest, half in recognition, Chrissy joins in. Alderman Stockdale's car, like a swift sly cat, slides at speed through the gateway and snares them in brilliance for a dazzling second – two raving and abandoned creatures, who fall

345

heart-sinkingly still as the car swings into the garage.

'Oh, bugger,' says Chrissy. 'Quick, let's go in.'

'No, let him go in first, then we'll know where he is,' says Liz, meaning that then they can be sure of avoiding him.

They dawdle towards the steps. Alderman Stockdale's footsteps come up briskly behind. He goes by without pausing, snarls a curt 'Good evening'.

'Good evening,' replies Liz.

Chrissy says nothing. When he's gone, she asks, 'Why does he speak like that? I know he's never been quite the same with us since the Mr Poole business, but he got over it, he was even jolly for a time. Remember last summer, how he had us laughing over that cake I made, the one that sunk in the middle and your mum trying to make out it was supposed to look like that? He had us splitting our sides. Now he barks "Good morning", "Good evening", like he can hardly stand the sight of us. You don't think it's because he thinks I'm a scrounger, always coming here?'

'I'm absolutely sure he doesn't. And he knows Mummy adores having you. No it's me. Becoming a psychology student has really rubbed it in, that I didn't turn out as he wanted and never will. He'll never see *Alderman and Mrs Stockdale and their charming daughter Elizabeth* reported in the *Evening Telegraph*.'

Chrissy is still doubtful. 'Maybe I do take coming here for granted. I ought to say "thank you" more often.'

'Don't be an idiot. Maybe if I tried to interest him in what I'm doing . . . But he's been so scornful on the subject, I've tried to keep off it. I'll give it another go. After all, he is funding me.'

They go into the house, introspectively hunting for personal fault and methods of appeasement. He's harsh to us, so what are we doing wrong? they wonder, as women will. It never occurs to them to ask whether this harshness stems from fault of his own.

346

*   *   *

Eight months later. Nine thirty in the morning. Dark as night outside because of the rain. In their dingy digs, they grate on each other's nerves; they wish they'd gone home for the vacation.

Liz finished her breakfast some time ago and is now swotting from lecture notes in one of the two easy chairs (if such basic comfort can be termed 'easy' – just two plastic covered spongy rectangles lain on springs stretched across wooden frames, one to sit on, one to lean against). Chrissy is still at the table in a corner of the room, munching her way through a second bowl of cereal. She, too, is swotting, from a file of notes propped against a cake tin. Liz has taken to bolting her food, the quicker to escape from the table where it's impossible not to get hooked by the wallpaper design – thin squiggly lines in hard black and red, criss-crossing over a white background. These lines drive her mad, make her head seize up, sear her eyeballs, screw her nerves. When she's sitting at the table, her eyes get drawn to them like obsessive voyeurs to a scene of carnage, and with Chrissy chomping and groaning beside her, she begins to imagine losing control, perhaps snatching up Chrissy's cornflakes bowl, hurling it at the wall; perhaps snatching up the eternal cake tin, bringing it down hard on Chrissy's head (at least silencing the chomping). She looks up from her notes, cautiously lifts the lid from her throbbing irritation and allows the escape of one small puff of steam – 'You don't think you could manage to eat more quietly?'

Chrissy doesn't answer; perhaps didn't hear, engrossed as she is in mastication. This provokes a further build up, forcing Liz to continue in a tight voice, 'And must you *groan* as you chew? Sounds like you're having sex or something, you know, pleasuring yourself. It's so frankly farmyard it wouldn't amaze me to hear pigs grunting.' Then she clamps her lips shut, keeps them closed till shame washes over her and she feels impelled to take the sting out of her sarcasm with a reasonably couched request. 'Please try and keep the volume down.'

Chrissy carries on eating, but discreetly and without the groans. When she's finished she takes her bowl and mug to the sink (in another corner of the room), swills them out.

Staying up was a ghastly mistake, thinks Liz, wishing they'd gone home like most students. Too late now, nothing for it but to sweat it out.

Fortunately, this being the Easter vacation (of their second university year), it's of short duration. They jumped at the chance at the end of their first year to move out of hall and become relatively independent. Reasonable lodgings were found here with Mrs Bisset (plus Mr Bisset and two Bisset children, rarely seen): two rooms, one on the ground floor with cooking facilities, one upstairs containing two beds and a washbasin, plus shared use (with the Bisset family) of bathroom and WC. Mrs Bisset confidently allocated each of them a weekly bath night, since when they've spent a great deal of energy devising means of sneaking a few inches of hot water when it's not their bath night but some other member of the household's. By and large, Mrs Bisset is a decent enough landlady, leaves them to their own devices, doesn't overly regulate or complain. During term time, they hardly notice being on top of one another; most days and evenings are spent going about their own business, often meeting up only at breakfast time and late at night. During the Christmas vacation they went home, as usual. However, with exams for Part One of their degrees coming up next term, it seemed a sound idea to remain at Mrs Bisset's and close to the university library. Mrs Stockdale protested that she would willingly set aside two study bedrooms and keep them supplied with sustenance; but they demurred, said, thanks all the same, but they needed to make use of university facilities. They're very short of money, so in fact can no longer afford the bus fare to the library; on fine days they walk there, but often it's too wet. Luckily, Mrs Stockdale sends regular food parcels.

It's the first time in her life that Liz has felt negatively towards Chrissy. She falls to imagining how prisoners feel locked up with one another in tiny cells for twenty-three hours out of twenty-four. It's a wonder they don't murder one another. Perhaps they do and it gets hushed up – this is something she must look into. If only it would stop raining. Having the electric light on all the time adds to the prison-cell atmosphere. There are french windows in this room, but it's so dark outside, they feel cut off from the world; they could be anywhere, adrift at sea, or marooned on an uninhabited rain-drenched island. Bet it's really stuffy in here, she thinks, only we're too cooped up to notice. It might be a good idea to take her notes upstairs and sit against the headboard on her bed. She can't just walk out on Chrissy, though, after speaking to her like that. 'Want a coffee?' she asks, as a peace offering.

'All right,' shrugs Chrissy.

Liz lights the gas ring, fills the kettle, drops a teaspoon of coffee powder into each of two mugs, pours on half an inch of milk from a near-empty bottle. When the kettle threatens to whistle, she pours on the hot water and stirs. She carries one of the mugs to the table, leans across Chrissy to set it down on a mat.

'Whoof,' says Chrissy, jerking back. 'I wondered what the pong was in here. Smelt it in the bathroom, too. It's your hair, stinks like a sheep. Why the hell don't you wash it?'

'Run out of shampoo,' mumbles Liz, endeavouring to lessen the offence with swift steps backwards.

'Then be my guest,' growls Chrissy. 'There's a bottle of Vosene in my toilet bag.'

'Didn't realize, sorry.' She gathers her notes under her arm, collects her coffee mug, goes somewhat huffily out of the room.

Twenty minutes later there's a knock on the front door. Recalling that the Bissets have gone to Doncaster for the weekend to stay with Grandma Bisset, Chrissy runs to answer it. It's the postman with a parcel. 'From your mum,' she yells joyfully up the stairs. 'Come down and open it.'

'You open it,' comes back the faint reply.

'But it's addressed to you.' Chrissy contemplates the parcel – still Liz doesn't come; at length, unable to restrain herself, rips it open. A fruit cake, a curd tart, a square of gingerbread – and an envelope. Seizing this last, Chrissy dashes upstairs to the bedroom, thrusts it at Liz (whose newly washed hair is swathed in a towel). Liz opens her mother's letter, counts out the contents. 'Ten pounds.'

'*Ten pounds.*' It's a fortune, and it goes without saying it's a fiver each. 'Let's go to John Taylor's party tonight. We're getting frowsty stuck in here.'

'All right,' agrees Liz. 'What're we going to wear, though? My dress has had it, and all the sweaters are mucky.'

'At least now we can afford the launderette.'

'Sweaters won't dry in time.'

'No.' Chrissy sits down on the edge of the bed to think it over. Her eyes light on Mrs Bisset's curtains. 'How about them?'

'What?'

'The curtains. Those net ones there, and those brocade ones downstairs. We could drape them round, pin them on. I bet they'd look ravishing.'

'Do you think so?'

'I do.'

'How'd we get there in all this wet?'

'Ring for a taxi on the Bissets' phone,' says Chrissy looking at the money.

'OK. It'd be nice to see people for a change, have a bit of fun.'

They don't waste time discussing how they'll get home.

Mrs Bisset's private quarters get thoroughly worked over (what they're searching for is safety pins to secure and shape her curtains), her electricity is stolen (they go into one of the Bisset children's bedrooms, open the airing cupboard door, switch on the immersion heater), her bath-night rule is flouted (they have a full bath each, extra hot). Finally, when her curtains are down and wound like mummies' bandages round her tenants' persons, her phone is commandeered for the purpose of summoning transport.

A toot of a horn signals the taxi's arrival. They feel like film stars tripping down the path in the rain, coats slung over their shoulders. In the back of the vehicle they try sitting in their bindings for the first time, discover that their feet shoot up, they can't sit up properly, have to laugh so hard they're unable to clearly indicate their destination.

'Gutteridge Street,' manages Chrissy.

'Number?' the cabbie asks wearily.

They turn to one another, collapse again. 'Sorry, don't know. Go down the street slowly, and, oh, God . . .'

'We'll point it out,' finishes Liz, choking over 'if we recognize it.'

'You students?' he sneers, thinking of his taxes.

'Oh no,' weeps Chrissy, as Liz's silent convulsion ends in a hoot. 'She's an opera singer.'

'And she's a dress designer.' With which the power of speech altogether escapes them, until rekindled a few minutes later by the sight of the house where their host has an attic flat.

'You've passed it,' Chrissy complains. 'It's the corner one back there.'

'Think I'm a mind reader? I drew in soon as you said.'

Liz wriggles forward, pleads piteously, her voice gone soft and charming, 'But we'll get wet if you don't go back. Please?'

He sighs, shoves the gear stick into reverse, backs up.

'You are kind. Thanks ever so.' Liz hands him a pound note, waits with a trusting smile for every penny of change.

Bumping into one another hilariously, they chase-hobble up the path, wrench open the unlocked door, climb two flights of stairs (pausing now and then to laugh weakly); at last gain the upper landing from where all the noise is coming and toss their coats on to a pile of other people's. Going into the room they adjust their personas, become poised, Chrissy tall and svelte in her orange brocade drapery, half her auburn curls piled high on her head, half left to tumble down her neck; Liz like a Spanish princess, black thick hair glossy from recent cleansing, creamy skin swathed in creamy lace. Not a glance in the room remains uncaptured; everyone – talkers, dancers, sprawlers, drinkers – everyone looks and stares.

Chrissy's hands fly out in greeting. She stays upright, turns herself, so that points north, south, east and west get equal advantage; is very soon surrounded. Liz, who has looked immediately for some safe place to sit, walks over to a settee, hitches up the lower reaches of her ensemble, carefully lowers bum to moquette. Competition ensues between two men she knows vaguely to sit beside her, the loser settling for the floor near her feet. The men exchange banter, Liz listens; she knows it's for her benefit. Then a man she's never seen before comes over with two glasses of red wine, hands her one. 'For me?' She's genuinely surprised. Mostly, it's get your own round here. His gesture strikes her as sophisticated, as does his way of settling on the arm of the settee with his face towards her which has the effect of cutting out the other two men.

'What a wonderful dress,' he remarks over his wineglass. 'And your friend's. Did you make them yourselves?'

'Er, mm,' she says vaguely.

'They're stunning. You're art students, I suppose. In fashion design?'

'No, neither.' She drops her head to hide a grin, and as she does so inhales a tell-tale whiff of window grime. Evidently her body has warmed up her casing, to malodorous effect. God knows how strongly she's going to end up ponging. Better make it clear now that the smell's not hers personally. 'Actually, it's curtains.'

It takes him a few moments to work this out. 'You mean the dress?'

'Yes. My landlady's. They pong a bit, I'm afraid. Chrissy and I hadn't anything to wear, so we improvised.'

He's obviously very taken with her explanation, and no less admiring. When the other two men give her up as a bad job and wander away, she moves up on the settee so that her new friend can sit more comfortably beside her. 'I haven't seen you around the university,' she says, as he sinks down.

'No. I'm at Imperial. I'm a friend of John's, we were at school together. I'm staying with him for the weekend.'

'Imperial College, London? I've a friend studying in London at Bedford College.'

'And does she favour curtains, too?'

'Possibly, when pushed.'

'I'm Nathan Learman, by the way.'

'I'm Liz Stockdale.'

In silence, they take time taking one another in. They've known each other less than five minutes, but already the future tingles their nerve ends; there's a sense of something huge building, something momentous, far-reaching – like the years ahead weighing on some sixth sense as the past weighs on memory.

Two hours later, having talked together without interruption, they get up to dance – a slow shuffle from foot to foot, more an excuse to hold one another. This clasping of the other's body shuts their minds down, becomes all they're aware of.

In the centre of the room, Chrissy has quite forgotten her dependence on safety pins. Dancing vigorously, disaster strikes; a corner of curtain trails to the floor, some heavy-footed bloke treads on it. As Chrissy yelps and flounders, the brocade looses its tethers, gravity takes its effect. Joe Johnson, who has spent the evening in an armchair, is galvanized, has never been known to move so swiftly, or even swiftly at all. He's by Chrissy's side in a trice, scooping up brocade, shielding her across the room into the bedroom. Alerted by her friend's cry of distress, Liz observes their flight; it crosses her mind to go and offer assistance, but Joe's looking after her, she reasons, who is like a brother to Chrissy (according to Chrissy). She closes her eyes, moves closer to Nathan.

It's three o'clock. Most people have gone. 'I ought to get back,' says Liz, looking doubtfully at the bedroom door which has not opened since Joe and Chrissy closed it.

'I'll give you a lift.'

So he's got a car: there seems no end to his attractions. 'Thanks. I'll just see if I can, er, tell my friend.'

'She can come too, of course.'

'Right.' Liz goes to the bedroom door, taps on it nervously, calls, 'Chrissy? It's Liz. Time to go home. There's a lift here, if you want one.'

Silence. After a few moments, the door opens a crack. 'Um, Liz? Don't think I'll come back tonight if you

don't mind. Is that OK? Will you be all right? Perhaps
Maureen'll stay with you . . .'

'No, no. I'll be fine. But will you?'

'Of course.'

'See you, then.'

'Yes, see you.'

It's a battered little car, but it starts first time. The car
doors close, the engine throbs, they turn to look at one
another: it's their first moment of being alone. Mouths
and hands meet over the gear stick. On the journey,
Liz gives Nathan directions, Nathan drives: this is all
they do – the atmosphere in the car feels super-charged,
superfluous exertion might set off something.

'Come in,' she says when they arrive.

He follows her inside.

Chrissy returns in the early afternoon, opens the french
windows, comes tiptoeing in pulling an 'Is it OK – or
am I interrupting something?' face. Liz tells her that
Nathan has gone to square matters with John with
whom he is supposed to be spending this weekend and
will soon be back, whereupon Chrissy seizes her in a
ballroom clinch, marches with her across the room and
back, tango style. Liz shoves her off, they sink grinning
at each other in the plasticky armchairs. Chrissy demands the details, Liz supplies them. 'Love at first
sight,' marvels Chrissy. 'Everyone felt it, the current
going between you two.'

'What about you and Joe?'

'I'm moving in with him. I've come back for some
things.'

'Oh, gosh, Chrissy,' says Liz, conveying, 'Do you
think that's wise?' After everything Chrissy's confided
about Joe, Liz is convinced it isn't. Joe has explained
how he's unable to connect sex with love, how he visits
prostitutes in the dock area; that, fond though he is of
Chrissy, a serious relationship between them is out of
the question. Chrissy, it seemed, had accepted this.

355

'Look, I've dreamt of getting this chance. I knew the bastard fancied me, whatever he said. He admitted caring about me, so it was just a matter of bringing him to the boil – not that I hadn't despaired of succeeding. So don't think I'm letting go now.'

'Does he want you to move in?'

Chrissy doesn't answer, bends over her holdall, starts dragging out Mrs Bisset's brocade curtain. 'He won't stop me,' she says at last. 'Deep down he'll probably be glad. But it's my decision. Give us a hand with this.' She holds out an end of the curtain.

'Hell, Chrissy, it needs pressing.'

'Rubbish. The creases will soon drop out. Where did we put the hooks?'

'It's all right for you, it's me who'll be around when Mrs Bisset blows a gasket.'

'Stop fussing. She'll never notice. You'd better tell her I've gone home, by the way, for the rest of the holiday. When term starts I'll make it look like I'm still living here.' (This will certainly be necessary; the age of enlightenment for cohabiting unmarried students has not yet dawned; getting caught by an irate landlady and subsequently reported to the university authorities invariably leads to rustication.) 'You'll help, won't you?'

'Yes, but be careful, Chrissy.' Liz finds she is more concerned about her friend getting involved with the enigmatic Joe Johnson than keeping the wool pulled over Mrs Bisset's eyes; doesn't feel, though, that she can mention this again.

When the curtains have been rehung, when Chrissy has crammed some of her belongings into her holdall, they hang about awkwardly in the downstairs room, unable to give adequate expression to all the anxieties chasing through their minds.

'Better write down Joe's address for me.'

'Oh, yes,' agrees Chrissy, leaning to scribble on a file holder. She straightens. 'Well.'

'Well.'

'Your turn to write to Nell.'

'Yes.'

'Plenty of news this time.'

'I'll say.'

Footsteps are coming down the side of the house. Liz's heart leaps.

They both look to the french windows. The next moment there's a dark blue duffel coat, a bright red scarf, and Nathan's face grinning in, kindliness crinkling his eyes.

'He's lovely,' murmurs Chrissy. 'I'm glad. You deserve someone super.'

Liz hurries to let him in.

She's full of contradictions: happy-miserable, hopeful-fearful, trying to work hard, not finding it easy to concentrate. Nathan is partly to blame. She lives for their phone calls, for the next time he comes up in his car to stay with John. He's been back twice; on a calendar over her bed she ticks off the days to his next visit. They write daily, anything from pages of hastily written scrawl to two or three line messages.

It's Chrissy who's firing her with hope one day, downing her with gloom the next. Chrissy is like a bird gliding on air currents, too blissfully preoccupied to come down to earth and pay attention to mundane matters, such as paying the rent, collecting her mail, attending the odd lecture. It's a full-time job covering up for her. Chrissy's intoxication can be infectious – Chrissy and Joe are hitting it off, so what else matters? Liz can believe for a few hours, before it wears off. Then she starts worrying whether Chrissy's neglecting her work. Most of all she worries about Chrissy crashing from her stratosphere when Joe ditches her, for in cold sober moments Liz feels sure this is what he'll do.

Last time Nathan came for the weekend, he and Liz cooked a meal for Chrissy and Joe. (Nathan is a wizard

357

at cooking, yet another amazing attribute.) Chrissy, Liz suspects, had problems persuading Joe to take part in this cosy scenario, but he came all the same, looking sheepishly willing to compensate for the derogatory comments he'd probably made beforehand; he talked quite a bit, asked questions, even praised the food.

'What do you think?' asked Liz afterwards.

'I think,' Nathan said slowly, 'Chrissy's in love.'

'And?'

'Joe loves Joe.'

'Ah,' sighed Liz, putting her arms round him, holding her own dear certainty close to soothe her pain for Chrissy.

She's written to Nell begging for her opinion. Could she suggest what Liz might say or do to forearm Chrissy against certain heartbreak? Nell writes back to say Liz is being ridiculously pessimistic, she's noticed this trait in her before. How can Liz *know* it's going to end in tears, might there possibly be a touch of class prejudice creeping in here? Just because Joe's a bit rough . . .

'I never said he was rough – where've you got that from?' she wrote back indignantly. 'If our letters are so boring you have to embroider them, maybe we just shouldn't bother.'

No direct reply is ever made to this. Nell writes to Chrissy next (it's her turn), a letter full of amusingly written anecdotes about nothing much. When she writes again to Liz it's in similar vain and contains only passing, irritatingly anodyne, reference to Chrissy's affair. Does she even read what we write? wonders Liz – but not for long: tomorrow she sits the first of her Part One papers.

She works till eleven, writes a goodnight note to Nathan, goes to bed – shifting a few of Chrissy's belongings for Mrs Bisset's benefit, in case, full of pre-examination nerves, she omits to do this in the morning.

When finals are over, Joe says he has job interviews in Birmingham and Leicester; while he's away Chrissy should return to her digs. This is fine by Chrissy: for one thing, Liz will be in London with Nathan celebrating the end of finals, so won't be around to allay Mrs Bisset's suspicions; for another, Chrissy has fallen behind with her work, she's been granted an extended deadline for an essay which ought to have been handed in before exams started and must now be submitted without fail three days hence.

For two days she works solidly at Mrs Bisset's. On the third day she takes the completed essay to meet the twelve o'clock deadline. This accomplished, heaving a sigh of relief, she ambles over to Arts Block to inspect her pigeon hole. Not much correspondence – a letter from Auntie Julie, a circular, a note. This note, which is not in an envelope but simply a piece of paper folded over, is from Joe.

Chrissy, my sweet,
   Don't bother coming back. I'm leaving the flat myself in a couple of weeks, so there's no point.
   See you around, Joe.

The circular and Auntie Julie's letter remain unread.

Joe's flat is above a shop. The shopkeeper is unloading boxes of vegetables when Chrissy comes charging along. 'Hello, duck,' he says, recognizing her. Her reply gets stuck in her throat.

As usual, the door at the side of the shop is unlocked; she lets herself in, runs up the narrow staircase towards the sound of a jazz record playing softly in the living room. The living-room door is ajar; she pushes it open, stands on the threshold, observes Joe sitting with his legs splayed in the cracked leather armchair, and a woman lolling on the saggy settee with her feet up. This woman stares back at Chrissy, lifts a cigarette to her mouth between fingers with bright red nails. Her hair looks like pale straw; she's got on tight trousers patterned leopard skin, a black top with a V neck showing freckled cleavage and mules with high heels. When she leans forward to flick ash over a tin tray with 'Hewitt's Ales' written on the side, several chunky bracelets slide down her arm. Chrissy's eyes report everything in meticulous detail, in starkly outstanding colour and form.

Looking at ease, Joe says, 'Hi.'

Chrissy takes a step into the room. 'Who's she?'

'Sylvie. Sylvie – Chrissy, Chrissy – Sylvie.'

'Get her out.'

'I invited her in.'

Chrissy drops the bag she's holding, moves on Sylvie. 'Then I'll throw her out.'

'I shouldn't bother,' says Joe. 'There's plenty more where she came from.' A remark Sylvie finds hilarious; her laugh cracks up in a smoker's cough, 'Pardon *me*,' she chokes, thumping her chest.

The sea starts singing in Chrissy's head, breakers gather, roll and roar, whoosh backwards, re-gather: it's her most compelling reality; Joe and Sylvie, the room, her own body seem hardly there. In a dream she turns away, goes into the bedroom, unhooks her kimono dressing gown from the bedroom door, looks round: there's nothing else; returns to the living room, stoops to retrieve her Stan Getz records, catches sight of a paperback belonging to her; stuffs all these items into her bag, walks out of the room, down the stairs. Her body does all this; her mind's gone off somewhere for a doze.

'All right, duck?' calls the shopkeeper.

She walks by, passes the bus-stop, just keeps walking.

Liz returns weightless with happiness from four whole days spent with Nathan. When term ends they're going on holiday together. (She plans to tell her parents she's going with a group from the psychology department.) Afterwards, Nathan will go to Newcastle to take up his job with the large firm that sponsored his degree course at Imperial. Newcastle sounds almost as far away as London to Liz, but Nathan says he'll have a better car and a decent flat, so they'll have good times during her final year at university. 'Then we'll get married, don't you think?' he asked casually as they strolled hand in hand one evening along the Embankment. 'Sure – perfect timing,' she replied, calmly enough, but her heart started thumping, energy built up, in a moment she broke away to go sprinting over imaginary hurdles. He chased after her, seized and pulled her round. They whooped in the other's face, celebrating the event they hadn't yet put a name to. Now, walking up the path at the side of the Bisset house, she decides to keep their agreement anonymous; 'engagement' hits the wrong note; from their very first evening together they've assumed mutual commitment.

She fumbles for her key, inserts and turns it in the lock, opens the french window, steps in.

The room's a mess. There's a sour smell. This could emanate from any number of things – the gaping waste bin, discarded food on the table, a sink full of gungy bowls and plates. She turns round slowly, taking it in. Enervation washes over her, she can't face it, wouldn't know where to start. Grimly, she goes upstairs.

Chrissy's on the bed, fully clothed. She struggles to sit up when Liz comes in. 'Hello,' she says with weak brightness, her eyes glittery, her face pale.

Liz puts down her bag.

'Sorry about the mess. I was just going to clear up.' She flops back down. 'Nice time?'

Liz studies her. 'So what's been happening?'

There's a pause before Chrissy tells her the bald facts, that the affair's over.

Liz's pulse quickens. Frightened of making the wrong move, she stands there tongue-tied.

'Don't worry, it was inevitable; I can see that now. I wasn't up to it. Basically I'm pretty drippy, pretty feeble. I've been lying here trying to picture what might have been – probably wouldn't have amounted to much, me trailing after him, landing up in some strange town, me in some God-awful job, Joe playing nights with a band, women constantly flitting in and out of his life. He still had other women, you know, while I was with him. Sooner or later I'd've cracked. I'm too conventional, always was. You and Nell were the interesting ones, the rebels. I just played along . . .'

'Will you shut up?' cries Liz, darting on her, turning quickly away. She's never felt so impelled to slap anyone in her life, she's so livid with Chrissy she can't stand looking at her. 'Don't ever, *ever* speak like that about yourself to me again. It's lies. You're the strongest, liveliest person I know. And the best looking. If you ever get mixed up with a piece of shit like Joe Johnson again, I'll kill you. How dare you take on *his* estimation?' With which she sits down suddenly on the edge of the bed.

Chrissy gropes for her hand.

Liz still can't look at her. 'I'm famished,' she says at last. 'Had anything to eat lately?'

'No.'

'Right.' She stands up. 'I'll go and make a start on that mess downstairs, then I'll get us something.'

'I'll come and help.'

'Great,' says Liz, walking out.

Over the next few days, Liz tries to stay close to Chrissy. She doesn't trust her false brightness. Despite these efforts, perhaps because Liz can't speak as kindly as the situation demands, Chrissy evades her. One lunch time, Liz is standing in the refectory queue when a woman she knows fairly well comes up to her. This woman has seen Chrissy on the top deck of a number twenty-two bus, just sitting there with tears streaming down her face. In fact, Chrissy's face and jacket were sopping with tears; she seemed incapable of replying to a sympathetic enquiry, just shook her head, smiled even, and went on weeping. The conductor reported that she'd been riding on the bus all afternoon, going from terminus to terminus. He wanted her off, but there was nothing the woman could do, not knowing Chrissy all that well, and in any case, her own stop came up just then. What she wonders is, is Chrissy OK? – it was so weird, her crying and smiling and just sitting there . . .

'Don't worry, she got home all right,' says Liz bleakly. 'But thanks for telling me.'

Arriving at the counter, Liz takes a tray, then reaches for salad, cheese roll, glass of water. After paying, she walks between chairs and tables looking not for a space but for a sighting of Chrissy. No sign of her. She eats, talks half-heartedly to her neighbour, excuses herself, goes out. Marching round the campus, she determines that once she finds Chrissy she'll stick like her shadow. Guilt quickens her footsteps – she's been harsh, mean; she couldn't bring herself to be unconditionally sympathetic. She understands why and is to a degree self-forgiving. It's because Chrissy running herself down like that, abasing herself before the wretched Joe Johnson, made Liz feel her own worth was under attack, that in the eyes of some men she's less deserving of consideration simply by virtue of being female. She still churns with rage remembering how Chrissy casually mentioned that Joe had other women while he was with involved with her, as if it were a duty of love to put up with them. Liz knows what she'd do – tell the Joe Johnsons of this world to go shoot up their own backsides. However, better stop thinking about it; better encourage the right frame of mind to be staunch for Chrissy, because if anything happens to her . . .

Liz finds her sitting on the grass in the quadrangle, her cheeks wet and smiling, a book lying face down by her side.

Later, she writes about the problem to Nathan. His reply comes back promptly. Of course Chrissy must join them on their holiday, he agrees bravely, plenty of room in the car; make it a foursome if Chrissy will feel more comfortable.

Liz gives his Basildon Bond a smacking kiss (generosity, as she might have known, is yet another of his wonderful attributes), hastens to find Chrissy and break the good news.

'For Pete's sake help me out,' Chrissy begs in a letter to Nell. 'I know you'll be tied up with the *Evening Telegraph* this vac, but please, *please* write and convince Liz you'll keep a beady eye on me while she's away with Nathan. It's lovely of them to ask me, but I couldn't stand it. Can you imagine – two love birds trying to hide their perfect bliss for fear of discomfiting bruised third party? In any case, Liz and Nathan ought to have some time together. I promise not to be a nuisance to you. OK, I *am* bloody miserable, but I'm not, as Liz seems to fear, likely to top myself. You could manage a few jars with me, couldn't you, between assignments?'

Nell sends a sweetly sensitive reply. She's longing, she writes, to hear the full saga of Chrissy's affair. She's so sad to think of Chrissy being hurt, but knows that Chrissy, who is strong and resourceful, will rise like a phoenix and soon, with her terrific looks (of which, Nell admits, she has always been secretly jealous) will be fighting off the chaps as usual. She promises to make a point of not working flat out while Liz is away so that she and Chrissy can really chew the fat. As for Liz, as usual she has all the luck. Thoroughly deserved, of course. Good heavens, the things that happen to Liz and Chrissy, whereas nothing ever happens to drear dull Nell.

'It's great of her – specially considering she's after a big story this vac, one that'll get syndicated,' says Chrissy earnestly to Liz. 'Oh, I'm really looking forward to seeing old Nell. Couldn't possibly turn her down – think how hurt she'd be. So just go and enjoy yourself with Nathan.'

Liz gives in. She's been rather on top of Chrissy lately, so Nell will come as a tonic, no doubt. She goes off to telephone Nathan, to communicate his reward.

iii

Nell . . . Chrissy and Liz smiled to one another as their friend went heavily through the hall and up the stairs to her rest: good old off-beat, funny-sharp, nice-nasty Nell. They didn't say this, their smiles conveyed it.

'Half an hour in the garden?' Chrissy invited. 'Then I shall have to make sure there's something for the hoard to eat tonight.'

It seemed a pity to Liz that Chrissy couldn't go out for a meal without labouring to feed other people beforehand, but she didn't say so. 'Lovely,' is what she said, adding, 'I'll just go and fetch my book.'

They sat on the edge of the lawn in the dappled shade of the horse chestnut tree, Liz with an open book face down on her lap, Chrissy without any such pretence, dozing.

'Liz,' murmured Chrissy eventually, 'I know Tony was horrid last night in the pub – to Nell, I mean; well, not horrid exactly, more snide, a bit unkind. Basically, though, he's not unkind. What you have to remember is, in the past *we've* been jolly mean to him. I expect he remembers this when we're all together. He likes to pretend it was just you two, and I had nothing to do with it.' She raised her sun-glasses, looking straight at Liz to show her message was keenly felt. 'I'm just telling you, because I don't like you to think badly of him.'

'Of course I don't.'

'Oh, good,' said Chrissy, dropping her sun-glasses on to her nose, closing her eyes behind them, settling back with her lips in smile.

Chrissy being 'only fair' again, thought Liz. Her eyes drifted from her friend, over the lawn to the grey stone house. She raked her memory – how mean had she personally been to Tony? She could recall the three of them sneering as schoolgirls, but surely it was Chrissy who always rounded on him? Later on came her and Nell's horrified reaction to the news that Chrissy was seeing him, followed by some feeble attempts on their part to dissuade her. But at least she had tried to make amends. As Chrissy's matron of honour, she'd borne a very difficult family situation. Nell, on the other hand, had declined to attend the wedding, claiming an urgent assignment prevented her . . .

Chrissy's wedding – what a day. Chrissy married from the Stockdales' home in Wold Enderby church, Alderman Stockdale giving her away, Mrs Stockdale crying like a proper bride's mother. (Liz had never been able to decide whether her mother's tears were for the sadness of having a member of the awkward squad for a daughter instead of lovely accommodating Chrissy, or because the very suitable Tony Duckenfield was marrying Chrissy and not their Elizabeth.) All things considered, it was nice of her parents to make such a great day for Chrissy, especially after the way Liz and Nathan had got married – early one morning in a Newcastle registry office, strangers inveigled in off the street to act as witnesses. She and Nathan had had a wedding to suit themselves and not their parents. Looked at another way, perhaps Chrissy's wedding to Tony came as a sort of consolation prize, for apart from her mother's sniffles, her abiding impression of the day was of rejoicing and pride. Tony, of course, was bursting with pride; and Chrissy gorgeous in oceans of frothy ivory lace. She herself had done her bit, looking fresh and dainty in a diminished version of the bride's dress, also in ivory but relieved by embroidered sprigs of tiny blue flowers. And her father so handsome with Chrissy on his arm, Liz suddenly recalled, her throat swelling. What a pity Nell hadn't come; it would have made the day more complete if she had. At least poor Auntie Julie made it (only just: a few months later she was dead from a stroke); her commentary had punctuated the proceedings, and Nathan's soothing agreement with everything she said had murmured round the church like echoes. (Dear Nathan, of course, had been assigned to look after her.) And at the reception afterwards, like the sun beaming, Chrissy's presiding smile. Lovely day.

'Right,' said Chrissy, sitting up. 'Better go in and see to things. What time has Nell booked for tonight, do you know?'

'She didn't say. Help, I've just thought: what the dickens am I going to wear? I've only brought shorts and jeans, and T-shirts and jumpers.'

Chrissy frowned. 'We'll find you something. I've got a nice silk shirt you could borrow. Possibly I could find you a skirt to fit . . .'

'Oh, not a skirt,' groaned Liz.

'My trousers would be far too long. You could wear a pair of Amanda's sawn-off clingy jobs, though – might look good under a long silk shirt.'

'Perfect,' said Liz comfortably, and took up her book.

iv

Auntie Julie's lips slacken; her cigarette droops but is held in place by the welding that has occurred between paper and skin, its smoke curls upwards to continue the work of thousands of predecessors – staining her white hair nicotine orange. 'Chrissy,' she yells, having taken the measure of the caller on the doorstep, 'someone to see you.'

A thud sounds overhead as Chrissy jerks out of her

367

dismal reverie and the book she hasn't been reading slides off the bed on to the floor.

'A fella,' adds Auntie Julie, as if coming to this conclusion.

Chrissy opens her bedroom door. 'Who is it?'

'Don't know. Never set eyes on him.'

'Tony Duckenfield,' supplies the caller helpfully.

Auntie Julie looks dubious. 'Tony? You don't look much like a Tony to me. More of a Cecil. Reckons he's called Tony, though to my eyes he's got the look of a Cecil,' she yells, turning from doorstep to staircase – 'or Hubert,' she adds, more to herself, turning back for another squint.

'I don't know any Cecil,' says Chrissy, coming wearily downstairs. 'Oh – Tony. Honestly, Auntie.' She smiles. 'Sorry.'

It's the nicest she's ever been to him. Emboldened, he steps in. 'Hello, Chrissy. I heard you were home. I wondered if you'd care for a drive out?'

'You've got a car?' She can barely conceive of him unattached to a bicycle.

'It's my mother's. I have the use of it.'

He sounds different, more confident, less deferential. Also, he's grown – not quite to her height, but taller than he was and he's filled out.

'Where to?' demands Auntie Julie.

'Wherever Chrissy fancies. Along the coast, over the wolds, perhaps have tea somewhere.'

Having recovered from her surprise, Chrissy finds the idea attractive. Liz is still on holiday with Nathan, she's seen Nell once or twice, most of the time she's been studying hard and striving to banish thoughts of Joe Johnson: this long vacation has begun to drag. 'It's very nice of you. Is there a bit of a breeze out there? – I'll just get a coat.' She runs back upstairs.

Tony and Auntie Julie are left observing one another.

'You must have money to burn.'

'I beg your pardon?'

368

'I say you must have money to burn, lad – "ride out", "tea". She'll cost you.'

'No, no, I'm sure. I mean, a very simple . . .'

'Sandwiches, scones, cake – she's got the appetite of a horse. I've known her of an evening demolish a whole packet of Sunblest. Me and her dad hardly get a look in. Aye, she'll cost.'

'I have adequate funds, thank you.'

'You think you have, lad, but you don't know the half of it. I often says to her dad, you and me could starve, I say, before that girl'd stint herself. Oh, so that's what you're wearing.' Auntie Julie, unabashed by her niece's arrival, is concerned only to disassociate herself from the collarless round-necked white cotton coat that Chrissy is wearing.

'Charming,' says Tony heartily.

'Thanks,' says Chrissy, grinning at her aunt. 'Looks like a tent?' she suggests, gently prompting her memory.

'Aye, it does,' says Auntie Julie, glad to be reminded of her first pronouncement on the garment. 'And with your legs, it looks like a tent on sticks,' she embellishes, chortling as Chrissy shuts the front door on her.

'Thank you, Auntie,' says Chrissy lightly to Tony, going down the path. And Tony, who can remember lurid primary school gossip about this aunt, whispers behind Chrissy's back, taunts to her face and Chrissy standing hang-dog taking it (for it was only with Liz's and Nell's friendship that she developed her later confidence), chances a knowing smile in response. Which is received with equanimity, for nowadays her aunt's oddity inspires in Chrissy the sort of affectionate pride some people feel for a cussed old dog or an unpredictable ancient car.

Tony's vehicle is up to the minute. 'A Mini,' she breathes stopping in her tracks.

'Nice aren't they? Ever ridden in one?' He goes ahead to open the passenger door.

'No.' Frankly delighted, she jumps in.

He gathers her skirt up to make sure none gets caught in the door. 'Where would you like to go?' he asks, getting in behind the wheel.

'Anywhere. Though tea in the country might be nice.'

The little car darts up Lister Avenue towards the traffic lights, nipping in and out of more staid traffic. Chrissy squeaks with pleasure. 'Gosh, this is *fun*.'

Liz and Nathan have returned from their holiday, Nathan has spent a weekend at Wold Enderby meeting Liz's parents, now Liz is visiting the Learmans in Leeds.

Chrissy gets a phone call from Mrs Stockdale.

'Oh, Chrissy, love, how are you? – lovely to hear your voice. I'm not well at all, dear, nothing physical, it's all the upset. I suppose you've met Elizabeth's young man? Yes, I dare say he is, dear, very nice, but he's not quite the sort of young man me and Elizabeth's daddy could ever *take to*, if you know what I mean. I've nothing against him personally. Not as such. You know, Chrissy, I can't think what's got into our Elizabeth. She used to be such a good little thing, so pretty and clever, a proper credit to us. Then almost overnight she turns somersault, gives up her piano, refuses to do music at university, takes up this funny subject . . . What dear? I'm sure it is, very interesting. Trouble is, it doesn't sound quite nice. I'll give you a little example, shall I? Mrs Garth, when I told her what Elizabeth was studying, said "Oo, that's all about sex." Now I know Mrs Garth is a bit of a feather brain, but you take my point? It's the *impression* it gives. And I'm sure Mrs Garth isn't the only one, not by a long shot. Of course, dear, I'm sure it's a most respectable subject, but it's not like music, you grant me that? With music and – what is it you're taking? – yes, history; with those sort of subjects you know what you're getting. You can't blame us for being disappointed. And now she brings this, well, this *Nathan* home. Honestly, Chrissy,

I sometimes think she does it on purpose. Her daddy hasn't been himself for a long while, and I can't see this boyfriend improving matters. Oh, I wish you'd come out and see me, Chrissy. I know it's difficult with the buses, perhaps, if Alderman Stockdale . . . What, dear? Would he really? How kind, you are a dark horse. Of course, dear, and he sounds a very nice friend. You must both stay for tea. And you and I can have a nice long chat . . .'

It's a relief after her dismal thoughts (which still take hold now and then), to know that Tony will be calling for her this afternoon. (He always calls on Wednesday and Saturday afternoons; these are the days he has the use of his mother's car.) It's a relief to know that for the next five or six hours, dismal thoughts won't get a finger to her; Tony and the Mini just aren't conducive, in fact Joe Johnson hardly seems credible in such brisk, trim company. There is also solid satisfaction (similar to the effect of a good meal) in the knowledge that wherever she chooses to go, Tony will be only too delighted to take her.

In the event, he is not only delighted, but excited, overwhelmed. His spectacles mist over; 'I didn't realize you were a friend of the family,' he says, whipping them off to polish with a handkerchief. 'I knew you were friendly with Liz, of course. Alderman Stockdale is a very influential man in these parts.'

'It's Mrs Stockdale I'm going to see.'

'Yes, yes. Will he be there at tea, do you suppose?'

'I expect so. He usually is on a Saturday. But will you give Mrs Stockdale and me an hour together first? I think she wants a private chat.'

'Of course, delighted to. I'll go and look in the church.' (Tony is keen on local history.)

He drops her discreetly at the gate, drives on to the church. Chrissy walks up the drive.

Mrs Stockdale hears her step, comes running. 'Oh, has he gone? But he'll be back for tea? I've made a chocolate Swiss roll, you were always partial to my chocolate Swiss roll. Will your friend like a nice ham salad, do you think? Men usually do, they go more for savouries. You are looking nice. What a pretty frock. I despair of our Elizabeth. If she's not in those horrid tight trousers, she's in baggy shorts. Come in dear, I'll put the kettle on.'

At tea, Tony makes a big impression, calls Alderman Stockdale 'sir', is gallant to Mrs Stockdale; shows keen interest in and reverence for local commerce, for town development is the coming thing and is the area of work he hopes to become involved with. He does not make the mistake of pretending undue modesty. 'That's right,' notes Alderman Stockdale, 'never sell yourself short, Tony, lad. I'll introduce you to the firm I use if you like – could prove useful for when you've finished your studies. People in my line of work can always use a bright lawyer.'

Mrs Stockdale is overjoyed by this visible improvement in her husband's mood. 'We haven't had such a nice tea time for, oh, I don't know how long,' she confides to Chrissy afterwards. 'I tell you, dear, sometimes he can't bear to come to the table, takes his tea on a tray in the study. Now you bring Tony again, he's such a nice boy. You will, promise?'

'Yes, all right,' says Chrissy, kindly. It gives her real pleasure these days to make others happy. It's as if, having had her own desires painfully thwarted, it's a relief, a victory of sorts, to clear the way so far as she can for the progress of other people's.

Nell and Liz learn from separate (though related) sources about Chrissy seeing Tony Duckenfield. Nell hears it from her lover, Bertie. Liz hears it from her mother (who is Bertie's wife). Nell and Bertie have quite a row about it. 'That little squirt? Bright? – you must be barking. He's utterly hideous, smarmy, revolting.' When Bertie gets hot under the collar in defence of the ghastly

Duckenfield, she drops her eyelids, pretends to stand corrected, for she depends, she recalls, rather heavily on Bertie's generosity and his ability to pull strings. Besides, there are more ways than one of killing a cat.

Liz is hardly less incredulous. 'Came to tea, with that creep, here? God, she really has flipped. I thought she was better. How could she? Oh, Mummy, I'm sorry, I didn't mean to upset you. Please don't start crying. It's just that I don't get it, she always loathed him. Well, if Daddy likes him, what can I say? He must have turned into a flipping marvel.' Faithfully promising her mother never to say nasty things about Tony again, and certainly never to Chrissy, she gets on the phone to Nell in the *Evening Telegraph* office.

When Nell has pretended to be shocked and surprised, when they've finished bad-mouthing Tony, they agree that his influence may be disastrous for Chrissy, who is very vulnerable at the moment and whose ego has obviously been more seriously damaged by her broken love affair than they appreciated. They decide to tackle her, delicately but firmly; kindly as close friends should.

'I've been meaning to tell you,' Nell interrupts casually when Liz suggests calling for her tomorrow evening so that they can call on Chrissy together, 'I'm not living at home any more; I've got a flat.'

'A flat?' Liz can't believe it: this is an impoverished student talking.

'I had to get away from Dad. It's a long story, tell you about it tomorrow. Will you take down the address?'

'Sure.' Dazed, Liz fumbles for pad and pencil.

'8A, Abbey Court, Abbey Drive. It's on the number six bus route. Get off at the park, turn left.'

'Hey, posh. Have you come into money or something?'

'I am earning, unlike you two.' (Liz and Chrissy haven't taken jobs this summer because they have dissertations to write as part of their degree finals.) 'Doing quite well, actually; I'm on to a big story at last – which is why I had to flee Maud Street. It's about a scam on the docks. Tell you about it tomorrow. Look, let's all meet here, about eight. Will you phone Chrissy?'

'Yes, all right. See you tomorrow.'

Liz sits staring across the hall which is full of afternoon brightness, sun streaming through the high window over the staircase, rays streaking and misting the farther recesses – a case of light casting a veil rather than making things clear. Like Nell's explanation of how she can afford to live in the most expensive area of town – on a temporary cub reporter's wage? Then she gets it: of course, it's a short let, for in four weeks' time the universities go up; someone at work is probably away for a short time and pleased to let the flat for peanuts. Satisfied with this conclusion, Liz dials Chrissy's number. Auntie Julie answers, says Chrissy has gone out with that Cecil but will be back later on. Frowning, Liz says she'll phone again this evening.

Now she's peering once more into the dim and mysterious end of the hall. Cecil? No-one tells her anything any more. Still, looking on the bright side, at least Chrissy's not confining herself to the awful Tony Duckenfield.

It's a great evening. It shouldn't be – with Nell on tenterhooks lest, despite Bertie's assurances to the contrary, Liz could be aware that this block of flats is a Stockdale property; with Liz full of guilt for neglecting Chrissy while selfishly consumed with passion for Nathan; with Chrissy sensing they've guessed she's seeing Tony and feeling defensive like she used to as a hockey-playing fifth-former subject to severe censure from the other two for her liking of games – it shouldn't be at all a great evening; nevertheless, this is how it turns out.

The Tony business is got out of the way briskly. Chrissy admits to seeing him. He's teaching her to drive his mother's Mini, she explains, talking animatedly of clutch control, of three-point turns. They hear her out in silence, decide the relationship is merely an innocent diversion from the rigours of study. Tony is working flat out, too, she reports. He's been tipped for a first. 'Really? Fancy,' they murmur, unable to work up enthusiasm for any aspect of Tony Quacker Duckenfield, who persists in their minds as the thick-skinned twerp with equally thick spectacles, who would trail after them uninvited, ignoring requests to depart. Their minds jib obstinately at the picture painted by Chrissy – Tony in nippy white Mini; their stern expressions reflect internal images – Tony of the wet red lips and plastered-down hair waiting doggedly outside school in his bicycle clips. However, it's a relief to see Chrissy's heart is clearly safe and sound and in the right place: it's the Mini she's smitten with.

They move on to the subject of Nathan, smile and look dreamy as Liz expounds. Wonderful, they exclaim, an absolute dreamboat, the perfect man. 'He'd have to be,' confirms Liz. 'After that business with you-know-who, I vowed to steer clear of further involvements; if he hadn't been perfect I'd never have succumbed. Mind you, I knew he was the moment he came up and spoke to me.'

'Trust Liz to spot class,' sighs Nell. She gets up, opens a bottle of wine, pours it into their rinsed-out coffee mugs. 'Here's to my brilliant story,' she offers. 'May it be syndicated.'

They drink eagerly, watching her; they're all ears.

Nell's story is of institutionalized thieving by dockers, a process with rules, with overlords, with an organization of its own. It's been going on for years; there are no big blatant thefts, just a small steady prudent trickle. Nell has long had an inkling about it without being overly impressed by her knowledge. (In his cups, her father is a loud-mouth; sober, he has always enjoyed boasting to his most clever and admired child.) Nell glosses over her original source (though this does not prevent Liz from getting anxious about Mr Nelson's rage and sense of betrayal when the story is printed and the consequent suffering of poor Mrs Nelson), and she glosses over her means of obtaining a dock pass (once again, Bertie was instrumental); instead, she concentrates on her cunning in gaining confidences, her persistence in asking questions; she whets their appetites with one or two quotes from her snappy prose. They're agog. Lazy-looking Nell, they think, always knew those dreamy eyes hid a razor-sharp mind. Their reactions are so pleasing, Nell privately presages that this, now, is the best moment: the story will be printed (when she is safely in London), it will be bought and syndicated by bigger newspapers and this will earn her in due course a junior job on a national paper; none of which will recover the sheer pleasure of regaling Liz and Chrissy.

They get up to go. Saying goodbye results in a mildly tipsy threeway hug. They feel empowered, exhilarated – the old triangular magic at work again.

Two years on, Liz is married to Nathan and combining clinical work with a master's degree at Newcastle, Nell has secured her coveted job on a London newspaper, Chrissy has completed her Dip Ed course and is waiting to take up her first teaching post at their old school.

Not a prospect Chrissy relishes. However, her father died last winter, Auntie Julie's oddities have become more pronounced; Chrissy remembers how Auntie Julie came to the rescue when her mother deserted and feels she has no other course than to return to live at home. She has a tender feeling of responsibility for Auntie Julie, a need to protect her.

She's had other lovers since Joe Johnson, but quickly, casually, to ward off insidious spinsterhood. Liz and Nell would ridicule and laugh at her if she admitted to this; nevertheless, there are times when, catching

376

herself frowning in the mirror, she detects definite touches of Auntie Julie.

Tony's still around, of course, but not as a lover. After a splendid degree he came home as planned and joined the firm of solicitors recommended by Alderman Stockdale. Tony is a good and reliable friend. His mother's nice, too. Having at first viewed Chrissy coldly as the girl who plays fast and loose with her darling's affections, she is now relaxed towards her. Mrs Duckenfield is a resilient widow. Left comfortably off in her young middle age, she works as a general practitioner's secretary, devotes her spare time to amateur theatricals.

Tony is very good with Auntie Julie. He gamely responds to the sobriquet 'Cecil', bears kindly with long expositions on the merits and drawbacks of various herbal preparations, takes her out in his car for long stares at the sea front, never getting huffy afterwards because she's stunk it out with cigarette smoke.

Tony, although Chrissy refuses to think about it, is a considerable part of her life.

She's at the tea table at Wold Enderby when it occurs to her: right now, in this place, with these people, she is purely, simply happy. This lovely house, the dear Stockdales, Tony at her side treated like a favourite son by the alderman, fussy Mrs Stockdale indulging her with all that unused-up motherliness, the grandfather clock beating steadily in the hall, flower scent and bird song wafting through the open windows, the cosy timeless family feeling – it's happiness. You can keep your thrills, your sexy passion: this is *me*, she thinks.

'Try one of these cheesy scones,' wheedles Mrs Stockdale. 'Mrs Garth gave me the recipe. I'd value your opinion.'

'Thank you, I will.' She cuts it in two, butters it, takes a thoughtful bite.

'Too salty? Go on, Chrissy love, you can say.'

'You might be right,' says Chrissy, reaching for the homemade blackberry jam. 'But I've a feeling it might just need . . .,' she spreads a dollop of black preserve, takes a second bite, 'mm, yes, I think that does it. See what you think.' She finishes the confection, licks her fingers.

'You're right,' cries Mrs Stockdale in pleased wonderment. 'Daddy, Chrissy's worked out what's wrong with these scones of Ada's. They're crying out for a bit of jam.'

'Blackberry jam,' says Chrissy solemnly. 'I don't think strawberry would fit the bill.'

'Try one, Tony.'

'Thank you. I don't mind if I do.'

'Daddy?'

'Oh, go on, then. So, Tony lad; you and me'll pop off after tea and take a look at those new houses.'

'Would you like to come?' asks Tony, turning to Chrissy. 'And Mrs Stockdale? The feminine point of view would be very valuable. House builders neglect it at their peril, in my opinion.'

'You may be right there,' concedes Alderman Stockdale, to whom this potential selling angle has not until now occurred.

Mrs Stockdale looks pleased. Her pleasure being a thing Chrissy is keen to promote, she quickly accepts on their joint behalf. 'That'd be nice, Tony.'

After tea, they set off in Alderman Stockdale's brand new Rover.

Mrs Stockdale and Chrissy find a great deal to say, mostly concerning kitchen and bathroom.

'Mind you,' says Chrissy, gazing out of the master-bedroom window at the pleasing aspect over Rusthorpe Meadows, 'I wouldn't turn my nose up at it any old how. Must be a dream living in a place like this, bright and airy, these lovely big windows, polished wood flooring, everything fitting nicely, loads and loads of

lovely space . . .' She's talking to herself really. But it's
Tony who overhears, Mrs Stockdale having detained
her husband in the bathroom on the subject of mixer
taps.

'A good family house,' agrees Tony. 'Plenty of room
for the kids.' This is true; there are five bedrooms, a
good size garden.

But Chrissy is struck by the comment. 'A good family
house,' she repeats slowly, weighing the words. 'I think
that's what I'd like most of all from life – a good
family.'

At long last Tony thinks he spies the winning post.
'Exactly what I'd like, too. Several kids; three,' he
hazards, watching her closely, trying to hit on the
number, 'four.'

Chrissy is now staring at him fixedly. 'At least four.'
'At least.'
'I didn't know you were keen on large families.'
'Definitely,' declares Tony.

There's a pause, footsteps sound; Tony's tongue darts
over his lips. 'I say, Chrissy. Will you marry me?'

In the doorway, Alderman and Mrs Stockdale hold
their breath . . .

'Yes, all right.' (But her eyes are stern: 'It's a bargain,'
they warn.) . . . then rush forward, clasp, kiss, wring
hands, quite beside themselves with joy.

V

Time to set off for their evening jaunt. In the hall,
they fell to arguing over which car they'd go in, who
would drive. Then Nell said she'd ring for a taxi; that
way no-one would be disadvantaged. Tony, who was
listening to this from the study, rose from his chair
and came to join them. 'Might I make a suggestion?
Let me drive you there, get a taxi back. I would offer
to fetch you as well, but I must get to bed early. Got to
be on the golf course by seven.'

379

'Done,' said Nell after a moment's thought during which she turned on him one of her half-veiled stares. 'Thanks, you're a sport.'

'That's very kind of you, Tony,' his wife declared; and Liz smiled murmured agreement, feeling like a rude child putting on an act of grown-up politeness, which was the effect being nice to Tony often had on her due to the artifice involved.

'He loves to be helpful,' Chrissy remarked happily, slipping her arm through Nell's, hoping this aspect of Tony would predominate rather than last night's nasty one.

Nell blinked and smiled. In another moment, the car was heard reversing up the gravel drive to the front door. Nell got into the front beside Tony – after all, it was her treat, she was in charge – Chrissy and Liz sat in the back.

They began reminding one another of their school-girl impressions of Court's Hotel: strolling past of a summer's evening, gazing in from their place among the fish-and-chip brigade on the sea front promenade at the elegant diners, the tables with stiff white linen, glistening glasses, flowers in silver vases, candelabra. Nell professed herself nervous still at the idea of actually going inside; expensive dinners in famous restaurants and hotels of international renown had failed to dispel her childish awe. That's because childhood impressions are so intensely felt, Liz said, however high you rise, feelings of inadequacy merely lie dormant and are easily triggered by associations. Which might explain the phenomenon often observed in restaurants of some people, usually men, behaving boorishly or super-critically.

Listening to Liz and Nell, the two foreigners, Tony said he hoped they realized Court's was one of the few high-class family hotels still operating as such in England. The Court family had owned and run it for three generations. Which explained an independent outlook and certain idiosyncrasies some visitors found amusing. For example, one firm Tony was professionally associated with (Midlands based) liked to send its executives to Court's for bracing 'think-tank' sessions. On one of these occasions, it came to the hotel management's notice that the bed belonging to one of the party (female) had not been slept in while the room of another (male) bore signs of double, mixed sex, occupancy. Whereupon the parties concerned were asked to leave and a stiff letter dispatched to the firm's directors.

'My goodness,' said Nell. 'You mean to say adultery doesn't occur in this part of the world?'

'It may well occur,' said Tony, completing a nifty overtaking manoeuvre, 'but under conditions of strict discretion. Perhaps Court's was exercised by the affront to its chambermaids. It's a point of view. This is not London, or Birmingham – nor even Newcastle,' he added, acknowledging Liz via the driving mirror.

Liz thought she'd remind him of her local ante-cedents. 'I remember being taken to Court's once or twice by Mummy and Daddy. Of course, they went there a great deal, every wedding anniversary, I should imagine. Daddy used to say that the moment the bar-man spotted Mummy entering the lounge, his hand reached automatically for the Harvey's Bristol Cream.'

'And I never went there at all, coming from Maud Street,' said Nell, thinking to herself that Court's was clearly the place where wealthy adulterers treat their wives.

'Oh, it's not as stuffy as Tony makes out,' said Chrissy, to whom a ladies' luncheon at the hotel was a monthly event. 'And in any case, the cooking's tremendous. I think I'll have one of their outsize Dover soles – if that's OK, Nell,' she added hurriedly.

'Anything, flower,' promised Nell, shaking her clutchbag at them like a tambourine. 'Loadsamoney.'

When Tony swung the car into the covered parking

area at the rear of the hotel, the uniformed man on the door stiffened to attention. 'Good evening, sir,' he called as Tony jumped out.

'Evening, Charles. Not stopping, I'm afraid. It's ladies' *only* night, tonight.' (As opposed to 'Ladies' Night', when you chaps run the show and wives know their place, thought Liz and Nell, smugly decoding.)

'I see, sir,' said Charles, bearing his disappointment well. He jerked and held open the door for the female diners to pass through, but maintained his gaze on Tony getting into his car and belting up, and as soon as decency permitted let the door swing shut on them to free his hand for a smart salute to the departing BMW.

Nell turned, peered at him through the glass door, rapped on it.

'Yes, madam?'

'Our coats,' she snarled. 'Where d'we put 'em?'

He came indoors, led the way.

'Thank you, Charles,' said Nell sweetly, sweeping past him into the cloakroom.

The lounge brought a different atmosphere; whether this was due to everyone recognizing Mrs Duckenfield was impossible to say, but no staff could have been more discreetly obliging. Nell, though, was still edgy. 'Bet you anything we don't get the window table I stipulated. I shall play merry hell if we don't,' she warned, 'it's what we're here for, dammit. Sod their good cooking, sod their Dover soles . . .'

'Oh Nell, just relax,' begged Chrissy, and Liz advised her to swallow her whisky and have another one, quick.

Nell did this, but lit a cigarette as well. When they groaned, she took two deep drags then stubbed it out. – 'Sorry.'

In the event they were shown to the best-placed window table in the dining room. 'See?' murmured Chrissy to Nell, smiling to the waiter as she slid into the chair he was holding for her. Liz and Nell turned at once to stare out of the window. Passing holiday-makers stared frankly back. Liz soon turned her head away; Nell stared on. Eventually, the novelty wore off. Wine flowed, food arrived and was well disposed of.

Laying down knife and fork at the conclusion of her second course, Liz became insightful. 'You know, the miracle isn't that here we sit, three erstwhile peasants who once gazed in in wonderment; it's that here we sit, the three of us together, *still* the three of us together after all these years – and with pretty disparate lives at that.'

This clever observation called for a second bottle of wine. 'Here's to us,' proposed Chrissy, when it arrived.

'And to us as we were,' added Liz dramatically, with a nod towards the window.

As they drank, their eyes which had gone to the promenade outside were blind to the strolling passers-by, to the bronze statue of the lad holding up a leaking boot, to the illuminated peacock and seal whose flashing bulbs made them appear to move so that the seal repeatedly caught a ball on its nose while the peacock raised and spread its tail feathers; they seemed instead to see their schoolgirl selves sauntering abreast in habitually disordered fashion, jostling together then swinging apart and occupying more than their fair share of the crowded pavement, heading home perhaps after a stint at the Sea Gull Café, maybe just beating the bounds, establishing themselves as persons who belonged and were not to be taken lightly. Liz could remember the wild taste (iodine and salt as the North Sea wind filled mouths and nostrils) of being abroad with her two friends, under their own governance.

Nell was the first to return to the present. 'Would you say,' she asked, peering into her wine glass, 'that we're perfectly safe now, friendship-wise? I mean, that as we've come this far, nothing could drive a wedge between us?'

They turned to her – what did she mean? What was she talking about?

'For instance, if it was discovered that one of us had done something utterly beyond the pale?'

'Like murdered someone?' asked Chrissy.

'But Nell already has. She's been murdering people on and off in her column for years,' Liz observed.

'Very droll.'

'Good lord, Nell, we've survived all the major gear changes – moving miles away from one another, careers, dramas, marriages, kids and so forth; surely now we've reached the coasting stage,' said Chrissy, greeting her *crème brûlée* with keen approval. Nell took up a silver spoon and with it scraped curling slivers from a glistening mound of lemon sorbet.

Liz chose some cheese to nibble with her wine. 'Choices made by little girls,' she mused, 'such a mystery. Who'd have thought, seeing us squatting together on the netball-court steps, that what we were about would have consequences for the rest of our lives? Adults make friends with people who share the same interests and concerns, usually from similar backgrounds. Kids don't care about such things, they go more on instinct. Which is why, I suppose, childhood friendships often fade – at least in the modern world, with people usually moving away from where they grew up. So why did ours last?'

'You tell us,' said Nell.

Liz sipped her wine. 'Well, for one thing we never got jealous. Remember when Nell first came on the scene, Chrissy? Neither of us felt threatened, did we?'

Chrissy shook her head, went on eating.

'And our different home backgrounds didn't bother us. They were intriguing, but no difficulty. I suppose we've just gone on being accepting. Well, we have, haven't we? – with one or two minor hiccups. I mean, I admit I've not always agreed with everything Nell's written, even got quite hot under the collar sometimes,

384

but it's been pure delight seeing her become so successful, vindicating what we always knew about her. And we think it's just marvellous, don't we, Nell, that Chrissy owns the most desirable house in the whole world?'

'Absolutely. And Chrissy and I have always been stunned with admiration for what you do, Liz, and adored lovely Nathan. What a memory you have. But of course, you're right – no jealousy,' Nell beamed.

'I do feel,' said Liz, pausing to take more wine, 'I'm seeing things particularly clearly tonight.' She drained her glass. 'Probably because I've stopped worrying about Rosie. And because I'm feeling less guilty about Mrs Poole after you set me thinking last night. I feel light as air, clean as crystal.'

Chrissy, who had finished her pudding, and now found herself free to offer her opinion, said, 'It was because we were like a family.' They looked at her. 'The reason we lasted,' she reminded them, reaching for her glass. 'We preferred each other to our relations.' She drank deeply, carefully. 'We've always identified with one another,' she added, putting down her glass.

'That's it.'

'Got it in one,' cried Nell, raising her glass which unfortunately proved empty. At which point a hovering waiter stepped forward to recommend fresh coffee in the lounge.

'What do you think?'

'Perhaps we'd better.'

'Might as well.'

Disengaging somewhat clumsily from their dining chairs, hanging on to one another (because legs had gone to sleep, the carpet was a bit catchy for Chrissy's heels, Liz felt the top of her head had slipped, and Nell was more than usually short-sighted), they progressed to the end of the dining room, through the hall, into the lounge where they sank into easy chairs.

'Terrific meal, Nell.'

'Yes, Nell, thanks. Bright idea, bringing us here.'

'Pleasure,' said Nell, hauling herself forward to lift the coffee pot.

vi

Nell has always imagined she's going to enjoy telling old Bertie where to stick it. It's added enormously to her enjoyment knowing that one day she's going to disappoint him, no doubt because the nub of her pleasure has always been the power she exercises. An essentially cerebral woman, Nell has taken other lovers on purpose to try and isolate Bertie's magic ingredient. Why are other men, younger, better looking and better equipped, more practiced and expert in the art of pleasing, utter wash-outs? Technically satisfying in the physical sense, but quite unable to provide the thrills she gets with Bertie? What has Alderman Stockdale got that other men haven't? Well, Mrs Stockdale, for a start; also daughter Liz. And enormous power and social standing in a rather isolated corner of North-East England (but a corner, nevertheless, of considerable emotional significance to Nell). Someone becoming acquainted with the facts of the case (and not knowing Nell) might suppose she would play down these facts in her mind, pretend to herself that Mrs Stockdale and Liz and aldermanic prestige have nothing whatever to do with it. On the contrary, it is Nell's delight to be fiercely objective, to explore every crevice of possibility, to ponder long on these qualities which are unique to Alderman Stockdale and the way they perhaps nudge her psyche.

Another factor in her thrill quota may be his being so prone to helpless desperation for her. This powerful man, this pillar of a rather staid community, this man who plays his cards close to his chest and values beyond rubies his reputation, can, at a given signal (such as Nell leaning forward and affording a glimpse

386

of her ample underwired bosom, or sitting so as to reveal sheer black stocking tops constrained by suspenders) be turned to quivering grovelling jelly. Oh yes, she's got his number – unlike personable personal secretary, Carol, stashed away in a neat little Stockdale property these past fifteen years and so wholesome you could eat off her. Bertie has simply made use of Carol in order to reserve Mrs Stockdale for purposes other than sexual. Nell (in spite of her virgin state when she came to him) opened up a whole new world, bred lusts he'd never dreamed of (but then Nell, as she is fond of remarking whenever she can worm it into a conversation was born *femme sérieuse*).

Initially, of course, her thoroughness was inspired by Bertie's indispensability. But since she landed her job on a national paper, an added thrill has been anticipating Bertie's reaction when naughty nights in London are arbitrarily withdrawn, when she acquaints him of her decision, for his own good he must understand, that he may be a big operator but only within the orbit of a rather small town.

Now, suddenly, she's not so sure. Try as she might, it's been impossible to find an adequate substitute. The question arises: does she really want to? How about – at this point Nell falls into one of her trances, forgets about her cigarette until it burns her fingers, doesn't hear the phone – how about depriving Mrs Stockdale and that staid old northeastern backwater of Bertie *altogether*? Claiming him all for herself? When the cigarette nips her fingers and the phone jolts by ceasing to ring, she asks, has she been pursuing this outcome all along, and imagining scenes of sending him packing merely as titillation? The more she thinks it over, the more certain she becomes: having Bertie to herself is essential for her happiness and wellbeing.

(Hey – wicked little joke: whatever will Liz make of it? She can see it now, her letter of explanation, signed 'your loving step-mummy'.)

*   *   *

Nell discovers the limits of her power the moment she raises the subject. Bertie has no intention of turning Mrs Stockdale out of The Mount, for the very good reason that Mrs Stockdale forms an indispensable part of its furnishing; he has no intention of living elsewhere; nor to discontinue Tuesday evenings at Carol's – though he refers to Carol and Tuesday evenings euphemistically as 'people who depend on me' and 'can't turn my back on them'. But Nell knows what he means. Too bloody comfortable, she rails at him. Be dead to all intents and purposes before he's sixty. He thinks he'd be dead within the twelvemonth were he daft enough to live with her full time – a chain smoking, hard drinking, sexually insatiable London newspaper woman. (On journeys back home to the North East – tired, jaded, memories rising like curdled evidence of over indulgence the night before to hang in his brain provoking shame similar to that of being caught by the steely light of morning in ridiculous party garb – on these weary journeys home he usually brands her as sexually insatiable. When he recovers his verve and the time draws near for another visit, he recalls the epithet pleasurably, as a recómmendation.) But Nell as a daily diet? Folk would conclude he'd lost his marbles. They'd be right.

Ordinarily, about any other matter, having received and understood the message, Nell would accept it and make other arrangements – witness her settling for the job of reporting gossipy matters (woman's province) rather than pursuing her hard-line investigative stuff (man's). The mature Nell dislikes the effect of banging her head against brick walls, prefers a steady view of the winning post. However, in this matter of Bertie, older emotions reassert their hold, emotions derived from her sense of inferiority as a girl, un-reasonable, unappeasable; the sort of emotions that prompted her refusal to oblige her headmistress and

388

remove an offending word from a piece for the school magazine, that allowed her to feel totally worthless and her life ruined when wretched Mogsy chucked her. She won't accept his verdict. Getting Bertie all to herself is suddenly seen as her life's goal. She cajoles, schemes, promises anything; makes herself softer, more of a helpless female hopelessly in love – whose only effect is to dampen Bertie's ardour. Where's the vamp? he wants to cry out with all the hurt passion of a chap shelling out brass. But he doesn't. Just turns morose on her, makes the mistake of discussing the pros and cons (with every intention of rubbishing the pros and promoting the cons) since if they're not making love they've got to do something to pass the time.

Chrissy's already had her first baby (nine months and a day after her wedding night); now Liz gives birth. Both babies are boys.

Doesn't Bertie regret not having a son? she asks one evening, smoothing his shirt front, peering up at him.

Bertie is non-committal.

Surely he must have wanted a son to carry on the business and the famous Stockdale name?

Bertie admits it might have been nice, but there was such a ballyhoo over Elizabeth getting born he jibbed at putting Mrs Stockdale to the same trouble again.

Nell smiles to herself. She thinks she now knows how to play a trump card.

Bertie arranging to meet her in a hotel foyer (not one of their haunts) to tell her in no uncertain terms that if she wants to go on seeing him she'd better get rid of it forthwith, mentioning his solicitor and grave doubts as to paternity, slapping money down on the table, is like waking from a silly sentimental dream. She sits and blinks, first at him, then at the envelope full of money. She doesn't say anything, so he repeats himself, even more forcefully.

Did she really, she is asking herself, propose to throw

her life away, waste her talent, her brilliant chances, on this seedy old bloke with the spent stomach muscles? (OK, tall rich old bloke with a blurred resemblance to the film star Jack Hawkins – well past his prime, nevertheless.) Has she actually saddled her body with his bastard child? Which – oh my God, oh my God, gibbers the idiot voice in her brain – has to come out one way or another, now or full term. Talk about madness. Hasn't she always dreaded pain, gone out of her way to avoid it? What's happened to her, for pity's sake? She had more sense as a fifteen year old passionately refusing to engage in hockey practice on the grounds that someone might hurt her, in which case she would sue the school. Now, messy humiliation and certain agony stare her in the face. God, but she loathes him. Too right he can pay. She snatches up the envelope, snaps her bag over it like predatory teeth. Gets up, starts walking.

'Nell,' he calls, half out of concern for her, half wishing to get everything cut and dried.

Her heart leaping makes her hesitate.

But it's too late. Breaking through the fudgy sweetness of fatuous dreams has allowed her to see ahead with brilliant clarity, as if the future's been personally painted for her by Max Ernst or some other Surrealist: she spies a sucking obstacle here, a tentacled hurdle there, the fiery pain, the cold blue humiliation – all to be surmounted or cleared from her path if she's to reach the golden horizon. So she steels herself, goes on walking, out through the revolving doors to the street, where she hails a taxi because her legs are trembling.

Rage buoys her up during the day. Evenings catch her at a low ebb. She's got so used to Bertie as a comfort blanket – the knowledge that he's there in the background ready to give life a nudge in the right direction – that she can't get through the night without first making herself fuddled on whisky. Also, dammit, she loves him (at least at this time of night), suspects she'll never feel the same with anyone else. Either way, viewed briskly in the career-orientated light of day, aching in the lost light of evening, the message is the same: she's got to get rid of thingy inside her; if she doesn't her life is needlessly burdened, if she doesn't Bertie will never come near her again.

She makes enquiries, is given an address; learns she'd better get a move on, also certain physical details. Panic sets in.

She writes to Chrissy, writes to Liz. Implores that if they ever loved her, if they feel for her the tiniest remnant of regard, to come at once. She's in mortal terror. It's an emergency.

They arrive – at her flat on the top floor of a tall Edwardian North London semi – fortunately without their babies (though Chrissy is pregnant with Amanda). Nell has a hard time getting them to understand the urgency; they will keep going back to the beginning. Is she sure? Absolutely? Yes, yes, moans Nell, and it's got to be got rid of, double quick.

Chrissy just won't see it. 'Tony and I will adopt it,' she cries triumphantly when other solutions have been dismissed.

This stuns Nell into silence while she contemplates all the deliciously embarrassing consequences. She's almost tempted. Liz and Chrissy stare in disbelief as Nell appears to enjoy a private joke. 'It's not funny,' screams an enraged Chrissy. And Liz wants to shake her for behaving like a callous thickhead. 'For Christ's sake couldn't you have used something? Getting caught at your age – it's pathetic.'

'I didn't get caught as you hatefully put it. It was a deliberate act. I was trying, in time-honoured fashion, to hook my man.'

'Well, where *is* your man since you mention him?'

'At home with his wife I imagine.'

'Oh. Married.'

'Yes. Married.'

For Liz, the problem instantly dissolves, slowly

reassembles. *Tell Mrs Poole I'm sorry* rings in her head like the warning clanging of a fire bell: it seems like her life's theme. For years she's felt personal responsibility for betrayed wives; her stomach is in the habit of contracting at any chance mention of the subject; when patients fall into this category she's uncomfortable looking them straight in the eye. So there's a wife in the background, she thinks, who is liable to suffer because of Nell's scheming, just as Mrs Poole suffered as a result of hers. Unless Nell can be prevented. 'So this man isn't interested?' she asks, playing for time while her new perspective of the situation settles into focus, her voice sounding to her as though it's rebounding in a stoppered jar.

'*This man* insists I get rid of it,' Nell expostulates. '*This man* will make plenty trouble if I don't. Now do you see? In any case, I *want* rid of it. I want the whole mess over and done with, everything to be like it never happened. What I'm trying to tell you is the process of achieving this state of affairs is scaring me witless.' She's shouting, beginning to shake. 'It's going to *hurt*, for Christ's sake. I need you with me. I need you to help me, to stick around and make sure I don't bleed to death or something.'

'I can't,' bursts out Chrissy, hiding her face in her hands. 'I can't, I can't,' comes her sobbing whimper.

'Oh – wonderful,' says Nell, turning away.

'She can't,' Liz says decisively. 'Don't worry though, I'll stay and hold your hand. Chrissy had better go home.'

'I'm so sorry, letting you down,' moans Chrissy. 'But this . . . Look,' she raises her tear-stained face, stares at them like a condemned person pleading for reprieve, 'if we, if we, oh surely, there's *something* . . .' But she can't think of anything, couldn't get it out if she could. Things are going too fast for her. She's going to fail, fail Nell, fail this baby, she foresees, clutching her throat which is thick and aching.

'I'm going to phone Tony now, tell him to meet the next train,' says Liz, who thinks Chrissy should be out of here as soon as possible. 'Where's the nearest?'

'Payphone in the hall,' says Nell. 'Turn right at the bottom of the stairs.'

Liz collects her purse, goes out.

'Bloody hell, Chrissy,' complains Nell. 'It's me who's in for it. I know you're up the spout, too, but at least Tony wants it; and you know what's coming, and you'll get the best of attention . . .'

'Going to the loo,' mumbles Chrissy, scrambling to her feet, making a dash for it. After a few minutes, she creeps down the three flights of stairs. 'Liz?' she calls softly, craning over the banisters.

Liz looks up. 'It's OK. A train leaves at six twenty. Tony's going to meet it. I told him you weren't feeling too good.'

'Liz . . .' She keeps going down to the bottom, hurries, seizes her arm. 'Liz, promise you'll try and talk her out of it.'

Liz collects her change, shuts it in her purse. 'I'll try and make sure she thinks about it,' she says at last. 'Seriously and quietly from all the angles. But if she's still of the same mind, I shall stick by her. One of us must.'

This starts Chrissy's tears up again.

'Oh, I didn't mean it like that, I'm not criticizing; I think Nell's the limit bringing you here. Look, I'll do my best. If it comes to it, I'll hate it, too. But we can't just turn our backs on her.'

'I feel such a let down.'

'Shush. Come on.' Hearts sinking, they trudge back upstairs to Nell.

They take Chrissy by taxi to King's Cross. Put her on the train. Wait on the platform watching the tears fall down Chrissy's face. Watch her mouthing 'Sorry,' and shake her head as the train moves. Watch her glide away, dissolving in moisture and grimy glass.

Liz closes her eyes to dispel the distressed ghost of one friend, opens them and turns to the quaking mass of fear that is her other.

The ghastliness of what follows coupled with Liz's staunch solidarity – going with her to the seedy clinic (so-called), waiting around, enduring the nightmare taxi ride home, summoning and facing a hostile GP when Nell's temperature soars, putting up with her moaning and groaning, waiting on her – drives Nell to make a solemn covenant with herself. She will for ever spare Liz the truth. No matter how tempted, how drunk, how bored and desperate for diversion, she will never ever tell her. It's a promise.

After a few weeks Nell is back to normal. A residue of bitterness over Bertie's behaviour (she's let him know she never wants to see him again) gives her writing extra bite. As a result, a rival newspaper offers her more money and greater exposure. The golden horizon looms up close.

Sometimes, Chrissy's tear-washed face flashes in Nell's inner eye. The image is blurred, trembly, as if moving beneath the surface of water or wavy glass. She herself has never shed tears for the lost baby. Glimpsing Chrissy's grief gives her a sweet sad relieved feeling, like consolation.

vii

Several coffees (and a brandy for Nell) later, the door-man, Charles, was prevailed upon to call for a taxi. Nell now changed her mind about Charles, perceived him to be a perfect sweetie, anxious to demonstrate the old-fashioned courtesy appreciated by the hotel's regular customers and to do his best for new ones whose requirements were less easy to gauge. Accordingly, as

394

Liz and Chrissy piled into the back of the car, Nell held everyone up by rummaging short-sightedly in her clutch-bag for an appropriate sum with which to tip him. 'Just half a mo, driver, got it somewhere. Bugger it – don't go, Charles. Oh hell – Charles, *stay*. Here,' she cried triumphantly.

Liz turned her head away. Chrissy closed her eyes muttering, 'I'll kill her.'

At last Nell sat heavily down on the front seat, still explaining herself to the driver, who let up the clutch in silence, in silence drove out on to the road, along by the prom, turned right at the Winter Gardens, headed for dark open country.

'I suppose we should be thankful she didn't kiss him,' murmured Liz in her friend's ear.

'So should he,' whispered Chrissy, discreetly opening her purse in order to settle the taxi fare promptly on arrival at The Old Rectory.

When the taxi drew up and Chrissy leaned forward, Nell started to object. Liz nipped out, opened Nell's door. 'Come on,' she commanded. 'People haven't got all night. You can always pay Chrissy back.'

Huffing a bit, Nell got out. The night air smote her, sharp, cool, dew-laden. No warmth in it or familiar tobacco fumes, just cruel pure air coming much too suddenly upon her unsuspecting lungs. She gasped, crumpled; wheezing and gagging, she was unable to walk unaided. The taxi driver jumped out and came to help. When they reached the front door, Chrissy dispatched him. 'Thank you, we'll manage now.'

Just in time. As the car drove away, Nell's convulsions, coming so soon upon an unusually ample meal, brought up a prodigious portion. The sight of vomit on her doorstep seemed to derange Chrissy; she darted inside, made across the hall.

'Where're you going? Don't leave me, you idiot,' Liz called.

'Bucket of water,' said Chrissy. 'Don't want Tony to see . . .'

'Later, for Pete's sake. Let's get her upstairs. In any case, it's not nasty, you can see it's undigested.'

'Rather not if it's all the same,' muttered Chrissy, taking Nell's other arm.

They got her up the long flight to the landing — suggested the bathroom, but she shook her head — brought her into her room and on to her bed; piled plumped-up pillows behind her, offered water, pills.

Nell, who was unable to utter a word, pointed to her mouth, shook a finger at her suitcase. Inside, they found an inhaler. Three squirts into her throat seemed restorative. In a moment, she asked for her pills and a glass of water.

'Want any help getting into bed?' Liz asked, some minutes later.

Nell shook her head.

'In that case I'll say goodnight,' said Chrissy, free at last to go and sluice the doorstep.

Liz pulled off Nell's shoes, then sat beside her on the bed. 'I'll stay for a while,' she said, recalling how fearful Nell had always been of sickness and pain. She remembered sitting on Nell's bed all those years ago, trying to calm her certain terror that she would bleed to death like the victims of men's wickedness in Mrs Nelson's library books, which Nell as a nine or ten year old had read avidly while her mother was slaving in the kitchen. '*Argh, ouwoo*,' Liz remembered her shrieking, when it was necessary to prop her up or help her to the bathroom, clutching her stomach, rolling her eyes, so that no-one, as Liz pointed out at the time, would take her seriously if she were dying.

'It must be very alarming,' she suggested now, diplomatically, 'feeling you can't breathe, can't get enough air. Trouble is, panicking is bound to make it worse.'

Nell looked at her through her eyelashes, growled, 'I'm not imagining it.'

'What is it, exactly?'

'Bronchitis,' Nell said shortly, after a pause. 'Bloody London pollution. Everyone's getting it – bronchitis or asthma.'

Liz nodded, not wishing to revive Nell's difficulties by drawing her into argument. 'Just the same, I should get yourself thoroughly checked out; see if something can be done to help. I'll come with you if you like,' she offered casually.

Nell's eyelids fluttered. She seemed to hesitate, then looked down at the counterpane.

Liz couldn't tell whether her offer had been accepted or turned down. She rose, deciding to mention it again in the morning. 'Night, night, then. Sing out, or bang on the wall if you want anything. I'm only next door.'

'Thanks. Goodnight.'

7
A TRIANGLE IS A STRONG SHAPE

i

In Liz's dream, Nell was coughing her lungs out. Liz heard her: hack, hack, hack. She was desperate to find her, but it was proving impossible, everywhere black or dull clay grey.

The hacking grew worse, Liz more despairing. On hands and knees, she felt her way through matted tangles which felt like the unyielding twine of ancient convolvulus. Exhausting work. No time to rest, though; Nell's noise was beginning to sound like choking. Then her hands touched smoothness, traced a long smooth stone rectangle with grass inside, and at its head, smooth stone steps. An obstacle prevented her from raising her head to peer through the gloom, but it didn't matter, she knew this place: it was the grave with the guardian angel. Where Nell lay – her hands made Nell out. She had to get help.

Someone was coming along the path. Very dimly, black against grey, Liz discerned a moving figure. Was it Chrissy? Oh, it must be. 'Help,' she called. 'Help me with Nell.' The figure drew level. Would it stop? Liz's blood zoomed and roared like an incoming tide, everything, the whole world, seemed to depend on it. The figure *did* pause; turned; and as Liz's heart quietened, and relief and certainty flowed through her veins like warm honey, came gliding over. It wasn't Chrissy.

'I'll help you,' said Mrs Poole. She knelt down on the far side of Nell and looked across at Liz; who, gradually through the gloom, saw she was smiling, laughing almost, teasing.

'I liked you so much,' Liz remembered. 'Then something happened and I forgot that I liked you.'

'I know,' said Mrs Poole, 'and it's quite all right.'

At which, Liz awoke, suddenly and cleanly, and opened her eyes. *Tell Mrs Poole I'm sorry* rang in her head sounding all used up, like the sentiments conveyed in an old fashioned song, understood in another time. As Mrs Poole had understood. Yes, she was sure of this now . . .

Nell was coughing, she remembered. I heard her in my sleep which made me dream it. No sound of it now. When a night creature screamed she thought, maybe that was what I heard. She drifted, alternately straining her ears and giving in to dream fragments washing over her, tugging, releasing, like waves.

Nell had indeed had an attack of coughing. It had woken her from uneasy sleep. She drank all the unpleasantly warm water remaining in the glass on her bedside table, then, still feeling parched and prickly hot (too much booze last night), decided to go downstairs and look in the fridge, see if there was a bottle of properly cold mineral water, fizzy, the way she liked it. She put on her dressing gown, collected the glass (and as a security measure the little pyramid of smoking equipment which she stashed in her pocket, thinking, you never know, might sneak a puff on the back doorstep, or maybe open a window and risk it indoors); quietly opened her door, felt her way to the banister and down the stairs.

Out of long habit (for this was her home, she the mother of its children), Chrissy awoke and raised her head; saw the strip of light showing under her door, swung her legs out of bed. Then recalled that two adults were occupying the rooms opposite at the moment and lay back down. Beside her, Tony moaned, tossed, fell still.

Nell was awfully poorly at bedtime; perhaps she

ought to go and check she was all right. From Tony's breathing, she deduced he was soundly asleep. This time she got out of bed more cautiously, reached for her dressing gown, stealthily let herself out of the room, crept downstairs to investigate a light showing across the far corner of the hall.

The kitchen window was open. Nell, at the head of the table, was occupying the tall wooden armchair where Tony always sat to eat his breakfast; before her on the table a half-filled glass of water, ashtray, cigarettes, lighter. She was neither drinking nor smoking when Chrissy came in, just sitting with her head resting against the chair back. 'God, you gave me a fright,' she said, without any change of bodily position or facial expression to back up this claim.

Chrissy walked round her. 'What's up? Can't sleep?'

'Mm, I was thirsty, came down for a drink, er, was just sitting here, wool gathering. I say, did I ever tell you . . .?' And off she went. As if they hadn't done enough reminiscing for one evening, thought Chrissy, yawning behind her hand. It seemed there would be no stopping her. 'Mm,' 'Really?' Chrissy put in now and then without any trace of enthralment, and 'I say,' as the hall clock struck two. Nell must be working up to something, she decided, trying to cast her tiredness aside by pottering about the kitchen, which bore evidence of everyone going to bed before the mistress of the house arrived home to chivvy them into tidying it. She collected a half-full carton of orange juice from the draining board, put it away in the fridge. Bent down to retrieve a newspaper – yesterday's agony she thought, folding it on the distraught face of a displaced woman of Bosnia, dropping it in the waste bin; there'd be more tomorrow, a starving face from Somalia, a weeping victim of violence at home.

Nell was still rabbitting. Though confident now of her ability to remain awake, Chrissy felt bone weariness steal over her; she drew back a chair from the side of the table, sat on it – her back to the Aga, her face towards the hall.

Nell's waxen face with inadequately removed make-up still smudging her eyes put Chrissy in mind of a pallid fruit – one of those white albino-looking peaches – with thumb bruises. Her dread, when Nell first arrived, of witnessing her minus her war paint now struck her as odd, though she could see what it was she'd dreaded: Nell's sickliness revealed. Nell was smiling at a little joke she'd made, a typical Nell joke against herself. Chrissy, returning the smile, felt a pang. Nell was clearly ill, and Nell being Nell, would be too terrified to admit it. Perhaps this was the point she was endeavouring to reach via inconsequential chatter; perhaps she was working herself up to confess and face how truly sick she was. It'll be some humiliating thing wrong with her, guessed Chrissy, recalling how humiliation was always Nell's bugbear. 'So humiliating I wanted to *die*,' she could recall her wailing – probably over some daft lad turning her down, or her father behaving drunkenly in the street. She and Liz, dazzled by all her glitzy glory of telly appearances and a name in the papers, tended to overlook Nell's vulnerabilities; but it was they who were the secure ones. It occurred to her that in her mental image of their triangle, she and Liz were always the points at either end of the base line, Nell was always at the apex; she and Liz rock solid, Nell high above, a wavering inspirational star. Maternal-type guilt smote her; they had made too many assumptions – 'Oh, you know old Nell. Just Nell being Nell. Trust Nell, she'll come out of it grinning, as usual.' From now on they must look out for her.

'I never told you, did I, about my affair with Liz's father?'

In the following silence, Nell peered at Chrissy, and Chrissy tested Nell's words for sensible meaning. Chrissy's good intentions seemed to turn on her mockingly. (Just Nell being Nell?) '*What*?'

'I remember you two accusing me of not letting on about my first lover. Well, that was why, because it was Bertie. Oh – Bertie.' Between 'Oh' and 'Bertie' all her body heaved up, collapsed in a profound sigh. 'The only bloke I ever lost my heart to. Do I mean "loved"?' She put her head on one side. 'Yes, I really think I do. Didn't start out as love – unless you count schoolgirl infatuation. Mind you, that's a commodity not to be lightly underestimated, as we three have reason to know, eh?' She looked sideways at Chrissy as if to check she was following closely.

Chrissy did not yet feel equal to any response. In any case, Nell had gone sweeping on.

'Remember when we were kids, going to tea at Liz's? Wasn't he the most devastating man you ever saw? And not on a silver screen, but flesh and blood, giving you the third degree at the tea table. Didn't your stomach scrunch when he looked at you? Wasn't it agony trying to eat? Ah – I suppose you were immune, stuck down the other end, busy filling your face and earning brownie points from Mummy Stockdale.'

'What the hell are you on about? Are you trying to make out . . .?'

'Oh, Chrissy petal, not "making out"; Bertie Stockdale was my first, last, my only love. A very dirty trick fate played on me there, I've always thought. You see, I'd fondly imagined I was in control, having done the picking up, allowed him measured and limited access, got precisely what I was after, and always intended and quite looked forward to giving him the heave-ho. Then on the very point of chucking him, fell in love. Maybe I always was, who knows? I remember, when we were kids, being quite terrified of him in a thrilling sort of way, he being so truly powerful – as opposed to my dad who was just a swaggering no-account bully. I thought all those questions he used to fire at me were a way of sneering at my background. When it dawned on me that he was throwing out a challenge, I was thrilled to little pieces, started saying things on purpose to get his interest. Around about, oh, seventeen I should think, I knew it wasn't just my intellect he found fascinating. So when the time came for a bit of a leg up – I needed someone to put in a word for me at the *Telegraph*, I cashed in, dangled my fatal speciality before him, schoolgirl freshness crossed with siren sophistication – how could he resist? Mind you, he wasn't in the habit of resisting, he was at it all the time we knew him. Oh, yes. Remember that neat little seccy-lady – what was her name? – Carol. He'd got her installed in a semi off Fairfield Road. That sort of bloke's always at it; never be fooled by male eminence. I sometimes think they cultivate it deliberately – that boring sober-suited worthiness, "weight of the world's problems on my shoulders" look – as an aphrodisiac. Certainly seems to work for 'em – fatties with spots and greasy hair, specs and pates and paunches – anything goes so long as they're flexing the old power muscles.'

'Hang on a minute. You're honestly telling me that you and Alderman Stockdale . . .?'

'Haven't you been listening?'

'I simply don't believe you; you're making it up.' It was a statement of faith, of disinclination. Having made it, she set her mind busily to supply good reasons. For instance, that Nell was so used to making stuff up for her column, it'd become a habit; that what Nell was really about was procrastinating, finding improbable diversions from owning up about her sickness.

'Oh well, then,' shrugged Nell, reaching for the cigarette packet. 'Look, I must have a puff, OK? I've opened the window.'

It crossed Chrissy's mind, remembering all the coughing and choking earlier, to object on these grounds, but she couldn't be bothered. The clock struck the half hour. She felt super-awake, the sort of awake you feel after a death or similar shock when it's necessary to keep going for days on end and you're running on pure adrenalin. An urge rose to feed herself, get something from the fridge, glass of milk maybe, or put the kettle on for coffee. She resisted it, suddenly dreaded making a noise. Which might wake Liz – all they needed was Liz coming down and getting an earful of this rubbish. Oh my God . . . She started, jolted her chair – it screeched on the floor tiles, but she scarcely noticed. 'You haven't told Liz?'

'Ah,' said Nell, blowing out smoke. 'So you do believe me.'

'Just answer me, will you? Have you told her?'

'No,' said Nell after a pause. 'No, I haven't as a matter of fact.'

This at least was good news. The whole point of them being here was to help Liz sort out her problems. The Rosie business was resolved, they'd even managed to ease Liz's scrupulous guilt over Mrs Poole; Chrissy was damned if Nell was now going to ruin everything by landing her with further stress. Better Nell told her story (as she seemed determined to do) with Liz out of earshot. 'How old were you when this business started?'

'Eighteen. Just left school.'

'God, what a hypocrite,' Chrissy couldn't hold back from exclaiming. 'All the fuss he made about *his* schoolgirl daughter being harmed, threatening to do likewise to poor little Alison . . .'

'Ah, but you forget. I wasn't *that* sort of daughter, the sort men insult one another by harming. I was a docker's daughter – when Dad could stand upright.' Making the point, she flicked her cigarette.

'You shouldn't smoke so much, you know.'

'I do know. I can't help it.'

'So how long did it last?'

'Over five years. Right through university . . .'

'That explains a lot.'

'. . .right through my first job, almost through my second. It was getting pregnant that finished it off.'

The remark, casually made, hung on gaining intensity. 'Oh, Nell,' Chrissy whispered, 'it wasn't . . .?'

'Of course it was. I told you at the time the father was married and insisted I got rid of it. Not that I was keen to do otherwise, once I knew having it wouldn't do me any good. Since then, though . . . Oh, hell,' she sighed, propping her head on a hand. 'Sometimes, last night for instance, when Clare was trying to get round you (oh I *do* like that kid, Chrissy, I think she's my favourite), she was leaning against you, and you put your arm round her . . . Times like that I almost wish . . . Then at other times I think, at least I'd have had a part of him. Because I really missed him, you know. Not straight away, I was much too busy. Later.' She shuddered, stubbed her cigarette out. 'Even after he died.'

But Chrissy wasn't listening any more. Implications were swimming in her mind like leaves caught in a whirlpool drawing closer and closer to the central point. 'In that case,' she said slowly, a dry throat producing a harsh tone, 'it would have been Liz's . . .'

Nell looked at her sadly. 'Yeah, Liz's step-thingy,' she confirmed, wincing at the flippancy. 'Indeed,' she added coolly, trying to steady her feelings.

Chrissy's feelings could not be unsteadier. She snatched one of Nell's cigarettes, stuck it in her mouth, lit it – simply the nearest form of oral comfort; drew on it, choking on the acrid inhalation and the wild idea that had come to her mind that *this* was where Nell had been heading all along: she wanted to make a clean breast of it to Liz. Well, she wouldn't let her. It'd be devastating. 'Don't ever,' she got out with difficulty, shakily jabbing the cigarette in Nell's face, 'don't ever tell Liz.'

'Don't tell Liz what?' demanded an indignant voice; and Liz came into the doorway.

Stunned, Nell squinted at her, then, looking dreamily at Chrissy, almost absently reached for a fresh cigarette; while Chrissy, frowning at Nell, endeavoured to convey every silent threat she could muster.

Liz, who had come to a halt on the far side of the table, plopped her hands on it impatiently. 'Well?'

ii

They're in a cafeteria-cum-waiting-room belonging to one of the largest hospitals in the North East. Tony is paying for the operation, he insisted on it, if anything goes wrong he wants to be able to blame somebody. But it's obvious to Chrissy that he's wasting his money, the surgeon would carry out the operation full steam ahead in any case, in the main hospital with the usual crack team. The only difference will come afterwards, when as soon as she's well enough to leave the recovery ward they'll move her into a private room or a nursing home, depending on how radical the surgery is. This is something that will not be known until the breast is opened. If things look good the surgeon will remove the lump and stitch her up; if not, he'll remove the entire breast.

Tony is at home with the kids and Mrs Stockdale. Chrissy was glad to accept Mrs Stockdale's offer, feels she can be relied on to keep the sustenance flowing. Tony was persuaded to keep in touch by phone, to visit her when the outcome is known. 'My mind will be at rest, knowing you're looking after the kids,' Chrissy told him, instead of the truth – that the only people she wants to face this with are Liz and Nell. Now they three are together she feels relaxed, almost detached from what is about to happen. The old feeling of invulnerability has taken over. They've had a few laughs, a bit of a gossip, they are themselves. Which puts even this hospital in its place, subdues all its threatening emanations – the medical smells wafting through swinging doors, the squeak of trolleys in endless corridors, the light-hearted passage of doctors and nurses who will soon render her naked and helpless. Chrissy is grateful and relieved beyond measure that her friends dropped everything to join her.

There's a great deal of green in this room, covering the lower half of the walls, the doors, the floor tiles – unpleasantly dark, the colour of rank grass on a sunless day. It's making Liz feel faintly queasy. Though perhaps her unease is due to the rush she's had getting here. They've arrived from different points of the compass. This is where they agreed to meet. Surreptitiously, under cover of the table, Liz looks at her watch. An hour to go, then Chrissy must present herself upstairs in the ward.

Nell lays her lighted cigarette against the side of the ashtray. She doodles in the specs of sugar on the Formica table top, shifts in her seat to unstick her thin skirt and plump thighs from the tacky plastic chair. This place is ghastly, but she's determined not to let it get to her. 'If he does decide to remove the breast,' she drawls, as though the ifs and buts of the operation have formed their topic of conversation, whereas in fact Chrissy has been telling them about bumping into Angie Hutchings and hardly recognizing her, she was so plain and dumpy; 'if that *is* the outcome, why not tell him in advance to remove both breasts? Much better *aesthetically*, don't you think? You could cultivate the boyish look, like that flat-chested French actress. It's got a certain appeal,' she muses, lifting her own ample bosom and resting it with her forearms on the table, hands clasped, peering earnestly at Chrissy. 'False ones are so disgusting. If I were you I'd tell him in advance: one off, both off. One off is crippling, two off is a statement.'

Not a muscle of Chrissy's moves.

Liz is staring at Nell's hands in the centre of the table and the smouldering cigarette beside them in the ashtray. Suddenly, without any conscious premeditation, she snatches the latter, screws its lighted end as hard as she can into the crevice between two of Nell's knuckles.

Nell gasps, but it's Chrissy who yells – '*Liz*,' and puts her hands to her face. There's a distinct smell of scorched flesh. Liz drops the screwed and now extinguished cigarette into the ashtray. Nell sits hypnotized by the deepening circle of redness.

'Ice,' cries Chrissy, leaping to her feet, seizing Nell's arm, dragging her to the counter. Liz watches as a crowd gathers. Then a woman shepherds Chrissy and Nell out of the room. Liz stays where she is. People turn and glance at her, look away quickly. Eventually, Chrissy puts her head round the door. 'Come on, Liz; bring our things.'

Liz bends down and collects their bags, hurries after Chrissy.

This room is predominantly brown, easy chairs covered in brown scratchy fabric, brown ribbed carpet, beige-brown walls. It's the room where relatives wait to be given bad news – 'the counselling room,' somebody called it.

They sit not looking at one another. Nell's hand has a gauze dressing on it.

Liz can't believe what she's done. As far as she can remember she has never before committed an act of violence. Already, her training and expertise, personified by a soothing professional voice, are at work in her head explaining that Nell's callousness was a defence against these surroundings which terrify her (for she has never conquered her pathetic dread of physical distress); that her own action was a response to pain inflicted on Chrissy, like watching a child torture a kitten, bursting with anger, saying 'what you are doing *hurts*; here, *feel* it.' The important thing, now, is to apologize, get the drama behind them, establish a supportive atmosphere.

Chrissy is searching for words to tell them that none of it matters – that is, so far as she is concerned. Nell was just being Nell; she wouldn't want her to be less.

408

Liz acted out of affronted love; Chrissy is touched by it. Trouble is, she can't say any of this for fear of upsetting one or the other. It only matters that we are here together, she wants to tell them.

Nell isn't thinking a thing as far as she knows. She feels as though she's been rescued from an ordeal, blissfully cosseted, warm, woozy, like the effect of swallowing two double whiskies.

'Help, I've got to go,' Chrissy says, looking at her watch. 'Coming up with me?'

Liz leaps to her feet. Nell has a struggle to rise. 'Are you OK?' Liz asks her.

'Mm, fine.'

'I really am very sorry.'

'Don't be sorry, petal, be proud. You were magnificent.'

Chrissy lets out her breath. They're going to be all right. She can submit to anaesthesia with her mind at peace.

The surgeon performs a lumpectomy. The surrounding tissue is healthy, the prognosis good. Ten years later this verdict still holds. Chrissy has virtually forgotten she's ever had surgery; it's behind her, over with, chapter closed.

iii

As Liz waited for an answer, and neither of them responded, indignation turned to disbelief. Not since they were kids, that time at the Sea Gull Café when Nell and Chrissy started something with the grammar-school boys and she couldn't join in, had Liz felt shut out, excluded. She had almost forgotten it happened, never imagined it happening since. Hateful childish hurt swept over her (they were avoiding her gaze, just sitting there with their heads bowed, staring at the table), her face felt on fire.

409

'Actually,' drawled Nell at last, then paused to draw on her cigarette, 'I was merely admitting to mild regret in my old age over that abortion. Chrissy thought it would be ungracious of me to mention it to you, you having supported me in my hour of need.'

She sounded glib, Liz thought, looking from Nell to Chrissy, who, in her profound relief at Nell not mentioning Alderman Stockdale, nodded vehemently, waving her cigarette.

The sight was jolting. 'What the hell do you think you're doing?' Liz cried, snatching the cigarette away, banging it lighted head down into the ashtray. 'Trying to get lung cancer?'

'Oh,' Chrissy gasped, suddenly brought up against the fact of her smoking. 'Can't think why I . . . It must have been Nell talking about her abortion – you know how that upset me.'

This was true, and eased Liz's suspicions, but before she could make any reply, Nell cut in, sounding not at all drawling and sophisticated, but hurt, on the brink of tears. 'So it doesn't matter to you if *I* get lung cancer?'

'A bit late in the day to stop *you* smoking,' Liz returned, fatigue letting her speak without thinking.

Stillness fell, even the air seemed to become stationary. No further words passed, no looks, yet they suddenly knew – as if the germ of their knowledge had been lodged in their brains all along and only now, liberated by its name being spoken, flowered and seized their attention. Liz's legs threatened to buckle; she slid into a chair. 'Why didn't you tell us before?' she asked, leaning forward and very gently depriving Nell of her cigarette. As she screwed it into the ashtray, a memory rose of doing this before. It was when Chrissy was being admitted to hospital. Now, she supposed with a sense of fatality, it was Nell's turn.

Not speaking, they sat with their eyes on Nell's smoking paraphernalia. After a moment, Chrissy lent abruptly over the table and gathered it up, rose and went to the waste bin, dropped in the whole lot – cigarette packet, lighter, ashtray. The bin lid plopped down with a thin clack. She returned to her chair.

On and on they sat, Nell at the table's head, Liz on her right, Chrissy on her left. The refrigerator motor clicked off, shuddered into silence, left a hush like an expanding blanket, pressing, stuffing itself into corners, all but stifling the faint rustle of leaves against the kitchen window, the far away beat of the hall clock. So we're not inviolate after all, thought Liz. This is how we get our come-uppance, this is how we're broken. Her heart felt raw, as if it were suddenly exposed to dry air.

'Tell us, Nell,' urged Chrissy at last.

'Got to report at the hospital on Tuesday. Biopsy, or something – wasn't attending too closely, but I think that's what he said – some mention of a probing needle at which I cut off. Definitely Tuesday, though. And definitely a growth in the lung. I guess cancer is what he was trying to indicate.'

'Tuesday. We'll be there, too, won't we Liz?'

'Of course. With you all the way, Nell.'

They looked earnestly into her face while they mentally re-arranged their lives. Oh, Nathan, thought Liz, with the sweet-sharp longing of one who must face a protracted parting but knows it will only be temporary. Fortunately, he was very well able to look after himself; and he and Rosie were friends again, thank heaven, and Jon said something about coming for a few days with Sushma, which would be company for him. Chrissy was going over in her mind how she'd devote the whole day to baking – lots of nourishing meals in the freezer, Maisie from over the road dropping in regularly – they'd be all right, of course they would.

So it's really true, really happening, thought Nell, feeling as if someone had turned on an unnaturally bright light in her head. She'd done it, been brave at last, let the truth stand, resisted the temptation to evade it a while longer by pursuing a juicy confession which

411

would have devastated Liz. Instead, she'd made Liz a gift of her silence. Acted selflessly, damn it. Good grief, she thought, blinking incredulously at the table top, I'm a decent person. She began to shake. A noise like teeth chattering sounded – belatedly she understood that it was coming from her own mouth.

They grabbed her nearest hand; then, as if the crisis facing them impelled them to seize every available grain of strength, reached across the table and completed the link up.

Chrissy's eyes roamed from one pair of linked hands to the next. Probably all lies about Alderman Stockdale, she thought comfortably; just another example of Nell's famous diversionary tactics. And in this case, who would blame her? We're all frail humanity, doing our best to cope. Anyway, no harm done; a nasty half hour, but at least she didn't try the story out on Liz. The important thing is, we're here, ready and willing to stand by her.

Liz, too, was transfixed by their joined hands. Of course we can't be broken, she thought; so long as one of us remains to hobble about the earth, we go on, fixed in the last one's identity. Their arms, she saw, formed a triangle over the table top. Warmth charged her, like a foretaste of tomorrow's sunrise. A triangle, she remembered, is a strong shape.

THE END

BETWEEN FRIENDS
Kathleen Rowntree

'THE FUNNIEST PORTRAIT OF VILLAGE TRIVIA
SINCE E.M. DELAFIELD'S *DIARY OF A PROVINCIAL
LADY*'
Cosmopolitan

Wychwood was a charming and enthusiastically
organized village. The women, with their pine-fitted
kitchens and glowing Agas, ran everything with tireless
efficiency, from the W.I. meetings (Dress a Wooden
Spoon, and How to Decorate an Egg) to Brasso-ing the
church lectern and making mock-crab sandwiches for
the Christmas Bazaar. One hardly expected a *liaison* to
flourish in such exemplary surroundings.

But when Tessa Brierley discovered that her husband
was having an affair with Maddy Storr, she was
doubly perturbed – for Maddy was not only the
life and soul of the village and President of the
W.I., but was also her very best friend, a friend
whom Tessa did not want to lose.

Stoically, resourcefully, observed by a community
celebrating crises, tragedies, and local festivities in its
own eccentric Wychwood way, Tessa began to plan
how she would keep both her husband and her friend.

'A HUMDINGER – SHARP AND DELIGHTFULLY
ENTERTAINING. A VILLAGE STORY IN THE
SPLENDID TRADITION OF JOANNA TROLLOPE'
Publishing News

'SPARKLING . . . A DELIGHTFUL SOCIAL COMEDY
WITH UNDERTONES OF REAL PAIN'
Cosmopolitan

0 552 99506 1

BLACK SWAN

THE QUIET WAR OF REBECCA SHELDON
Kathleen Rowntree

When Rebecca Sheldon married George Ludbury, she found herself at war with his grotesquely funny family as well as with the hypocrisy of the Edwardian society in which she lived. The Ludburys – an affluent Midlands farming clan – were snobbish, possessive, malicious, and in the case of Pip, downright mad. The matriarchal Mrs Harold Ludbury was enraged when George – for whom she had planned better things – insisted on marrying Rebecca, dismissed by Mrs Ludbury as a 'shop girl'. From that moment on the family did their best to wreck the marriage, win George back to the family farm, and alienate Rebecca's children from her.

It took thirty years of gentle compliance and evasive pleasantness before Rebecca won her private war and achieved exactly what she wanted.

0 552 99325 5

BLACK SWAN

BRIEF SHINING
Kathleen Rowntree

The sequel to *The Quiet War of Rebecca Sheldon*.

'CAPTURES THOSE PERFECT ENDLESS SUMMERS
OF CHILDHOOD . . . THE RUSTIC STYLE OF LAURIE
LEE'S NOSTALGIC PROSE IS MIXED WITH PUNGENT
STABS REMINISCENT OF KATHERINE MANSFIELD'
She

To Sally and Anne, Willow Dasset was a place of
sun and poppy fields and haymaking, and Grandpa
Ludbury striding across the farmyard to welcome
them. Everything was perfect at Willow Dasset,
except their parents. Meg and Henry brought all
their tensions and resentments with them, and
their pervading restlessness somehow damaged the
enchantment of summer at the farm.

As Sally, the elder, changed from a child into
a young girl, she realized that the tension came
from her mother. Meg was a Ludbury, with all the
strangeness, the greeds and longings of that curious
clan. But now Meg's jealousy and resentment was
centred on her own daughter. Sally, reaching for a
life of her own, realized that if she wanted any kind
of happiness, she had to fight her mother any way she
could. And the one thing she never forgot was her
grandmother – for Rebecca too had had to fight the
Ludburys – and Rebecca had won.

'THE NARRATIVE IS QUIETLY HAUNTING WITH
MEMORABLE CHARACTERS'
Publishers Weekly

0 552 99584 3

BLACK SWAN

A SELECTED LIST OF FINE NOVELS
AVAILABLE FROM BLACK SWAN

THE PRICES SHOWN BELOW WERE CORRECT AT THE TIME OF GOING TO PRESS.
HOWEVER TRANSWORLD PUBLISHERS RESERVE THE RIGHT TO SHOW NEW
RETAIL PRICES ON COVERS WHICH MAY DIFFER FROM THOSE PREVIOUSLY
ADVERTISED IN THE TEXT OR ELSEWHERE.

❐	99537 1	GUPPIES FOR TEA	*Marika Cobbold*	£5.99
❐	99593 2	A RIVAL CREATION	*Marika Cobbold*	£5.99
❐	99467 7	MONSIEUR DE BRILLANCOURT	*Clare Harkness*	£4.99
❐	99387 5	TIME OF GRACE	*Clare Harkness*	£5.99
❐	99590 8	OLD NIGHT	*Clare Harkness*	£5.99
❐	99506 1	BETWEEN FRIENDS	*Kathleen Rowntree*	£5.99
❐	99325 5	THE QUIET WAR OF REBECCA SHELDON	*Kathleen Rowntree*	£5.99
❐	99584 3	BRIEF SHINING	*Kathleen Rowntree*	£5.99
❐	99529 0	OUT OF THE SHADOWS	*Titia Sutherland*	£5.99
❐	99460 x	THE FIFTH SUMMER	*Titia Sutherland*	£4.99
❐	99574 6	ACCOMPLICE OF LOVE	*Titia Sutherland*	£5.99
❐	99494 4	THE CHOIR	*Joanna Trollope*	£5.99
❐	99410 3	A VILLAGE AFFAIR	*Joanna Trollope*	£5.99
❐	99442 1	A PASSIONATE MAN	*Joanna Trollope*	£5.99
❐	99470 7	THE RECTOR'S WIFE	*Joanna Trollope*	£5.99
❐	99492 8	THE MEN AND THE GIRLS	*Joanna Trollope*	£5.99
❐	99082 5	JUMPING THE QUEUE	*Mary Wesley*	£5.99
❐	99548 7	HARNESSING PEACOCKS	*Mary Wesley*	£5.99
❐	99304 2	NOT THAT SORT OF GIRL	*Mary Wesley*	£5.99
❐	99355 7	SECOND FIDDLE	*Mary Wesley*	£5.99
❐	99393 x	A SENSIBLE LIFE	*Mary Wesley*	£5.99
❐	99258 5	THE VACILLATIONS OF POPPY CAREW	*Mary Wesley*	£5.99
❐	99126 0	THE CAMOMILE LAWN	*Mary Wesley*	£5.99
❐	99495 2	A DUBIOUS LEGACY	*Mary Wesley*	£5.99
❐	99591 6	A MISLAID MAGIC	*Joyce Windsor*	£4.99

All Black Swan Books are available at your bookshop or newsagent, or can be
ordered from the following address:
Black Swan Books
Cash Sales Department
P.O. Box 11, Falmouth, Cornwall TR10 9EN

UK and B.F.P.O. customers please send a cheque or postal order (no currency) and
allow £1.00 for postage and packing for the first book plus 50p for the second book
and 30p for each additional book to a maximum charge of £3.00 (7 books plus).

Overseas customers, including Eire, please allow £2.00 for postage and packing for
the first book plus £1.00 for the second book and 50p for each subsequent title
ordered.

NAME (Block letters) ....

ADDRESS ....

....